The
WHISPERERS
& Other Stories

The
WHISPERERS
& Other Stories

A LIFETIME OF THE
SUPERNATURAL

by
Algernon Blackwood

Edited by
MIKE ASHLEY

THE BRITISH LIBRARY

This collection first published in 2022 by
The British Library
96 Euston Road
London NW1 2DB

Introduction, selection and notes © 2022 Mike Ashley
Volume copyright © 2022 The British Library Board

Cataloguing in Publication Data
A catalogue record for this publication is available from the British Library

ISBN 978 0 7123 5426 4

Frontispiece illustration by Władysław T. Benda from 'The Wings
of Horus' in *The Century Magazine*, November 1914.

Endpaper illustrations by W. Graham Robertson from the Algernon Blackwood
collections *The Lost Valley* (Eveleigh Nash, 1910) and *Pan's Garden* (Macmillan, 1912).

Cover design by Mauricio Villamayor with illustration by Mag Ruhig.

Text design and typesetting by Tetragon, London.
Printed in Malta by Gutenberg Press.

MIX
Paper from
responsible sources
FSC
www.fsc.org   FSC® C022612

CONTENTS

To the memory of
MICHAEL POINTON
(1941–2021)
My companion in pursuit of the truth.

INTRODUCTION

A Lifetime of the Supernatural

Towards the end of his long life, and in response to an enthusiastic letter from a devoted fan, Algernon Blackwood revealed that everything he had ever written, all his stories and novels, were "more or less autobiographical". Here was someone who did not simply imagine the magic and mystery in his stories, he had experienced it all.

When I read that letter, which I found amongst the few surviving papers left by Blackwood after his death, I knew that I would have to write his biography, though I had no idea at that time that the research would take me over twenty years. Even then the first edition of *Starlight Man*, published in 2001, still admitted gaps in my research, much, but not all, of which I was able to complete over the next twenty years for the revised edition.

A biography is all very well, but for people to fully appreciate the work of Blackwood, and to see how it fitted into his life, it's necessary to read those stories. He was quite prolific. Over 230 stories, twelve novels, plus children's books, stage and radio plays, so there is much to read, and this volume can present only a small fraction. But I have selected sixteen stories which in one way or another reflect aspects of Blackwood's outlook and experiences and I have put them in context, so you can see how they related directly to his life.

I have provided a continuing narrative to connect the stories so that you can follow his life which I hope will encourage you to read more of his work and understand its significance. Although most of Blackwood's work was written a hundred or more years ago it has not lost any of its power or vision and that is because from Blackwood's perspective, it was written from life. During his lifetime many recognised Blackwood's talent. It is well known that H. P. Lovecraft held Blackwood in high esteem and amongst his effusions, when writing his essay "Supernatural Horror in Literature" in 1927, he called Blackwood "the one absolute and unquestioned master of weird atmosphere". In the late 1940s a young Swiss student, Peter Penzoldt, was researching for his thesis later published as *The Supernatural in Fiction* (1952) and he dedicated the book to Blackwood, calling him "the greatest of them all". Genre expert E. F. Bleiler remarked in *The Guide to Supernatural Fiction* (1983) that "No one else has come closer to expressing the ineffable…".

I could go on because it is not difficult to find examples of critics' recognition of Blackwood's abilities and his unique contribution to weird fiction. Although he did write some fairly straightforward ghost stories, such as "The Empty House", which opens this collection, Blackwood did not like being labelled as such. When he began telling strange stories on BBC radio in the 1930s and on television in the 1940s, he became labelled "the Ghost Man", which he found derogatory. Blackwood's primary fascination was with Nature—with a capital N. The "supernatural" was not something apart. It was always there, and someone with a heightened sensitivity could find themselves immersed in the realities of the world, ruled by the spirit of the Earth itself—what the Greeks called Gaia—and which manifests itself in many forms of Nature, which we may now think of as Pan. "The Man Who Played Upon the Leaf", included here, is a potent example of Blackwood's idea of Nature-worship.

There are many stories I might have included, but Blackwood was often at his best in longer works such as "The Willows" and "The Wendigo" and as these are already included in the British Library Tales of the Weird volume *Roarings from Further Out*, along with the John Silence occult detective story "Ancient Sorceries" and the powerful Nature story "The Man Whom the Trees Loved", I have decided to set them aside. It allows me space to include several little-known stories and so demonstrate both the depth and breadth of Blackwood's vision.

The stories here, therefore, represent the complete range of Blackwood's short fiction, from the early ghost stories to his experiences with the occult society the Hermetic Order of the Golden Dawn, to the impressions on his psyche created by his experiences in the remote wilds of the Caucasus and Egypt, to the nightmares caused by his service as a secret agent during the First World War to his rather more personal reflections upon his own life and his close friends. They are all clues to his lifetime of the supernatural.

MIKE ASHLEY

A NOTE FROM THE PUBLISHER

The original short stories reprinted in the British Library's classic fiction series were written and published in a period ranging across the nineteenth and twentieth centuries. There are many elements of these stories which continue to entertain modern readers; however, in some cases there are also uses of language, instances of stereotyping and some attitudes expressed by narrators or characters which may not be endorsed by the publishing standards of today. We acknowledge therefore that some elements in the stories selected for reprinting may continue to make uncomfortable reading for some of our audience. With these new editions British Library Publishing aims to offer a new readership a chance to read some of the rare material of the British Library's collections in an affordable format, to enjoy their merits and to look back into the worlds of the past two centuries as portrayed by their writers. It is not possible to separate these stories from the history of their writing and as such the following stories are presented as they were originally published with the inclusion of minor edits made for consistency of style and sense, and with pejorative terms of an extremely offensive nature partly obscured. We welcome feedback from our readers, which can be sent to the following address:

British Library Publishing
The British Library
96 Euston Road
London, NW1 2DB
United Kingdom

THE EMPTY HOUSE

Algernon Henry Blackwood was born on 14 March 1869 at Shooter's Hill in Kent. He was the fourth of five children with two elder sisters, Cecilia and Beatrice, an elder brother, Stevenson, and two years later a younger sister, Ada. Their father, Sir Arthur Blackwood, who was Head of the Post Office, had undergone a religious conversion during the Crimean War and developed the zeal and passion of an evangelist, determined to save souls. It instilled in young Algie a tangible fear of hell and damnation and, because he did not believe in the religious conviction of his parents, a constant sense of guilt.

Blackwood was also descended from the aristocracy. His three times great grandfather, Sir Robert Blackwood, had been made a baronet with land in Northern Ireland. From him was descended the Lords Dufferin. His great grandfather was Vice-Admiral Sir Henry Blackwood, the first Baronet Blackwood, who had fought with Horatio Nelson at Trafalgar and escorted his body home. Blackwood's mother had been married before and had a daughter, Blackwood's elder half-sister. She had married the Earl of Kintore. Blackwood always felt this weight of history and responsibility upon his shoulders and though these connections would help him later in life, it still made him feel inadequate.

Perhaps it was no surprise that Blackwood sought refuge in Nature. He loved to explore the grounds at their later home in Crayford, Kent, and took every opportunity to take long walks, sometimes at night. As he wrote later, his love of Nature grew in intensity every year, "bringing comfort, companionship, inspiration, joy... a truly magical spell." Blackwood also explored other

13

religions, first Buddhism and then the teachings of Helena Blavatsky known as theosophy. This horrified Blackwood's father who became convinced his son's soul was doomed.

It might seem strange, therefore, that Blackwood Sr. was interested in psychic phenomena. Whilst he had no patience for spiritualism, he was interested in the scientific study of ghosts or apparent hauntings being undertaken by the Society for Psychical Research (SPR) which had been established in 1882 and counted amongst its members the future Archbishop of Canterbury Edward White Benson, the future prime minister Arthur Balfour and the future Professor in Moral and Political Philosophy, Henry Sidgwick. This was a serious organisation and Blackwood's father wanted to know what they might discover in relation to the works of God or the Devil.

One of the leading researchers for the SPR was Frank Podmore who worked as a senior clerk in Sir Arthur's offices in London. It was through Podmore that the young Algernon learned of reported hauntings or strange phenomena. Precisely when Blackwood went on his first investigation is uncertain but his last television broadcast referred to exploring a house in Knightsbridge probably in late June 1888, before he went to Edinburgh University in October to study agriculture. Blackwood may have investigated other hauntings at that time because he wrote about one such as "A Mysterious House", his first published story, in 1889. Another possibility was the basis for the following story. Podmore knew of a house in Hove, near Brighton, which had a reputation for being haunted. Blackwood had family friends in Brighton and he makes out in this story that he was accompanied on his adventure by an aunt. Years later he admitted that it was a "charming lady who had persuaded herself that I would make a good husband". It certainly is surprising that Blackwood, when only nineteen, would be allowed to enter an apparently haunted house with a young lady, unchaperoned, so we must assume the following events are after his return from New York. Here then is Blackwood's adapted account of that early haunting, which became the title story of his first book, The Empty House, *in 1906.*

C ERTAIN houses, like certain persons, manage somehow to pro-
claim at once their character for evil. In the case of the latter, no
particular feature need betray them; they may boast an open
countenance and an ingenuous smile; and yet a little of their company
leaves the unalterable conviction that there is something radically amiss
with their being: that they are evil. Willy nilly, they seem to communicate
an atmosphere of secret and wicked thoughts which makes those in their
immediate neighbourhood shrink from them as from a thing diseased.

And, perhaps, with houses the same principle is operative, and it is
the aroma of evil deeds committed under a particular roof, long after the
actual doers have passed away, that makes the gooseflesh come and the hair
rise. Something of the original passion of the evil-doer, and of the horror
felt by his victim, enters the heart of the innocent watcher, and he becomes
suddenly conscious of tingling nerves, creeping skin, and a chilling of the
blood. He is terror-stricken without apparent cause.

There was manifestly nothing in the external appearance of this particular house to bear out the tales of the horror that was said to reign
within. It was neither lonely nor unkempt. It stood, crowded into a corner
of the square, and looked exactly like the houses on either side of it. It had
the same number of windows as its neighbours; the same balcony over-
looking the gardens; the same white steps leading up to the heavy black
front door; and, in the rear, there was the same narrow strip of green, with
neat box borders, running up to the wall that divided it from the backs of
the adjoining houses. Apparently, too, the number of chimney pots on the

roof was the same; the breadth and angle of the eaves; and even the height of the dirty area railings.

And yet this house in the square, that seemed precisely similar to its fifty ugly neighbours, was as a matter of fact entirely different—horribly different.

Wherein lay this marked, invisible difference is impossible to say. It cannot be ascribed wholly to the imagination, because persons who had spent some time in the house, knowing nothing of the facts, had declared positively that certain rooms were so disagreeable they would rather die than enter them again, and that the atmosphere of the whole house produced in them symptoms of a genuine terror; while the series of innocent tenants who had tried to live in it and been forced to decamp at the shortest possible notice, was indeed little less than a scandal in the town.

When Shorthouse arrived to pay a "week-end" visit to his Aunt Julia in her little house on the sea-front at the other end of the town, he found her charged to the brim with mystery and excitement. He had only received her telegram that morning, and he had come anticipating boredom; but the moment he touched her hand and kissed her apple-skin wrinkled cheek, he caught the first wave of her electrical condition. The impression deepened when he learned that there were to be no other visitors, and that he had been telegraphed for with a very special object.

Something was in the wind, and the "something" would doubtless bear fruit; for this elderly spinster aunt, with a mania for psychical research, had brains as well as will power, and by hook or by crook she usually managed to accomplish her ends. The revelation was made soon after tea, when she sidled close up to him as they paced slowly along the sea-front in the dusk.

"I've got the keys," she announced in a delighted, yet half awesome voice. "Got them till Monday!"

"The keys of the bathing-machine, or—?" he asked innocently, looking from the sea to the town. Nothing brought her so quickly to the point as feigning stupidity.

"Neither," she whispered. "I've got the keys of the haunted house in the square—and I'm going there tonight."

Shorthouse was conscious of the slightest possible tremor down his back. He dropped his teasing tone. Something in her voice and manner thrilled him. She was in earnest.

"But you can't go alone—" he began.

"That's why I wired for you," she said with decision.

He turned to look at her. The ugly, lined, enigmatical face was alive with excitement. There was the glow of genuine enthusiasm round it like a halo. The eyes shone. He caught another wave of her excitement, and a second tremor, more marked than the first, accompanied it.

"Thanks, Aunt Julia," he said politely; "thanks awfully."

"I should not dare to go quite alone," she went on, raising her voice; "but with you I should enjoy it immensely. You're afraid of nothing, I know."

"Thanks *so* much," he said again. "Er—is anything likely to happen?"

"A great deal *has* happened," she whispered, "though it's been most cleverly hushed up. Three tenants have come and gone in the last few months, and the house is said to be empty for good now."

In spite of himself Shorthouse became interested. His aunt was so very much in earnest.

"The house is very old indeed," she went on, "and the story—an unpleasant one—dates a long way back. It has to do with a murder committed by a jealous stableman who had some affair with a servant in the house. One night he managed to secrete himself in the cellar, and when every one was asleep, he crept upstairs to the servants' quarters, chased the girl down to the next landing, and before anyone could come to the rescue threw her bodily over the banisters into the hall below."

"And the stableman—?"

"Was caught, I believe, and hanged for murder; but it all happened a century ago, and I've not been able to get more details of the story."

Shorthouse now felt his interest thoroughly aroused; but, though he was not particularly nervous for himself, he hesitated a little on his aunt's account.

"On one condition," he said at length.

"Nothing will prevent my going," she said firmly; "but I may as well hear your condition."

"That you guarantee your power of self-control if anything really horrible happens. I mean—that you are sure you won't get too frightened."

"Jim," she said scornfully, "I'm not young, I know, nor are my nerves; but *with you* I should be afraid of nothing in the world!"

This, of course, settled it, for Shorthouse had no pretensions to being other than a very ordinary young man, and an appeal to his vanity was irresistible. He agreed to go.

Instinctively, by a sort of subconscious preparation, he kept himself and his forces well in hand the whole evening, compelling an accumulative reserve of control by that nameless inward process of gradually putting all the emotions away and turning the key upon them—a process difficult to describe, but wonderfully effective, as all men who have lived through severe trials of the inner man well understand. Later, it stood him in good stead.

But it was not until half-past ten, when they stood in the hall, well in the glare of friendly lamps and still surrounded by comforting human influences, that he had to make the first call upon this store of collected strength. For, once the door was closed, and he saw the deserted silent street stretching away white in the moonlight before them, it came to him clearly that the real test that night would be in dealing with *two fears* instead of one. He would have to carry his aunt's fear as well as his own. And, as he glanced down at her sphinx-like countenance and realised that it might assume no pleasant aspect in a rush of real terror, he felt satisfied with only one thing in the whole adventure—that he had confidence in his own will and power to stand against any shock that might come.

Slowly they walked along the empty streets of the town; a bright autumn moon silvered the roofs, casting deep shadows; there was no breath of wind; and the trees in the formal gardens by the sea-front watched them silently as they passed along. To his aunt's occasional remarks Shorthouse made no reply, realising that she was simply surrounding herself with mental buffers—saying ordinary things to prevent herself thinking of extraordinary things. Few windows showed lights, and from scarcely a single chimney came smoke or sparks. Shorthouse had already begun to notice everything, even the smallest details. Presently they stopped at the street corner and looked up at the name on the side of the house full in the moonlight, and with one accord, but without remark, turned into the square and crossed over to the side of it that lay in shadow.

"The number of the house is thirteen," whispered a voice at his side; and neither of them made the obvious reference, but passed across the broad sheet of moonlight and began to march up the pavement in silence.

It was about half-way up the square that Shorthouse felt an arm slipped quietly but significantly into his own, and knew then that their adventure had begun in earnest, and that his companion was already yielding imperceptibly to the influences against them. She needed support.

A few minutes later they stopped before a tall, narrow house that rose before them into the night, ugly in shape and painted a dingy white. Shutterless windows, without blinds, stared down upon them, shining here and there in the moonlight. There were weather streaks in the wall and cracks in the paint, and the balcony bulged out from the first floor a little unnaturally. But, beyond this generally forlorn appearance of an unoccupied house, there was nothing at first sight to single out this particular mansion for the evil character it had most certainly acquired.

Taking a look over their shoulders to make sure they had not been followed, they went boldly up the steps and stood against the huge black door that fronted them forbiddingly. But the first wave of nervousness was now upon them, and Shorthouse fumbled a long time with the key before he could fit it into the lock at all. For a moment, if truth were told, they both hoped it would not open, for they were a prey to various unpleasant emotions as they stood there on the threshold of their ghostly adventure. Shorthouse, shuffling with the key and hampered by the steady weight on his arm, certainly felt the solemnity of the moment. It was as if the whole world—for all experience seemed at that instant concentrated in his own consciousness—were listening to the grating noise of that key. A stray puff of wind wandering down the empty street woke a momentary rustling in the trees behind them, but otherwise this rattling of the key was the only sound audible; and at last it turned in the lock and the heavy door swung open and revealed a yawning gulf of darkness beyond.

With a last glance at the moonlit square, they passed quickly in and the door slammed behind them with a roar that echoed prodigiously through empty halls and passages. But, instantly, with the echoes, another sound made itself heard, and Aunt Julia leaned suddenly so heavily upon him that he had to take a step backwards to save himself from falling.

A man had coughed close beside them—so close that it seemed they must have been actually by his side in the darkness.

With the possibility of practical jokes in his mind, Shorthouse at once swung his heavy stick in the direction of the sound; but it met nothing more solid than air. He heard his aunt give a little gasp beside him.

"There's someone here," she whispered; "I heard him."

"Be quiet!" he said sternly. "It was nothing but the noise of the front door."

"Oh! get a light—quick!" she added, as her nephew, fumbling with a box of matches, opened it upside down and let them all fall with a rattle on to the stone floor.

The sound, however, was not repeated; and there was no evidence of retreating footsteps. In another minute they had a candle burning, using an empty end of a cigar case as a holder; and when the first flare had died down he held the impromptu lamp aloft and surveyed the scene. And it was dreary enough in all conscience, for there is nothing more desolate in all the abodes of men than an unfurnished house dimly lit, silent, and forsaken, and yet tenanted by rumour with the memories of evil and violent histories.

They were standing in a wide hall-way; on their left was the open door of a spacious dining-room, and in front the hall ran, ever narrowing, into a long, dark passage that led apparently to the top of the kitchen stairs. The broad uncarpeted staircase rose in a sweep before them, everywhere draped in shadows, except for a single spot about half-way up where the moonlight came in through the window and fell in a bright patch on the boards. This shaft of light shed a faint radiance above and below it, lending to the objects within its reach a misty outline that was infinitely more suggestive and ghostly than complete darkness. Filtered moonlight always seems to paint faces on the surrounding gloom, and as Shorthouse peered up into the well of darkness and thought of the countless empty rooms and passages in the upper part of the old house, he caught himself longing again for the safety of the moonlit square, or the cosy, bright drawing-room they had left half-an-hour before. Then realising that these thoughts were dangerous, he thrust them away again and summoned all his energy for concentration on the present.

"Aunt Julia," he said aloud, severely, "we must now go through the house from top to bottom and make a thorough search."

The echoes of his voice died away slowly all over the building, and in the intense silence that followed he turned to look at her. In the candlelight he saw that her face was already ghastly pale; but she dropped his arm for a moment and said in a whisper, stepping close in front of him—

"I agree. We must be sure there's no one hiding. That's the first thing."

She spoke with evident effort, and he looked at her with admiration.

"You feel quite sure of yourself? It's not too late—"

"I think so," she whispered, her eyes shifting nervously toward the shadows behind. "Quite sure, only one thing—"

"What's that?"

"You must never leave me alone for an instant."

"As long as you understand that any sound or appearance must be investigated at once, for to hesitate means to admit fear. That is fatal."

"Agreed," she said, a little shakily, after a moment's hesitation. "I'll try—"

Arm in arm, Shorthouse holding the dripping candle and the stick, while his aunt carried the cloak over her shoulders, figures of utter comedy to all but themselves, they began a systematic search.

Stealthily, walking on tiptoe and shading the candle lest it should betray their presence through the shutterless windows, they went first into the big dining-room. There was not a stick of furniture to be seen. Bare walls, ugly mantel-pieces and empty grates stared at them. Everything, they felt, resented their intrusion, watching them, as it were, with veiled eyes; whispers followed them; shadows flitted noiselessly to right and left; something seemed ever at their back, watching, waiting an opportunity to do them injury. There was the inevitable sense that operations which went on when the room was empty had been temporarily suspended till they were well out of the way again. The whole dark interior of the old building seemed to become a malignant Presence that rose up, warning them to desist and mind their own business; every moment the strain on the nerves increased.

Out of the gloomy dining-room they passed through large folding doors into a sort of library or smoking-room, wrapt equally in silence, darkness, and dust; and from this they regained the hall near the top of the back stairs.

Here a pitch black tunnel opened before them into the lower regions, and—it must be confessed—they hesitated. But only for a minute. With the worst of the night still to come it was essential to turn from nothing. Aunt

Julia stumbled at the top step of the dark descent, ill lit by the flickering candle, and even Shorthouse felt at least half the decision go out of his legs.

"Come on!" he said peremptorily, and his voice ran on and lost itself in the dark, empty spaces below.

"I'm coming," she faltered, catching his arm with unnecessary violence.

They went a little unsteadily down the stone steps, a cold, damp air meeting them in the face, close and malodorous. The kitchen, into which the stairs led along a narrow passage, was large, with a lofty ceiling. Several doors opened out of it—some into cupboards with empty jars still standing on the shelves, and others into horrible little ghostly back offices, each colder and less inviting than the last. Black beetles scurried over the floor, and once, when they knocked against a deal table standing in a corner, something about the size of a cat jumped down with a rush and fled, scampering across the stone floor into the darkness. Everywhere there was a sense of recent occupation, an impression of sadness and gloom.

Leaving the main kitchen, they next went towards the scullery. The door was standing ajar, and as they pushed it open to its full extent Aunt Julia uttered a piercing scream, which she instantly tried to stifle by placing her hand over her mouth. For a second Shorthouse stood stock-still, catching his breath. He felt as if his spine had suddenly become hollow and someone had filled it with particles of ice.

Facing them, directly in their way between the doorposts, stood the figure of a woman. She had dishevelled hair and wildly staring eyes, and her face was terrified and white as death.

She stood there motionless for the space of a single second. Then the candle flickered and she was gone—gone utterly—and the door framed nothing but empty darkness.

"Only the beastly jumping candle-light," he said quickly, in a voice that sounded like someone else's and was only half under control. "Come on, aunt. There's nothing there."

He dragged her forward. With a clattering of feet and a great appearance of boldness they went on, but over his body the skin moved as if crawling ants covered it, and he knew by the weight on his arm that he was supplying the force of locomotion for two. The scullery was cold, bare, and empty; more like a large prison cell than anything else. They went round it, tried the door into the yard, and the windows, but found them all fastened securely. His aunt moved beside him like a person in a dream. Her eyes were tightly shut, and she seemed merely to follow the pressure of his arm. Her courage filled him with amazement. At the same time he noticed that a certain odd change had come over her face, a change which somehow evaded his power of analysis.

"There's nothing here, aunty," he repeated aloud quickly. "Let's go upstairs and see the rest of the house. Then we'll choose a room to wait up in."

She followed him obediently, keeping close to his side, and they locked the kitchen door behind them. It was a relief to get up again. In the hall there was more light than before, for the moon had travelled a little further down the stairs. Cautiously they began to go up into the dark vault of the upper house, the boards creaking under their weight.

On the first floor they found the large double drawing-rooms, a search of which revealed nothing. Here also was no sign of furniture or recent occupancy; nothing but dust and neglect and shadows. They opened the big folding doors between front and back drawing-rooms and then came out again to the landing and went on upstairs.

They had not gone up more than a dozen steps when they both simultaneously stopped to listen, looking into each other's eyes with a new apprehension across the flickering candle flame. From the room they had left hardly ten seconds before came the sound of a door quietly closing. It was beyond all question; they heard the booming noise that accompanies the shutting of heavy doors, followed by the sharp catching of the latch.

"We must go back and see," said Shorthouse briefly, in a low tone, and turning to go downstairs again.

Somehow she managed to drag after him, her feet catching in her dress, her face livid.

When they entered the front drawing-room it was plain that the folding doors had been closed—half a minute before. Without hesitation Shorthouse opened them. He almost expected to see someone facing him in the back room; but only darkness and cold air met him. They went through both rooms, finding nothing unusual. They tried in every way to make the doors close of themselves, but there was not wind enough even to set the candle flame flickering. The doors would not move without strong pressure. All was silent as the grave. Undeniably the rooms were utterly empty, and the house utterly still.

"It's beginning," whispered a voice at his elbow which he hardly recognised as his aunt's.

He nodded acquiescence, taking out his watch to note the time. It was fifteen minutes before midnight; he made the entry of exactly what had occurred in his notebook, setting the candle in its case upon the floor in order to do so. It took a moment or two to balance it safely against the wall.

Aunt Julia always declared that at this moment she was not actually watching him, but had turned her head towards the inner room, where she fancied she heard something moving; but, at any rate, both positively agreed that there came a sound of rushing feet, heavy and very swift—and the next instant the candle was out!

But to Shorthouse himself had come more than this, and he has always thanked his fortunate stars that it came to him alone and not to his aunt too. For, as he rose from the stooping position of balancing the candle, and before it was actually extinguished, a face thrust itself forward so close to his own that he could almost have touched it with his lips. It was a face working with passion; a man's face, dark, with thick features, and angry, savage eyes. It belonged to a common man, and it was evil in its ordinary normal expression, no doubt, but as he saw it, alive with intense, aggressive emotion, it was a malignant and terrible human countenance.

There was no movement of the air; nothing but the sound of rushing feet—stockinged or muffled feet; the apparition of the face; and the almost simultaneous extinguishing of the candle.

In spite of himself, Shorthouse uttered a little cry, nearly losing his balance as his aunt clung to him with her whole weight in one moment of real, uncontrollable terror. She made no sound, but simply seized him bodily. Fortunately, however, she had seen nothing, but had only heard the rushing feet, for her control returned almost at once, and he was able to disentangle himself and strike a match.

The shadows ran away on all sides before the glare, and his aunt stooped down and groped for the cigar case with the precious candle. Then they discovered that the candle had not been *blown* out at all; it had been *crushed* out. The wick was pressed down into the wax, which was flattened as if by some smooth, heavy instrument.

How his companion so quickly overcame her terror, Shorthouse never properly understood; but his admiration for her self-control increased tenfold, and at the same time served to feed his own dying flame—for which he was undeniably grateful. Equally inexplicable to him was the evidence of physical force they had just witnessed. He at once suppressed the memory of stories he had heard of "physical mediums" and their dangerous phenomena; for if these were true, and either his aunt or himself was unwittingly a physical medium, it meant that they were simply aiding to focus the forces of a haunted house already charged to the brim. It was like walking with unprotected lamps among uncovered stores of gunpowder.

So, with as little reflection as possible, he simply relit the candle and went up to the next floor. The arm in his trembled, it is true, and his own tread was often uncertain, but they went on with thoroughness, and after a search revealing nothing they climbed the last flight of stairs to the top floor of all.

Here they found a perfect nest of small servants' rooms, with broken pieces of furniture, dirty cane-bottomed chairs, chests of drawers, cracked mirrors, and decrepit bedsteads. The rooms had low sloping ceilings already hung here and there with cobwebs, small windows, and badly plastered walls—a depressing and dismal region which they were glad to leave behind.

It was on the stroke of midnight when they entered a small room on the third floor, close to the top of the stairs, and arranged to make themselves comfortable for the remainder of their adventure. It was absolutely bare, and was said to be the room—then used as a clothes closet—into which the infuriated groom had chased his victim and finally caught her. Outside, across the narrow landing, began the stairs leading up to the floor above, and the servants' quarters where they had just searched.

In spite of the chilliness of the night there was something in the air of this room that cried for an open window. But there was more than this. Shorthouse could only describe it by saying that he felt less master of himself here than in any other part of the house. There was something that acted directly on the nerves, tiring the resolution, enfeebling the will. He was conscious of this result before he had been in the room five minutes, and it was in the short time they stayed there that he suffered the wholesale depletion of his vital forces, which was, for himself, the chief horror of the whole experience.

They put the candle on the floor of the cupboard, leaving the door a few inches ajar, so that there was no glare to confuse the eyes, and no shadow to shift about on walls and ceiling. Then they spread the cloak on the floor and sat down to wait, with their backs against the wall.

Shorthouse was within two feet of the door on to the landing; his position commanded a good view of the main staircase leading down into the darkness, and also of the beginning of the servants' stairs going to the floor above; the heavy stick lay beside him within easy reach.

The moon was now high above the house. Through the open window they could see the comforting stars like friendly eyes watching in the sky. One by one the clocks of the town struck midnight, and when the sounds died away the deep silence of a windless night fell again over everything. Only the boom of the sea, far away and lugubrious, filled the air with hollow murmurs.

Inside the house the silence became awful; awful, he thought, because any minute now it might be broken by sounds portending terror. The strain of waiting told more and more severely on the nerves; they talked in whispers when they talked at all, for their voices aloud sounded queer and unnatural. A chilliness, not altogether due to the night air, invaded the room, and made them cold. The influences against them, whatever these might be, were slowly robbing them of self-confidence, and the power of decisive action; their forces were on the wane, and the possibility of real fear took on a new and terrible meaning. He began to tremble for the elderly woman by his side, whose pluck could hardly save her beyond a certain extent.

He heard the blood singing in his veins. It sometimes seemed so loud that he fancied it prevented his hearing properly certain other sounds that were beginning very faintly to make themselves audible in the depths of the house. Every time he fastened his attention on these sounds, they instantly ceased. They certainly came no nearer. Yet he could not rid himself of the idea that movement was going on somewhere in the lower regions of the house. The drawing-room floor, where the doors had been so strangely closed, seemed too near; the sounds were further off than that. He thought of the great kitchen, with the scurrying black beetles, and of the dismal little scullery; but, somehow or other, they did not seem to come from there either. Surely they were not *outside* the house!

Then, suddenly, the truth flashed into his mind, and for the space of a minute he felt as if his blood had stopped flowing and turned to ice.

The sounds were not downstairs at all; they were *upstairs*—upstairs, somewhere among those horrid gloomy little servants' rooms with their bits of broken furniture, low ceilings, and cramped windows—upstairs where the victim had first been disturbed and stalked to her death.

And the moment he discovered where the sounds were, he began to hear them more clearly. It was the sound of feet, moving stealthily along the passage overhead, in and out among the rooms, and past the furniture.

He turned quickly to steal a glance at the motionless figure seated beside him, to note whether she had shared his discovery. The faint candle-light coming through the crack in the cupboard door, threw her strongly-marked face into vivid relief against the white of the wall. But it was something else that made him catch his breath and stare again. An extraordinary something had come into her face and seemed to spread over her features like a mask; it smoothed out the deep lines and drew the skin everywhere a little tighter so that the wrinkles disappeared; it brought into the face—with the sole exception of the old eyes—an appearance of youth and almost of childhood.

He stared in speechless amazement—amazement that was danger- ously near to horror. It was his aunt's face indeed, but it was her face of forty years ago, the vacant innocent face of a girl. He had heard stories of that strange effect of terror which could wipe a human countenance clean of other emotions, obliterating all previous expressions; but he had never realised that it could be literally true, or could mean anything so simply horrible as what he now saw. For the dreadful signature of overmastering fear was written plainly in that utter vacancy of the girlish face beside him; and when, feeling his intense gaze, she turned to look at him, he instinc- tively closed his eyes tightly to shut out the sight.

Yet, when he turned a minute later, his feelings well in hand, he saw to his intense relief another expression; his aunt was smiling, and though the face was deathly white, the awful veil had lifted and the normal look was returning.

"Anything wrong?" was all he could think of to say at the moment. And the answer was eloquent, coming from such a woman.

"I feel cold—and a little frightened," she whispered.

He offered to close the window, but she seized hold of him and begged him not to leave her side even for an instant.

"It's upstairs, I know," she whispered, with an odd half laugh; "but I can't possibly go up."

But Shorthouse thought otherwise, knowing that in action lay their best hope of self-control.

He took the brandy flask and poured out a glass of neat spirit, stiff enough to help anybody over anything. She swallowed it with a little shiver. His only idea now was to get out of the house before her collapse became inevitable; but this could not safely be done by turning tail and running from the enemy. Inaction was no longer possible; every minute he was growing less master of himself, and desperate, aggressive measures were imperative without further delay. Moreover, the action must be taken *towards* the enemy, not away from it; the climax, if necessary and unavoidable, would have to be faced boldly. He could do it now; but in ten minutes he might not have the force left to act for himself, much less for both!

Upstairs, the sounds were meanwhile becoming louder and closer, accompanied by occasional creaking of the boards. Someone was moving stealthily about, stumbling now and then awkwardly against the furniture.

Waiting a few moments to allow the tremendous dose of spirits to produce its effect, and knowing this would last but a short time under the circumstances, Shorthouse then quietly got on his feet, saying in a determined voice—

"Now, Aunt Julia, we'll go upstairs and find out what all this noise is about. You must come too. It's what we agreed."

He picked up his stick and went to the cupboard for the candle. A limp form rose shakily beside him breathing hard, and he heard a voice say very faintly something about being "ready to come." The woman's courage amazed him; it was so much greater than his own; and, as they advanced, holding aloft the dripping candle, some subtle force exhaled from this trembling, white-faced old woman at his side that was the true source of his inspiration. It held something really great that shamed him and gave him the support without which he would have proved far less equal to the occasion.

They crossed the dark landing, avoiding with their eyes the deep black space over the banisters. Then they began to mount the narrow staircase to meet the sounds which, minute by minute, grew louder and nearer. About half-way up the stairs Aunt Julia stumbled and Shorthouse turned to catch her by the arm, and just at that moment there came a terrific crash in the servants' corridor overhead. It was instantly followed by a shrill, agonised scream that was a cry of terror and a cry for help melted into one.

Before they could move aside, or go down a single step, someone came rushing along the passage overhead, blundering horribly, racing madly, at full speed, three steps at a time, down the very staircase where they stood. The steps were light and uncertain; but close behind them sounded the heavier tread of another person, and the staircase seemed to shake.

Shorthouse and his companion just had time to flatten themselves against the wall when the jumble of flying steps was upon them, and two persons, with the slightest possible interval between them, dashed past at full speed. It was a perfect whirlwind of sound breaking in upon the midnight silence of the empty building.

The two runners, pursuer and pursued, had passed clean through them where they stood, and already with a thud the boards below had received first one, then the other. Yet they had seen absolutely nothing—not a hand, or arm, or face, or even a shred of flying clothing.

There came a second's pause. Then the first one, the lighter of the two, obviously the pursued one, ran with uncertain footsteps into the little room which Shorthouse and his aunt had just left. The heavier one followed. There was a sound of scuffling, gasping, and smothered screaming; and then out on to the landing came the step—of a single person *treading weightily.*

A dead silence followed for the space of half a minute, and then was heard a rushing sound through the air. It was followed by a dull, crashing thud in the depths of the house below—on the stone floor of the hall.

Utter silence reigned after. Nothing moved. The flame of the candle was steady. It had been steady the whole time, and the air had been undisturbed by any movement whatsoever. Palsied with terror, Aunt Julia, without waiting for her companion, began fumbling her way downstairs; she was crying gently to herself, and when Shorthouse put his arm round her and half carried her, he felt that she was trembling like a leaf. He went into the little room and picked up the cloak from the floor, and, arm in arm, walking very slowly, without speaking a word or looking once behind them, they marched down the three flights into the hall.

In the hall they saw nothing, but the whole way down the stairs they were conscious that someone followed them; step by step; when they went faster IT was left behind, and when they went more slowly IT caught them up. But never once did they look behind to see; and at each turning of the staircase they lowered their eyes for fear of the following horror they might see upon the stairs above.

With trembling hands Shorthouse opened the front door, and they walked out into the moonlight and drew a deep breath of the cool night air blowing in from the sea.

A HAUNTED ISLAND

Blackwood's studies at Edinburgh University proved unsuccessful—he spent more time in the pathology laboratory, attending seances and furthering his studies of theology and hypnotism. Algernon's elder brother, Stevie, was also at Edinburgh, so his exploits were reported back to his father, who despaired. In April 1890, young Blackwood was despatched to Canada with an annual allowance of £100, there to become a farmer. Sir Arthur had used his family connections, not least the influence of Lord Dufferin, who had been Governor-General of Canada, to obtain Algernon a job either on the Canadian Pacific Railway or in insurance as a financial base before setting himself up on a farm. All this proved rather futile. Blackwood did work for a while as a sub-editor on the Canadian Methodist Magazine, *which published some of his earliest writings about his travels in the Black Forest, France and Italy, but when he found work on a farm just outside Toronto, it was a disaster. Blackwood had entered into a partnership with a local dairy farmer and his father sent him the rest of his capital to invest. All worked well for a few months but then the milk turned sour, trade crashed and the partnership was dissolved.*

Blackwood invested such money as he salvaged into a hotel. When his father, a staunch temperance man, learned of this he held his head in his hands and declared that Algie's soul was lost and he would go to Hell. It further tested his father's spiritual strength when he learned that Algernon had joined the Theosophical Society. Alas, for Algernon his abilities as a businessman again proved disastrous and after a few months the hotel failed with huge debts.

Blackwood and his friend Johann Pauw did a moonlight flit, fleeing to the lakes and woods. They spent the summer of 1892 on an island in Lake Rosseau which Blackwood found idyllic. They survived mostly on fish and Blackwood spent the time reading and writing. He planned a book about his adventures, which was never completed.

The wilds of northern Canada freed Blackwood's inner soul and it is where his communion with Nature really started. It inspired several stories of which the best known is "The Wendigo" where the spirit of the wild seeks its revenge upon those who invade its territories. Though Blackwood later moved on to New York he returned to Canada when opportunity allowed and stayed again at his magical island in 1898. It was probably then that he set down the follow-ing story, which was one of his first to be published upon his return to England, in 1899.

Although this story might seem to portray the native Americans in a mur-derous light, it was invoking the fears of the English settlers and the events of recent history. It had only been a little more than twenty years earlier when the Province of Ontario passed the Free Land Grant and Homestead Act which encouraged settlers and dispossessed the native tribes who were granted a small reservation. Little wonder that the settlers feared the Indians—as they were always known in Blackwood's lifetime—would seek out their old lands.

In fact, Blackwood felt a close affinity with native Americans. Over the years he and others noted how his weathered face and slightly hooked nose took on the appearance of a native American man. Whilst at Edinburgh University he had attended seances run by one of the fellow doctors, whose wife was a medium, and at one point she reveals that she was in touch with an Indian medicine man who commented that Blackwood was one too, adding "You have great healing power." At the time he believed in reincarnation and wondered whether his soul might have once been that of an Algonquin native.

Blackwood had read about the history and beliefs of the native Americans and wrote about them in two articles "The Vanishing Redskins" and "Kuloskap *the Master" published in* The Boy's Own Paper *in 1907. There was a curious incident after he had returned to England and was visited by Mrs. Kent, an old lady who had befriended him in New York. One evening as he was taking his leave, she suddenly seemed startled. Looking back, Blackwood saw a vision of her as an Indian squaw. It was not until his next visit that he learned that at the same moment Mrs. Kent had seen him as a native American.*

T HE following events occurred on a small island of isolated position in a large Canadian lake, to whose cool waters the inhabitants of Montreal and Toronto flee for rest and recreation in the hot months. It is only to be regretted that events of such peculiar interest to the genuine student of the psychical should be entirely uncorroborated. Such unfortunately, however, is the case.

Our own party of nearly twenty had returned to Montreal that very day, and I was left in solitary possession for a week or two longer, in order to accomplish some important "reading" for the law which I had foolishly neglected during the summer.

It was late in September, and the big trout and maskinonge were stirring themselves in the depths of the lake, and beginning slowly to move up to the surface waters as the north winds and early frosts lowered their temperature. Already the maples were crimson and gold, and the wild laughter of the loons echoed in sheltered bays that never knew their strange cry in the summer.

With a whole island to oneself, a two-storey cottage, a canoe, and only the chipmunks, and the farmer's weekly visit with eggs and bread, to disturb one, the opportunities for hard reading might be very great. It all depends!

The rest of the party had gone off with many warnings to beware of Indians, and not to stay late enough to be the victim of a frost that thinks nothing of forty below zero. After they had gone, the loneliness of the situation made itself unpleasantly felt. There were no other islands within six or seven miles, and though the mainland forests lay a couple of miles behind me, they stretched for a very great distance unbroken by any signs of human habitation. But, though the island was completely deserted and silent, the rocks and trees that had echoed human laughter and voices almost every hour of the day for two months could not fail to retain some memories of it all; and I was not surprised to fancy I heard a shout or a cry as I passed from rock to rock, and more than once to imagine that I heard my own name called aloud.

In the cottage there were six tiny little bedrooms divided from one another by plain unvarnished partitions of pine. A wooden bedstead, a mattress, and a chair, stood in each room, but I only found two mirrors, and one of these was broken.

The boards creaked a good deal as I moved about, and the signs of occupation were so recent that I could hardly believe I was alone. I half expected to find someone left behind, still trying to crowd into a box more than it would hold. The door of one room was stiff, and refused for a moment to open, and it required very little persuasion to imagine someone was holding the handle on the inside, and that when it opened I should meet a pair of human eyes.

A thorough search of the floor led me to select as my own sleeping quarters a little room with a diminutive balcony over the verandah roof. The room was very small, but the bed was large, and had the best mattress of them all. It was situated directly over the sitting-room where I should live and do my "reading," and the miniature window looked out to the rising sun. With the exception of a narrow path which led from the front door and verandah through the trees to the boat-landing, the island was densely covered with maples, hemlocks, and cedars. The trees gathered in round the cottage so closely that the slightest wind made the branches scrape the roof and tap the wooden walls. A few moments after sunset the darkness became impenetrable, and ten yards beyond the glare of the lamps that shone through the sitting-room windows—of which there were four—you could not see an inch before your nose, nor move a step without running up against a tree.

The rest of that day I spent moving my belongings from my tent to the sitting-room, taking stock of the contents of the larder, and chopping enough wood for the stove to last me for a week. After that, just before sunset, I went round the island a couple of times in my canoe for precaution's sake. I had never dreamed of doing this before, but when a man is alone he does things that never occur to him when he is one of a large party.

How lonely the island seemed when I landed again! The sun was down, and twilight is unknown in these northern regions. The darkness comes up at once. The canoe safely pulled up and turned over on her face, I groped my way up the little narrow pathway to the verandah. The six lamps were soon burning merrily in the front room; but in the kitchen, where I "dined," the shadows were so gloomy, and the lamplight was so inadequate, that the stars could be seen peeping through the cracks between the rafters.

I turned in early that night. Though it was calm and there was no wind, the creaking of my bedstead and the musical gurgle of the water over the rocks below were not the only sounds that reached my ears. As I lay awake, the appalling emptiness of the house grew upon me. The corridors and vacant rooms seemed to echo innumerable footsteps, shufflings, the rustle of skirts, and a constant undertone of whispering. When sleep at length overtook me, the breathings and noises, however, passed gently to mingle with the voices of my dreams.

A week passed by, and the "reading" progressed favourably. On the tenth day of my solitude, a strange thing happened. I awoke after a good night's sleep to find myself possessed with a marked repugnance for my room. The air seemed to stifle me. The more I tried to define the cause of this dislike, the more unreasonable it appeared. There was something about the room that made me afraid. Absurd as it seems, this feeling clung to me obstinately while dressing, and more than once I caught myself shivering, and conscious of an inclination to get out of the room as quickly as possible. The more I tried to laugh it away, the more real it became; and when at last I was dressed, and went out into the passage, and downstairs into the kitchen, it was with feelings of relief, such as I might imagine would accompany one's escape from the presence of a dangerous contagious disease.

While cooking my breakfast, I carefully recalled every night spent in the room, in the hope that I might in some way connect the dislike I now felt with some disagreeable incident that had occurred in it. But the only thing I could recall was one stormy night when I suddenly awoke and heard the boards creaking so loudly in the corridor that I was convinced there were people in the house. So certain was I of this, that I had descended the stairs, gun in hand, only to find the doors and windows securely fastened, and the mice and black-beetles in sole possession of the floor. This was certainly not sufficient to account for the strength of my feelings.

The morning hours I spent in steady reading; and when I broke off in the middle of the day for a swim and luncheon, I was very much surprised, if not a little alarmed, to find that my dislike for the room had, if anything, grown stronger. Going upstairs to get a book, I experienced the most marked aversion to entering the room, and while within I was conscious all the time of an uncomfortable feeling that was half uneasiness and half apprehension. The result of it was that, instead of reading, I spent the afternoon on the water paddling and fishing, and when I got home about sundown, brought with me half a dozen delicious black bass for the supper-table and the larder.

As sleep was an important matter to me at this time, I had decided that if my aversion to the room was so strongly marked on my return as it had been before, I would move my bed down into the sitting-room, and sleep there. This was, I argued, in no sense a concession to an absurd and fanciful fear, but simply a precaution to ensure a good night's sleep. A bad night involved the loss of the next day's reading,—a loss I was not prepared to incur.

I accordingly moved my bed downstairs into a corner of the sitting-room facing the door, and was moreover uncommonly glad when the operation was completed, and the door of the bedroom closed finally upon the shadows, the silence, and the strange *fear* that shared the room with them.

The croaking stroke of the kitchen clock sounded the hour of eight as I finished washing up my few dishes, and closing the kitchen door behind me, passed into the front room. All the lamps were lit, and their reflectors, which I had polished up during the day, threw a blaze of light into the room.

Outside the night was still and warm. Not a breath of air was stirring; the waves were silent, the trees motionless, and heavy clouds hung like an oppressive curtain over the heavens. The darkness seemed to have rolled up with unusual swiftness, and not the faintest glow of colour remained to show where the sun had set. There was present in the atmosphere that ominous and overwhelming silence which so often precedes the most violent storms.

I sat down to my books with my brain unusually clear, and in my heart the pleasant satisfaction of knowing that five black bass were lying in the ice-house, and that tomorrow morning the old farmer would arrive with fresh bread and eggs. I was soon absorbed in my books.

As the night wore on the silence deepened. Even the chipmunks were still; and the boards of the floors and walls ceased creaking. I read on steadily till, from the gloomy shadows of the kitchen, came the hoarse sound of the clock striking nine. How loud the strokes sounded! They were like blows of a big hammer. I closed one book and opened another, feeling that I was just warming up to my work.

This, however, did not last long. I presently found that I was reading the same paragraphs over twice, simple paragraphs that did not require such effort. Then I noticed that my mind began to wander to other things, and the effort to recall my thoughts became harder with each digression. Concentration was growing momentarily more difficult. Presently I discovered that I had turned over two pages instead of one, and had not noticed my mistake until I was well down the page. This was becoming serious. What was the disturbing influence? It could not be physical fatigue. On the contrary, my mind was unusually alert, and in a more receptive condition than usual. I made a new and determined effort to read, and for a short time succeeded in giving my whole attention to my subject. But in a very few moments again I found myself leaning back in my chair, staring vacantly into space.

Something was evidently at work in my subconsciousness. There was something I had neglected to do. Perhaps the kitchen door and windows were not fastened. I accordingly went to see, and found that they were! The fire perhaps needed attention. I went in to see, and found that it was all right! I looked at the lamps, went upstairs into every bedroom in turn, and then went round the house, and even into the ice-house. Nothing was wrong; everything was in its place. Yet something *was* wrong! The conviction grew stronger and stronger within me.

When I at length settled down to my books again and tried to read, I became aware, for the first time, that the room seemed growing cold. Yet the day had been oppressively warm, and evening had brought no relief. The six big lamps, moreover, gave out heat enough to warm the room pleasantly. But a chilliness, that perhaps crept up from the lake, made itself felt in the room, and caused me to get up to close the glass door opening on to the verandah.

For a brief moment I stood looking out at the shaft of light that fell from the windows and shone some little distance down the pathway, and out for a few feet into the lake.

As I looked, I saw a canoe glide into the pathway of light, and immediately crossing it, pass out of sight again into the darkness. It was perhaps a hundred feet from the shore, and it moved swiftly.

I was surprised that a canoe should pass the island at that time of night, for all the summer visitors from the other side of the lake had gone home weeks before, and the island was a long way out of any line of water traffic.

My reading from this moment did not make very good progress, for somehow the picture of that canoe, gliding so dimly and swiftly across the narrow track of light on the black waters, silhouetted itself against the background of my mind with singular vividness. It kept coming between my eyes and the printed page. The more I thought about it the more surprised I became. It was of larger build than any I had seen during the past summer months, and was more like the old Indian war canoes with the high curving bows and stern and wide beam. The more I tried to read, the less success attended my efforts; and finally I closed my books and went out on the verandah to walk up and down a bit, and shake the chilliness out of my bones.

The night was perfectly still, and as dark as imaginable. I stumbled down the path to the little landing wharf, where the water made the very faintest of gurgling under the timbers. The sound of a big tree falling in the mainland forest, far across the lake, stirred echoes in the heavy air, like the first guns of a distant night attack. No other sound disturbed the stillness that reigned supreme.

As I stood upon the wharf in the broad splash of light that followed me from the sitting-room windows, I saw another canoe cross the pathway of uncertain light upon the water, and disappear at once into the impenetrable gloom that lay beyond. This time I saw more distinctly than before. It was like the former canoe, a big birch-bark, with high-crested bows and stern and broad beam. It was paddled by two Indians, of whom the one in the stern—the steerer—appeared to be a very large man. I could see this very plainly; and though the second canoe was much nearer the island than the first, I judged that they were both on their way home to the Government Reservation, which was situated some fifteen miles away upon the mainland.

I was wondering in my mind what could possibly bring any Indians down to this part of the lake at such an hour of the night, when a third canoe, of precisely similar build, and also occupied by two Indians, passed silently round the end of the wharf. This time the canoe was very much nearer shore, and it suddenly flashed into my mind that the three canoes were in reality one and the same, and that only one canoe was circling the island!

This was by no means a pleasant reflection, because, if it were the correct solution of the unusual appearance of the three canoes in this lonely part of the lake at so late an hour, the purpose of the two men could only reasonably be considered to be in some way connected with myself. I had never known of the Indians attempting any violence upon the settlers who shared the wild, inhospitable country with them; at the same time, it was not beyond the region of possibility to suppose... But then I did not care even to think of such hideous possibilities, and my imagination immediately sought relief in all manner of other solutions to the problem, which indeed came readily enough to my mind, but did not succeed in recommending themselves to my reason.

Meanwhile, by a sort of instinct, I stepped back out of the bright light in which I had hitherto been standing, and waited in the deep shadow of a rock to see if the canoe would again make its appearance. Here I could see, without being seen, and the precaution seemed a wise one.

After less than five minutes the canoe, as I had anticipated, made its fourth appearance. This time it was not twenty yards from the wharf, and I saw that the Indians meant to land. I recognised the two men as those who had passed before, and the steerer was certainly an immense fellow. It was unquestionably the same canoe. There could be no longer any doubt that for some purpose of their own the men had been going round and round the island for some time, waiting for an opportunity to land. I strained my eyes to follow them in the darkness, but the night had completely swallowed them up, and not even the faintest swish of the paddles reached my ears as the Indians plied their long and powerful strokes. The canoe would be round again in a few moments, and this time it was possible that the men might land. It was well to be prepared. I knew nothing of their intentions, and two to one (when the two are big Indians!) late at night on a lonely island was not exactly my idea of pleasant intercourse.

In a corner of the sitting-room, leaning up against the back wall, stood my Marlin rifle, with ten cartridges in the magazine and one lying snugly in the greased breech. There was just time to get up to the house and take up a position of defence in that corner. Without an instant's hesitation I ran up to the verandah, carefully picking my way among the trees, so as to avoid being seen in the light. Entering the room, I shut the door leading to the verandah, and as quickly as possible turned out every one of the six lamps. To be in a room so brilliantly lighted, where my every movement could be observed from outside, while I could see nothing but impenetrable darkness at every window, was by all laws of warfare an unnecessary concession to the enemy. And this enemy, if enemy it was to be, was far too wily and dangerous to be granted any such advantages.

I stood in the corner of the room with my back against the wall, and my hand on the cold rifle-barrel. The table, covered with my books, lay between me and the door, but for the first few minutes after the lights were out the darkness was so intense that nothing could be discerned at all. Then, very gradually, the outline of the room became visible, and the framework of the windows began to shape itself dimly before my eyes.

After a few minutes the door (its upper half of glass), and the two windows that looked out upon the front verandah, became specially distinct; and I was glad that this was so, because if the Indians came up to the house I should be able to see their approach, and gather something of their plans. Nor was I mistaken, for there presently came to my ears the peculiar hollow sound of a canoe landing and being carefully dragged up over the rocks. The paddles I distinctly heard being placed underneath, and the silence that ensued thereupon I rightly interpreted to mean that the Indians were stealthily approaching the house...

While it would be absurd to claim that I was not alarmed—even frightened—at the gravity of the situation and its possible outcome, I speak the whole truth when I say that I was not overwhelmingly afraid for myself. I was conscious that even at this stage of the night I was passing into a psychical condition in which my sensations seemed no longer normal. Physical fear at no time entered into the nature of my feelings; and though I kept my hand upon my rifle the greater part of the night, I was all the time conscious that its assistance could be of little avail against the terrors that I had to face. More than once I seemed to feel most curiously that I was in no real sense a part of the proceedings, nor actually involved in them, but that I was playing the part of a spectator—a spectator, moreover, on a psychic rather than on a material plane. Many of my sensations that night were too vague for definite description and analysis, but the main feeling that will stay with me to the end of my days is the awful horror of it all, and the miserable sensation that if the strain had lasted a little longer than was actually the case my mind must inevitably have given way.

Meanwhile I stood still in my corner, and waited patiently for what was to come. The house was as still as the grave, but the inarticulate voices of the night sang in my ears, and I seemed to hear the blood running in my veins and dancing in my pulses.

If the Indians came to the back of the house, they would find the kitchen door and window securely fastened. They could not get in there without making considerable noise, which I was bound to hear. The only mode of getting in was by means of the door that faced me, and I kept my eyes glued on that door without taking them off for the smallest fraction of a second.

My sight adapted itself every minute better to the darkness. I saw the table that nearly filled the room, and left only a narrow passage on each side. I could also make out the straight backs of the wooden chairs pressed up against it, and could even distinguish my papers and inkstand lying on the white oilcloth covering. I thought of the gay faces that had gathered round that table during the summer, and I longed for the sunlight as I had never longed for it before.

Less than three feet to my left the passage-way led to the kitchen, and the stairs leading to the bedrooms above commenced in this passage-way, but almost in the sitting-room itself. Through the windows I could see the dim motionless outlines of the trees: not a leaf stirred, not a branch moved.

A few moments of this awful silence, and then I was aware of a soft tread on the boards of the verandah, so stealthy that it seemed an impression directly on my brain rather than upon the nerves of hearing. Immediately afterwards a black figure darkened the glass door, and I perceived that a face was pressed against the upper panes. A shiver ran down my back, and my hair was conscious of a tendency to rise and stand at right angles to my head.

It was the figure of an Indian, broad-shouldered and immense; indeed, the largest figure of a man I have ever seen outside of a circus hall. By some power of light that seemed to generate itself in the brain, I saw the strong dark face with the aquiline nose and high cheek-bones flattened against the glass. The direction of the gaze I could not determine; but faint gleams of light as the big eyes rolled round and showed their whites, told me plainly that no corner of the room escaped their searching.

For what seemed fully five minutes the dark figure stood there, with the huge shoulders bent forward so as to bring the head down to the level of the glass; while behind him, though not nearly so large, the shadowy form of the other Indian swayed to and fro like a bent tree. While I waited in an agony of suspense and agitation for their next movement little currents of icy sensation ran up and down my spine and my heart seemed alternately to stop beating and then start off again with terrifying rapidity. They must have heard its thumping and the singing of the blood in my head! Moreover, I was conscious, as I felt a cold stream of perspiration trickle down my face, of a desire to scream, to shout, to bang the walls like a child, to make a noise, or do anything that would relieve the suspense and bring things to a speedy climax.

It was probably this inclination that led me to another discovery, for when I tried to bring my rifle from behind my back to raise it and have it pointed at the door ready to fire, I found that I was powerless to move. The muscles, paralysed by this strange fear, refused to obey the will. Here indeed was a terrifying complication!

There was a faint sound of rattling at the brass knob, and the door was pushed open a couple of inches. A pause of a few seconds, and it was pushed open still further. Without a sound of footsteps that was appreciable to my ears, the two figures glided into the room, and the man behind gently closed the door after him.

They were alone with me between the four walls. Could they see me standing there, so still and straight in my corner? Had they, perhaps, already seen me? My blood surged and sang like the roll of drums in an orchestra; and though I did my best to suppress my breathing, it sounded like the rushing of wind through a pneumatic tube.

My suspense as to the next move was soon at an end—only, however, to give place to a new and keener alarm. The men had hitherto exchanged no words and no signs, but there were general indications of a movement across the room, and whichever way they went they would have to pass round the table. If they came my way they would have to pass within six inches of my person. While I was considering this very disagreeable possibility, I perceived that the smaller Indian (smaller by comparison) suddenly raised his arm and pointed to the ceiling. The other fellow raised his head and followed the direction of his companion's arm. I began to understand at last. They were going upstairs, and the room directly overhead to which they pointed had been until this night my bedroom. It was the room in which I had experienced that very morning so strange a sensation of fear, and but for which I should then have been lying asleep in the narrow bed against the window.

The Indians then began to move silently around the room; they were going upstairs, and they were coming round my side of the table. So stealthy were their movements that, but for the abnormally sensitive state of the nerves, I should never have heard them. As it was, their cat-like tread was distinctly audible. Like two monstrous black cats they came round the table toward me, and for the first time I perceived that the smaller of the two dragged something along the floor behind him. As it trailed along over the floor with a soft, sweeping sound, I somehow got the impression that it was a large dead thing with outstretched wings, or a large, spreading cedar branch. Whatever it was, I was unable to see it even in outline, and I was too terrified, even had I possessed the power over my muscles, to move my neck forward in the effort to determine its nature.

Nearer and nearer they came. The leader rested a giant hand upon the table as he moved. My lips were glued together, and the air seemed to burn in my nostrils. I tried to close my eyes, so that I might not see as they passed me; but my eyelids had stiffened, and refused to obey. Would they never get by me? Sensation seemed also to have left my legs, and it was as if I were standing on mere supports of wood or stone. Worse still, I was conscious that I was losing the power of balance, the power to stand upright, or even to lean backwards against the wall. Some force was drawing me forward, and a dizzy terror seized me that I should lose my balance, and topple forward against the Indians just as they were in the act of passing me.

Even moments drawn out into hours must come to an end some time, and almost before I knew it the figures had passed me and had their feet upon the lower step of the stairs leading to the upper bedrooms. There could not have been six inches between us, and yet I was conscious only of a current of cold air that followed them. They had not touched me, and I was convinced that they had not seen me. Even the trailing thing on the floor behind them had not touched my feet, as I had dreaded it would, and on such an occasion as this I was grateful even for the smallest mercies.

The absence of the Indians from my immediate neighbourhood brought little sense of relief. I stood shivering and shuddering in my corner, and, beyond being able to breathe more freely, I felt no whit less uncomfortable. Also, I was aware that a certain light, which, without apparent source or rays, had enabled me to follow their every gesture and movement, had gone out of the room with their departure. An unnatural darkness now filled the room, and pervaded its every corner so that I could barely make out the positions of the windows and the glass doors.

As I said before, my condition was evidently an abnormal one. The capacity for feeling surprise seemed, as in dreams, to be wholly absent. My senses recorded with unusual accuracy every smallest occurrence, but I was able to draw only the simplest deductions.

The Indians soon reached the top of the stairs, and there they halted for a moment. I had not the faintest clue as to their next movement. They appeared to hesitate. They were listening attentively. Then I heard one of them, who by the weight of his soft tread must have been the giant, cross the narrow corridor and enter the room directly overhead—my own little bedroom. But for the insistence of that unaccountable dread I had experienced there in the morning, I should at that very moment have been lying in the bed with the big Indian in the room standing beside me.

For the space of a hundred seconds there was silence, such as might have existed before the birth of sound. It was followed by a long quivering shriek of terror, which rang out into the night, and ended in a short gulp before it had run its full course. At the same moment the other Indian left his place at the head of the stairs, and joined his companion in the bedroom. I heard the "thing" trailing behind him along the floor. A thud followed, as of something heavy falling, and then all became as still and silent as before.

It was at this point that the atmosphere, surcharged all day with the electricity of a fierce storm, found relief in a dancing flash of brilliant lightning simultaneously with a crash of loudest thunder. For five seconds every article in the room was visible to me with amazing distinctness, and through the windows I saw the tree trunks standing in solemn rows. The thunder pealed and echoed across the lake and among the distant islands, and the floodgates of heaven then opened and let out their rain in streaming torrents.

The drops fell with a swift rushing sound upon the still waters of the lake, which leaped up to meet them, and pattered with the rattle of shot on the leaves of the maples and the roof of the cottage. A moment later, and another flash, even more brilliant and of longer duration than the first, lit up the sky from zenith to horizon, and bathed the room momentarily in dazzling whiteness. I could see the rain glistening on the leaves and branches outside. The wind rose suddenly, and in less than a minute the storm that had been gathering all day burst forth in its full fury.

Above all the noisy voices of the elements, the slightest sounds in the room overhead made themselves heard, and in the few seconds of deep silence that followed the shriek of terror and pain I was aware that the movements had commenced again. The men were leaving the room and approaching the top of the stairs. A short pause, and they began to descend. Behind them, tumbling from step to step, I could hear that trailing "thing" being dragged along. It had become ponderous!

I awaited their approach with a degree of calmness, almost of apathy, which was only explicable on the ground that after a certain point Nature applies her own anæsthetic, and a merciful condition of numbness supervenes. On they came, step by step, nearer and nearer, with the shuffling sound of the burden behind growing louder as they approached.

They were already half-way down the stairs when I was galvanised afresh into a condition of terror by the consideration of a new and horrible possibility. It was the reflection that if another vivid flash of lightning were to come when the shadowy procession was in the room, perhaps when it was actually passing in front of me, I should see everything in detail, and worse, be seen myself! I could only hold my breath and wait—wait while the minutes lengthened into hours, and the procession made its slow progress round the room.

The Indians had reached the foot of the staircase. The form of the huge leader loomed in the doorway of the passage, and the burden with an ominous thud had dropped from the last step to the floor. There was a moment's pause while I saw the Indian turn and stoop to assist his companion. Then the procession moved forward again, entered the room close on my left, and began to move slowly round my side of the table. The leader was already beyond me, and his companion, dragging on the floor behind him the burden, whose confused outline I could dimly make out, was exactly in front of me, when the cavalcade came to a dead halt. At the same moment, with the strange suddenness of thunderstorms, the splash of the rain ceased altogether, and the wind died away into utter silence.

For the space of five seconds my heart seemed to stop beating, and then the worst came. A double flash of lightning lit up the room and its contents with merciless vividness.

The huge Indian leader stood a few feet past me on my right. One leg was stretched forward in the act of taking a step. His immense shoulders were turned toward his companion, and in all their magnificent fierceness I saw the outline of his features. His gaze was directed upon the burden his companion was dragging along the floor; but his profile, with the big aquiline nose, high cheek-bone, straight black hair and bold chin, burnt itself in that brief instant into my brain, never again to fade.

Dwarfish, compared with this gigantic figure, appeared the proportions of the other Indian, who, within twelve inches of my face, was stooping over the thing he was dragging in a position that lent to his person the additional horror of deformity. And the burden, lying upon a sweeping cedar branch which he held and dragged by a long stem, was the body of a white man. The scalp had been neatly lifted, and blood lay in a broad smear upon the cheeks and forehead.

Then, for the first time that night, the terror that had paralysed my muscles and my will lifted its unholy spell from my soul. With a loud cry I stretched out my arms to seize the big Indian by the throat, and, grasping only air, tumbled forward unconscious upon the ground.

I had recognised the body, and *the face was my own!*...

It was bright daylight when a man's voice recalled me to consciousness. I was lying where I had fallen, and the farmer was standing in the room with the loaves of bread in his hands. The horror of the night was still in my heart, and as the bluff settler helped me to my feet and picked up the rifle which had fallen with me, with many questions and expressions of condolence, I imagine my brief replies were neither self-explanatory nor even intelligible.

That day, after a thorough and fruitless search of the house, I left the island, and went over to spend my last ten days with the farmer; and when the time came for me to leave, the necessary reading had been accomplished, and my nerves had completely recovered their balance.

On the day of my departure the farmer started early in his big boat with my belongings to row to the point, twelve miles distant, where a little steamer ran twice a week for the accommodation of hunters. Late in the afternoon I went off in another direction in my canoe, wishing to see the island once again, where I had been the victim of so strange an experience.

In due course I arrived there, and made a tour of the island. I also made a search of the little house, and it was not without a curious sensation in my heart that I entered the little upstairs bedroom. There seemed nothing unusual.

Just after I re-embarked, I saw a canoe gliding ahead of me around the curve of the island. A canoe was an unusual sight at this time of the year, and this one seemed to have sprung from nowhere. Altering my course a little, I watched it disappear around the next projecting point of rock. It had high curving bows, and there were two Indians in it. I lingered with some excitement, to see if it would appear again round the other side of the island; and in less than five minutes it came into view. There were less than two hundred yards between us, and the Indians, sitting on their haunches, were paddling swiftly in my direction.

I never paddled faster in my life than I did in those next few minutes. When I turned to look again, the Indians had altered their course, and were again circling the island.

The sun was sinking behind the forests on the mainland, and the crimson-coloured clouds of sunset were reflected in the waters of the lake, when I looked round for the last time, and saw the big bark canoe and its two dusky occupants still going round the island. Then the shadows deepened rapidly; the lake grew black, and the night wind blew its first breath in my face as I turned a corner, and a projecting bluff of rock hid from my view both island and canoe.

MAX HENSIG

Bacteriologist and Murderer:
A Story of New York

As autumn arrived Blackwood and Pauw decided to leave their idyllic surroundings but rather than return to Toronto and face their creditors they
headed for New York. They arrived on 14 September 1892 with no real plans.
Pauw went in search of work in the theatre whilst Blackwood, mindful of his
achievements at the Methodist Magazine in Toronto, visited the offices of
Harper's. He was assigned a job about a cargo of wild animals which had just
arrived for the New York Zoo which he wrote for Harper's Young People
but no further assignments came. However, thanks to people he met at a local
cricket match, he was given an introduction to the editor of the New York
Sun, an influential and at one time notorious newspaper because of its delight
in running hoax stories and scandals. The editor passed Blackwood over to the
Evening Sun where he was employed at $15 a week. He was given the role as
crime reporter at the notorious Tombs Police Court, a posting that other reporters avoided. Blackwood reported on various trials and interviewed prisoners,
seeking the personal angle, sometimes getting a story from a convicted criminal
about to be executed in the electric chair.

The first major story upon which Blackwood reported was that of Carlyle
Harris, a medical student who had been convicted of murdering his wife
with morphine. Harris had appealed, and Blackwood reported upon that

appeal which began in late November 1892. He interviewed Harris and, even thirty years later, when writing his autobiography Episodes Before Thirty, *he remembered it vividly: "Carlyle Harris, calm, indifferent, cold as ice, I still see, as he peered past the iron in Murderers' Row, protesting his innocence with his steely blue eyes fixed on mine." Blackwood interviewed many criminals, which made a vivid, even terrifying impression. They were of many races and cultures reflecting the melting pot of all those struggling to survive in New York. He remained the Tombs reporter for, what he recalled as, "… a loathed, distressing, horror-laden year."*

Those experiences were impossible to forget and fifteen years later he distilled it all into the following story. It includes words, phrases and descriptions we find disconcerting these days but which reflect the multicultural, almost suffocating world in which Blackwood struggled to make a living.

I

BESIDES the departmental men on the New York *Vulture*, there were about twenty reporters for general duty, and Williams had worked his way up till he stood easily among the first half-dozen; for, in addition to being accurate and painstaking, he was able to bring to his reports of common things that touch of imagination and humour which just lifted them out of the rut of mere faithful recording. Moreover, the city editor (*anglice* news editor) appreciated his powers, and always tried to give him assignments that did himself and the paper credit, and he was justified now in expecting to be relieved of the hack jobs that were usually allotted to new men.

He was therefore puzzled and a little disappointed one morning as he saw his inferiors summoned one after another to the news desk to receive the best assignments of the day, and when at length his turn came, and the city editor asked him to cover the "Hensig story," he gave a little start of vexation that almost betrayed him into asking what the devil the "Hensig story" was. For it is the duty of every morning newspaper man—in New York at least—to have made himself familiar with all the news of the day before he shows himself at the office, and though Williams had already done this, he could not recall either the name or the story.

"You can run to a hundred or a hundred and fifty, Mr. Williams. Cover the trial thoroughly, and get good interviews with Hensig and the lawyers. There'll be no night assignment for you till the case is over."

Williams was going to ask if there were any private "tips" from the District Attorney's office, but the editor was already speaking with Weekes, who wrote the daily "weather story," and he went back slowly to his desk, angry and disappointed, to read up the Hensig case and lay his plans for the day accordingly. At any rate, he reflected, it looked like "a soft job," and as there was to be no second assignment for him that night, he would get off by eight o'clock, and be able to dine and sleep for once like a civilised man. And that was something.

It took him some time, however, to discover that the Hensig case was only a murder story. And this increased his disgust. It was tucked away in the corners of most of the papers, and little importance was attached to it. A murder trial is not first-class news unless there are very special features connected with it, and Williams had already covered scores of them. There was a heavy sameness about them that made it difficult to report them interestingly, and as a rule they were left to the tender mercies of the "flimsy" men—the Press Associations—and no paper sent a special man unless the case was distinctly out of the usual. Moreover, a hundred and fifty meant a column and a half, and Williams, not being a space man, earned the same money whether he wrote a stickful or a page; so that he felt doubly aggrieved, and walked out into the sunny open spaces opposite Newspaper Row heaving a deep sigh and cursing the boredom of his trade.

Max Hensig, he found, was a German doctor accused of murdering his second wife by injecting arsenic. The woman had been buried several weeks when the suspicious relatives got the body exhumed, and a quantity of the poison had been found in her. Williams recalled something about the arrest, now he came to think of it; but he felt no special interest in it, for ordinary murder trials were no longer his legitimate work, and he scorned them. At first, of course, they had thrilled him horribly, and some of his interviews with the prisoners, especially just before execution, had deeply impressed his imagination and kept him awake at night. Even now he could not enter the gloomy Tombs Prison, or cross the Bridge of Sighs leading from it to the courts, without experiencing a real sensation, for its huge Egyptian columns and massive walls closed round him like death; and the first time he walked down Murderers' Row, and came in view of the cell doors, his throat was dry, and he had almost turned and run out of the building.

The first time, too, that he covered the trial of a n—o and listened to the man's hysterical speech before sentence was pronounced, he was absorbed with interest, and his heart leaped. The wild appeals to the Deity, the long invented words, the ghastly pallor under the black skin, the rolling eyes, and the torrential sentences all seemed to him to be something tremendous to describe for his sensational sheet; and the stickful that was eventually printed—written by the flimsy man too—had given him quite a new standard of the relative value of news and of the quality of the satiated public palate. He had reported the trials of a Chinaman, stolid as wood; of an Italian who had been too quick with his knife; and of a farm girl who had done both her parents to death in their beds, entering their room stark naked, so that no stains should betray her; and at the beginning these things haunted him for days.

But that was all months ago, when he first came to New York. Since then his work had been steadily in the criminal courts, and he had grown a second skin. An execution in the electric chair at Sing Sing could still unnerve him somewhat, but mere murder no longer thrilled or excited him, and he could be thoroughly depended on to write a good "murder story"—an account that his paper could print without blue pencil.

Accordingly he entered the Tombs Prison with nothing stronger than the feeling of vague oppression that gloomy structure always stirred in him, and certainly with no particular emotion connected with the prisoner he was about to interview; and when he reached the second iron door, where a warder peered at him through a small grating, he heard a voice behind him, and turned to find the *Chronicle* man at his heels.

"Hullo, Senator! What good trail are you following down here?" he cried, for the other got no small assignments, and never had less than a column on the *Chronicle* front page at space rates.

"Same as you, I guess—Hensig," was the reply.

"But there's no space in Hensig," said Williams with surprise. "Are you back on salary again?"

"Not much," laughed the Senator—no one knew his real name, but he was always called Senator. "But Hensig's good for two hundred easy. There's a whole list of murders behind him, we hear, and this is the first time he's been caught."

"Poison?"

The Senator nodded in reply, turning to ask the warder some question about another case, and Williams waited for him in the corridor, impatiently rather, for he loathed the musty prison odour. He watched the Senator as he talked, and was distinctly glad he had come. They were good friends: he had helped Williams when he first joined the small army of newspaper men and was not much welcomed, being an Englishman. Common origin and good-heartedness mixed themselves delightfully in his face, and he always made Williams think of a friendly, honest cart-horse—stolid, strong, with big and simple emotions.

"Get a hustle on, Senator," he said at length impatiently.

The two reporters followed the warder down the flagged corridor, past a row of dark cells, each with its occupant, until the man, swinging his keys in the direction indicated, stopped and pointed:

"Here's your gentleman," he said, and then moved on down the corridor, leaving them staring through the bars at a tall, slim young man, pacing to and fro. He had flaxen hair and very bright blue eyes; his skin was white, and his face wore so open and innocent an expression that one would have said he could not twist a kitten's tail without wincing.

"From the *Chronicle* and *Vulture*," explained Williams, by way of introduction, and the talk at once began in the usual way.

The man in the cell ceased his restless pacing up and down, and stopped opposite the bars to examine them. He stared straight into Williams's eyes for a moment, and the reporter noted a very different expression from the one he had first seen. It actually made him shift his position and stand a little to one side. But the movement was wholly instinctive. He could not have explained why he did it.

"Guess you vish me to say I did it, and then egsplain to you *how* I did it," the young doctor said coolly, with a marked German accent. "But I haf no copy to gif you shust now. You see at the trial it is nothing but spite— and shealosy of another woman. I lofed my vife. I vould not haf gilled her for anything in the world—"

"Oh, of course, of course, Dr. Hensig," broke in the Senator, who was more experienced in the ways of difficult interviewing. "We quite understand that. But, you know, in New York the newspapers try a man as much as the courts, and we thought you might like to make a statement to the public which we should be very glad to print for you. It may help your case—"

"Nothing can help my case in this tamned country where shustice is to be pought mit tollars!" cried the prisoner, with a sudden anger and an expression of face still further belying the first one; "nothing except a lot of money. But I tell you now two things you may write for your public: One is, no motive can be shown for the murder, because I lofed Zinka and vished her to live alvays. And the other is—" He stopped a moment and stared steadily at Williams making shorthand notes—"that with my knowledge—my egceptional knowledge—of poisons and pacteriology I could have done it in a dozen ways without pumping arsenic into her body. That is a fool's way of killing. It is clumsy and childish and sure of discofery! See?"

He turned away, as though to signify that the interview was over, and sat down on his wooden bench.

"Seems to have taken a fancy to you," laughed the Senator, as they went off to get further interviews with the lawyers. "He never looked at me once."

"He's got a bad face—the face of a devil. I don't feel complimented," said Williams shortly. "I'd hate to be in his power."

"Same here," returned the other. "Let's go into Silver Dollars and wash the dirty taste out."

So, after the custom of reporters, they made their way up the Bowery and went into a saloon that had gained a certain degree of fame because the Tammany owner had let a silver dollar into each stone of the floor. Here they washed away most of the "dirty taste" left by the Tombs atmosphere and Hensig, and then went on to Steve Brodie's, another saloon a little higher up the same street.

"There'll be others there," said the Senator, meaning drinks as well as reporters, and Williams, still thinking over their interview, silently agreed.

Brodie was a character; there was always something lively going on in his place. He had the reputation of having once jumped from the Brooklyn Bridge and reached the water alive. No one could actually deny it, and no one could prove that it really happened; and anyhow, he had enough imagination and personality to make the myth live and to sell much bad liquor on the strength of it. The walls of his saloon were plastered with lurid oil-paintings of the bridge, the height enormously magnified, and Steve's body in mid-air, an expression of a happy puppy on his face.

Here, as expected, they found "Whitey" Fife, of the *Recorder*, and Galusha Owen, of the *World*. "Whitey," as his nickname implied, was an albino, and clever. He wrote the daily "weather story" for his paper, and the way he spun a column out of rain, wind, and temperature was the envy of every one except the Weather Clerk, who objected to being described as "Farmer Dunne, cleaning his rat-tail file," and to having his dignified office referred to in the public press as "a down-country farm." But the public liked it, and laughed, and "Whitey" was never really spiteful.

Owen, too, when sober, was a good man who had long passed the rubicon of hack assignments. Yet both these men were also on the Hensig story. And Williams, who had already taken an instinctive dislike to the case, was sorry to see this, for it meant frequent interviewing and the possession, more or less, of his mind and imagination. Clearly, he would have much to do with this German doctor. Already, even at this stage, he began to hate him.

The four reporters spent an hour drinking and talking. They fell at length to discussing the last time they had chanced to meet on the same assignment—a private lunatic asylum owned by an incompetent quack without a licence, and where most of the inmates, not mad in the first instance, and all heavily paid for by relatives who wished them out of the way, had gone mad from ill-treatment. The place had been surrounded before dawn by the Board of Health officers, and the quasi-doctor arrested as he opened his front door. It was a splendid newspaper "story," of course.

"My space bill ran to sixty dollars a day for nearly a week," said Whitey Fife thickly, and the others laughed, because Whitey wrote most of his stuff by cribbing it from the evening papers.

"A dead cinch," said Galusha Owen, his dirty flannel collar poking up through his long hair almost to his ears. "I 'faked' the whole of the second day without going down there at all."

He pledged Whitey for the tenth time that morning, and the albino leered happily across the table at him, and passed him a thick compliment before emptying his glass.

"Hensig's going to be good, too," broke in the Senator, ordering a round of gin-fizzes, and Williams gave a little start of annoyance to hear the name brought up again. "He'll make good stuff at the trial. I never saw a cooler hand. You should've heard him talk about poisons and bacteriology, and boasting he could kill in a dozen ways without fear of being caught. I guess he was telling the truth right enough!"

"That so?" cried Galusha and Whitey in the same breath, not having done a stroke of work so far on the case.

"Run down to the Tombsh angetaninerview," added Whitey, turning with a sudden burst of enthusiasm to his companion. His white eyebrows and pink eyes fairly shone against the purple of his tipsy face.

"No, no," cried the Senator; "don't spoil a good story. You're both as full as ticks. I'll match with Williams which of us goes. Hensig knows us already, and we'll all 'give up' in this story right along. No 'beats.'"

So they decided to divide news till the case was finished, and to keep no exclusive items to themselves; and Williams, having lost the toss, swallowed his gin-fizz and went back to the Tombs to get a further talk with the prisoner on his knowledge of expert poisoning and bacteriology.

Meanwhile his thoughts were very busy elsewhere. He had taken no part in the noisy conversation in the bar-room, because something lay at the back of his mind, bothering him, and claiming attention with great persistence. Something was at work in his deeper consciousness, something that had impressed him with a vague sense of unpleasantness and nascent fear, reaching below that second skin he had grown.

And, as he walked slowly through the malodorous slum streets that lay between the Bowery and the Tombs, dodging the pullers-in outside the Jew clothing stores, and nibbling at a bag of pea-nuts he caught up off an Italian push-cart *en route*, this "something" rose a little higher out of its obscurity, and began to play with the roots of the ideas floating higgledy-piggledy on the surface of his mind. He thought he knew what it was, but could not make quite sure. From the roots of his thoughts it rose a little higher, so that he clearly felt it as something disagreeable. Then, with a sudden rush, it came to the surface, and poked its face before him so that he fully recognised it.

The blond visage of Dr. Max Hensig rose before him, cool, smiling, and implacable.

Somehow, he had expected it would prove to be Hensig—this unpleasant thought that was troubling him. He was not really surprised to have labelled it, because the man's personality had made an unwelcome impression upon him at the very start. He stopped nervously in the street, and looked round. He did not expect to see anything out of the way, or to find that he was being followed. It was not that exactly. The act of turning was merely the outward expression of a sudden inner discomfort, and a man with better nerves, or nerves more under control, would not have turned at all.

But what caused this tremor of the nerves? Williams probed and searched within himself. It came, he felt, from some part of his inner being he did not understand; there had been an intrusion, an incongruous intrusion, into the stream of his normal consciousness. Messages from this region always gave him pause; and in this particular case ne saw no reason why he should think specially of Dr. Hensig with alarm—this light-haired stripling with blue eyes and drooping moustache. The faces of other murderers had haunted him once or twice because they were more than ordinarily bad, or because their case possessed unusual features of horror. But there was nothing so very much out of the way about Hensig—at least, if there was, the reporter could not seize and analyse it. There seemed no adequate reason to explain his emotion. Certainly, it had nothing to do with the fact that he was merely a murderer, for that stirred no thrill in him at all, except a kind of pity, and a wonder how the man would meet his execution. It must, he argued, be something to do with the *personality* of the man, apart from any particular deed or characteristic.

Puzzled, and still a little nervous, he stood in the road, hesitating. In front of him the dark walls of the Tombs rose in massive steps of granite. Overhead white summer clouds sailed across a deep blue sky; the wind sang cheerfully among the wires and chimney-pots, making him think of fields and trees; and down the street surged the usual cosmopolitan New York crowd of laughing Italians, surly n——oes, Hebrews chattering Yiddish, tough-looking hooligans with that fighting lurch of the shoulders peculiar to New York roughs, Chinamen, taking little steps like boys—and every other sort of nondescript imaginable. It was early June, and there were faint odours of the sea and of sea-beaches in the air. Williams caught himself shivering a little with delight at the sight of the sky and scent of the wind.

Then he looked back at the great prison, rightly named the Tombs, and the sudden change of thought from the fields to the cells, from life to death, somehow landed him straight into the discovery of what caused this attack of nervousness:

Hensig was no ordinary murderer! That was it. There was something quite out of the ordinary about him. The man was a horror, pure and simple, standing apart from normal humanity. The knowledge of this rushed over him like a revelation, bringing unalterable conviction in its train. Something of it had reached him in that first brief interview, but without explaining itself sufficiently to be recognised, and since then it had been working in his system, like a poison, and was now causing a disturbance, not having been assimilated. A quicker temperament would have labelled it long before.

Now, Williams knew well that he drank too much, and had more than a passing acquaintance with drugs; his nerves were shaky at the best of times. His life on the newspapers afforded no opportunity of cultivating pleasant social relations, but brought him all the time into contact with the seamy side of life—the criminal, the abnormal, the unwholesome in human nature. He knew, too, that strange thoughts, *idées fixes* and what not, grew readily in such a soil as this, and, not wanting these, he had formed a habit—peculiar to himself—of deliberately sweeping his mind clean once a week of all that had haunted, obsessed, or teased him, of the horrible or unclean, during his work; and his eighth day, his holiday, he invariably spent in the woods, walking, building fires, cooking a meal in the open, and getting all the country air and the exercise he possibly could. He had in this way kept his mind free from many unpleasant pictures that might otherwise have lodged there abidingly, and the habit of thus cleansing his imagination had proved more than once of real value to him.

So now he laughed to himself, and turned on those whizzing brooms of his, trying to forget these first impressions of Hensig, and simply going in, as he did a hundred other times, to get an ordinary interview with an ordinary prisoner. This habit, being nothing more nor less than the practice of suggestion, was more successful sometimes than others. This time—since fear is less susceptible to suggestion than other emotions—it was less so.

Williams got his interview, and came away fairly creeping with horror. Hensig was all that he had felt, and more besides. He belonged, the reporter felt convinced, to that rare type of deliberate murderer, cold-blooded and calculating, who kills for a song, delights in killing, and gives its whole intellect to the consideration of each detail, glorying in evading detection and revelling in the notoriety of the trial, if caught. At first he had answered reluctantly, but as Williams plied his questions intelligently, the young doctor warmed up and became enthusiastic with a sort of cold intellectual enthusiasm, till at last he held forth like a lecturer, pacing his cell, gesticulating, explaining with admirable exposition how easy murder could be to a man who knew his business.

And *he* did know his business! No man, in these days of inquests and post-mortem examination, would inject poisons that might be found weeks afterwards in the viscera of the victim. No man who knew his business!

"What is more easy," he said, holding the bars with his long white fingers and gazing into the reporter's eyes, "than to take a disease germ ['cherm' he pronounced it] of typhus, plague, or any cherm you blease, and make so virulent a culture that no medicine in the vorld could counteract it; a really powerful microbe—and then scratch the skin of your victim with a pin? And who could drace it to you, or accuse you of murder?"

Williams, as he watched and heard, was glad the bars were between them; but, even so, something invisible seemed to pass from the prisoner's atmosphere and lay an icy finger on his heart. He had come into contact with every possible kind of crime and criminal, and had interviewed scores of men who, for jealousy, greed, passion, or other comprehensible emotion, had killed and paid the penalty of killing. He understood that. Any man with strong passions was a potential killer. But never before had he met a man who in cold blood, deliberately, under no emotion greater than boredom, would destroy a human life and then boast of his ability to do it. Yet this, he felt sure, was what Hensig had done, and what his vile words shadowed forth and betrayed. Here was something outside humanity, something terrible, monstrous; and it made him shudder. This young doctor, he felt, was a fiend incarnate, a man who thought less of human life than of the lives of flies in summer, and who would kill with as steady a hand and cool a brain as though he were performing a common operation in the hospital.

Thus the reporter left the prison gates with a vivid impression in his mind, though exactly how his conclusion was reached was more than he could tell. This time the mental brooms failed to act. The horror of it remained.

On the way out into the street he ran against Policeman Dowling of the ninth precinct, with whom he had been fast friends since the day he wrote a glowing account of Dowling's capture of a "greengoods-man," when Dowling had been so drunk that he nearly lost his prisoner altogether. The policeman had never forgotten the good turn; it had promoted him to plain clothes; and he was always ready to give the reporter any news he had.

"Know of anything good today?" he asked by way of habit.

"Bet your bottom dollar I do," replied the coarse-faced Irish policeman; "one of the best, too. I've got Hensig!"

Dowling spoke with pride and affection. He was mighty pleased, too, because his name would be in the paper every day for a week or more, and a big case helped the chances of promotion.

Williams cursed inwardly. Apparently there was no escape from this man Hensig.

"Not much of a case, is it?" he asked.

"It's a jim dandy, that's what it is," replied the other, a little offended. "Hensig may miss the Chair because the evidence is weak, but he's the worst I've ever met. Why, he'd poison you as soon as spit in your eye, and if he's got a heart at all he keeps it on ice."

"What makes you think that?"

"Oh, they talk pretty freely to us sometimes," the policeman said, with a significant wink. "Can't be used against them at the trial, and it kind o' relieves their mind, I guess. But I'd just as soon not have heard most of what that guy told me—see? Come in," he added, looking round cautiously; "I'll set 'em up and tell you a bit."

Williams entered the side-door of a saloon with him, but not too willingly.

"A glarss of Scotch for the Englishman," ordered the officer facetiously, "and I'll take a horse's collar with a dash of peach bitters in it—just what you'd notice, no more." He flung down a half-dollar, and the bar-tender winked and pushed it back to him across the counter.

"What's yours, Mike?" he asked him.

"I'll take a cigar," said the bar-tender, pocketing the proffered dime and putting a cheap cigar in his waistcoat pocket, and then moving off to allow the two men elbow-room to talk in.

They talked in low voices with heads close together for fifteen minutes, and then the reporter set up another round of drinks. The bar-tender took *his* money. Then they talked a bit longer, Williams rather white about about the gills and the policeman very much in earnest.

"The boys are waiting for me up at Brodie's," said Williams at length. "I must be off."

"That's so," said Dowling, straightening up. "We'll just liquor up again to show there's no ill-feeling. And mind you see me every morning before the case is called. Trial begins tomorrow."

They swallowed their drinks, and again the bar-tender took a ten-cent piece and pocketed a cheap cigar.

"Don't print what I've told you, and don't give it up to the other reporters," said Dowling as they separated. "And if you want confirmation jest take the cars and run down to Amityville, Long Island, and you'll find what I've said is O.K. every time."

Williams went back to Steve Brodie's, his thoughts whizzing about him like bees in a swarm. What he had heard increased tenfold his horror of the man. Of course, Dowling may have lied or exaggerated, but he thought not. It was probably all true, and the newspaper offices knew something about it when they sent good men to cover the case. Williams wished to Heaven he had nothing to do with the thing; but meanwhile he could not write what he had heard, and all the other reporters wanted was the result of his interview. That was good for half a column, even expurgated.

He found the Senator in the middle of a story to Galusha, while Whitey Fife was knocking cocktail glasses off the edge of the table and catching them just before they reached the floor, pretending they were Steve Brodie jumping from the Brooklyn Bridge. He had promised to set up the drinks for the whole bar if he missed, and just as Williams entered a glass smashed to atoms on the stones, and a roar of laughter went up from the room. Five or six men moved up to the bar and took their liquor, Williams included, and soon after Whitey and Galusha went off to get some lunch and sober up, having first arranged to meet Williams later in the evening and get the "story" from him.

"Get much?" asked the Senator.

"More than I care about," replied the other, and then told his friend the story.

The Senator listened with intense interest, making occasional notes from time to time, and asking a few questions. Then, when Williams had finished, he said quietly:

"I guess Dowling's right. Let's jump on a car and go down to Amityville, and see what they think about him down there."

Amityville was a scattered village some twenty miles away on Long Island, where Dr. Hensig had lived and practised for the last year or two, and where Mrs. Hensig No. 2 had come to her suspicious death. The neighbours would be sure to have plenty to say, and though it might not prove of great value, it would be certainly interesting. So the two reporters went down there, and interviewed any one and every one they could find, from the man in the drug-store to the parson and the undertaker, and the stories they heard would fill a book.

"Good stuff," said the Senator, as they journeyed back to New York on the steamer, "but nothing we can use, I guess." His face was very grave, and he seemed troubled in his mind.

"Nothing the District Attorney can use either at the trial," observed Williams.

"It's simply a devil—not a man at all," the other continued, as if talking to himself. "Utterly unmoral! I swear I'll make McSweater put me on another job."

For the stories they had heard showed Dr. Hensig as a man who openly boasted that he could kill without detection; that no enemy of his lived long; that, as a doctor, he had, or ought to have, the right over life and death; and that if a person was a nuisance, or a trouble to him, there was no reason he should not put them away, provided he did it without rousing suspicion. Of course he had not shouted these views aloud in the market-place, but he had let people know that he held them, and held them seriously. They had fallen from him in conversation, in unguarded moments, and were clearly the natural expression of his mind and views. And many people in the village evidently had no doubt that he had put them into practice more than once.

"There's nothing to give up to Whitey or Galusha, though," said the Senator decisively, "and there's hardly anything we can use in our story."

"I don't think I should care to use it anyhow," Williams said, with rather a forced laugh.

The Senator looked round sharply by way of question.

"Hensig *may be acquitted and get out,*" added Williams.

"Same here. I guess you're dead right," he said slowly, and then added more cheerfully, "Let's go and have dinner in Chinatown, and write our copy together."

So they went down Pell Street, and turned up some dark wooden stairs into a Chinese restaurant, smelling strongly of opium and of cooking not Western. Here at a little table on the sanded floor they ordered chou chop suey and chou om dong in brown bowls, and washed it down with frequent doses of the fiery white whisky, and then moved into a corner and began to cover their paper with pencil writing for the consumption of the great American public in the morning.

"There's not much to choose between Hensig and *that,*" said the Senator, as one of the degraded white women who frequent Chinatown entered the room and sat down at an empty table to order whisky. For, with four thousand Chinamen in the quarter, there is not a single Chinese woman.

"All the difference in the world," replied Williams, following his glance across the smoky room. "She's been decent once, and may be again some day, but that damned doctor has never been anything but what he is—a soulless, intellectual devil. He doesn't belong to humanity at all. I've got a horrid idea that—"

"How do you spell 'bacteriology,' two r's or one?" asked the Senator, going on with his scrawly writing of a story that would be read with interest by thousands next day.

"Two r's and one k," laughed the other. And they wrote on for another hour, and then went to turn it in to their respective offices in Park Row.

II

The trial of Max Hensig lasted two weeks, for his relations supplied money, and he got good lawyers and all manner of delays. From a newspaper point of view it fell utterly flat, and before the end of the fourth day most of the papers had shunted their big men on to other jobs more worthy of their powers.

From Williams's point of view, however, it did not fall flat, and he was kept on it till the end. A reporter, of course, has no right to indulge in editorial remarks, especially when a case is still *sub judice*, but in New York journalism and the dignity of the law have a standard all their own, and into his daily reports there crept the distinct flavour of his own conclusions. Now that new men, with whom he had no agreement to "give up," were covering the story for the other papers, he felt free to use any special knowledge in his possession, and a good deal of what he had heard at Amityville and from officer Dowling somehow managed to creep into his writing. Something of the horror and loathing he felt for this doctor also betrayed itself, more by inference than actual statement, and no one who read his daily column could come to any other conclusion than that Hensig was a calculating, cool-headed murderer of the most dangerous type.

This was a little awkward for the reporter, because it was his duty every morning to interview the prisoner in his cell, and get his views on the conduct of the case in general and on his chances of escaping the Chair in particular.

Yet Hensig showed no embarrassment. All the newspapers were supplied to him, and he evidently read every word that Williams wrote. He must have known what the reporter thought about him, at least so far as his guilt or innocence was concerned, but he expressed no opinion as to the fairness of the articles, and talked freely of his chances of ultimate escape. The very way in which he glorified in being the central figure of a matter that bulked so large in the public eye seemed to the reporter an additional proof of the man's perversity. His vanity was immense. He made most careful toilets, appearing every day in a clean shirt and a new tie, and never wearing the same suit on two consecutive days. He noted the descriptions of his personal appearance in the Press, and was quite offended if his clothes and bearing in court were not referred to in detail. And he was unusually delighted and pleased when any of the papers stated that he looked smart and self-possessed, or showed great self-control—which some of them did.

"They make a hero of me," he said one morning when Williams went to see him as usual before court opened, "and if I go to the Chair—which I tink I not do, you know—you shall see some thing fine. Berhaps they electrocute a corpse only!"

And then, with dreadful callousness, he began to chaff the reporter about the tone of his articles for the first time.

"I only report what is said and done in court," stammered Williams, horribly uncomfortable, "and I am always ready to write anything you care to say—"

"I haf no fault to find," answered Hensig, his cold blue eyes fixed on the reporter's face through the bars, "none at all. You tink I haf killed, and you show it in all your sendences. Haf you ever seen a man in the Chair, I ask you?"

Williams was obliged to say he had.

"*Ach was!* You haf indeed!" said the doctor coolly.

"It's instantaneous, though," the other added quickly, "and must be quite painless." This was not exactly what he thought, but what else could he say to the poor devil who might presently be strapped down into it with that horrid band across his shaved head!

Hensig laughed, and turned away to walk up and down the narrow cell. Suddenly he made a quick movement and sprang like a panther close up to the bars, pressing his face between them with an expression that was entirely new. Williams started back a pace in spite of himself.

"There are worse ways of dying than that," he said in a low voice, with a diabolical look in his eyes; "slower ways that are bainful much more. I shall get oudt. I shall not be conficted. I shall get oudt, and then perhaps I come and tell you apout them."

The hatred in his voice and expression was unmistakable, but almost at once the face changed back to the cold pallor it usually wore, and the extraordinary doctor was laughing again and quietly discussing his lawyers and their good or bad points.

After all, then, that skin of indifference was only assumed, and the man really resented bitterly the tone of his articles. He liked the publicity, but was furious with Williams for having come to a conclusion and for letting that conclusion show through his reports.

The reporter was relieved to get out into the fresh air. He walked briskly up the stone steps to the court-room, still haunted by the memory of that odious white face pressing between the bars and the dreadful look in the eyes that had come and gone so swiftly. And what did those words mean exactly? Had he heard them right? Were they a threat?

"There are slower and more painful ways of dying, and if I get out I shall perhaps come and tell you about them."

The work of reporting the evidence helped to chase the disagreeable vision, and the compliments of the city editor on the excellence of his "story," with its suggestion of a possible increase of salary, gave his mind quite a different turn; yet always at the back of his consciousness there remained the vague, unpleasant memory that he had roused the bitter hatred of this man, and, as he thought, of a man who was a veritable monster.

There may have been something hypnotic, a little perhaps, in this obsessing and haunting idea of the man's steely wickedness, intellectual and horribly skilful, moving freely through life with something like a god's power and with a list of unproved and unprovable murders behind him. Certainly it impressed his imagination with very vivid force, and he could not think of this doctor, young, with unusual knowledge and out-of-the-way skill, yet utterly unmoral, free to work his will on men and women who displeased him, and almost safe from detection—he could not think of it all without a shudder and a crawling of the skin. He was exceedingly glad when the last day of the trial was reached and he no longer was obliged to seek the daily interview in the cell, or to sit all day in the crowded court watching the detestable white face of the prisoner in the dock and listening to the web of evidence closing round him, but just failing to hold him tight enough for the Chair. For Hensig was acquitted, though the jury sat up all night to come to a decision, and the final interview Williams had with the man immediately before his release into the street was the pleasantest and yet the most disagreeable of all.

"I knew I get oudt all right," said Hensig with a slight laugh, but without showing the real relief he must have felt. "No one peliefed me guilty but my vife's family and yourself, Mr. *Vulture* reporter. I read efery day your repordts. You chumped to a conglusion too quickly, I tink—"

"Oh, we write what we're told to write—"

"Berhaps some day you write anozzer story, or berhaps you read the story some one else write of your own trial. Then you understand better what you make me feel."

Williams hurried on to ask the doctor for his opinion of the conduct of the trial, and then inquired what his plans were for the future. The answer to the question caused him genuine relief.

"Ach! I return of course to Chermany," he said. "People here are now afraid of me a liddle. The newspapers haf killed me instead of the Chair. Goot-bye, Mr. *Vulture* reporter, goot-bye!"

And Williams wrote out his last interview with as great a relief, probably, as Hensig felt when he heard the foreman of the jury utter the words "Not guilty"; but the line that gave him most pleasure was the one announcing the intended departure of the acquitted man for Germany.

III

The New York public want sensational reading in their daily life, and they get it, for the newspaper that refused to furnish it would fail in a week, and New York newspaper proprietors do not pose as philanthropists. Horror succeeds horror, and the public interest is never for one instant allowed to faint by the way.

Like any other reporter who betrayed the smallest powers of description, Williams realised this fact with his very first week on the *Vulture*. His daily work became simply a series of sensational reports of sensational happenings; he lived in a perpetual whirl of exciting arrests, murder trials, cases of blackmail, divorce, forgery, arson, corruption, and every other kind of wickedness imaginable. Each case thrilled him a little less than the preceding one; excess of sensation had simply numbed him; he became, not callous, but irresponsive, and had long since reached the stage when excitement ceases to betray judgment, as with inexperienced reporters it was apt to do.

The Hensig case, however, for a long time lived in his imagination and haunted him. The bald facts were buried in the police files at Mulberry Street headquarters and in the newspaper office "morgues," while the public, thrilled daily by fresh horrors, forgot the very existence of the evil doctor a couple of days after the acquittal of the central figure.

But for Williams it was otherwise. The personality of the heartless and calculating murderer—the intellectual poisoner, as he called him— had made a deep impression on his imagination, and for many weeks his memory kept him alive as a moving and actual horror in his life. The words he had heard him utter, with their covert threats and ill-concealed animosity, helped, no doubt, to vivify the recollection and to explain why Hensig stayed in his thoughts and haunted his dreams with a persistence that reminded him of his very earliest cases on the paper.

With time, however, even Hensig began to fade away into the confused background of piled up memories of prisoners and prison scenes, and at length the memory became so deeply buried that it no longer troubled him at all.

The summer passed, and Williams came back from his hard-earned holiday of two weeks in the Maine backwoods. New York was at its best, and the thousands who had been forced to stay and face its torrid summer heats were beginning to revive under the spell of the brilliant autumn days. Cool sea breezes swept over its burnt streets from the Lower Bay, and across the splendid flood of the Hudson River the woods on the Palisades of New Jersey had turned to crimson and gold. The air was electric, sharp, sparkling, and the life of the city began to pulse anew with its restless and impetuous energy. Bronzed faces from sea and mountains thronged the streets, health and light-heartedness showed in every eye, for autumn in New York wields a potent magic not to be denied, and even the East Side slums, where the unfortunates crowd in their squalid thousands, had the appearance of having been swept and cleansed. Along the water-fronts especially the powers of sea and sun and scented winds combined to work an irresistible fever in the hearts of all who chafed within their prison walls.

And in Williams, perhaps more than in most, there was something that responded vigorously to the influences of hope and cheerfulness everywhere abroad. Fresh with the vigour of his holiday and full of good resolutions for the coming winter he felt released from the evil spell of irregular living, and as he crossed one October morning to Staten Island in the big double-ender ferry-boat, his heart was light, and his eye wandered to the blue waters and the hazy line of woods beyond with feelings of pure gladness and delight.

He was on his way to Quarantine to meet an incoming liner for the *Vulture*. A Jew-baiting member of the German Reichstag was coming to deliver a series of lectures in New York on his favourite subject, and the newspapers who deemed him worthy of notice at all were sending him fair warning that his mission would be tolerated perhaps, but not welcomed. The Jews were good citizens and America a "free country," and his meetings in the Cooper Union Hall would meet with derision certainly, and violence possibly.

The assignment was a pleasant one, and Williams had instructions to poke fun at the officious and interfering German, and advise him to return to Bremen by the next steamer without venturing among flying eggs and dead cats on the platform. He entered fully into the spirit of the job and was telling the Quarantine doctor about it as they steamed down the bay in the little tug to meet the huge liner just anchoring inside Sandy Hook.

The decks of the ship were crowded with passengers watching the arrival of the puffing tug, and just as they drew alongside in the shadow Williams suddenly felt his eyes drawn away from the swinging rope ladder to some point about half-way down the length of the vessel. There, among the intermediate passengers on the lower deck, he saw a face staring at him with fixed intentness. The eyes were bright blue, and the skin, in that row of bronzed passengers, showed remarkably white. At once, and with a violent rush of blood from the heart, he recognised Hensig.

In a moment everything about him changed: the blue waters of the bay turned black, the light seemed to leave the sun, and all the old sensations of fear and loathing came over him again like the memory of some great pain. He shook himself, and clutched the rope ladder to swing up after the Health Officer, angry, yet genuinely alarmed at the same time, to realise that the return of this man could so affect him. His interview with the Jew-baiter was of the briefest possible description, and he hurried through to catch the Quarantine tug back to Staten Island, instead of steaming up the bay with the great liner into dock, as the other reporters did. He had caught no second glimpse of the hated German, and he even went so far as to harbour a faint hope that he might have been deceived, and that some trick of resemblance in another face had caused a sort of subjective hallucination. At any rate, the days passed into weeks, and October slipped into November, and there was no recurrence of the distressing vision. Perhaps, after all, it was a stranger only; or, if it was Hensig, then he had forgotten all about the reporter, and his return had no connection necessarily with the idea of revenge.

None the less, however, Williams felt uneasy. He told his friend Dowling, the policeman.

"Old news," laughed the Irishman. "Headquarters are keeping an eye on him as a suspect. Berlin wants a man for two murders—goes by the name of Brunner—and from their description we think it's this feller Hensig. Nothing certain yet, but we're on his trail. *I'm* on his trail," he added proudly, "and don't you forget it! I'll let you know anything when the time comes, but mum's the word just now!"

One night, not long after this meeting, Williams and the Senator were covering a big fire on the West Side docks. They were standing on the out-skirts of the crowd watching the immense flames that a shouting wind seemed to carry half-way across the river. The surrounding shipping was brilliantly lit up and the roar was magnificent. The Senator, having come out with none of his own, borrowed his friend's overcoat for a moment to protect him from spray and flying cinders while he went inside the fire lines for the latest information obtainable. It was after midnight, and the main story had been telephoned to the office; all they had now to do was to send in the latest details and corrections to be written up at the news desk.

"I'll wait for you over at the corner!" shouted Williams, moving off through a scene of indescribable confusion and taking off his fire badge as he went. This conspicuous brass badge, issued to reporters by the Fire Department, gave them the right to pass within the police cordon in the pursuit of information, and at their own risk. Hardly had he unpinned it from his coat when a hand dashed out of the crowd surging up against him and made a determined grab at it. He turned to trace the owner, but at that instant a great lurching of the mob nearly carried him off his feet, and he only just succeeded in seeing the arm withdrawn, having failed of its object, before he was landed with a violent push upon the pavement he had been aiming for.

The incident did not strike him as particularly odd, for in such a crowd there are many who covet the privilege of getting closer to the blaze. He simply laughed and put the badge safely in his pocket, and then stood to watch the dying flames until his friend came to join him with the latest details.

Yet, though time was pressing and the Senator had little enough to do, it was fully half an hour before he came lumbering up through the darkness. Williams recognised him some distance away by the check ulster he wore—his own.

But *was* it the Senator, after all? The figure moved oddly and with a limp, as though injured. A few feet off it stopped and peered at Williams through the darkness.

"That you, Williams?" asked a gruff voice.

"I thought you were some one else for a moment," answered the reporter, relieved to recognise his friend, and moving forward to meet him. "But what's wrong? Are you hurt?"

The Senator looked ghastly in the lurid glow of the fire. His face was white, and there was a little trickle of blood on the forehead.

"Some fellow nearly did for me," he said; "deliberately pushed me clean off the edge of the dock. If I hadn't fallen on to a broken pile and found a boat, I'd have been drowned sure as God made little apples. Think I know who it was, too. *Think!* I mean I *know*, because I saw his damned white face and heard what he said."

"Who in the world was it? What did he want?" stammered the other.

The Senator took his arm, and lurched into the saloon behind them for some brandy. As he did so he kept looking over his shoulder.

"Quicker we're off from this dirty neighbourhood, the better," he said.

Then he turned to Williams, looking oddly at him over the glass, and answering his questions.

"Who was it?—why, it was Hensig! And what did he want?—well, he wanted *you!*"

"Me! Hensig!" gasped the other.

"Guess he mistook me for you," went on the Senator, looking behind him at the door. "The crowd was so thick I cut across by the edge of the dock. It was quite dark. There wasn't a soul near me. I was running.

Suddenly what I thought was a stump got up in front of me, and, Gee whiz, man! I tell you it was Hensig, or I'm a drunken Dutchman. I looked bang into his face. 'Good-pye, Mr. *Vulture* reporter,' he said, with a damned laugh, and gave me a push that sent me backwards clean over the edge."

The Senator paused for breath, and to empty his second glass.

"*My* overcoat!" exclaimed Williams faintly.

"Oh, he'd been following you right enough, I guess."

The Senator was not really injured, and the two men walked back towards Broadway to find a telephone, passing through a region of dimly-lighted streets known as Little Africa, where the n——oes lived, and where it was safer to keep the middle of the road, thus avoiding sundry dark alley-ways opening off the side. They talked hard all the way.

"He's after you, no doubt," repeated the Senator. "I guess he never forgot your report of his trial. Better keep your eye peeled!" he added with a laugh.

But Williams didn't feel a bit inclined to laugh, and the thought that it certainly *was* Hensig he had seen on the steamer, and that he was following him so closely as to mark his check ulster and make an attempt on his life, made him feel horribly uncomfortable, to say the least. To be stalked by such a man was terrible. To realise that he was marked down by that white-faced, cruel wretch, merciless and implacable, skilled in the manifold ways of killing by stealth—that somewhere in the crowds of the great city he was watched and waited for, hunted, observed: here was an obsession really to torment and become dangerous. Those light-blue eyes, that keen intelligence, that mind charged with revenge, had been watching him ever since the trial, even from across the sea. The idea terrified him. It brought death into his thoughts for the first time with a vivid sense of nearness and reality far greater than anything he had experienced when watching others die.

That night, in his dingy little room in the East Nineteenth Street boarding-house, Williams went to bed in a blue funk, and for days afterwards he went about his business in a continuation of the same blue funk. It was useless to deny it. He kept his eyes everywhere, thinking he was being watched and followed. A new face in the office, at the boarding-house table, or anywhere on his usual beat, made him jump. His daily work was haunted; his dreams were all nightmares; he forgot all his good resolutions, and plunged into the old indulgences that helped him to forget his distress. It took twice as much liquor to make him jolly, and four times as much to make him reckless.

Not that he really was a drunkard, or cared to drink for its own sake, but he moved in a thirsty world of reporters, policemen, reckless and loose-living men and women, whose form of greeting was "What'll you take?" and method of reproach "Oh, he's sworn off!" Only now he was more careful how much he took, counting the cocktails and fizzes poured into him during the course of his day's work, and was anxious never to lose control of himself. He must be on the watch. He changed his eating and drinking haunts, and altered any habits that could give a clue to the devil on his trail. He even went so far as to change his boarding-house. His emotion—the emotion of fear—changed everything. It tinged the outer world with gloom, draping it in darker colours, stealing something from the sunlight, reducing enthusiasm, and acting as a heavy drag, as it were, upon all the normal functions of life.

The effect upon his imagination, already diseased by alcohol and drugs, was, of course, exceedingly strong. The doctor's words about developing a germ until it became too powerful to be touched by any medicine, and then letting it into the victim's system by means of a pin-scratch—this possessed him more than anything else. The idea dominated his thoughts; it seemed so clever, so cruel, so devilish. The "accident" at the fire had been, of course, a real accident, conceived on the spur of the moment—the result of a chance meeting and a foolish mistake. Hensig had no need to resort to such clumsy methods. When the right moment came he would adopt a far simpler, *safer* plan.

Finally, he became so obsessed by the idea that Hensig was following him, waiting for his opportunity, that one day he told the news editor the whole story. His nerves were so shaken that he could not do his work properly.

"That's a good story. Make two hundred of it," said the editor at once. "Fake the name, of course. Mustn't mention Hensig, or there'll be a libel suit."

But Williams was in earnest, and insisted so forcibly that Treherne, though busy as ever, took him aside into his room with the glass door.

"Now, see here, Williams, you're drinking too much," he said; "that's about the size of it. Steady up a bit on the wash, and Hensig's face will disappear." He spoke kindly, but sharply. He was young himself, awfully keen, with much knowledge of human nature and a rare "nose for news." He understood the abilities of his small army of men with intuitive judgment. That they drank was nothing to him, provided they did their work. Everybody in that world drank, and the man who didn't was looked upon with suspicion.

Williams explained rather savagely that the face was no mere symptom of delirium tremens, and the editor spared him another two minutes before rushing out to tackle the crowd of men waiting for him at the news desk.

"That so? You don't say!" he asked, with more interest. "Well, I guess Hensig's simply trying to razzle-dazzle you. You tried to kill him by your reports, and he wants to scare you by way of revenge. But he'll never dare *do* anything. Throw him a good bluff, and he'll give in like a baby. Everything's pretence in this world. But I rather like the idea of the germs. That's original!"

Williams, a little angry at the other's flippancy, told the story of the Senator's adventure and the changed overcoat.

"May be, may be," replied the hurried editor; "but the Senator drinks Chinese whisky, and a man who does that might imagine anything on God's earth. Take a tip, Williams, from an old hand, and let up a bit on the liquor. Drop cocktails and keep to straight whisky, and never drink on an empty stomach. Above all, *don't mix!*"

He gave him a keen look and was off.

"Next time you see this German," cried Treherne from the door, "go up and ask him for an interview on what it feels like to escape from the Chair—just to show him you don't care a red cent. Talk about having him watched and followed—suspected man—and all that sort of flim-flam. Pretend to warn him. It'll turn the tables and make him digest a bit. See?"

Williams sauntered out into the street to report a meeting of the Rapid Transit Commissioners, and the first person he met as he ran down the office steps was—Max Hensig.

Before he could stop, or swerve aside, they were face to face. His head swam for a moment and he began to tremble. Then some measure of self-possession returned, and he tried instinctively to act on the editor's advice. No other plan was ready, so he drew on the last force that had occupied his mind. It was that—or running.

Hensig, he noticed, looked prosperous; he wore a fur overcoat and cap. His face was whiter than ever, and his blue eyes burned like coals.

"Why! Dr. Hensig, you're back in New York!" he exclaimed. "When did you arrive? I'm glad—I suppose—I mean—er—will you come and have a drink?" he concluded desperately. It was very foolish, but for the life of him he could think of nothing else to say. And the last thing in the world he wished was that his enemy should know that he was afraid.

"I tink not, Mr. *Vulture* reporder, tanks," he answered coolly; "but I sit py and vatch you drink." His self-possession was perfect, as it always was.

But Williams, more himself now, seized on the refusal and moved on, saying something about having a meeting to go to.

"I walk a liddle way with you, berhaps," Hensig said, following him down the pavement.

It was impossible to prevent him, and they started side by side across City Hall Park towards Broadway. It was after four o'clock; the dusk was falling; the little park was thronged with people walking in all directions, every one in a terrific hurry as usual. Only Hensig seemed calm and unmoved among that racing, tearing life about them. He carried an atmosphere of ice about with him: it was his voice and manner that produced this impression; his mind was alert, watchful, determined, always sure of itself.

Williams wanted to run. He reviewed swiftly in his mind a dozen ways of getting rid of him quickly, yet knowing well they were all futile. He put his hands in his overcoat pockets—the check ulster—and watched sideways every movement of his companion.

"Living in New York again, aren't you?" he began.

"Not as a doctor any more," was the reply. "I now teach and study. Also I write sciendific books a liddle—"

"What about?"

"Cherms," said the other, looking at him and laughing. "Disease cherms, their culture and development." He put the accent on the "op."

Williams walked more quickly. With a great effort he tried to put Treherne's advice into practice.

"You care to give me an interview any time—on your special subjects?" he asked, as naturally as he could.

"Oh yes; with much bleasure. I lif in Harlem now, if you will call von day—"

"Our office is best," interrupted the reporter. "Paper, desks, library, all handy for use, you know."

"If you're afraid—" began Hensig. Then, without finishing the sentence, he added with a laugh, "I haf no arsenic there. You not tink me any more a pungling boisoner? You haf changed your mind about all dat?"

Williams felt his flesh beginning to creep. How could he speak of such a matter! His own wife, too!

He turned quickly and faced him, standing still for a moment so that the throng of people deflected into two streams past them. He felt it absolutely imperative upon him to say something that should convince the German he was not afraid.

"I suppose you are aware, Dr. Hensig, that the police know you have returned, and that you are being watched probably?" he said in a low voice, forcing himself to meet the odious blue eyes.

"And why not, bray?" he asked imperturbably.

"They may suspect something—"

"Susbected—already again? *Ach was!*" said the German.

"I only wished to warn you—" stammered Williams, who always found it difficult to remain self-possessed under the other's dreadful stare.

"No boliceman see what I do—or catch me again," he laughed quite horribly. "But I tank you all the same."

Williams turned to catch a Broadway car going at full speed. He could not stand another minute with this man, who affected him so disagreeably.

"I call at the office one day to gif you interview!" Hensig shouted as he dashed off, and the next minute he was swallowed up in the crowd, and Williams, with mixed feelings and a strange inner trembling, went to cover the meeting of the Rapid Transit Board.

But, while he reported the proceedings mechanically, his mind was busy with quite other thoughts. Hensig was at his side the whole time. He felt quite sure, however unlikely it seemed, that there was no fancy in his fears, and that he had judged the German correctly. Hensig hated him, and would put him out of the way if he could. He would do it in such a way that detection would be almost impossible. He would not shoot or poison in the ordinary way, or resort to any clumsy method. He would simply follow, watch, wait his opportunity, and then act with utter callousness and remorseless determination. And Williams already felt pretty certain of the means that would be employed: "*Cherms!*"

This meant proximity. He must watch every one who came close to him in trains, cars, restaurants—anywhere and everywhere. It could be done in a second: only a slight scratch would be necessary, and the disease would be in his blood with such strength that the chances of recovery would be slight. And what could he do? He could not have Hensig watched or arrested. He had no story to tell to a magistrate, or to the police, for no one would listen to such a tale. And, if he were stricken down by sudden illness, what was more likely than to say he had caught the fever in the ordinary course of his work, since he was always frequenting noisome dens and the haunts of the very poor, the foreign and filthy slums of the East Side, and the hospitals, morgues, and cells of all sorts and conditions of men? No; it was a disagreeable situation, and Williams, young, shaken in nerve, and easily impressionable as he was, could not prevent its obsession of his mind and imagination.

"If I get suddenly ill," he told the Senator, his only friend in the whole city, "and send for you, look carefully for a scratch on my body. Tell Dowling, and tell the doctor the story."

"You think Hensig goes about with a little bottle of plague germs in his vest pocket," laughed the other reporter, "ready to scratch you with a pin?"

"Some damned scheme like that, I'm sure."

"Nothing could be proved anyway. He wouldn't keep the evidence in his pocket till he was arrested, would he?"

During the next week or two Williams ran against Hensig twice—accidentally. The first time it happened just outside his own boarding-house—the *new one*. Hensig had his foot on the stone steps as if just about to come up, but quick as a flash he turned his face away and moved on down the street. This was about eight o'clock in the evening, and the hall light fell through the opened door upon his face. The second time it was not so clear: the reporter was covering a case in the courts, a case of suspicious death in which a woman was chief prisoner, and he thought he saw the doctor's white visage watching him from among the crowd at the back of the court-room. When he looked a second time, however, the face had disappeared, and there was no sign afterwards of its owner in the lobby or corridor.

That same day he met Dowling in the building; he was promoted now, and was always in plain clothes. The detective drew him aside into a corner. The talk at once turned upon the German.

"We're watching him too," he said. "Nothing you can use yet, but he's changed his name again, and never stops at the same address for more than a week or two. I guess he's Brunner right enough, the man Berlin's looking for. He's a holy terror if ever there was one."

Dowling was happy as a schoolboy to be in touch with such a promising case.

"What's he up to now in particular?" asked the other.

"Something pretty black," said the detective. "But I can't tell you yet awhile. He calls himself Schmidt now, and he's dropped the 'Doctor.' We may take him any day—just waiting for advices from Germany."

Williams told his story of the overcoat adventure with the Senator, and his belief that Hensig was waiting for a suitable opportunity to catch him alone.

"That's dead likely too," said Dowling, and added carelessly, "I guess we'll have to make some kind of a case against him anyway, just to get him out of the way. He's too dangerous to be around huntin' on the loose."

IV

So gradual sometimes are the approaches of fear that the processes by which it takes possession of a man's soul are often too insidious to be recognised, much less to be dealt with, until their object has been finally accomplished and the victim has lost the power to act. And by this time the reporter, who had again plunged into excess, felt so nerveless that, if he met Hensig face to face, he could not answer for what he might do. He might assault his tormentor violently—one result of terror—or he might find himself powerless to do anything at all but yield, like a bird fascinated before a snake.

He was always thinking now of the moment when they would meet, and of what would happen; for he was just as certain that they must meet eventually, and that Hensig would try to kill him, as that his next birthday would find him twenty-five years old. That meeting, he well knew, could be delayed only, not prevented, and his changing again to another boarding-house, or moving altogether to a different city, could only postpone the final accounting between them. It was bound to come.

A reporter on a New York newspaper has one day in seven to himself. Williams's day off was Monday, and he was always glad when it came. Sunday was especially arduous for him, because in addition to the unsatisfactory nature of the day's assignments, involving private interviewing which the citizens pretended to resent on their day of rest, he had the task in the evening of reporting a difficult sermon in a Brooklyn church. Having only a column and a half at his disposal, he had to condense as he went along, and the speaker was so rapid, and so fond of lengthy quotations, that the reporter found his shorthand only just equal to the task. It was usually after half-past nine o'clock when he left the church, and there was still the labour of transcribing his notes in the office against time.

The Sunday following the glimpse of his tormentor's face in the court-room he was busily condensing the wearisome periods of the preacher, sitting at a little table immediately under the pulpit, when he glanced up during a brief pause and let his eye wander over the congregation and up to the crowded galleries. Nothing was farther at the moment from his much-occupied brain than the doctor of Amityville, and it was such an unexpected shock to encounter his fixed stare up there among the occupants of the front row, watching him with an evil smile, that his senses temporarily deserted him. The next sentence of the preacher was wholly lost, and his shorthand during the brief remainder of the sermon was quite illegible, he found, when he came to transcribe it at the office.

It was after one o'clock in the morning when he finished, and he went out feeling exhausted and rather shaky. In the all-night drug store at the corner he indulged accordingly in several more glasses of whisky than usual, and talked a long time with the man who guarded the back room and served liquor to the few who knew the pass-word, since the shop had really no licence at all. The true reason for this delay he recognised quite plainly: he was afraid of the journey home along the dark and emptying streets. The lower end of New York is practically deserted after ten o'clock: it has no residences, no theatres, no *cafés*, and only a few travellers from late ferries share it with reporters, a sprinkling of policemen, and the ubiquitous ne'er-do-wells who haunt the saloon doors. The newspaper world of Park Row was, of course, alive with light and movement, but once outside that narrow zone and the night descended with an effect of general darkness.

Williams thought of spending three dollars on a cab, but dismissed the idea because of its extravagance. Presently Galusha Owens came in—too drunk to be of any use, though, as a companion. Besides, he lived in Harlem, which was miles beyond Nineteenth Street, where Williams had to go. He took another rye whisky—his fourth—and looked cautiously through the coloured glass windows into the street. No one was visible. Then he screwed up his nerves another twist or two, and made a bolt for it, taking the steps in a sort of flying leap—and running full tilt into a man whose figure seemed almost to have risen out of the very pavement.

He gave a cry and raised his fists to strike.

"Where's your hurry?" laughed a familiar voice. "Is the Prince of Wales dead?" It was the Senator, most welcome of all possible appearances.

"Come in and have a horn," said Williams, "and then I'll walk home with you." He was immensely glad to see him, for only a few streets separated their respective boarding-houses.

"But he'd never sit out a long sermon just for the pleasure of watching you," observed the Senator after hearing his friend's excited account.

"That man'll take any trouble in the world to gain his end," said the other with conviction. "He's making a study of all my movements and habits. He's not the sort to take chances when it's a matter of life and death. I'll bet he's not far away at this moment."

"Rats!" exclaimed the Senator, laughing in rather a forced way. "You're getting the jumps with your Hensig and death. Have another rye."

They finished their drinks and went out together, crossing City Hall Park diagonally towards Broadway, and then turning north. They crossed Canal and Grand Streets, deserted and badly lighted. Only a few drunken loiterers passed them. Occasionally a policeman on the corner, always close to the side-door of a saloon, of course, recognised one or other of them and called good-night. Otherwise there was no one, and they seemed to have this part of Manhattan Island pretty well to themselves. The presence of the Senator, ever cheery and kind, keeping close to his friend all the way, the effect of the half-dozen whiskies, and the sight of the guardians of the law, combined to raise the reporter's spirits somewhat; and when they reached Fourteenth Street, with its better light and greater traffic, and saw Union Square lying just beyond, close to his own street, he felt a distinct increase of courage and no objection to going on alone.

"Good-night!" cried the Senator cheerily. "Get home safe; I turn off here anyway." He hesitated a moment before turning down the street, and then added, "You feel O.K., don't you?"

"You may get double rates for an exclusive bit of news if you come on and see me assaulted," Williams replied, laughing aloud, and then waiting to see the last of his friend.

But the moment the Senator was gone the laughter disappeared. He went on alone, crossing the square among the trees and walking very quickly. Once or twice he turned to see if anybody were following him, and his eyes scanned carefully as he passed every occupant of the park benches where a certain number of homeless loafers always find their night's lodging. But there was nothing apparently to cause him alarm, and in a few minutes more he would be safe in the little back bedroom of his own house. Over the way he saw the lights of Burbacher's saloon, where respectable Germans drank Rhine wine and played chess till all hours. He thought of going in for a night-cap, hesitating for a moment, but finally going on. When he got to the end of the square, however, and saw the dark opening of East Eighteenth Street, he thought after all he would go back and have another drink. He hovered for a moment on the kerbstone and then turned; his will often slipped a cog now in this way.

It was only when he was on his way back that he realised the truth: that his real reason for turning back and avoiding the dark open mouth of the street was because he was afraid of something its shadows might conceal. This dawned upon him quite suddenly. If there had been a light at the corner of the street he would never have turned back at all. And as this passed through his mind, already somewhat fuddled with what he had drunk, he became aware that the figure of a man had slipped forward out of the dark space he had just refused to enter, and was following him down the street. The man was pressing, too, close into the houses, using any protection of shadow or railing that would enable him to move unseen.

But the moment Williams entered the bright section of pavement opposite the wine-room windows he knew that this man had come close up behind him, with a little silent run, and he turned at once to face him. He saw a slim man with dark hair and blue eyes, and recognised him instantly.

"It's very late to be coming home," said the man at once. "I thought I recognised my reporder friend from the *Vulture*." These were the actual words, and the voice was meant to be pleasant, but what Williams thought he heard, spoken in tones of ice, was something like, "At last I've caught you! You are in a state of collapse nervously, and you are exhausted. I can do what I please with you." For the face and the voice were those of Hensig the Tormentor, and the dyed hair only served to emphasise rather grotesquely the man's features and make the pallor of the skin greater by contrast.

His first instinct was to turn and run, his second to fly at the man and strike him. A terror beyond death seized him. A pistol held to his head, or a waving bludgeon, he could easily have faced; but this odious creature, slim, limp, and white of face, with his terrible suggestion of cruelty, literally appalled him so that he could think of nothing intelligent to do or to say. This accurate knowledge of his movements, too, added to his distress— this waiting for him at night when he was tired and foolish from excess. At that moment he knew all the sensations of the criminal a few hours before his execution: the bursts of hysterical terror, the inability to realise his position, to hold his thoughts steady, the helplessness of it all. Yet, in the end, the reporter heard his own voice speaking with a rather weak and unnatural kind of tone and accompanied by a gulp of forced laughter— heard himself stammering the ever-ready formula: "I was going to have a drink before turning in—will you join me?"

The invitation, he realised afterwards, was prompted by the one fact that stood forth clearly in his mind at the moment—the thought, namely, that whatever he did or said, he must never let Hensig for one instant imagine that he felt afraid and was so helpless a victim.

Side by side they moved down the street, for Hensig had acquiesced in the suggestion, and Williams already felt dazed by the strong, persistent will of his companion. His thoughts seemed to be flying about somewhere outside his brain, beyond control, scattering wildly. He could think of nothing further to say, and had the smallest diversion furnished the opportunity he would have turned and run for his life through the deserted streets.

"A glass of lager," he heard the German say, "I take berhaps that with you. You know me in spite of—" he added, indicating by a movement the changed colour of his hair and moustache. "Also, I gif you now the interview you asked for, if you like."

The reporter agreed feebly, finding nothing adequate to reply. He turned helplessly and looked into his face with something of the sensations a bird may feel when it runs at last straight into the jaws of the reptile that has fascinated it. The fear of weeks settled down upon him, focussing about his heart. It was, of course, an effect of hypnotism, he remembered thinking vaguely through the befuddlement of his drink—this culminating effect of an evil and remorseless personality acting upon one that was diseased and extra receptive. And while he made the suggestion and heard the other's acceptance of it, he knew perfectly well that he was falling in with the plan of the doctor's own making, a plan that would end in an assault upon his person, perhaps a technical assault only—a mere touch—still, an assault that would be at the same time an attempt at murder. The alcohol buzzed in his ears. He felt strangely powerless. He walked steadily to his doom, side by side with his executioner.

Any attempt to analyse the psychology of the situation was utterly beyond him. But, amid the whirl of emotion and the excitement of the whisky, he dimly grasped the importance of *two fundamental things.*

And the first was that, though he was now muddled and frantic, yet a moment would come when his will would be capable of one supreme effort to escape, and that therefore it would be wiser for the present to waste no atom of volition on temporary half-measures. He would play dead dog. The fear that now paralysed him would accumulate till it reached the point of saturation: that would be the time to strike for his life. For just as the coward may reach a stage where he is capable of a sort of frenzied heroism that no ordinarily brave man could compass, so the victim of fear, at a point varying with his balance of imagination and physical vigour, will reach a state where fear leaves him and he becomes numb to its effect from sheer excess of feeling it. It is the point of saturation. He may then turn suddenly calm and act with a judgment and precision that simply bewilder the object of the attack. It is, of course, the inevitable swing of the pendulum, the law of equal action and reaction.

Hazily, tipsily perhaps, Williams was conscious of this potential power deep within him, below the superficial layers of smaller emotions—could he but be *sufficiently terrified to reach it* and bring it to the surface where it must result in action.

And, as a consequence of this foresight of his sober subliminal self, he offered no opposition to the least suggestion of his tormentor, but made up his mind instinctively to agree to all that he proposed. Thus he lost no atom of the force he might eventually call upon, by friction over details which in any case he would yield in the end. And at the same time he felt intuitively that his utter weakness might even deceive his enemy a little and increase the chances of his single effort to escape when the right moment arrived.

That Williams was able to "imagine" this true psychology, yet wholly unable to analyse it, simply showed that on occasion he could be psychically active. His deeper subliminal self, stirred by the alcohol and the stress of emotion, was guiding him, and would continue to guide him in proportion as he let his fuddled normal self slip into the background without attempt to interfere.

And the second fundamental thing he grasped—due even more than the first to psychic intuition—was the certainty that he could drink more, up to a certain point, with distinct advantage to his power and lucidity— but up to a given point only. After that would come unconsciousness, a single sip too much and he would cross the frontier—a very narrow one. It was as though he knew intuitively that "the drunken consciousness is one bit of the mystic consciousness." At present he was only fuddled and fear- ful, but additional stimulant would inhibit the effects of the other emo- tions, give him unbounded confidence, clarify his judgment and increase his capacity to a stage far beyond the normal. Only—he must stop in time.

His chances of escape, therefore, so far as he could understand, depended on these two things: he must drink till he became self-confident and arrived at the abnormally clear-minded stage of drunkenness; and he must wait for the moment when Hensig had so filled him up with fear that he no longer could react to it. Then would be the time to strike. Then his will would be free and have judgment behind it.

These were the two things standing up clearly somewhere behind that great confused turmoil of mingled fear and alcohol.

Thus for the moment, though with scattered forces and rather wildly feeble thoughts, he moved down the street beside the man who hated him and meant to kill him. He had no purpose at all but to agree and to wait. Any attempt he made now could end only in failure.

They talked a little as they went, the German calm, chatting as though he were merely an agreeable acquaintance, but behaving with the obvious knowledge that he held his victim secure, and that his struggles would prove simply rather amusing. He even laughed about his dyed hair, saying by way of explanation that he had done it to please a woman who told him it would make him look younger. Williams knew this was a lie, and that the police had more to do with the change than a woman; but the man's vanity showed through the explanation, and was a vivid little self-revelation.

He objected to entering Burbacher's, saying that he (Burbacher) paid no blackmail to the police, and might be raided for keeping open after hours.

"I know a nice quiet blace on T'ird Avenue. We go there," he said.

Williams, walking unsteadily and shaking inwardly, still groping, too, feebly after a way of escape, turned down the side street with him. He thought of the men he had watched walking down the short corridor from the cell to the "Chair" at Sing Sing, and wondered if they felt as he did. It was just like going to his own execution.

"I haf a new disgovery in bacteriology—in cherms," the doctor went on, "and it will make me famous, for it is very imbortant. I gif it you egsclusive for the *Vulture*, as you are a friend." He became technical, and the reporter's mind lost itself among such words as "toxins," "alkaloids," and the like. But he realised clearly enough that Hensig was playing with him and felt absolutely sure of his victim. When he lurched badly, as he did more than once, the German took his arm by way of support, and at the vile touch of the man it was all Williams could do not to scream or strike out blindly.

They turned up Third Avenue and stopped at the side-door of a cheap saloon. He noticed the name of Schumacher over the porch, but all lights were out except a feeble glow that came through the glass fanlight. A man pushed his face cautiously round the half-opened door, and after a brief examination let them in with a whispered remark to be quiet. It was the usual formula of the Tammany saloon-keeper, who paid so much a month to the police to be allowed to keep open all night, provided there was no noise or fighting. It was now well after one o'clock in the morning, and the streets were deserted.

The reporter was quite at home in the sort of place they had entered; otherwise the sinister aspect of a drinking "joint" after hours, with its gloom and general air of suspicion, might have caused him some extra alarm. A dozen men, unpleasant of countenance, were standing at the bar, where a single lamp gave just enough light to enable them to see their glasses. The bar-tender gave Hensig a swift glance of recognition as they walked along the sanded floor.

"Come," whispered the German; "we go to the back room, I know the bass-word," he laughed, leading the way.

They walked to the far end of the bar and opened a door into a brightly lit room with about a dozen tables in it, at most of which men sat drinking with highly painted women, talking loudly, quarrelling, singing, and the air thick with smoke. No one took any notice of them as they went down the room to a table in the corner farthest from the door—Hensig chose it; and when the single waiter came up with "Was nehmen die Herren?" and a moment later brought the rye whisky they both asked for, Williams swallowed his own without the "chaser" of soda water, and ordered another on the spot.

"It'sh awfully watered," he said rather thickly to his companion, "and I'm tired."

"Cocaine, under the circumstances, would help you quicker, berhaps!" replied the German with an expression of amusement. Good God! was there nothing about him the man had not found out? He must have been shadowing him for days; it was at least a week since Williams had been to the First Avenue drug store to get the wicked bottle refilled. Had he been on his trail every night when he left the office to go home? This idea of remorseless persistence made him shudder.

"Then we finish quickly if you are tired," the doctor continued, "and tomorrow you can show me your repordt for gorrections if you make any misdakes berhaps. I gif you the address tonight pefore we leave."

The increased ugliness of his speech and accent betrayed his growing excitement. Williams drank his whisky, again without water, and called for yet another, clinking glasses with the murderer opposite, and swallowing half of this last glass, too, while Hensig merely tasted his own, looking straight at him over the performance with his evil eyes.

"I can write shorthand," began the reporter, trying to appear at his ease.

"*Ach*, I know, of course."

There was a mirror behind the table, and he took a quick glance round the room while the other began searching in his coat pocket for the papers he had with him. Williams lost no single detail of his movements, but at the same time managed swiftly to get the "note" of the other occupants of the tables. Degraded and besotted faces he saw, almost without exception, and not one to whom he could appeal for help with any prospect of success. It was a further shock, too, to realise that he preferred the more or less bestial countenances round him to the intellectual and ascetic face opposite. They were at least human, whereas *he* was something quite outside the pale; and this preference for the low creatures, otherwise loathsome to him, brought his mind by sharp contrast to a new and vivid realisation of the personality before him. He gulped down his drink, and again ordered it to be refilled.

But meanwhile the alcohol was beginning to key him up out of the dazed and negative state into which his first libations and his accumulations of fear had plunged him. His brain became a shade clearer. There was even a faint stirring of the will. He had already drunk enough under normal circumstances to be simply reeling, but tonight the emotion of fear inhibited the effects of the alcohol, keeping him singularly steady. Provided he did not exceed a given point, he could go on drinking till he reached the moment of high power when he could combine all his forces into the single consummate act of cleverly calculated escape. If he missed this psychological moment he would collapse.

A sudden crash made him jump. It was behind him against the other wall. In the mirror he saw that a middle-aged man had lost his balance and fallen off his chair, foolishly intoxicated, and that two women were ostensibly trying to lift him up, but really were going swiftly through his pockets as he lay in a heap on the floor. A big man who had been asleep the whole evening in the corner stopped snoring and woke up to look and laugh, but no one interfered. A man must take care of himself in such a place and with such company, or accept the consequences. The big man composed himself again for sleep, sipping his glass a little first, and the noise of the room continued as before. It was a case of "knock-out drops" in the whisky, put in by the women, however, rather than by the saloon-keeper. Williams remembered thinking he had nothing to fear of that kind. Hensig's method would be far more subtle and clever—*cherms!* A scratch with a pin and a germ!

"I haf zome notes here of my disgovery," he went on, smiling significantly at the interruption, and taking some papers out of an inner pocket. "But they are written in Cherman, so I dranslate for you. You haf paper and benzil?"

The reporter produced the sheaf of office copy paper he always carried about with him, and prepared to write. The rattle of the elevated trains outside and the noisy buzz of drunken conversation inside formed the background against which he heard the German's steely insistent voice going on ceaselessly with the "dranslation and egsplanation." From time to time people left the room, and new customers reeled in. When the clatter of incipient fighting and smashed glasses became too loud, Hensig waited till it was quiet again. He watched every new arrival keenly. They were very few now, for the night had passed into early morning and the room was gradually emptying. The waiter took snatches of sleep in his chair by the door; the big man still snored heavily in the angle of the wall and window. When he was the only one left, the proprietor would certainly close up.

He had not ordered a drink for an hour at least. Williams, however, drank on steadily, always aiming at the point when he would be at the top of his power, full of confidence and decision. That moment was undoubtedly coming nearer all the time. Yes, but so was the moment Hensig was waiting for. He, too, felt absolutely confident, encouraging his companion to drink more, and watching his gradual collapse with unmasked glee. He betrayed his gloating quite plainly now: he held his victim too securely to feel anxious; when the big man reeled out they would be alone for a brief minute or two unobserved—and meanwhile he allowed himself to become a little too *careless* from over-confidence. And Williams noted that too.

For slowly the will of the reporter began to assert itself, and with this increase of intelligence he of course appreciated his awful position more keenly, and therefore, *felt more fear*. The two main things he was waiting for were coming perceptibly within reach: to reach the saturation point of terror and the culminating moment of the alcohol. Then, action and escape!

Gradually, thus, as he listened and wrote, he passed from the stage of stupid, negative terror into that of active, positive terror. The alcohol kept driving hotly at those hidden centres of imagination within, which, once touched, begin to reveal; in other words, he became observant, critical, alert. Swiftly the power grew. His lucidity increased till he became almost conscious of the workings of the other man's mind, and it was like sitting opposite a clock whose wheels and needles he could just hear clicking. His eyes seemed to spread their power of vision all over his skin; he could see what was going on without actually looking. In the same way he heard all that passed in the room without turning his head. Every moment he became clearer in mind. He almost touched clairvoyance. The presentiment earlier in the evening that this stage would come was at last being actually fulfilled.

From time to time he sipped his whisky, but more cautiously than at first, for he knew that this keen psychical activity was the forerunner of helpless collapse. Only for a minute or two would he be at the top of his power. The frontier was a dreadfully narrow one, and already he had lost control of his fingers, and was scrawling a shorthand that bore no resemblance to the original system of its inventor.

As the white light of this abnormal perceptiveness increased, the horror of his position became likewise more and more vivid. He knew that he was fighting for his life with a soulless and malefic being who was next door to a devil. The sense of fear was being magnified now with every minute that passed. Presently the power of *perceiving* would pass into *doing*; he would strike the blow for his life, whatever form that blow might take.

Already he was sufficiently master of himself to act—to act in the sense of deceiving. He exaggerated his drunken writing and thickness of speech, his general condition of collapse; and this power of *hearing* the workings of the other man's mind showed him that he was successful. Hensig was a little deceived. He proved this by increased carelessness, and by allowing the expression of his face to become plainly exultant.

Williams's faculties were so concentrated upon the causes operating in the terrible personality opposite to him, that he could spare no part of his brain for the explanations and sentences that came from his lips. He did not hear or understand a hundredth part of what the doctor was saying, but occasionally he caught up the end of a phrase and managed to ask a blundering question out of it; and Hensig, obviously pleased with his increasing obfuscation, always answered at some length, quietly watching with pleasure the reporter's foolish hieroglyphics upon the paper.

The whole thing, of course, was an utter blind. Hensig had no discovery at all. He was talking scientific jargon, knowing full well that those shorthand notes would never be transcribed, and that he himself would be out of harm's way long before his victim's senses had cleared sufficiently to tell him that he was in the grasp of a deadly sickness which no medicines could prevent ending in death.

Williams saw and felt all this clearly. It somehow came to him, rising up in that clear depth of his mind that was stirred by the alcohol, and yet beyond the reach, so far, of its deadly confusion. He understood perfectly well that Hensig was waiting for a moment to act; that he would do nothing violent, but would carry out his murderous intention in such an innocent way that the victim would have no suspicions at the moment, and would only realise later that he had been poisoned and—

Hark! What was that? There was a change. Something had happened. It was like the sound of a gong, and the reporter's fear suddenly doubled. Hensig's scheme had moved forward a step. There was no sound actually, but his senses seemed grouped together into one, and for some reason his perception of the change came by way of audition. Fear brimmed up perilously near the breaking point. But the moment for action had not quite come yet, and he luckily saved himself by the help of another and contrary emotion. He emptied his glass, spilling half of it purposely over his coat, and burst out laughing in Hensig's face. The vivid picture rose before him of Whitey Fife catching cocktail glasses off the edge of Steve Brodie's table.

The laugh was admirably careless and drunken, but the German was startled and looked up suspiciously. He had not expected this, and through lowered eyelids Williams observed an expression of momentary uncertainty on his features, as though he felt he was not absolutely master of the situation after all, as he imagined.

"Su'nly thought of Whitey Fife knocking Steve-brodie off'sh Brooklyn Bridsh in a co—cock'tail glashh—" Williams explained in a voice hopelessly out of control. "You know Whhhiteyfife, of coursh, don't you?—ha, ha, ha!"

Nothing could have helped him more in putting Hensig off the scent. His face resumed its expression of certainty and cold purpose. The waiter, wakened by the noise, stirred uneasily in his chair, and the big man in the corner indulged in a gulp that threatened to choke him as he sat with his head sunk upon his chest. But otherwise the empty room became quiet again. The German resumed his confident command of the situation. Williams, he saw, was drunk enough to bring him easily into his net.

None the less, the reporter's perception had not been at fault. There *was* a change. Hensig was about to do something, and his mind was buzzing with preparations.

The victim, now within measuring distance of his supreme moment—the point where terror would release his will, and alcohol would inspire him beyond possibility of error—saw everything as in the clear light of day. Small things led him to the climax: the emptied room; the knowledge that shortly the saloon would close; the grey light of day stealing under the chinks of door and shutter; the increased vileness of the face gleaming at him opposite in the paling gas glare. Ugh! how the air reeked of stale spirits, the fumes of cigar smoke, and the cheap scents of the vanished women. The floor was strewn with sheets of paper, absurdly scrawled over. The table had patches of wet, and cigarette ashes lay over everything. His hands and feet were icy, his eyes burning hot. His heart thumped like a soft hammer.

Hensig was speaking in quite a changed voice now. He had been leading up to this point for hours. No one was there to see, even if anything was to be seen—which was unlikely. The big man still snored; the waiter was asleep too. There was silence in the outer room, and between the walls of the inner there was—*Death*.

"Now, Mr. *Vulture* reporder, I *show* you what I mean all this time to egsplain," he was saying in his most metallic voice.

He drew a blank sheet of the reporter's paper towards him across the little table, avoiding carefully the wet splashes.

"Lend me your bencil von moment, please. Yes?"

Williams, simulating almost total collapse, dropped the pencil and shoved it over the polished wood as though the movement was about all he could manage. With his head sunk forward upon his chest he watched stupidly. Hensig began to draw some kind of outline; his touch was firm, and there was a smile on his lips.

"Here, you see, is the human arm," he said, sketching rapidly; "and here are the main nerves, and here the artery. Now, my discovery, as I haf peen egsplaining to you, is simply—" He dropped into a torrent of meaningless scientific phrases, during which the other purposely allowed his hand to lie relaxed upon the table, knowing perfectly well that in a moment Hensig would seize it—for the purposes of illustration.

His terror was so intense that, for the first time this awful night, he was within an ace of action. The point of saturation had been almost reached. Though apparently sodden drunk, his mind was really at the highest degree of clear perception and judgment, and in another moment—the moment Hensig actually began his final assault—the terror would provide the reporter with the extra vigour and decision necessary to strike his one blow. Exactly how he would do it, or what precise form it would take, he had no idea; that could be left to the inspiration of the moment; he only knew that his strength would last just long enough to bring this about, and that then he would collapse in utter intoxication upon the floor.

Hensig dropped the pencil suddenly: it clattered away to a corner of the room, showing it had been propelled with force, not merely allowed to fall, and he made no attempt to pick it up. Williams, to test his intention, made a pretended movement to stoop after it, and the other, as he imagined he would, stopped him in a second.

"I haf another," he said quickly, diving into his inner pocket and producing a long dark pencil. Williams saw in a flash, through his half-closed eyes, that it was sharpened at one end, while the other end was covered by a little protective cap of transparent substance like glass, a third of an inch long. He heard it click as it struck a button of the coat, and also saw that by a very swift motion of the fingers, impossible to be observed by a drunken man, Hensig removed the cap so that the end was free. Something gleamed there for a moment, something like a point of shining metal—the point of a pin.

"Gif me your hand von minute and I drace the nerve up the arm I speak apout," the doctor continued in that steely voice that showed no sign of nervousness, though he was on the edge of murder. "So, I show you much petter vot I mean."

Without a second's hesitation—for the moment for action had not quite come—he lurched forward and stretched his arm clumsily across the table. Hensig seized the fingers in his own and turned the palm uppermost. With his other hand he pointed the pencil at the wrist, and began moving it a little up towards the elbow, pushing the sleeve back for the purpose. His touch was the touch of death. On the point of the black pin, engrafted into the other end of the pencil, Williams knew there clung the germs of some deadly disease, germs unusually powerful from special culture; and that within the next few seconds the pencil would turn and the pin would *accidentally* scratch his wrist and let the virulent poison into his blood.

He knew this, yet at the same time he managed to remain master of himself. For he also realised that at last, just in the nick of time, the moment he had been waiting for all through these terrible hours had actually arrived, and he was ready to act.

And the little unimportant detail that furnished the extra quota of fear necessary to bring him to this point was—*touch*. It was the touch of Hensig's hand that did it, setting every nerve a-quiver to its utmost capacity, filling him with a black horror that reached the limits of sensation.

In that moment Williams regained his self-control and became absolutely sober. Terror removed its paralysing inhibitions, having led him to the point where numbness succeeds upon excess, and sensation ceases to register in the brain. The emotion of fear was dead, and he was ready to act with all the force of his being—that force, too, raised to a higher power after long repression.

Moreover, he could make no mistake, for at the same time he had reached the culminating effect of the alcohol, and a sort of white light filled his mind, showing him clearly what to do and how to do it. He felt master of himself, confident, capable of anything. He followed blindly that inner guidance he had been dimly conscious of the whole night, and what he did he did instinctively, as it were, without deliberate plan.

He was *waiting for the pencil to turn* so that the pin pointed at his vein. Then, when Hensig was wholly concentrated upon the act of murder, and thus oblivious of all else, he would find his opportunity. For at this supreme moment the German's mind would be focussed on the one thing. He would notice nothing else round him. He would be open to successful attack. But this supreme moment would hardly last more than five seconds at most!

The reporter raised his eyes and stared for the first time steadily into his opponent's eyes, till the room faded out and he saw only the white skin in a blaze of its own light. Thus staring, he caught in himself the full stream of venom, hatred, and revenge that had been pouring at him across the table for so long—caught and held it for one instant, and then returned it into the other's brain with all its original force and the added impetus of his own recovered will behind it.

Hensig felt this, and for a moment seemed to waver; he was surprised out of himself by the sudden change in his victim's attitude. The same instant, availing himself of a diversion caused by the big man in the corner waking noisily and trying to rise, he slowly *turned the pencil round* so that the point of the pin was directed at the hand lying in his. The sleepy waiter was helping the drunken man to cross to the door, and the diversion was all in his favour.

But Williams knew what he was doing. He did not even tremble.

"When that pin scratches me," he said aloud in a firm, sober voice, "it means—death."

The German could not conceal his surprise on hearing the change of voice, but he still felt sure of his victim, and clearly wished to enjoy his revenge thoroughly. After a moment's hesitation he replied, speaking very low:

"You tried, I tink, to get me conficted, and now I punish you, dat is all."

His fingers moved, and the point of the pin descended a little lower. Williams felt the faintest imaginable prick on his skin—or thought he did. The German had lowered his head again to direct the movement of the pin properly. But the moment of Hensig's concentration was also the moment of his own attack. And it had come.

"But the alcohol will counteract it!" he burst out, with a loud and startling laugh that threw the other completely off his guard. The doctor lifted his face in amazement. That same instant the hand that lay so helplessly and tipsily in his turned like a flash of lightning, and, before he knew what had happened, their positions were reversed. Williams held his wrist, pencil and all, in a grasp of iron. And from the reporter's other hand the German received a terrific smashing blow in the face that broke his glasses and dashed him back with a howl of pain against the wall.

There was a brief passage of scramble and wild blows, during which both table and chairs were sent flying, and then Williams was aware that a figure behind him had stretched forth an arm and was holding a bright silvery thing close to Hensig's bleeding face. Another glance showed him that it was a pistol, and that the man holding it was the big drunken man who had apparently slept all night in the corner of the room. Then, in a flash, he recognised him as Dowling's partner—a headquarters detective.

The reporter stepped back, his head swimming again. He was very unsteady on his feet.

"I've been watching your game all the evening," he heard the headquarters man saying as he slipped the handcuffs over the German's unresisting wrists. "We have been on your trail for weeks, and I might jest as soon have taken you when you left the Brooklyn church a few hours ago, only I wanted to see what you were up to—see? You're wanted in Berlin for one or two little dirty tricks, but our advices only came last night. Come along now."

"You'll get nozzing," Hensig replied very quietly, wiping his bloody face with the corner of his sleeve. "See, I have scratched myself!"

The detective took no notice of this remark, not understanding it, probably, but Williams noticed the direction of the eyes, and saw a scratch on his wrist, slightly bleeding. Then he understood that in the struggle the pin had accidentally found another destination than the one intended for it.

But he remembered nothing more after that, for the reaction set in with a rush. The strain of that awful night left him utterly limp, and the accumulated effect of the alcohol, now that all was past, overwhelmed him like a wave, and he sank in a heap upon the floor, unconscious.

The illness that followed was simply "nerves," and he got over it in a week or two, and returned to his work on the paper. He at once made inquiries, and found that Hensig's arrest had hardly been noticed by the papers. There was no interesting feature about it, and New York was already in the throes of a new horror.

But Dowling, that enterprising Irishman—always with an eye to promotion and the main chance—Dowling had something to say about it.

"No luck, Mr. English," he said ruefully, "no luck at all. It would have been a mighty good story, but it never got in the papers. That damned German, Schmidt, alias Brunner, alias Hensig, died in the prison hospital before we could even get him remanded for further inquiries—"

"What did he die of?" interrupted the reporter quickly.

"Black typhus, I think they call it. But it was terribly swift, and he was dead in four days. The doctor said he'd never known such a case."

"I'm glad he's out of the way," observed Williams.

"Well, yes," Dowling said hesitatingly; "but it was a jim dandy of a story, an' he might have waited a little bit longer jest so as I got something out of it for meself."

THE OLD MAN OF VISIONS

Whilst on the island in Lake Rosseau, Blackwood had injured himself diving into the lake and hitting a rock. By late November the wound had turned septic and he was confined to bed. It was at this time he fell victim to a new room-mate, whom he called Arthur Boyde, whom he had met at that same cricket match that landed him a job at the Evening Sun. *Boyde—his real name was Bigge—was a confidence trickster and a thief and he was soon milking Blackwood of whatever funds he could find. Once Blackwood realised the truth, he dragged himself off his sick bed and hunted Bigge through the snow-covered New York streets and, with the help of a policeman he knew from the Tombs, had him arrested. Even then Blackwood felt guilty and did so for many years.*

Once Blackwood had recovered he returned to his reporting duties at the Evening Sun *and amongst the trials he covered was that of Lizzie Borden, who was found not guilty of killing her parents, though Blackwood was convinced she had. He found the work arduous, especially in the boiling heat of a New York summer and he tried to escape whenever he could, either to Central Park or the Bronx Park or, at least once, back to Canada. Otherwise he found solace in writing stories, though chose not to seek publication and instead stored them in a cupboard. He was befriended by a fellow reporter (and traveller) Angus Hamilton who was interested in the stories and would later be a catalyst to Blackwood's getting into print.*

As the 1894 summer threatened Blackwood and his close friends became interested in a report that gold had been found in the Rainy Lake region on the

Canadian/US border in Minnesota. It was the chance of another adventure which Blackwood said he would report upon to his paper, but although it was a few weeks' escape, no one earned their fortune.

Back in New York, Blackwood continued to make interesting friends. Arguably the most profound was the English-born Alfred H. Louis, who had converted from the Jewish faith to Anglicanism. He was 65 when he met Blackwood on the river front by an olive-oil warehouse where they both drank a glass of the nutritious oil. Blackwood was soon under Louis's spell. He had been a politician but had fallen foul of William Gladstone and chose to self-exile in America. His calling was as a lawyer and barrister and he was an accomplished musician and a talented poet, but life had dealt him hard. He had married but his wife had died and soon after so did his second child. Something turned his mind and he became mystical and detached. Blackwood called him "a dignified, venerable and mysterious being," but also a "madman". Nevertheless, Blackwood found solace in Louis who became his mentor and there is little doubt that, mad or otherwise, Louis helped Blackwood keep his sanity during the darkest days. It was Louis who encouraged Blackwood to return home in 1899, and Louis was the last person Blackwood saw, waving to him from the quay as the ship departed. Later Blackwood and his friends helped finance Louis's return to Britain where he remained for the last decade of his life, dying in 1915 aged 86. Blackwood dedicated Episodes Before Thirty to him. He was also the inspiration for the following story, itself rather mystical, making the point that if you share too much of your dreams and visions much of the magic will be lost.

T HE image of Teufelsdröckh, sitting in his watch-tower "alone with the stars," leaped into my mind the moment I saw him; and the curious expression of his eyes proclaimed at once that here was a being who allowed the world of small effects to pass him by, while he himself dwelt among the eternal verities. It was only necessary to catch a glimpse of the bent grey figure, so slight yet so tremendous, to real-ise that he carried staff and wallet, and was travelling alone in a spiritual region, uncharted, and full of wonder, difficulty, and fearful joy.

The inner eye perceived this quite as clearly as the outer was aware of his Hebraic ancestry; but along what winding rivers, through what haunted woods, by the shores of what singing seas he pressed forward towards the mountains of his goal, no one could guess from a mere inspec-tion of that wonderful old face.

To have stumbled upon such a figure in the casual way I did seemed incredible to me even at the time, yet I at once caught something of the uplifting airs that followed this inhabitant of a finer world, and I spent days—and considered them well spent—trying to get into conversation with him, so that I might know something more than the thin disguise of his holding a reader's ticket for the Museum Library.

To reach the stage of intimacy where actual speech is a hindrance to close understanding, one need not in some cases have spoken at all: thus by merely setting my mind, and above all, my imagination, into tune with his, and by steeping myself so much in his atmosphere that I absorbed and then gave back to him with my own stamp the forces he exhaled, it was at length possible to persuade those vast-seeing eyes to turn in my direction; and our glances having once met, I simply rose when he rose, and followed him out of the little smoky restaurant so closely up the street that our clothes brushed, and I thought I could even catch the sound of his breathing.

Whether, having already weighed me, he accepted the office, or whether he was grateful for the arm to lean upon, with his many years' burden, I do not know; but the sympathy between us was such that, without a single word, we walked up that foggy London street to the door of his lodging in Bloomsbury, while I noticed that at the touch of his arm the noise of the town seemed to turn into deep singing, and even the hurrying passers-by seemed bent upon noble purposes; and though he barely reached to my shoulder, and his grey beard almost touched my glove as I bent my arm to hold his own, there was something immense about his figure that sent him with towering stature above me and filled my thoughts with enchanting dreams of grandeur and high beauty.

But it was only when the door had closed on him with a little rush of wind, and I was walking home alone, that I fully realised the shock of my return to earth; and on reaching my own rooms I shook with laughter to think I had walked a mile and a half with a complete stranger without uttering a single syllable. Then the laughter suddenly hushed as I caught my face in the glass with the expression of the soul still lingering about the eyes and forehead, and for a brief moment my heart leaped to a sort of noble fever in the blood, leaving me with the smart of the soul's wings stirring beneath the body's crushing weight. And when it passed I found myself dwelling upon the only words he had spoken when I left him at the door:

"I am the Old Man of Visions, and I am *at your service.*"

I think he never had a name—at least, it never passed his lips, and perhaps lay buried with so much else of the past that he clearly deemed unimportant. To me, at any rate, he became simply the Old Man of Visions, and to the little waiting-maid and the old landlady he was known simply as "Mister"—Mister, neither more nor less. The impenetrable veil that hung over his past never lifted for any vital revelations of his personal history, though he evidently knew all countries of the world, and had absorbed into his heart and brain the experience of all possible types of human nature; and there was an air about him not so much of "Ask me no questions," as "Do not ask me, for I cannot answer you *in words.*"

He could satisfy, but not in mere language; he would reveal, but by the wonderful words of silence only; for he was the Old Man of Visions, and visions need no words, being swift and of the spirit.

Moreover, the landlady—poor, dusty, faded woman—the landlady stood in awe, and disliked being probed for information in a passage-way down which he might any moment tread, for she could only tell me, "He just came in one night, years ago, and he's been here ever since!" And more than that I never knew. "Just came in—one night—years ago." This adequately explained him, for where he came *from,* or was journeying *to,* was something quite beyond the scope of ordinary limited language.

I pictured him suddenly turning aside from the stream of unimportant events, quietly stepping out of the world of straining, fighting, and shouting, and moving to take his rightful place among the forces of the still, spiritual region where he belonged by virtue of long pain and difficult attainment. For he was unconnected with any conceivable network of relations, friends, or family, and his terrible aloofness could not be disturbed by any one unless with his permission and by his express wish. Nor could he be imagined as "belonging" to any definite set of souls. He was apart from the world—and above it.

But it was only when I began to creep a little nearer to him, and our strange, silent intimacy passed from mental to spiritual, that I began really to understand more of this wonderful Old Man of Visions.

Steeped in the tragedy, and convulsed with laughter at the comedy, of life, he yet lived there in his high attic wrapped in silence as in a golden cloud; and so seldom did he actually speak to me that each time the sound of his voice, that had something elemental in it—something of winds and waters—thrilled me with the power of the first time. He lived, like Teufelsdröckh, "alone with the stars," and it seemed impossible, more and more, to link him on anywhere into practical dealings with ordinary men and women. Life somehow seemed to pass *below* him. Yet the small, selfish spirit of the recluse was far from him, and he was tenderly and deeply responsive to pain and suffering, and more particularly to genuine yearning for the far things of beauty. The unsatisfied longings of others could move him at once to tears.

"My relations with men are perfect," he said one night as we neared his dwelling. "I give them all sympathy out of my stores of knowledge and experience, and they give to me what kindness I need. My outer shell lies within impenetrable solitude, for only so can my inner life move freely along the paths and terraces that are thronged with the beings to whom I belong." And when I asked him how he maintained such deep sympathy with humanity, and had yet absolved himself apparently from action as from speech, he stopped against an area railing and turned his great eyes on to my face, as though their fires could communicate his thought without the husk of words:

"I have peered too profoundly into life and beyond it," he murmured, "to wish to express in language what I *know*. Action is not for all, always; and I am in touch with the cisterns of thought that lie behind action. I ponder the mysteries. What I may solve is not lost for lack either of speech or action, for the true mystic is ever the true man of action, and my thought will reach others as soon as they are ready for it in the same way that it reached you. All who strongly yearn must, sooner or later, find me and be comforted."

His eyes shifted from my face towards the stars, softly shining above the dark Museum roof, and a moment later he had disappeared into the hall-way of his house.

"An old poet who has strayed afield and lost his way," I mused; but through the door where he had just vanished the words came back to me as from a great distance: "A priest, rather, who has begun to find his way."

For a space I stood, pondering on his face and words:—that mercilessly intelligent look of the Hebrew woven in with the expression of the sadness of a whole race, yet touched with the glory of the spirit; and his utterance—that he had passed through all the traditions and no longer needed a formal, limited creed to hold to. I forget how I reached my own door several miles away, but it seemed to me that I flew.

In this way, and by unregistered degrees, we came to know each other better, and he accepted me and took me into his life. Always wrapped in the great calm of his delightful silence, he taught me more, and told me more, than could ever lie within the confines of mere words; and in moments of need, no matter when or where, I always knew exactly how to find him, reaching him in a few seconds by some swift way that disdained the means of ordinary locomotion.

Then at last one day he gave me the key of his house. And the first time I found my way into his eyrie, and realised that it was a haven I could always fly to when the yearnings of the heart and soul struggled vainly for recompense, the full meaning and importance of the Old Man of Visions became finally clear to me.

11

The room, high up creaky, darkened stairs in the ancient house, was bare and fireless, looking through a single patched window across a tumbled sea of roofs and chimneys; yet there was that in it which instantly proclaimed it a little holy place out of the world, a temple in which some one with spiritual vitality had worshipped, prayed, wept, and sung.

It was dusty and unswept, yet it was utterly *unsoiled*; and the Old Man of Visions who lived there, for all his shabby and stained garments, his uncombed beard and broken shoes, stood within its door revealed in his real self, moving in a sort of divine whiteness, iridescent, shining. And here, in this attic (lampless and unswept), high up under the old roofs of Bloomsbury, the window scarred with rain and the corners dropping cobwebs, I heard his silver whisper issue from the shadows:

"Here you may satisfy your soul's desire and may commune with the Invisibles; only, to find the Invisibles, you must first be able to lose yourself."

Ah! through that stained window-pane, the sight leaping at a single bound from black roofs up to the stars, what pictures, dreams, and visions the Old Man has summoned to my eyes! Distances, measureless and impossible hitherto, became easy, and from the oppression of dead bricks and the market-place he transported me in a moment to the slopes of the Mountains of Dream; leading me to little places near the summits where the pines grew thinly and the stars were visible through their branches, fading into the rose of dawn; where the winds tasted of the desert, and the voices of the wilderness fled upward with a sound of wings and falling streams. At his word houses melted away, and the green waves of all the seas flowed into their places; forests waved themselves into the coastline of dull streets; and the power of the old earth, with all her smells and flowers and wild life, thrilled down among the dead roofs and caught me away into freedom among the sunshine of meadows and the music of sweet pipings. And with the divine deliverance came the crying of sea-gulls, the glimmer of reedy tarns, the whispering of wind among grasses, and the healing scorch of a real sun upon the skin.

And poetry such as was never known or heard before clothed all he uttered, yet even then took no form in actual words, for it was of the substance of aspiration and yearning, voicing adequately all the busy, high-born dreams that haunt the soul yet never live in the uttered line. He breathed it about him in the air so that it filled my being. It was part of him—beyond words; and it sang my own longings, and sang them perfectly so that I was satisfied; for my own mood never failed to touch him instantly and to waken the right response. In its essence it was spiritual—the mystic poetry of heaven; still, the love of humanity informed it, for star-fire and heart's blood were about equally mingled there, while the mystery of unattainable beauty moved through it like a white flame.

With other dreams and longings, too, it was the same; and all the most beautiful ideas that ever haunted a soul undowered with expression here floated with satisfied eyes and smiling lips before one—floated in silence, unencumbered, unlimited, unrestrained by words.

In this dim room, never made ugly by artificial light, but always shadowy in a kind of gentle dusk, the Old Man of Visions had only to lead me to the window to bring peace. Music, that rendered the soul fluid, as it poured across the old roofs into the room, was summoned by him at need; and when one's wings beat sometimes against the prison walls and the yearning for escape oppressed the heart, I have heard the little room rush and fill with the sound of trees, wind among grasses, whispering branches, and lapping waters. The very odours of space and mountain-side came too, and the looming of noble hills seemed visible overhead against the stars, as though the ceiling had suddenly become transparent.

For the Old Man of Visions had the power of instantly satisfying an ideal when once that ideal created a yearning that could tear and burn its way out with sufficient force to set the will a-moving.

III

But as the time passed and I came to depend more and more upon the intimacy with my strange old friend, new light fell upon the nature and possibilities of our connection. I discovered, for instance, that though I held the key to his dwelling, and was familiar with the way, he was nevertheless not always available. Two things, in different fashion, rendered him inaccessible, or mute; and, for the first, I gradually learned that when life was prosperous, and the body singing loud, I could not find my way to his house. No amount of wandering, calculation, or persevering effort enabled me even to find the street again. With any burst of worldly success, however fleeting, the Old Man of Visions somehow slipped away into remote shadows and became unreal and misty. A merely passing desire to be with him, to seek his inspiration by a glimpse through that magic window-pane, resulted only in vain and tiresome pacing to and fro along ugly streets that produced weariness and depression; and after these periods it became, I noticed, less and less easy to discover the house, to fit the key in the door, or, having gained access to the temple, to realise the visions I *thought* I craved for.

Often, in this way, have I searched in vain for days, but only succeeded in losing myself in the murky purlieus of a quite strange Bloomsbury; stopping outside numberless counterfeit doors, and struggling vainly with locks that knew nothing of my little shining key.

But, on the other hand, pain, loneliness, sorrow—the merest whisper of spiritual affliction—and, lo, in a single moment the difficult geography became plain, and without hesitation, when I was unhappy or distressed, I found the way to his house as by a bird's instinctive flight, and the key slipped into the lock as though it loved it and was returning home.

The other cause to render him inaccessible, though not so determined—since it never concealed the way to the house—was even more distressing, for it depended wholly on myself; and I came to know how the least ugly action, involving a depreciation of ideals, so confused the mind that, when I got into the house, with difficulty, and found him in the little room after much searching, he was able to do or say scarcely anything at all for me. The mirror facing the door then gave back, I saw, no proper reflection of his person, but only a faded and wavering shadow with dim eyes and stooping, indistinct outline, and I even fancied I could see the pattern of the wall and shape of the furniture *through* his body, as though he had grown semi-transparent.

"You must not expect yearnings to weigh," came his whisper, like wind far overhead, "unless you lend to them *your own* substance; and your own substance you cannot both keep and lend. If you would know the Invisibles, forget yourself."

And later, as the years slipped away one after another into the mists, and the frontier between the real and the unreal began to shift amazingly with his teachings, it became more and more clear to me that he belonged to a permanent region that, with all the changes in the world's history, has itself never altered in any essential particular. This immemorial Old Man of Visions, as I grew to think of him, had existed always; he was old as the sea and coeval with the stars; and he dwelt beyond time and space, reaching out a hand to all those who, weary of the shadows and illusions of practical life, really call to him with their heart of hearts. To me, indeed, the touch of sorrow was always near enough to prevent his becoming often inaccessible, and after a while even his voice became so *living* that I sometimes heard it calling to me in the street and in the fields.

Oh, wonderful Old Man of Visions! Happy the days of disaster, since they taught me how to know you, the Unraveller of Problems, the Destroyer of Doubts, who bore me ever away with soft flight down the long, long vistas of the heart and soul!

And his loneliness in that temple attic under the stars, his loneliness, too, had a meaning I did not fail to understand later, and why he was always available for me and seemed to belong to no other.

"To every one who finds me," he said, with the strange smile that wrapped his whole being and not his face alone, "to every one I am the same, and yet different. I am not really ever alone. The whole world, nay"— his voice rose to a singing cry—"the whole universe lies in this room, or just beyond that window-pane; for here past and future meet and all real dreams find completeness. But remember," he added—and there was a sound as of soft wind and rain in the room with his voice—"no true dream can ever be shared, and should you seek to explain me to another you must lose me beyond recall. You have never asked my name, nor must you ever tell it. Each must find me in his own way."

Yet one day, for all my knowledge and his warnings, I felt so sure of my intimacy with this immemorial being, that I spoke of him to a friend who was, I had thought, so much a part of myself that it seemed no betrayal. And my friend, who went to search and found nothing, returned with the fool's laughter on his face, and swore that no street or number existed, for he had looked in vain, and had repeatedly *asked the way*.

And, from that day to this, the Old Man of Visions has neither called to me nor let his place be found; the streets are strange and empty, and I have even lost the little shining key.

THE LISTENER

When Blackwood returned to England in February 1899 there was a period of euphoria as he met again his close family, and especially his mother. His father had died six years before and, as ever, Blackwood felt guilty that he had not been able to reconcile himself with his father's beliefs and concerns. Thanks to his aristocratic connections, in particular Lord Kintore, he acquired a job in the City as a Company Secretary, something which was of no interest to him but which provided an income. For his last few years in New York he had served as the Private Secretary to the millionaire banker James Speyer, which had given him some status and enhanced his reputation amongst his family.

Nevertheless, Blackwood needed to escape and would often walk through Richmond Park at night or anywhere away from people. But he needed somewhere to stay and first found lodgings in Sussex Street in Belgravia and then in Halsey Street, Chelsea. This last place was near both his elder sisters and to the Kintores who, when in London, stayed at the Berkeley Hotel. Although they enticed Blackwood to enjoy nights at the theatre or dining out, Blackwood much preferred writing about his experiences in New York. It was a form of therapy and some of the writing took the form of stories. Along with those he had written in New York he had little thought of publishing them though a few found their way into popular magazines. "A Case of Eavesdropping", for example, is set in New York, in rooms where the lodger overhears ghosts re-enacting a murder, and it appeared in the December 1900 Pall Mall Magazine. *But most languished in his cupboard. Amongst them was the following story, written in*

1899, but not published until Blackwood's second book in 1907, which bore the same title, The Listener. *It shows how he was perfecting the art of creating a tangible atmosphere within an autobiographical setting.* The start of the story *reads very much how Blackwood would himself have kept track of his income and expenses, but how much of the rest is real, we will have to imagine.*

*S*EPT. 4—I have hunted all over London for rooms suited to my income—£120 a year—and have at last found them. Two rooms, without modern conveniences, it is true, and in an old, ramshackle building, but within a stone's throw of P—— Place and in an eminently respectable street. The rent is only £25 a year. I had begun to despair when at last I found them by chance. The chance was a mere chance, and unworthy of record. I had to sign a lease for a year, and I did so willingly. The furniture from our old place in H—shire, which has been stored so long, will just suit them.

Oct. 1.—Here I am in my two rooms, in the centre of London, and not far from the offices of the periodicals where occasionally I dispose of an article or two. The building is at the end of a *cul-de-sac*. The alley is well paved and clean, and lined chiefly with the backs of sedate and institutional-looking buildings. There is a stable in it. My own house is dignified with the title of "Chambers." I feel as if one day the honour must prove too much for it, and it will swell with pride—and fall asunder. It is very old. The floor of my sitting-room has valleys and low hills on it, and the top of the door slants away from the ceiling with a glorious disregard of what is usual. They must have quarrelled—fifty years ago—and have been going apart ever since.

Oct. 2.—My landlady is old and thin, with a faded, dusty face. She is uncommunicative. The few words she utters seem to cost her pain. Probably her lungs are half choked with dust. She keeps my rooms as free from this commodity as possible, and has the assistance of a strong girl who brings up the breakfast and lights the fire. As I have said already, she is not communicative. In reply to pleasant efforts on my part she informed me briefly that I was the only occupant of the house at present. My rooms had not been occupied for some years. There had been other gentlemen upstairs, but they had left.

She never looks straight at me when she speaks, but fixes her dim eyes on my middle waistcoat button, till I get nervous and begin to think it isn't on straight, or is the wrong sort of button altogether.

Oct. 8.—My week's book is nicely kept, and so far is reasonable. Milk and sugar 7d., bread 6d., butter 8d., marmalade 6d., eggs 1s. 8d., laundress 2s. 9d., oil 6d., attendance 5s.; total 12s. 2d.

The landlady has a son who, she told me, is "somethink on a homnibus." He comes occasionally to see her. I think he drinks, for he talks very loud, regardless of the hour of the day or night, and tumbles about over the furniture downstairs.

All the morning I sit indoors writing—articles; verses for the comic papers; a novel I've been "at" for three years, and concerning which I have dreams; a children's book, in which the imagination has free rein; and another book which is to last as long as myself, since it is an honest record of my soul's advance or retreat in the struggle of life. Besides these, I keep a book of poems which I use as a safety valve, and concerning which I have no dreams whatsoever. Between the lot I am always occupied. In the afternoons I generally try to take a walk for my health's sake, through Regent's Park, into Kensington Gardens, or farther afield to Hampstead Heath.

Oct. 10.—Everything went wrong today. I have two eggs for breakfast. This morning one of them was bad. I rang the bell for Emily. When she came in I was reading the paper, and, without looking up, I said, "Egg's bad." "Oh, is it, sir?" she said; "I'll get another one," and went out, taking the egg with her. I waited my breakfast for her return, which was in five minutes. She put the new egg on the table and went away. But, when I looked down, I saw that she had taken away the good egg and left the bad one—all green and yellow—in the slop basin. I rang again.

"You've taken the wrong egg," I said.

"Oh!" she exclaimed; "I thought the one I took down didn't smell so *very* bad." In due time she returned with the good egg, and I resumed my breakfast with two eggs, but less appetite. It was all very trivial, to be sure, but so stupid that I felt annoyed. The character of that egg influenced everything I did. I wrote a bad article, and tore it up. I got a bad headache. I used bad words—to myself. Everything was bad, so I "chucked" work and went for a long walk.

I dined at a cheap chop-house on my way back, and reached home about nine o'clock.

Rain was just beginning to fall as I came in, and the wind was rising. It promised an ugly night. The alley looked dismal and dreary, and the hall of the house, as I passed through it, felt chilly as a tomb. It was the first stormy night I had experienced in my new quarters. The draughts were awful. They came criss-cross, met in the middle of the room, and formed eddies and whirlpools and cold silent currents that almost lifted the hair of my head. I stuffed up the sashes of the windows with neckties and odd socks, and sat over the smoky fire to keep warm. First I tried to write, but found it too cold. My hand turned to ice on the paper.

What tricks the wind did play with the old place! It came rushing up the forsaken alley with a sound like the feet of a hurrying crowd of people who stopped suddenly at the door. I felt as if a lot of curious folk had arranged themselves just outside and were staring up at my windows. Then they took to their heels again and fled whispering and laughing down the lane, only, however, to return with the next gust of wind and repeat their impertinence. On the other side of my room a single square window opens into a sort of shaft, or well, that measures about six feet across to the back wall of another house. Down this funnel the wind dropped, and puffed and shouted. Such noises I never heard before. Between these two entertainments I sat over the fire in a great-coat, listening to the deep booming in the chimney. It was like being in a ship at sea, and I almost looked for the floor to rise in undulations and rock to and fro.

Oct. 12.—I wish I were not quite so lonely—and so poor. And yet I love both my loneliness and my poverty. The former makes me appreciate the companionship of the wind and rain, while the latter preserves my liver and prevents me wasting time in dancing attendance upon women. Poor, ill-dressed men are not acceptable "attendants."

My parents are dead, and my only sister is—no, not dead exactly, but married to a very rich man. They travel most of the time, he to find his health, she to lose herself. Through sheer neglect on her part she has long passed out of my life. The door closed when, after an absolute silence of five years, she sent me a cheque for £50 at Christmas. It was signed by her husband! I returned it to her in a thousand pieces and in an unstamped envelope. So at least I had the satisfaction of knowing that it cost her something! She wrote back with a broad quill pen that covered a whole page with three lines, "You are evidently as cracked as ever, and rude and ungrateful into the bargain." It had always been my special terror lest the insanity in my father's family should leap across the generations and appear in me. This thought haunted me, and she knew it. So after this little exchange of civilities the door slammed, never to open again. I heard the crash it made, and, with it, the falling from the walls of my heart of many little bits of china with their own peculiar value—rare china, some of it, that only needed dusting. The same walls, too, carried mirrors in which I used sometimes to see reflected the misty lawns of childhood, the daisy chains, the wind-torn blossoms scattered through the orchard by warm rains, the robbers' cave in the long walk, and the hidden store of apples in the hay-loft. She was my inseparable companion then—but, when the door slammed, the mirrors cracked across their entire length, and the visions they held vanished for ever. Now I am quite alone. At forty one cannot begin all over again to build up careful friendships, and all others are comparatively worthless.

Oct. 14.—My bedroom is 10 by 10. It is below the level of the front room, and a step leads down into it. Both rooms are very quiet on calm nights, for there is no traffic down this forsaken alley-way. In spite of the occasional larks of the wind, it is a most sheltered strip. At its upper end, below my windows, all the cats of the neighbourhood congregate as soon as darkness gathers. They lie undisturbed on the long ledge of a blind window of the opposite building, for after the postman has come and gone at 9.30, no footsteps ever dare to interrupt their sinister conclave, no step but my own, or sometimes the unsteady footfall of the son who "is somethink on a homnibus."

Oct. 15.—I dined at an "A.B.C." shop on poached eggs and coffee, and then went for a stroll round the outer edge of Regent's Park. It was ten o'clock when I got home. I counted no less than thirteen cats, all of a dark colour, crouching under the lee side of the alley walls. It was a cold night, and the stars shone like points of ice in a blue-black sky. The cats turned their heads and stared at me in silence as I passed. An odd sensation of shyness took possession of me under the glare of so many pairs of unblinking eyes. As I fumbled with the latch-key they jumped noiselessly down and pressed against my legs, as if anxious to be let in. But I slammed the door in their faces and ran quickly upstairs. The front room, as I entered to grope for the matches, felt as cold as a stone vault, and the air held an unusual dampness.

Oct. 17.—For several days I have been working on a ponderous article that allows no play for the fancy. My imagination requires a judicious rein; I am afraid to let it loose, for it carries me sometimes into appalling places beyond the stars and beneath the world. No one realises the danger more than I do. But what a foolish thing to write here—for there is no one to know, no one to realise! My mind of late has held unusual thoughts, thoughts I have never had before, about medicines and drugs and the treatment of strange illnesses. I cannot imagine their source. At no time in my life have I dwelt upon such ideas as now constantly throng my brain. I have had no exercise lately, for the weather has been shocking; and all my afternoons have been spent in the reading-room of the British Museum, where I have a reader's ticket.

I have made an unpleasant discovery: there are rats in the house. At night from my bed I have heard them scampering across the hills and valleys of the front room, and my sleep has been a good deal disturbed in consequence.

Oct. 19.—The landlady, I find, has a little boy with her, probably her son's child. In fine weather he plays in the alley, and draws a wooden cart over the cobbles. One of the wheels is off, and it makes a most distracting noise. After putting up with it as long as possible, I found it was getting on my nerves, and I could not write. So I rang the bell. Emily answered it.

"Emily, will you ask the little fellow to make less noise? It's impossible to work."

The girl went downstairs, and soon afterwards the child was called in by the kitchen door. I felt rather a brute for spoiling his play. In a few minutes, however, the noise began again, and I felt that he was the brute. He dragged the broken toy with a string over the stones till the rattling noise jarred every nerve in my body. It became unbearable, and I rang the bell a second time.

"That noise *must* be put a stop to!" I said to the girl, with decision.

"Yes, sir," she grinned, "I know; but one of the wheels is hoff. The men in the stable offered to mend it for 'im, but he wouldn't let them. He says he likes it that way."

"I can't help what he likes. The noise must stop. I can't write."

"Yes, sir; I'll tell Mrs. Monson."

The noise stopped for the day then.

Oct. 23.—Every day for the past week that cart has rattled over the stones, till I have come to think of it as a huge carrier's van with four wheels and two horses; and every morning I have been obliged to ring the bell and have it stopped. The last time Mrs. Monson herself came up, and said she was sorry I had been annoyed; the sounds should not occur again. With rare discursiveness she went on to ask if I was comfortable, and how I liked the rooms. I replied cautiously. I mentioned the rats. She said they were mice. I spoke of the draughts. She said, "Yes, it were a draughty 'ouse." I referred to the cats, and she said they had been as long as she could remember. By way of conclusion, she informed me that the house was over two hundred years old, and that the last gentleman who had occupied my rooms was a painter who "'ad real Jimmy Bueys and Raffles 'anging all hover the walls." It took me some moments to discern that Cimabue and Raphael were in the woman's mind.

Oct. 24.—Last night the son who is "somethink on a homnibus" came in. He had evidently been drinking, for I heard loud and angry voices below in the kitchen long after I had gone to bed. Once, too, I caught the singular words rising up to me through the floor, "Burning from top to bottom is the only thing that'll ever make this 'ouse right." I knocked on the floor, and the voices ceased suddenly, though later I again heard their clamour in my dreams.

These rooms are very quiet, almost too quiet sometimes. On windless nights they are silent as the grave, and the house might be miles in the country. The roar of London's traffic reaches me only in heavy, distant vibrations. It holds an ominous note sometimes, like that of an approaching army, or an immense tidal-wave very far away thundering in the night.

Oct. 27.—Mrs. Monson, though admirably silent, is a foolish, fussy woman. She does such stupid things. In dusting the room she puts all my things in the wrong places. The ash-trays, which should be on the writing-table, she sets in a silly row on the mantelpiece. The pen-tray, which should be beside the inkstand, she hides away cleverly among the books on my reading-desk. My gloves she arranges daily in idiotic array upon a half-filled book-shelf, and I always have to rearrange them on the low table by the door. She places my armchair at impossible angles between the fire and the light, and the tablecloth—the one with Trinity Hall stains—she puts on the table in such a fashion that when I look at it I feel as if my tie and all my clothes were on crooked and awry. She exasperates me. Her very silence and meekness are irritating. Sometimes I feel inclined to throw the inkstand at her, just to bring an expression into her watery eyes and a squeak from those colourless lips. Dear me! What violent expressions I am making use of! How very foolish of me! And yet it almost seems as if the words were not my own, but had been spoken into my ear—I mean, I never make use of such terms naturally.

Oct. 30.—I have been here a month. The place does not agree with me, I think. My headaches are more frequent and violent, and my nerves are a perpetual source of discomfort and annoyance.

I have conceived a great dislike for Mrs. Monson, a feeling I am certain she reciprocates. Somehow, the impression comes frequently to me that there are goings on in this house of which I know nothing, and which she is careful to hide from me.

Last night her son slept in the house, and this morning as I was standing at the window I saw him go out. He glanced up and caught my eye. It was a loutish figure and a singularly repulsive face that I saw, and he gave me the benefit of a very unpleasant leer. At least, so I imagined.

Evidently I am getting absurdly sensitive to trifles, and I suppose it is my disordered nerves making themselves felt. In the British Museum this afternoon I noticed several people at the readers' table staring at me and watching every movement I made. Whenever I looked up from my books I found their eyes upon me. It seemed to me unnecessary and unpleasant, and I left earlier than was my custom. When I reached the door I threw back a last look into the room, and saw every head at the table turned in my direction. It annoyed me very much, and yet I know it is foolish to take note of such things. When I am well they pass me by. I must get more regular exercise. Of late I have had next to none.

Nov. 2.—The utter stillness of this house is beginning to oppress me. I wish there were other fellows living upstairs. No footsteps ever sound overhead, and no tread ever passes my door to go up the next flight of stairs. I am beginning to feel some curiosity to go up myself and see what the upper rooms are like. I feel lonely here and isolated, swept into a deserted corner of the world and forgotten... Once I actually caught myself gazing into the long, cracked mirrors, trying to see the sunlight dancing beneath the trees in the orchard. But only deep shadows seemed to congregate there now, and I soon desisted.

It has been very dark all day, and no wind stirring. The fogs have begun. I had to use a reading-lamp all this morning. There was no cart to be heard today. I actually missed it. This morning, in the gloom and silence, I think I could almost have welcomed it. After all, the sound is a very human one, and this empty house at the end of the alley holds other noises that are not quite so satisfactory.

I have never once seen a policeman in the lane, and the postmen always hurry out with no evidence of a desire to loiter.

10 P.M.—As I write this I hear no sound but the deep murmur of the distant traffic and the low sighing of the wind. The two sounds melt into one another. Now and again a cat raises its shrill, uncanny cry upon the darkness. The cats are always there under my windows when the darkness falls. The wind is dropping into the funnel with a noise like the sudden sweeping of immense distant wings. It is a dreary night. I feel lost and forgotten.

Nov. 3.—From my windows I can see arrivals. When any one comes to the door I can just see the hat and shoulders and the hand on the bell. Only two fellows have been to see me since I came here two months ago. Both of them I saw from the window before they came up, and heard their voices asking if I was in. Neither of them ever came back.

I have finished the ponderous article. On reading it through, however, I was dissatisfied with it, and drew my pencil through almost every page. There were strange expressions and ideas in it that I could not explain, and viewed with amazement, not to say alarm. They did not sound like my *very own*, and I could not remember having written them. Can it be that my memory is beginning to be affected?

My pens are never to be found. That stupid old woman puts them in a different place each day. I must give her due credit for finding so many new hiding places; such ingenuity is wonderful. I have told her repeatedly, but she always says, "I'll speak to Emily, sir." Emily always says, "I'll tell Mrs. Monson, sir." Their foolishness makes me irritable and scatters all my thoughts. I should like to stick the lost pens into them and turn them out, blind-eyed, to be scratched and mauled by those thousand hungry cats.

Whew! What a ghastly thought! Where in the world did it come from? Such an idea is no more my own than it is the policeman's. Yet I felt I *had* to write it. It was like a voice singing in my head, and my pen wouldn't stop till the last word was finished. What ridiculous nonsense! I must and will restrain myself. I must take more regular exercise; my nerves and liver plague me horribly.

Nov. 4.—I attended a curious lecture in the French quarter on "Death," but the room was so hot and I was so weary that I fell asleep. The only part I heard, however, touched my imagination vividly. Speaking of suicides, the lecturer said that self-murder was no escape from the miseries of the present, but only a preparation of greater sorrow for the future. Suicides, he declared, cannot shirk their responsibilities so easily. They must return to take up life exactly where they laid it so violently down, but with the added pain and punishment of their weakness. Many of them wander the earth in unspeakable misery till they can *reclothe* themselves in the body of some one else—generally a lunatic, or weak-minded person, who cannot resist the hideous obsession. This is their only means of escape. Surely a weird and horrible idea! I wish I had slept all the time and not heard it at all. My mind is morbid enough without such ghastly fancies. Such mischievous propaganda should be stopped by the police. I'll write to the *Times* and suggest it. Good idea!

I walked home through Greek Street, Soho, and imagined that a hundred years had slipped back into place and De Quincey was still there, haunting the night with invocations to his "just, subtle, and mighty" drug. His vast dreams seemed to hover not very far away. Once started in my brain, the pictures refused to go away; and I saw him sleeping in that cold, tenantless mansion with the strange little waif who was afraid of its ghosts, both together in the shadows under a single horseman's cloak; or wandering in the companionship of the spectral Anne; or, later still, on his way to the eternal rendezvous at the foot of Great Titchfield Street, the rendezvous she never was able to keep. What an unutterable gloom, what an untold horror of sorrow and suffering comes over me as I try to realise something of what that man—boy he then was—must have taken into his lonely heart.

As I came up the alley I saw a light in the top window, and a head and shoulders thrown in an exaggerated shadow upon the blind. I wondered what the son could be doing up there at such an hour.

Nov. 5.—This morning, while writing, some one came up the creaking stairs and knocked cautiously at my door. Thinking it was the landlady, I said, "Come in!" The knock was repeated, and I cried louder, "Come in, come in!" But no one turned the handle, and I continued my writing with a vexed "Well, stay out, then!" under my breath. Went on writing? I tried to, but my thoughts had suddenly dried up at their source. I could not set down a single word. It was a dark, yellow-fog morning, and there was little enough inspiration in the air as it was, but that stupid woman standing just outside my door waiting to be told again to come in roused a spirit of vexation that filled my head to the exclusion of all else. At last I jumped up and opened the door myself.

"What do you want, and why in the world don't you come in?" I cried out. But the words dropped into empty air. There was no one there. The fog poured up the dingy staircase in deep yellow coils, but there was no sign of a human being anywhere.

I slammed the door, with imprecations upon the house and its noises, and went back to my work. A few minutes later Emily came in with a letter.

"Were you or Mrs. Monson outside a few minutes ago knocking at my door?"

"No, sir."

"Are you sure?"

"Mrs. Monson's gone to market, and there's no one but me and the child in the 'ole 'ouse, and I've been washing the dishes for the last hour, sir."

I fancied the girl's face turned a shade paler. She fidgeted towards the door with a glance over her shoulder.

"Wait, Emily," I said, and then told her what I had heard. She stared stupidly at me, though her eyes shifted now and then over the articles in the room.

"Who was it?" I asked when I had come to the end.

"Mrs. Monson says it's honly mice," she said, as if repeating a learned lesson.

"Mice!" I exclaimed; "it's nothing of the sort. Some one was feeling about outside my door. Who was it? Is the son in the house?"

Her whole manner changed suddenly, and she became earnest instead of evasive. She seemed anxious to tell the truth.

"Oh no, sir; there's no one in the house at all but you and me and the child, and there couldn't 'ave been nobody at your door. As for them knocks—" She stopped abruptly, as though she had said too much.

"Well, what about the knocks?" I said more gently.

"Of course," she stammered, "the knocks isn't mice, nor the footsteps neither, but then—" Again she came to a full halt.

"Anything wrong with the house?"

"Lor', no, sir; the drains is splendid!"

"I don't mean drains, girl. I mean, did anything—anything bad ever happen here?"

She flushed up to the roots of her hair, and then turned suddenly pale again. She was obviously in considerable distress, and there was something she was anxious, yet afraid to tell—some forbidden thing she was not allowed to mention.

"I don't mind what it was, only I should like to know," I said encouragingly.

Raising her frightened eyes to my face, she began to blurt out something about "that which 'appened once to a gentleman that lived hupstairs," when a shrill voice calling her name sounded below.

"Emily, Emily!" It was the returning landlady, and the girl tumbled downstairs as if pulled backward by a rope, leaving me full of conjectures as to what in the world could have happened to a gentleman *upstairs* that could in so curious a manner affect my ears *downstairs*.

Nov. 10.—I have done capital work; have finished the ponderous article and had it accepted for the —— *Review*, and another one ordered. I feel well and cheerful, and have had regular exercise and good sleep; no headaches, no nerves, no liver! Those pills the chemist recommended are wonderful. I can watch the child playing with his cart and feel no annoyance; sometimes I almost feel inclined to join him. Even the grey-faced landlady rouses pity in me; I am sorry for her: so worn, so weary, so oddly put together, just like the building. She looks as if she had once suffered some shock of terror, and was momentarily dreading another. When I spoke to her today very gently about not putting the pens in the ash-tray and the gloves on the book-shelf she raised her faint eyes to mine for the first time, and said with the ghost of a smile, "I'll try and remember, sir," I felt inclined to pat her on the back and say, "Come, cheer up and be jolly. Life's not so bad after all." Oh! I am much better. There's nothing like open air and success and good sleep. They build up as if by magic the portions of the heart eaten down by despair and unsatisfied yearnings. Even to the cats I feel friendly. When I came in at eleven o'clock tonight they followed me to the door in a stream, and I stooped down to stroke the one nearest to me. Bah! The brute hissed and spat, and struck at me with her paws. The claw caught my hand and drew blood in a thin line. The others danced sideways into the darkness, screeching, as though I had done them an injury. I believe these cats really hate me. Perhaps they are only waiting to be reinforced. Then they will attack me. Ha, ha! In spite of the momentary annoyance, this fancy sent me laughing upstairs to my room.

The fire was out, and the room seemed unusually cold. As I groped my way over to the mantelpiece to find the matches I realised all at once that there was another person standing beside me in the darkness. I could, of course, see nothing, but my fingers, feeling along the ledge, came into forcible contact with something that was at once withdrawn. It was cold and moist. I could have sworn it was somebody's hand. My flesh began to creep instantly.

"Who's that?" I exclaimed in a loud voice.

My voice dropped into the silence like a pebble into a deep well. There was no answer, but at the same moment I heard some one moving away from me across the room in the direction of the door. It was a confused sort of footstep, and the sound of garments brushing the furniture on the way. The same second my hand stumbled upon the matchbox, and I struck a light. I expected to see Mrs. Monson, or Emily, or perhaps the son who is something on an omnibus. But the flare of the gas jet illumined an empty room; there was not a sign of a person anywhere. I felt the hair stir upon my head, and instinctively I backed up against the wall, lest something should approach me from behind. I was distinctly alarmed. But the next minute I recovered myself. The door was open on to the landing, and I crossed the room, not without some inward trepidation, and went out. The light from the room fell upon the stairs, but there was no one to be seen anywhere, nor was there any sound on the creaking wooden staircase to indicate a departing creature.

I was in the act of turning to go in again when a sound overhead caught my ear. It was a very faint sound, not unlike the sigh of wind; yet it could not have been the wind, for the night was still as the grave. Though it was not repeated, I resolved to go upstairs and see for myself what it all meant. Two senses had been affected—touch and hearing—and I could not believe that I had been deceived. So, with a lighted candle, I went stealthily forth on my unpleasant journey into the upper regions of this queer little old house.

On the first landing there was only one door, and it was locked. On the second there was also only one door, but when I turned the handle it opened. There came forth to meet me the chill musty air that is characteristic of a long unoccupied room. With it there came an indescribable odour. I use the adjective advisedly. Though very faint, diluted as it were, it was nevertheless an odour that made my gorge rise. I had never smelt anything like it before, and I cannot describe it.

The room was small and square, close under the roof, with a sloping ceiling and two tiny windows. It was cold as the grave, without a shred of carpet or a stick of furniture. The icy atmosphere and the nameless odour combined to make the room abominable to me, and, after lingering a moment to see that it contained no cupboards or corners into which a person might have crept for concealment, I made haste to shut the door, and went downstairs again to bed. Evidently I had been deceived after all as to the noise.

In the night I had a foolish but very vivid dream. I dreamed that the landlady and another person, dark and not properly visible, entered my room on all fours, followed by a horde of immense cats. They attacked me as I lay in bed, and murdered me, and then dragged my body upstairs and deposited it on the floor of that cold little square room under the roof.

Nov. 11.—Since my talk with Emily—the unfinished talk—I have hardly once set eyes on her. Mrs. Monson now attends wholly to my wants. As usual, she does everything exactly as I don't like it done. It is all too utterly trivial to mention, but it is exceedingly irritating. Like small doses of morphine often repeated, she has finally a cumulative effect.

Nov. 12.—This morning I woke early, and came into the front room to get a book, meaning to read in bed till it was time to get up. Emily was laying the fire.

"Good morning!" I said cheerfully. "Mind you make a good fire. It's very cold."

The girl turned and showed me a startled face. It was not Emily at all!

"Where's Emily?" I exclaimed.

"You mean the girl as was 'ere before me?"

"Has Emily left?"

"I came on the 6th," she replied sullenly, "and she'd gone then." I got my book and went back to bed. Emily must have been sent away almost immediately after our conversation. This reflection kept coming between me and the printed page. I was glad when it was time to get up. Such prompt energy, such merciless decision, seemed to argue something of importance—to somebody.

Nov. 13.—The wound inflicted by the cat's claw has swollen, and causes me annoyance and some pain. It throbs and itches. I'm afraid my blood must be in poor condition, or it would have healed by now. I opened it with a penknife soaked in an antiseptic solution, and cleansed it thoroughly. I have heard unpleasant stories of the results of wounds inflicted by cats.

Nov. 14.—In spite of the curious effect this house certainly exercises upon my nerves, I like it. It is lonely and deserted in the very heart of London, but it is also for that reason quiet to work in. I wonder why it is so cheap. Some people might be suspicious, but I did not even ask the reason. No answer is better than a lie. If only I could remove the cats from the outside and the rats from the inside. I feel that I shall grow accustomed more and more to its peculiarities, and shall die here. Ah, that expression reads queerly and gives a wrong impression: I meant *live and die* here. I shall renew the lease from year to year till one of us crumbles to pieces. From present indications the building will be the first to go.

Nov. 16.—It is abominable the way my nerves go up and down with me—and rather discouraging. This morning I woke to find my clothes scattered about the room, and a cane chair overturned beside the bed. My coat and waistcoat looked just as if they had been *tried on* by some one in the night. I had horribly vivid dreams, too, in which some one covering his face with his hands kept coming close up to me, crying out as if in pain, "Where can I find covering? Oh, who will clothe me?" How silly, and yet it frightened me a little. It was so dreadfully real. It is now over a year since I last walked in my sleep and woke up with such a shock on the cold pavement of Earl's Court Road, where I then lived. I thought I was cured, but evidently not. This discovery has rather a disquieting effect upon me. Tonight I shall resort to the old trick of tying my toe to the bed-post.

Nov. 17.—Last night I was again troubled by most oppressive dreams. Some one seemed to be moving in the night up and down my room, sometimes passing into the front room, and then returning to stand beside the bed and stare intently down upon me. I was being watched by this person all night long. I never actually awoke, though I was often very near it. I suppose it was a nightmare from indigestion, for this morning I have one of my old vile headaches. Yet all my clothes lay about the floor when I awoke, where they had evidently been flung (had I so tossed them?) during the dark hours, and my trousers trailed over the step into the front room.

Worse than this, though—I fancied I noticed about the room in the morning that strange, fetid odour. Though very faint, its mere suggestion is foul and nauseating. What in the world can it be, I wonder?… In future I shall lock my door.

Nov. 26.—I have accomplished a lot of good work during this past week, and have also managed to get regular exercise. I have felt well and in an equable state of mind. Only two things have occurred to disturb my equanimity. The first is trivial in itself, and no doubt to be easily explained. The upper window where I saw the light on the night of November 4, with the shadow of a large head and shoulders upon the blind, is one of the windows in the square room under the roof. In reality it has *no blind at all!*

Here is the other thing. I was coming home last night in a fresh fall of snow about eleven o'clock, my umbrella low down over my head. Half-way up the alley, where the snow was wholly untrodden, I saw a man's legs in front of me. The umbrella hid the rest of his figure, but on raising it I saw that he was tall and broad and was walking, as I was, towards the door of my house. He could not have been four feet ahead of me. I had thought the alley was empty when I entered it, but might of course have been mistaken very easily.

A sudden gust of wind compelled me to lower the umbrella, and when I raised it again, not half a minute later, there was no longer any man to be seen. With a few more steps I reached the door. It was closed as usual. I then noticed with a sudden sensation of dismay that the surface of the freshly fallen snow was *unbroken.* My own footmarks were the only ones to be seen anywhere, and though I retraced my way to the point where I had first seen the man, I could find no slightest impression of any other boots. Feeling creepy and uncomfortable, I went upstairs, and was glad to get into bed.

Nov. 28.—With the fastening of my bedroom door the disturbances ceased. I am convinced that I walked in my sleep. Probably I untied my toe and then tied it up again. The fancied security of the locked door would alone have been enough to restore sleep to my troubled spirit and enable me to rest quietly.

Last night, however, the annoyance was suddenly renewed in another and more aggressive form. I woke in the darkness with the impression that some one was standing outside my bedroom door *listening*. As I became more awake the impression grew into positive knowledge. Though there was no appreciable sound of moving or breathing, I was so convinced of the propinquity of a listener that I crept out of bed and approached the door. As I did so there came faintly from the next room the unmistakable sound of some one retreating stealthily across the floor. Yet, as I heard it, it was neither the tread of a man nor a regular footstep, but rather, it seemed to me, a confused sort of crawling, almost as of some one on his hands and knees.

I unlocked the door in less than a second, and passed quickly into the front room, and I could feel, as by the subtlest imaginable vibrations upon my nerves, that the spot I was standing in had just that instant been vacated! The Listener had moved; he was now behind the other door, standing in the passage. Yet this door was also closed. I moved swiftly, and as silently as possible, across the floor, and turned the handle. A cold rush of air met me from the passage and sent shiver after shiver down my back. There was no one in the doorway; there was no one on the little landing; there was no one moving down the staircase. Yet I had been so quick that this midnight Listener could not be very far away, and I felt that if I persevered I should eventually come face to face with him. And the courage that came so opportunely to overcome my nervousness and horror seemed born of the unwelcome conviction that it was somehow necessary for my safety as well as my sanity that I should find this intruder and force his secret from him. For was it not the intent action of his mind upon my own, in concentrated listening, that had awakened me with such a vivid realisation of his presence?

Advancing across the narrow landing, I peered down into the well of the little house. There was nothing to be seen; no one was moving in the darkness. How cold the oilcloth was to my bare feet.

I cannot say what it was that suddenly drew my eyes upwards. I only know that, without apparent reason, I looked up and saw a person about half-way up the next turn of the stairs, leaning forward over the balustrade and staring straight into my face. It was a man. He appeared to be clinging to the rail rather than standing on the stairs. The gloom made it impossible to see much beyond the general outline, but the head and shoulders were seemingly enormous, and stood sharply silhouetted against the skylight in the roof immediately above. The idea flashed into my brain in a moment that I was looking into the visage of something monstrous. The huge skull, the mane-like hair, the wide-humped shoulders, suggested, in a way I did not pause to analyse, that which was scarcely human; and for some seconds, fascinated by horror, I returned the gaze and stared into the dark, inscrutable countenance above me, without knowing exactly where I was or what I was doing.

Then I realised in quite a new way that I was face to face with the secret midnight Listener, and I steeled myself as best I could for what was about to come.

The source of the rash courage that came to me at this awful moment will ever be to me an inexplicable mystery. Though shivering with fear, and my forehead wet with an unholy dew, I resolved to advance. Twenty questions leaped to my lips: What are you? What do you want? Why do you listen and watch? Why do you come into my room? But none of them found articulate utterance.

I began forthwith to climb the stairs, and with the first signs of my advance *he* drew himself back into the shadows and began to move too. He retreated as swiftly as I advanced. I heard the sound of his crawling motion a few steps ahead of me, ever maintaining the same distance. When I reached the landing he was half-way up the next flight, and when I was half-way up the next flight he had already arrived at the top landing. I then heard him open the door of the little square room under the roof and go in. Immediately, though the door did not close after him, the sound of his moving entirely ceased.

At this moment I longed for a light, or a stick, or any weapon whatsoever; but I had none of these things, and it was impossible to go back. So I marched steadily up the rest of the stairs, and in less than a minute found myself standing in the gloom face to face with the door through which this creature had just entered.

For a moment I hesitated. The door was about half-way open, and the Listener was standing evidently in his favourite attitude just behind it—listening. To search through that dark room for him seemed hopeless; to enter the same small space where he was seemed horrible. The very idea filled me with loathing, and I almost decided to turn back.

It is strange at such times how trivial things impinge on the consciousness with a shock as of something important and immense. Something—it may have been a beetle or a mouse—scuttled over the bare boards behind me. The door moved a quarter of an inch, closing. My decision came back with a sudden rush, as it were, and thrusting out a foot, I kicked the door so that it swung sharply back to its full extent, and permitted me to walk forward slowly into the aperture of profound blackness beyond. What a queer soft sound my bare feet made on the boards! How the blood sang and buzzed in my head!

I was inside. The darkness closed over me, hiding even the windows. I began to grope my way round the walls in a thorough search; but in order to prevent all possibility of the other's escape, I first of all *closed the door.*

There we were, we two, shut in together between four walls, within a few feet of one another. But with what, with whom, was I thus momentarily imprisoned? A new light flashed suddenly over the affair with a swift, illuminating brilliance—and I knew I was a fool, an utter fool! I was wide awake at last, and the horror was evaporating. My cursed nerves again; a dream, a nightmare, and the old result—walking in my sleep. The figure was a dream-figure. Many a time before had the actors in my dreams stood before me for some moments after I was awake… There was a chance match in my pyjamas' pocket, and I struck it on the wall. The room was utterly empty. It held not even a shadow. I went quickly down to bed, cursing my wretched nerves and my foolish, vivid dreams. But as soon as ever I was asleep again, the same uncouth figure of a man crept back to my bedside, and bending over me with his immense head close to my ear, whispered repeatedly in my dreams, "I want your body; I want its covering. I'm waiting for it, and listening always." Words scarcely less foolish than the dream.

But I wonder what that queer odour was up in the square room. I noticed it again, and stronger than ever before, and it seemed to be also in my bedroom when I woke this morning.

Nov. 29.—Slowly, as moonbeams rise over a misty sea in June, the thought is entering my mind that my nerves and somnambulistic dreams do not adequately account for the influence this house exercises upon me. It holds me as with a fine, invisible net. I cannot escape if I would. It draws me, and it means to keep me.

Nov. 30.—The post this morning brought me a letter from Aden, forwarded from my old rooms in Earl's Court. It was from Chapter, my former Trinity chum, who is on his way home from the East, and asks for my address. I sent it to him at the hotel he mentioned, "to await arrival."

As I have already said, my windows command a view of the alley, and I can see an arrival without difficulty. This morning, while I was busy writing, the sound of footsteps coming up the alley filled me with a sense of vague alarm that I could in no way account for. I went over to the window, and saw a man standing below waiting for the door to be opened. His shoulders were broad, his top-hat glossy, and his overcoat fitted beautifully round the collar. All this I could see, but no more. Presently the door was opened, and the shock to my nerves was unmistakable when I heard a man's voice ask, "Is Mr. —— still here?" mentioning my name. I could not catch the answer, but it could only have been in the affirmative, for the man entered the hall and the door shut to behind him. But I waited in vain for the sound of his steps on the stairs. There was no sound of any kind. It seemed to me so strange that I opened my door and looked out. No one was anywhere to be seen. I walked across the narrow landing, and looked through the window that commands the whole length of the alley. There was no sign of a human being, coming or going. The lane was deserted. Then I deliberately walked downstairs into the kitchen, and asked the grey-faced landlady if a gentleman had just that minute called for me.

The answer, given with an odd, weary sort of smile, was "*No!*"

Dec. 1.—I feel genuinely alarmed and uneasy over the state of my nerves. Dreams are dreams, but never before have I had dreams in broad daylight.

I am looking forward very much to Chapter's arrival. He is a capital fellow, vigorous, healthy, with no nerves, and even less imagination; and he has £2000 a year into the bargain. Periodically he makes me offers— the last was to travel round the world with him as secretary, which was a delicate way of paying my expenses and giving me some pocket-money— offers, however, which I invariably decline. I prefer to keep his friendship. Women could not come between us; money might—therefore I give it no opportunity. Chapter always laughed at what he called my "fancies," being himself possessed only of that thin-blooded quality of imagination which is ever associated with the prosaic-minded man. Yet, if taunted with this obvious lack, his wrath is deeply stirred. His psychology is that of the crass materialist—always a rather funny article. It will afford me genuine relief, none the less, to hear the cold judgment his mind will have to pass upon the story of this house as I shall have it to tell.

Dec. 2.—The strangest part of it all I have not referred to in this brief diary. Truth to tell, I have been afraid to set it down in black and white. I have kept it in the background of my thoughts, preventing it as far as possible from taking shape. In spite of my efforts, however, it has continued to grow stronger.

Now that I come to face the issue squarely, it is harder to express than I imagined. Like a half-remembered melody that trips in the head but vanishes the moment you try to sing it, these thoughts form a group in the background of my mind, *behind* my mind, as it were, and refuse to come forward. They are crouching ready to spring, but the actual leap never takes place.

In these rooms, except when my mind is strongly concentrated on my own work, I find myself suddenly dealing in thoughts and ideas that are not my own! New, strange conceptions, wholly foreign to my temperament, are for ever cropping up in my head. What precisely they are is of no particular importance. The point is that they are entirely apart from the channel in which my thoughts have hitherto been accustomed to flow. Especially they come when my mind is at rest, unoccupied; when I'm dreaming over the fire, or sitting with a book which fails to hold my attention. Then these thoughts which are not mine spring into life and make me feel exceedingly uncomfortable. Sometimes they are so strong that I almost feel as if some one were in the room beside me, thinking aloud.

Evidently my nerves and liver are shockingly out of order. I must work harder and take more vigorous exercise. The horrid thoughts never come when my mind is much occupied. But they are always there—waiting and as it were *alive*.

What I have attempted to describe above came first upon me gradually after I had been some days in the house, and then grew steadily in strength. The other strange thing has come to me only twice in all these weeks. *It appals me*. It is the consciousness of the propinquity of some deadly and loathsome disease. It comes over me like a wave of fever heat, and then passes off, leaving me cold and trembling. The air seems for a few seconds to become tainted. So penetrating and convincing is the thought of this sickness, that on both occasions my brain has turned momentarily dizzy, and through my mind, like flames of white heat, have flashed the ominous names of all the dangerous illnesses I know. I can no more explain these visitations than I can fly, yet I know there is no dreaming about the clammy skin and palpitating heart which they always leave as witnesses of their brief visit.

Most strongly of all was I aware of this nearness of a mortal sickness when, on the night of the 28th, I went upstairs in pursuit of the listening figure. When we were shut in together in that little square room under the roof, I felt that I was face to face with the actual essence of this invisible and malignant disease. Such a feeling never entered my heart before, and I pray to God it never may again.

There! Now I have confessed. I have given some expression at least to the feelings that so far have been afraid to see in my own writing. For—since I can no longer deceive myself—the experiences of that night (28th) were no more a dream than my daily breakfast is a dream; and the trivial entry in this diary by which I sought to explain away an occurrence that caused me unutterable horror was due solely to my desire not to acknowledge in words what I really felt and believed to be true. The increase that would have accrued to my horror by so doing might have been more than I could stand.

Dec. 3.—I wish Chapter would come. My facts are all ready marshalled, and I can see his cool, grey eyes fixed incredulously on my face as I relate them: the knocking at my door, the well-dressed caller, the light in the upper window and the shadow upon the blind, the man who preceded me in the snow, the scattering of my clothes at night, Emily's arrested confession, the landlady's suspicious reticence, the midnight listener on the stairs, and those awful subsequent words in my sleep; and above all, and hardest to tell, the presence of the abominable sickness, and the stream of thoughts and ideas that are not my own.

I can see Chapter's face, and I can almost hear his deliberate words, "You've been at the tea again, and underfeeding, I expect, as usual. Better see my nerve doctor, and then come with me to the south of France." For this fellow, who knows nothing of disordered liver or high-strung nerves, goes regularly to a great nerve specialist with the periodical belief that his nervous system is beginning to decay.

Dec. 5.—Ever since the incident of the Listener, I have kept a night-light burning in my bedroom, and my sleep has been undisturbed. Last night, however, I was subjected to a far worse annoyance. I woke suddenly, and saw a man in front of the dressing-table regarding himself in the mirror. The door was locked, as usual. I knew at once it was the Listener, and the blood turned to ice in my veins. Such a wave of horror and dread swept over me that it seemed to turn me rigid in the bed, and I could neither move nor speak. I noted, however, that the odour I so abhorred was strong in the room.

The man seemed to be tall and broad. He was stooping forward over the mirror. His back was turned to me, but in the glass I saw the reflection of a huge head and face illumined fitfully by the flicker of the night-light. The spectral grey of very early morning stealing in round the edges of the curtains lent an additional horror to the picture, for it fell upon hair that was tawny and mane-like, hanging loosely about a face whose swollen, rugose features bore the once seen never forgotten leonine expression of—I dare not write down that awful word. But, by way of corroborative proof, I saw in the faint mingling of the two lights that there were several bronze-coloured blotches on the cheeks which the man was evidently examining with great care in the glass. The lips were pale and very thick and large. One hand I could not see, but the other rested on the ivory back of my hair-brush. Its muscles were strangely contracted, the fingers thin to emaciation, the back of the hand closely puckered up. It was like a big grey spider crouching to spring, or the claw of a great bird.

The full realisation that I was alone in the room with this nameless creature, almost within arm's reach of him, overcame me to such a degree that, when he suddenly turned and regarded me with small beady eyes, wholly out of proportion to the grandeur of their massive setting, I sat bolt upright in bed, uttered a loud cry, and then fell back in a dead swoon of terror upon the bed.

Dec. 6.—… When I came to this morning, the first thing I noticed was that my clothes were strewn all over the floor… I find it difficult to put my thoughts together, and have sudden accesses of violent trembling. I determined that I would go at once to Chapter's hotel and find out when he is expected. I cannot refer to what happened in the night; it is too awful, and I have to keep my thoughts rigorously away from it. I feel light-headed and queer, couldn't eat any breakfast, and have twice vomited with blood. While dressing to go out, a hansom rattled up noisily over the cobbles, and a minute later the door opened, and to my great joy in walked the very subject of my thoughts.

The sight of his strong face and quiet eyes had an immediate effect upon me, and I grew calmer again. His very handshake was a sort of tonic. But, as I listened eagerly to the deep tones of his reassuring voice, and the visions of the night time paled a little, I began to realise how very hard it was going to be to tell him my wild, intangible tale. Some men radiate an animal vigour that destroys the delicate woof of a vision and effectually prevents its reconstruction. Chapter was one of these men.

We talked of incidents that had filled the interval since we last met, and he told me something of his travels. He talked and I listened. But, so full was I of the horrid thing I had to tell, that I made a poor listener. I was for ever watching my opportunity to leap in and explode it all under his nose.

Before very long, however, it was borne in upon me that he too was merely talking for time. He too held something of importance in the background of his mind, something too weighty to let fall till the right moment presented itself. So that during the whole of the first half-hour we were both waiting for the psychological moment in which properly to release our respective bombs; and the intensity of our minds' action set up opposing forces that merely sufficed to hold one another in check—and nothing more. As soon as I realised this, therefore, I resolved to yield. I renounced for the time my purpose of telling my story, and had the satisfaction of seeing that his mind, released from the restraint of my own, at once began to make preparations for the discharge of its momentous burden. The talk grew less and less magnetic; the interest waned; the descriptions of his travels became less alive. There were pauses between his sentences. Presently he repeated himself. His words clothed no living thoughts. The pauses grew longer. Then the interest dwindled altogether and went out like a candle in the wind. His voice ceased, and he looked up squarely into my face with serious and anxious eyes.

The psychological moment had come at last!

"I say—" he began, and then stopped short.

I made an unconscious gesture of encouragement, but said no word. I dreaded the impending disclosure exceedingly. A dark shadow seemed to precede it.

"I say," he blurted out at last, "what in the world made you ever come to this place—to these rooms, I mean?"

"They're cheap, for one thing," I began, "and central and—"

"They're too cheap," he interrupted. "Didn't you ask what made 'em so cheap?"

"It never occurred to me at the time."

There was a pause in which he avoided my eyes.

"For God's sake, go on, man, and tell it!" I cried, for the suspense was getting more than I could stand in my nervous condition.

"This was where Blount lived so long," he said quietly, "and where he—died. You know, in the old days I often used to come here and see him, and do what I could to alleviate his—" He stuck fast again.

"Well!" I said with a great effort. "*Please* go on—faster."

"But," Chapter went on, turning his face to the window with a perceptible shiver, "he finally got so terrible I simply couldn't stand it, though I always thought I could stand anything. It got on my nerves and made me dream, and haunted me day and night."

I stared at him, and said nothing. I had never heard of Blount in my life, and didn't know what he was talking about. But, all the same, I was trembling, and my mouth had become strangely dry.

"This is the first time I've been back here since," he said almost in a whisper, "and, 'pon my word, it gives me the creeps. I swear it isn't fit for a man to live in. I never saw you look so bad, old man."

"I've got it for a year," I jerked out, with a forced laugh; "signed the lease and all. I thought it was rather a bargain."

Chapter shuddered, and buttoned his overcoat up to his neck. Then he spoke in a low voice, looking occasionally behind him as though he thought some one was listening. I too could have sworn some one else was in the room with us.

"He did it himself, you know, and no one blamed him a bit; his sufferings were awful. For the last two years he used to wear a veil when he went out, and even then it was always in a closed carriage. Even the attendant who had nursed him for so long was at length obliged to leave. The extremities of both the lower limbs were gone, dropped off, and he moved about the ground on all fours with a sort of crawling motion. The odour, too, was—"

I was obliged to interrupt him here. I could hear no more details of that sort. My skin was moist, I felt hot and cold by turns, for at last I was beginning to understand.

"Poor devil," Chapter went on; "I used to keep my eyes closed as much as possible. He always begged to be allowed to take his veil off, and asked if I minded very much. I used to stand by the open window. He never touched me, though. He rented the whole house. Nothing would induce him to leave it."

"Did he occupy—these very rooms?"

"No. He had the little room on the top floor, the square one just under the roof. He preferred it because it was dark. These rooms were too near the ground, and he was afraid people might see him through the windows. A crowd had been known to follow him up to the very door, and then stand below the windows in the hope of catching a glimpse of his face."

"But there were hospitals."

"He wouldn't go near one, and they didn't like to force him. You know, they say it's *not* contagious, so there was nothing to prevent his staying here if he wanted to. He spent all his time reading medical books, about drugs and so on. His head and face were something appalling, just like a lion's."

I held up my hand to arrest further description.

"He was a burden to the world, and he knew it. One night I suppose he realised it too keenly to wish to live. He had the free use of drugs—and in the morning he was found dead on the floor. Two years ago, that was, and they said then he had still several years to live."

"Then, in Heaven's name!" I cried, unable to bear the suspense any longer, "tell me what it was he had, and be quick about it."

"I thought you knew!" he exclaimed, with genuine surprise. "I thought you knew!"

He leaned forward and our eyes met. In a scarcely audible whisper I caught the words his lips seemed almost afraid to utter:

"He was a leper!"

SMITH: AN EPISODE IN
A LODGING HOUSE

This story is set in Edinburgh, and may draw upon some incident or other whilst Blackwood was at University, though it could not have been written in the form it is until he had much greater knowledge to draw upon. While at Edinburgh he became friends with a Hindu medical student who instructed Blackwood in various forms of mental control. Mysteriously Blackwood noted that "We made curious and interesting experiments together." He does not name this individual but he drew upon his personality in creating the characters John Silence and Julius Le Vallon.

Whilst in North America, Blackwood continued his theosophical studies, joining first the Toronto branch of the society and then the New York branch. When he returned to England one of his first commitments was to join the London branch and it was through this that he met one of the leading lights in the Theosophical Society, the poet W. B. Yeats. Or rather, a one-time leading light, as Yeats's interest in theosophy had waned as he grew more interested in the occult. He joined the Hermetic Order of the Golden Dawn, which had been founded in 1888 for the study of the ancient alchemical tradition of the Hebrew kabbalah and magic. It was through Yeats that Blackwood was introduced to the Golden Dawn in October 1900. He took his studies seriously and within two years had reached the Zelator Grade, the top grade in the First Order. He did not proceed into the Second Order to become an adept, perhaps because he felt no need, as his communion with Nature provided more than enough wonder and magic. Nevertheless, his studies provided him with a deep understanding of the occult, sufficient to work into several of his books, notably The Human Chord. Also through the Golden Dawn he met others of a like interest, including fellow author Arthur Machen and most notoriously Aleister Crowley, who had become an adept in the Order and later founded his own society.

The following story draws upon Blackwood's hermetic studies and you wonder how much he may have encountered such events. There was a similar incident caused by Crowley at his flat in Chancery Lane in 1899, not long after Blackwood returned from New York. Crowley had conducted an experiment to summon certain forces which at first seemed unsuccessful. He left the flat but upon returning found the room disturbed with "semi-materialised beings" marching around.

"WHEN I was a medical student," began the doctor, half turning towards his circle of listeners in the firelight, "I came across one or two very curious human beings; but there was one fellow I remember particularly, for he caused me the most vivid, and I think the most uncomfortable, emotions I have ever known.

"For many months I knew Smith only by name as the occupant of the floor above me. Obviously his name meant nothing to me. Moreover I was busy with lectures, reading, cliniques and the like, and had little leisure to devise plans for scraping acquaintance with any of the other lodgers in the house. Then chance brought us curiously together, and this fellow Smith left a deep impression upon me as the result of our first meeting. At the time the strength of this first impression seemed quite inexplicable to me, but looking back at the episode now from a standpoint of greater knowledge I judge the fact to have been that he stirred my curiosity to an unusual degree, and at the same time awakened my sense of horror—whatever that may be in a medical student—about as deeply and permanently as these two emotions were capable of being stirred at all in the particular system and set of nerves called ME.

"How he knew that I was interested in the study of languages was something I could never explain, but one day, quite unannounced, he came quietly into my room in the evening and asked me point-blank if I knew enough Hebrew to help him in the pronunciation of certain words.

"He caught me along the line of least resistance, and I was greatly flattered to be able to give him the desired information; but it was only when he had thanked me and was gone that I realised I had been in the presence of an unusual individuality. For the life of me I could not quite seize and label the peculiarities of what I felt to be a very striking personality, but it was borne in upon me that he was a man apart from his fellows, a mind that followed a line leading away from ordinary human intercourse and human interests, and into regions that left in his atmosphere something remote, rarefied, chilling.

"The moment he was gone I became conscious of two things—an intense curiosity to know more about this man and what his real interests were, and secondly, the fact that my skin was crawling and that my hair had a tendency to rise."

The doctor paused a moment here to puff hard at his pipe, which, however, had gone out beyond recall without the assistance of a match; and in the deep silence, which testified to the genuine interest of his listeners, someone poked the fire up into a little blaze, and one or two others glanced over their shoulders into the dark distances of the big hall.

"On looking back," he went on, watching the momentary flames in the grate, "I see a short, thick-set man of perhaps forty-five, with immense shoulders and small, slender hands. The contrast was noticeable, for I remember thinking that such a giant frame and such slim finger bones hardly belonged together. His head, too, was large and very long, the head of an idealist beyond all question, yet with an unusually strong development of the jaw and chin. Here again was a singular contradiction, though I am better able now to appreciate its full meaning, with a greater experience in judging the values of physiognomy. For this meant, of course, an enthusiastic idealism balanced and kept in check by will and judgment— elements usually deficient in dreamers and visionaries.

"At any rate, here was a being with probably a very wide range of possibilities, a machine with a pendulum that most likely had an unusual length of swing.

"The man's hair was exceedingly fine, and the lines about his nose and mouth were cut as with a delicate steel instrument in wax. His eyes I have left to the last. They were large and quite changeable, not in colour only, but in character, size, and shape. Occasionally they seemed the eyes of someone else, if you can understand what I mean, and at the same time, in their shifting shades of blue, green, and a nameless sort of dark grey, there was a sinister light in them that lent to the whole face an aspect almost alarming. Moreover, they were the most luminous optics I think I have ever seen in any human being.

"There, then, at the risk of a wearisome description, is Smith as I saw him for the first time that winter's evening in my shabby student's rooms in Edinburgh. And yet the real part of him, of course, I have left untouched, for it is both indescribable and un-get-atable. I have spoken already of an atmosphere of warning and aloofness he carried about with him. It is impossible further to analyse the series of little shocks his presence always communicated to my being; but there was that about him which made me instantly on the *qui vive* in his presence, every nerve alert, every sense strained and on the watch. I do not mean that he deliberately suggested danger, but rather that he brought forces in his wake which automatically warned the nervous centres of my system to be on their guard and alert.

"Since the days of my first acquaintance with this man I have lived through other experiences and have seen much I cannot pretend to explain or understand; but, so far in my life, I have only once come across a human being who suggested a disagreeable familiarity with unholy things, and who made me feel uncanny and 'creepy' in his presence; and that unenviable individual was Mr. Smith.

"What his occupation was during the day I never knew. I think he slept until the sun set. No one ever saw him on the stairs, or heard him move in his room during the day. He was a creature of the shadows, who apparently preferred darkness to light. Our landlady either knew nothing, or would say nothing. At any rate she found no fault, and I have since wondered often by what magic this fellow was able to convert a common landlady of a common lodging-house into a discreet and uncommunicative person. This alone was a sign of genius of some sort.

"'He's been here with me for years—long before you come, an' I don't interfere or ask no questions of what doesn't concern me, as long as people pays their rent,' was the only remark on the subject that I ever succeeded in winning from that quarter, and it certainly told me nothing nor gave me any encouragement to ask for further information.

"Examinations, however, and the general excitement of a medical student's life for a time put Mr. Smith completely out of my head. For a long period he did not call upon me again, and for my part, I felt no courage to return his unsolicited visit.

"Just then, however, there came a change in the fortunes of those who controlled my very limited income, and I was obliged to give up my ground-floor and move aloft to more modest chambers on the top of the house. Here I was directly over Smith, and had to pass his door to reach my own.

"It so happened that about this time I was frequently called out at all hours of the night for the maternity cases which a fourth-year student takes at a certain period of his studies, and on returning from one of these visits at about two o'clock in the morning I was surprised to hear the sound of voices as I passed his door. A peculiar sweet odour, too, not unlike the smell of incense, penetrated into the passage.

"I went upstairs very quietly, wondering what was going on there at this hour of the morning. To my knowledge Smith never had visitors. For a moment I hesitated outside the door with one foot on the stairs. All my interest in this strange man revived, and my curiosity rose to a point not far from action. At last I might learn something of the habits of this lover of the night and the darkness.

"The sound of voices was plainly audible, Smith's predominating so much that I never could catch more than points of sound from the other, penetrating now and then the steady stream of his voice. Not a single word reached me, at least, not a word that I could understand, though the voice was loud and distinct, and it was only afterwards that I realised he must have been speaking in a foreign language.

"The sound of footsteps, too, was equally distinct. Two persons were moving about the room, passing and repassing the door, one of them a light, agile person, and the other ponderous and somewhat awkward. Smith's voice went on incessantly with its odd, monotonous droning, now loud, now soft, as he crossed and re-crossed the floor. The other person was also on the move, but in a different and less regular fashion, for I heard rapid steps that seemed to end sometimes in stumbling, and quick sudden movements that brought up with a violent lurching against the walls or furniture.

"As I listened to Smith's voice, moreover, I began to feel afraid. There was something in the sound that made me feel intuitively he was in a tight place, and an impulse stirred faintly in me—very faintly, I admit—to knock at the door and inquire if he needed help.

"But long before the impulse could translate itself into an act, or even before it had been properly weighed and considered by the mind, I heard a voice close beside me in the air, a sort of hushed whisper which I am certain was Smith speaking, though the sound did not seem to have come to me through the door. It was close in my very ear, as though he stood beside me, and it gave me such a start, that I clutched the banisters to save myself from stepping backwards and making a clatter on the stairs.

"'There is nothing you can do to help me,' it said distinctly, 'and you will be much safer in your own room.'

"I am ashamed to this day of the pace at which I covered the flight of stairs in the darkness to the top floor, and of the shaking hand with which I lit my candles and bolted the door. But, there it is, just as it happened.

"This midnight episode, so odd and yet so trivial in itself, fired me with more curiosity than ever about my fellow-lodger. It also made me connect him in my mind with a sense of fear and distrust. I never saw him, yet I was often, and uncomfortably, aware of his presence in the upper regions of that gloomy lodging-house. Smith and his secret mode of life and mysterious pursuits, somehow contrived to awaken in my being a line of reflection that disturbed my comfortable condition of ignorance. I never saw him, as I have said, and exchanged no sort of communication with him, yet it seemed to me that his mind was in contact with mine, and some of the strange forces of his atmosphere filtered through into my being and disturbed my equilibrium. Those upper floors became haunted for me after dark, and, though outwardly our lives never came into contact, I became unwillingly involved in certain pursuits on which his mind was centred. I felt that he was somehow making use of me against my will, and by methods which passed my comprehension.

"I was at that time, moreover, in the heavy, unquestioning state of materialism which is common to medical students when they begin to understand something of the human anatomy and nervous system, and jump at once to the conclusion that they control the universe and hold in their forceps the last word of life and death. I 'knew it all,' and regarded a belief in anything beyond matter as the wanderings of weak, or at best, untrained minds. And this condition of mind, of course, added to the strength of this upsetting fear which emanated from the floor below and began slowly to take possession of me.

"Though I kept no notes of the subsequent events in this matter, they made too deep an impression for me ever to forget the sequence in which they occurred. Without difficulty I can recall the next step in the adventure with Smith, for adventure it rapidly grew to be."

The doctor stopped a moment and laid his pipe on the table behind him before continuing. The fire had burned low, and no one stirred to poke it. The silence in the great hall was so deep that when the speaker's pipe touched the table the sound woke audible echoes at the far end among the shadows.

"One evening, while I was reading, the door of my room opened and Smith came in. He made no attempt at ceremony. It was after ten o'clock and I was tired, but the presence of the man immediately galvanised me into activity. My attempts at ordinary politeness he thrust on one side at once, and began asking me to vocalise, and then pronounce for him, certain Hebrew words; and when this was done he abruptly inquired if I was not the fortunate possessor of a very rare Rabbinical Treatise, which he named.

"How he knew that I possessed this book puzzled me exceedingly; but I was still more surprised to see him cross the room and take it out of my book-shelf almost before I had had time to answer in the affirmative. Evidently, he knew exactly where it was kept. This excited my curiosity beyond all bounds, and I immediately began asking him questions; and though, out of sheer respect for the man, I put them very delicately to him, and almost by way of mere conversation, he had only one reply for the lot. He would look up at me from the pages of the book with an expression of complete comprehension on his extraordinary features, would bow his head a little and say very gravely—

"'That, of course, is a perfectly proper question,'—which was absolutely all I could ever get out of him.

"On this particular occasion he stayed with me perhaps ten or fifteen minutes. Then he went quickly downstairs to his room with my Hebrew Treatise in his hand, and I heard him close and bolt his door.

"But a few moments later, before I had time to settle down to my book again, or to recover from the surprise his visit had caused me, I heard the door open, and there stood Smith once again beside my chair. He made no excuse for his second interruption, but bent his head down to the level of my reading lamp and peered across the flame straight into my eyes.

"'I hope,' he whispered, 'I hope you are never disturbed at night?'

"'Eh?' I stammered, 'disturbed at night? Oh no, thanks, at least, not that I know of—'

"'I'm glad,' he replied gravely, appearing not to notice my confusion and surprise at his question. 'But, remember, should it ever be the case, please let me know at once.'

"And he was gone down the stairs and into his room again.

"For some minutes I sat reflecting upon his strange behaviour. He was not mad, I argued, but was the victim of some harmless delusion that had gradually grown upon him as a result of his solitary mode of life; and from the books he used, I judged that it had something to do with mediaeval magic, or some system of ancient Hebrew mysticism. The words he asked me to pronounce for him were probably 'Words of Power,' which, when uttered with the vehemence of a strong will behind them, were supposed to produce physical results, or set up vibrations in one's own inner being that had the effect of a partial lifting of the veil.

"I sat thinking about the man, and his way of living, and the probable effects in the long-run of his dangerous experiments, and I can recall perfectly well the sensation of disappointment that crept over me when I realised that I had labelled his particular form of aberration, and that my curiosity would therefore no longer be excited.

"For some time I had been sitting alone with these reflections—it may have been ten minutes or it may have been half an hour—when I was aroused from my reverie by the knowledge that someone was again in the room standing close beside my chair. My first thought was that Smith had come back again in his swift, unaccountable manner, but almost at the same moment I realised that this could not be the case at all. For the door faced my position, and it certainly had not been opened again.

"Yet, someone was in the room, moving cautiously to and fro, watching me, almost touching me. I was as sure of it as I was of myself, and though at the moment I do not think I was actually afraid, I am bound to admit that a certain weakness came over me and that I felt that strange disinclination for action which is probably the beginning of the horrible paralysis of real terror. I should have been glad to hide myself, if that had been possible, to cower into a corner, or behind a door, or anywhere so that I could not be watched and observed.

"But, overcoming my nervousness with an effort of the will, I got up quickly out of my chair and held the reading lamp aloft so that it shone into all the corners like a searchlight.

"The room was utterly empty! It was utterly empty, at least, to the *eye*, but to the nerves, and especially to that combination of sense perception which is made up by all the senses acting together, and by no one in particular, there was a person standing there at my very elbow.

"I say 'person,' for I can think of no appropriate word. For, if it *was* a human being, I can only affirm that I had the overwhelming conviction that it was *not*, but that it was some form of life wholly unknown to me both as to its essence and its nature. A sensation of gigantic force and power came with it, and I remember vividly to this day my terror on realising that I was close to an invisible being who could crush me as easily as I could crush a fly, and who could see my every movement while itself remaining invisible.

"To this terror was added the certain knowledge that the 'being' kept in my proximity for a definite purpose. And that this purpose had some direct bearing upon my well-being, indeed upon my life, I was equally convinced; for I became aware of a sensation of growing lassitude as though the vitality were being steadily drained out of my body. My heart began to beat irregularly at first, then faintly. I was conscious, even within a few minutes, of a general drooping of the powers of life in the whole system, an ebbing away of self-control, and a distinct approach of drowsiness and torpor.

"The power to move, or to think out any mode of resistance, was fast leaving me, when there rose, in the distance as it were, a tremendous commotion. A door opened with a clatter, and I heard the peremptory and commanding tones of a human voice calling aloud in a language I could not comprehend. It was Smith, my fellow-lodger, calling up the stairs; and his voice had not sounded for more than a few seconds, when I felt something withdrawn from my presence, from my person, indeed from my *very skin*. It seemed as if there was a rushing of air and some large creature swept by me at about the level of my shoulders. Instantly the pressure on my heart was relieved, and the atmosphere seemed to resume its normal condition.

"Smith's door closed quietly downstairs, as I put the lamp down with trembling hands. What had happened I do not know; only, I was alone again and my strength was returning as rapidly as it had left me.

"I went across the room and examined myself in the glass. The skin was very pale, and the eyes dull. My temperature, I found, was a little below normal and my pulse faint and irregular. But these smaller signs of disturbance were as nothing compared with the feeling I had—though no outward signs bore testimony to the fact—that I had narrowly escaped a real and ghastly catastrophe. I felt shaken, somehow, shaken to the very roots of my being."

The doctor rose from his chair and crossed over to the dying fire, so that no one could see the expression on his face as he stood with his back to the grate, and continued his weird tale.

"It would be wearisome," he went on in a lower voice, looking over our heads as though he still saw the dingy top floor of that haunted Edinburgh lodging-house; "it would be tedious for me at this length of time to analyse my feelings, or attempt to reproduce for you the thorough examination to which I endeavoured then to subject my whole being, intellectual, emotional, and physical. I need only mention the dominant emotion with which this curious episode left me—the indignant anger against myself that I could ever have lost my self-control enough to come under the sway of so gross and absurd a delusion. This protest, however, I remember making with all the emphasis possible. And I also remember noting that it brought me very little satisfaction, for it was the protest of my reason only, when all the rest of my being was up in arms against its conclusions.

"My dealings with the 'delusion,' however, were not yet over for the night; for very early next morning, somewhere about three o'clock, I was awakened by a curiously stealthy noise in the room, and the next minute there followed a crash as if all my books had been swept bodily from their shelf on to the floor.

"But this time I was not frightened. Cursing the disturbance with all the resounding and harmless words I could accumulate, I jumped out of bed and lit the candle in a second, and in the first dazzle of the flaring match—but before the wick had time to catch—I was certain I *saw* a dark grey shadow, of ungainly shape, and with something more or less like a human head, drive rapidly past the side of the wall furthest from me and disappear into the gloom by the angle of the door.

"I waited one single second to be sure the candle was alight, and then dashed after it, but before I had gone two steps, my foot stumbled against something hard piled up on the carpet and I only just saved myself from falling headlong. I picked myself up and found that all the books from what I called my 'language shelf' were strewn across the floor. The room, meanwhile, as a minute's search revealed, was quite empty. I looked in every corner and behind every stick of furniture, and a student's bedroom on a top floor, costing twelve shillings a week, did not hold many available hiding-places, as you may imagine.

"The crash, however, was explained. Some very practical and physical force had thrown the books from their resting-place. That, at least, was beyond all doubt. And as I replaced them on the shelf and noted that not one was missing, I busied myself mentally with the sore problem of how the agent of this little practical joke had gained access to my room, and then escaped again. *For my door was locked and bolted.*

"Smith's odd question as to whether I was disturbed in the night, and his warning injunction to let him know at once if such were the case, now of course returned to affect me as I stood there in the early morning, cold and shivering on the carpet; but I realised at the same moment how impossible it would be for me to admit that a more than usually vivid nightmare could have any connection with himself. I would rather stand a hundred of these mysterious visitations than consult such a man as to their possible cause.

"A knock at the door interrupted my reflections, and I gave a start that sent the candle grease flying.

"'Let me in,' came in Smith's voice.

"I unlocked the door. He came in fully dressed. His face wore a curious pallor. It seemed to me to be under the skin and to shine through and almost make it luminous. His eyes were exceedingly bright.

"I was wondering what in the world to say to him, or how he would explain his visit at such an hour, when he closed the door behind him and came close up to me—uncomfortably close.

"'You should have called me at once,' he said in his whispering voice, fixing his great eyes on my face.

"I stammered something about an awful dream, but he ignored my remark utterly, and I caught his eye wandering next—if any movement of those optics can be described as 'wandering'—to the book-shelf. I watched him, unable to move my gaze from his person. The man fascinated me horribly for some reason. Why, in the devil's name, was he up and dressed at three in the morning? How did he know anything had happened unusual in my room? Then his whisper began again.

"'It's your amazing vitality that causes you this annoyance,' he said, shifting his eyes back to mine.

"I gasped. Something in his voice or manner turned my blood into ice.

"'That's the real attraction,' he went on. 'But if this continues one of us will have to leave, you know.'

"I positively could not find a word to say in reply. The channels of speech dried up within me. I simply stared and wondered what he would say next. I watched him in a sort of dream, and as far as I can remember, he asked me to promise to call him sooner another time, and then began to walk round the room, uttering strange sounds, and making signs with his arms and hands until he reached the door. Then he was gone in a second, and I had closed and locked the door behind him.

"After this, the Smith adventure drew rapidly to a climax. It was a week or two later, and I was coming home between two and three in the morning from a maternity case, certain features of which for the time being had very much taken possession of my mind, so much so, indeed, that I passed Smith's door without giving him a single thought.

"The gas jet on the landing was still burning, but so low that it made little impression on the waves of deep shadow that lay across the stairs. Overhead, the faintest possible gleam of grey showed that the morning was not far away. A few stars shone down through the skylight. The house was still as the grave, and the only sound to break the silence was the rushing of the wind round the walls and over the roof. But this was a fitful sound, suddenly rising and as suddenly falling away again, and it only served to intensify the silence.

"I had already reached my own landing when I gave a violent start. It was automatic, almost a reflex action in fact, for it was only when I caught myself fumbling at the door handle and thinking where I could conceal myself quickest that I realised a voice had sounded close beside me in the air. It was the same voice I had heard before, and it seemed to me to be calling for help. And yet the very same minute I pushed on into the room, determined to disregard it, and seeking to persuade myself it was the creaking of the boards under my weight or the rushing noise of the wind that had deceived me.

"But hardly had I reached the table where the candles stood when the sound was unmistakably repeated: 'Help! help!' And this time it was accompanied by what I can only describe as a vivid tactile hallucination. I was touched: the *skin* of my arm was clutched by fingers.

"Some compelling force sent me headlong downstairs as if the haunting forces of the whole world were at my heels. At Smith's door I paused. The force of his previous warning injunction to seek his aid without delay acted suddenly and I leant my whole weight against the panels, little dreaming that I should be called upon to give help rather than to receive it.

"The door yielded at once, and I burst into a room that was so full of a choking vapour, moving in slow clouds, that at first I could distinguish nothing at all but a set of what seemed to be huge shadows passing in and out of the mist. Then, gradually, I perceived that a red lamp on the mantel-piece gave all the light there was, and that the room which I now entered for the first time was almost empty of furniture.

"The carpet was rolled back and piled in a heap in the corner, and upon the white boards of the floor I noticed a large circle drawn in black of some material that emitted a faint glowing light and was apparently smoking. Inside this circle, as well as at regular intervals outside it, were curious-looking designs, also traced in the same black, smoking substance. These, too, seemed to emit a feeble light of their own.

"My first impression on entering the room had been that it was full of—*people*, I was going to say; but that hardly expresses my meaning. *Beings*, they certainly were, but it was borne in upon me beyond the pos-sibility of doubt, that they were not human beings. That I had caught a momentary glimpse of living, intelligent entities I can never doubt, but I am equally convinced, though I cannot prove it, that these entities were from some other scheme of evolution altogether, and had nothing to do with the ordinary human life, either incarnate or discarnate.

"But, whatever they were, the visible appearance of them was exceedingly fleeting. I no longer saw anything, though I still felt convinced of their immediate presence. They were, moreover, of the same order of life as the visitant in my bedroom of a few nights before, and their proximity to my atmosphere in numbers, instead of singly as before, conveyed to my mind something that was quite terrible and overwhelming. I fell into a violent trembling, and the perspiration poured from my face in streams.

"They were in constant motion about me. They stood close to my side; moved behind me; brushed past my shoulder; stirred the hair on my forehead; and circled round me without ever actually touching me, yet always pressing closer and closer. Especially in the air just over my head there seemed ceaseless movement, and it was accompanied by a confused noise of whispering and sighing that threatened every moment to become articulate in words. To my intense relief, however, I heard no distinct words, and the noise continued more like the rising and falling of the wind than anything else I can imagine.

"But the characteristic of these 'Beings' that impressed me most strongly at the time, and of which I have carried away the most permanent recollection, was that each one of them possessed what seemed to be a *vibrating centre* which impelled it with tremendous force and caused a rapid whirling motion of the atmosphere as it passed me. The air was full of these little vortices of whirring, rotating force, and whenever one of them pressed me too closely I felt as if the nerves in that particular portion of my body had been literally drawn out, absolutely depleted of vitality, and then immediately replaced—but replaced dead, flabby, useless.

"Then, suddenly, for the first time my eyes fell upon Smith. He was crouching against the wall on my right, in an attitude that was obviously defensive, and it was plain he was in extremities. The terror on his face was pitiable, but at the same time there was another expression about the tightly clenched teeth and mouth which showed that he had not lost all control of himself. He wore the most resolute expression I have ever seen on a human countenance, and, though for the moment at a fearful disadvantage, he looked like a man who had confidence in himself, and, in spite of the working of fear, was waiting his opportunity.

"For my part, I was face to face with a situation so utterly beyond my knowledge and comprehension, that I felt as helpless as a child, and as useless.

"'Help me back—quick—into that circle,' I heard him half cry, half whisper to me across the moving vapours.

"My only value appears to have been that I was not afraid to act. Knowing nothing of the forces I was dealing with I had no idea of the deadly perils risked, and I sprang forward and caught him by the arms. He threw all his weight in my direction, and by our combined efforts his body left the wall and lurched across the floor towards the circle.

"Instantly there descended upon us, out of the empty air of that smoke-laden room, a force which I can only compare to the pushing, driving power of a great wind pent up within a narrow space. It was almost explosive in its effect, and it seemed to operate upon all parts of my body equally. It fell upon us with a rushing noise that filled my ears and made me think for a moment the very walls and roof of the building had been torn asunder. Under its first blow we staggered back against the wall, and I understood plainly that its purpose was to prevent us getting back into the circle in the middle of the floor.

"Pouring with perspiration, and breathless, with every muscle strained to the very utmost, we at length managed to get to the edge of the circle, and at this moment, so great was the opposing force, that I felt myself actually torn from Smith's arms, lifted from my feet, and twirled round in the direction of the windows as if the wheel of some great machine had caught my clothes and was tearing me to destruction in its revolution.

"But, even as I fell, bruised and breathless, against the wall, I saw Smith firmly upon his feet in the circle and slowly rising again to an upright position. My eyes never left his figure once in the next few minutes.

"He drew himself up to his full height. His great shoulders squared themselves. His head was thrown back a little, and as I looked I saw the expression on his face change swiftly from fear to one of absolute command. He looked steadily round the room and then his voice began to *vibrate*. At first in a low tone, it gradually rose till it assumed the same volume and intensity I had heard that night when he called up the stairs into my room.

"It was a curiously increasing sound, more like the swelling of an instrument than a human voice; and as it grew in power and filled the room, I became aware that a great change was being effected slowly and surely. The confusion of noise and rushings of air fell into the roll of long, steady vibrations not unlike those caused by the deeper pedals of an organ. The movements in the air became less violent, then grew decidedly weaker, and finally ceased altogether. The whisperings and sighings became fainter and fainter, till at last I could not hear them at all; and, strangest of all, the light emitted by the circle, as well as by the designs round it, increased to a steady glow, casting their radiance upwards with the weirdest possible effect upon his features. Slowly, by the power of his voice, behind which lay undoubtedly a genuine knowledge of the occult manipulation of sound, this man dominated the forces that had escaped from their proper sphere, until at length the room was reduced to silence and perfect order again.

"Judging by the immense relief which also communicated itself to my nerves I then felt that the crisis was over and Smith was wholly master of the situation.

"But hardly had I begun to congratulate myself upon this result, and to gather my scattered senses about me, when, uttering a loud cry, I saw him leap out of the circle and fling himself into the air—as it seemed to me, into the empty air. Then, even while holding my breath for dread of the crash he was bound to come upon the floor, I saw him strike with a dull thud against a solid body in mid-air, and the next instant he was wrestling with some ponderous thing that was absolutely invisible to me, and the room shook with the struggle.

"To and fro *they* swayed, sometimes lurching in one direction, sometimes in another, and always in horrible proximity to myself, as I leaned trembling against the wall and watched the encounter.

"It lasted at most but a short minute or two, ending as suddenly as it had begun. Smith, with an unexpected movement, threw up his arms with a cry of relief. At the same instant there was a wild, tearing shriek in the air beside me and something rushed past us with a noise like the passage of a flock of big birds. Both windows rattled as if they would break away from their sashes. Then a sense of emptiness and peace suddenly came over the room, and I knew that all was over.

"Smith, his face exceedingly white, but otherwise strangely composed, turned to me at once.

"'God!—if you hadn't come— You deflected the stream; broke it up—' he whispered. 'You saved me.'"

The doctor made a long pause. Presently he felt for his pipe in the darkness, groping over the table behind us with both hands. No one spoke for a bit, but all dreaded the sudden glare that would come when he struck the match. The fire was nearly out and the great hall was pitch dark.

But the storyteller did not strike that match. He was merely gaining time for some hidden reason of his own. And presently he went on with his tale in a more subdued voice.

"I quite forget," he said, "how I got back to my own room. I only know that I lay with two lighted candles for the rest of the night, and the first thing I did in the morning was to let the landlady know I was leaving her house at the end of the week.

"Smith still has my Rabbinical Treatise. At least he did not return it to me at the time, and I have never seen him since to ask for it."

ENTRANCE AND EXIT

This story has its roots in Canada and became a key element in Blackwood's beliefs. While working at the dairy farm Blackwood was told a story by a visiting farmer. It seems that this farmer's younger brother had gone out one snowy evening to fetch water from the well and never returned. His footsteps in the snow went halfway to the well at which point were the buckets he'd taken with him. But of him there was no sign, though the farmer thought he heard his voice in the distance. It was never solved. Blackwood was intrigued by this because of his belief that our world is separated from another, or others, simply by vibrations and that at some point you might pass through into another dimension. He used that idea in his famous story, "The Willows", set on a remote island in the river Danube where two travellers are menaced by forces which seem to be in an adjoining world. And he used it in several others such as "Elsewhere and Otherwise" and "The Man Who Was Milligan", but it also became a regular story he told at parties, usually sitting around a fire at night. It formed one of his radio stories.

The strange thing about this story was that it was also heard by the American storyteller Ambrose Bierce who included it in his sequence of "Mysterious Disappearances" as "The Difficulty in Crossing a Field" in 1888. And the strange thing about Ambrose Bierce is that he too disappeared, either at the end of 1913 or early 1914 when he ventured into Mexico in the midst of a revolution. He said in a letter that he was heading off the next day "for an unknown destination". There have been many theories about where he went and what happened, but the fact remains that he was never seen again.

THESE three—the old physicist, the girl, and the young Anglican parson who was engaged to her—stood by the window of the country house. The blinds were not yet drawn. They could see the dark clump of pines in the field, with crests silhouetted against the pale wintry sky of the February afternoon. Snow, freshly fallen, lay upon lawn and hill. A big moon was already lighting up.

"Yes, that's the wood," the old man said, "and it was this very day fifty years ago—February 13—the man disappeared from its shadows; swept in this extraordinary, incredible fashion into invisibility—into *some other place*. Can you wonder the grove is haunted?" A strange impressiveness of manner belied the laugh following the words.

"Oh, please tell us," the girl whispered; "we're all alone now." Curiosity triumphed; yet a vague alarm betrayed itself in the questioning glance she cast for protection at her younger companion, whose fine face, on the other hand, wore an expression that was grave and singularly "rapt." He was listening keenly.

"As though Nature," the physicist went on, half to himself, "here and there concealed vacuums, gaps, holes in space (his mind was always speculative; more than speculative, some said), through which a man might drop into invisibility—a new direction, in fact, at right angles to the three known ones—'higher space,' as Bolyai, Gauss, and Hinton might call it; and what you, with your mystical turn"—looking toward the young priest—"might consider a spiritual change of condition, into a region where space and time do not exist, and where all dimensions are possible—because they are *one*."

"But, *please*, the story," the girl begged, not understanding these dark sayings, "although I'm not sure that Arthur ought to hear it. He's much too interested in such queer things as it is!" Smiling, yet uneasy, she stood closer to his side, as though her body might protect his soul.

"Very briefly, then, you shall hear what I remember of this haunting, for I was barely ten years old at the time. It was evening—clear and cold like this, with snow and moonlight—when someone reported to my father that a peculiar sound, variously described as crying, singing, wailing, was being heard in the grove. He paid no attention until my sister heard it too, and was frightened. Then he sent a groom to investigate. Though the night was brilliant the man took a lantern. We watched from this very window till we lost his figure against the trees, and the lantern stopped swinging suddenly, as if he had put it down. It remained motionless. We waited half an hour, and then my father, curiously excited, I remember, went out quickly, and I, utterly terrified, went after him. We followed his tracks, which came to an end beside the lantern, the last step being a stride almost impossible for a man to have made. All around the snow was unbroken by a single mark, but the man himself had vanished. Then we heard him calling for help—above, behind, beyond us; from all directions at once, yet from none, came the sound of his voice; but though we called back he made no answer, and gradually his cries grew fainter and fainter, as if going into tremendous distance, and at last died away altogether."

"And the man himself?" asked both listeners.

"Never returned—from that day to this has never been seen... At intervals for weeks and months afterwards reports came in that he was still heard crying, always crying for help. With time, even these reports ceased—for most of us," he added under his breath; "and that is all I know. A mere outline, as you see."

The girl did not quite like the story, for the old man's manner made it too convincing. She was half disappointed, half frightened.

"See! there are the others coming home," she exclaimed, with a note of relief, pointing to a group of figures moving over the snow near the pine trees. "Now we can think of tea!" She crossed the room to busy herself with the friendly tray as the servant approached to fasten the shutters. The young priest, however, deeply interested, talked on with their host, though in a voice almost too low for her to hear. Only the final sentences reached her, making her uneasy—absurdly so, she thought—till afterwards.

"—for matter, as we know, interpenetrates matter," she heard, "and two objects may conceivably occupy the same space. The odd thing really is that one should hear, but not see; that air-waves should bring the voice, yet ether-waves fail to bring the picture."

And then the older man: "—as if certain places in Nature, yes, invited the change—places where these extraordinary forces stir from the earth as from the surface of a living Being with organs—places like islands, mountain-tops, pine-woods, especially pines isolated from their kind. You know the queer results of digging absolutely virgin soil, of course—and that theory of the earth's being *alive*—" The voice dropped again.

"States of mind also helping the forces of the place," she caught the priest's reply in part; "such as conditions induced by music, by intense listening, by certain moments in the Mass even—by ecstasy or—"

"I say, what *do* you think?" cried a girl's voice, as the others came in with welcome chatter and odours of tweeds and open fields. "As we passed your old haunted pine-wood we heard *such* a queer noise. Like someone wailing or crying. Caesar howled and ran; and Harry refused to go in and investigate. He positively funked it!" They all laughed. "More like a rabbit in a trap than a person crying," explained Harry, a blush kindly concealing his startling pallor. "I wanted my tea too much to bother about an old rabbit."

It was some time after tea when the girl became aware that the priest had disappeared, and putting two and two together, ran in alarm to her host's study. Quite easily, from the hastily opened shutters, they saw his figure moving across the snow. The moon was very bright over the world, yet he carried a lantern that shone pale yellow against the white brilliance.

"Oh, for God's sake, quick!" she cried, pale with fear. "Quick! or we're too late! Arthur's simply wild about such things. Oh, I might have known—I might have guessed. And this is the very night. I'm terrified!"

By the time he had found his overcoat and slipped round the house with her from the back door, the lantern, they saw, was already swinging close to the pine-wood. The night was still as ice, bitterly cold. Breathlessly they ran, following the tracks. Half-way his steps diverged, and were plainly visible in the virgin snow by themselves. They heard the whispering of the branches ahead of them, for pines cry even when no airs stir. "Follow me close," said the old man sternly. The lantern, he already saw, lay upon the ground unattended; no human figure was anywhere visible.

"See! The steps come to an end here," he whispered, stooping down as soon as they reached the lantern. The tracks, hitherto so regular, showed an odd wavering—the snow curiously disturbed. Quite suddenly they stopped. The final step was a very long one—a stride, almost immense, "as though he was pushed forward from behind," muttered the old man, too low to be overheard, "or sucked forward from in front—as in a fall."

The girl would have dashed forward but for his strong restraining grasp. She clutched him, uttering a sudden dreadful cry. "Hark! I hear his voice!" she almost sobbed. They stood still to listen. A mystery that was more than the mystery of night closed about their hearts—a mystery that is beyond life and death, that only great awe and terror can summon from the deeps of the soul. Out of the heart of the trees, fifty feet away, issued a crying voice, half wailing, half singing, very faint. "Help! help!" it sounded through the still night; "for the love of God, pray for me!"

The melancholy rustling of the pines followed; and then again the singular crying voice shot past above their heads, now in front of them, now once more behind. It sounded everywhere. It grew fainter and fainter, fading away, it seemed, into distance that somehow was appalling... The grove, however, was empty of all but the sighing wind; the snow unbroken by any tread. The moon threw inky shadows; the cold bit; it was a terror of ice and death and this awful singing cry...

"But why *pray*?" screamed the girl, distracted, frantic with her bewildered terror. "Why *pray*? Let us *do* something to help—*do* something...!" She swung round in a circle, nearly falling to the ground. Suddenly she perceived that the old man had dropped to his knees in the snow beside her and was—praying.

"Because the forces of prayer, of thought, of the will to help, alone can reach and succour him where he now is," was all the answer she got. And a moment later both figures were kneeling in the snow, praying, so to speak, their very heart's life out...

The search may be imagined—the steps taken by police, friends, newspapers, by the whole country in fact... But the most curious part of this queer "Higher Space" adventure is the end of it—at least, the "end" so far as at present known. For after three weeks, when the winds of March were a-roar about the land, there crept over the fields towards the house the small dark figure of a man. He was thin, pallid as a ghost, worn and fearfully emaciated, but upon his face and in his eyes were traces of an astonishing radiance—a glory unlike anything ever seen... It may, of course, have been deliberate, or it may have been a genuine loss of memory only; none could say—least of all the girl whom his return snatched from the gates of death; but, at any rate, what had come to pass during the interval of his amazing disappearance he has never yet been able to reveal.

"And you must never ask me," he would say to her—and repeat even after his complete and speedy restoration to bodily health—"for I simply cannot tell. I know no language, you see, that could express it. I was near you all the time. But I was also—elsewhere and otherwise..."

THE WHISPERERS

*Blackwood had continued to place stories with various magazines but was not
seriously seeking publication. However, in early 1906 he was surprised to run into
his old friend from New York, the journalist and now noted war correspondent
Angus Hamilton who was briefly in London but soon to head off to China. They
went back to Blackwood's lodgings and Hamilton asked him if he was still writing
those stories. Blackwood opened a cupboard full of manuscripts. Hamilton asked
if he might borrow some. Blackwood did not see him again but was astounded,
if not a little annoyed, when a few weeks later a letter came from the publisher
Eveleigh Nash showing an interest in publishing them. Initially Blackwood was
fearful of appearing in print, but he met with the publisher and his reader who
had recommended the stories, Maude ffoulkes, and the rest, as they say, is history.*

That first book, The Empty House, *appeared in November 1906 to good
reviews and sales and was followed, a year later, by* The Listener. *The income
received by these sales was encouraging, but nothing compared to his third book,*
John Silence: Physician Extraordinary *published in September 1908. Nash
gave the book an unprecedented promotional campaign with images of the
mysterious doctor on hoardings and buses. Sales were phenomenal and gave
Blackwood the independence he needed. He gave in his job in the City and
became a full-time writer, and never looked back.*

*It was not quite so positive for Angus Hamilton who, despite his success,
developed severe depression. Whilst on a lecture tour in the United States in
June 1913 he cut his throat in a hotel room.*

Blackwood found his independence allowed him to travel throughout Europe, especially Switzerland which he loved. He settled in a small pension, or guest house in the village of Bôle, near the French border. This became his second home for many years. He would spend most days walking in the surrounding mountains and in the evening writing whatever took his imagination. Blackwood had loved books since his childhood and felt that it was through books that one could not only learn but be influenced, even helped, especially if you suffer a moment of writer's block.

T o be too impressionable is as much a source of weakness as to be hyper-sensitive: so many messages come flooding in upon one another that confusion is the result; the mind chokes, imagination grows congested.

Jones, as an imaginative writing man, was well aware of this, yet could not always prevent it; for if he dulled his mind to one impression, he ran the risk of blunting it to all. To guard his main idea, and picket its safe conduct through the seethe of additions that instantly flocked to join it, was a psychological puzzle that sometimes overtaxed his powers of critical selection. He prepared for it, however. An editor would ask him for a story—"about five thousand words, you know"; and Jones would answer, "I'll send it you with pleasure—when it comes." He knew his difficulty too well to promise more. Ideas were never lacking, but their length of treatment belonged to machinery he could not coerce. They were alive; they refused to come to heel to suit mere editors. Midway in a tale that started crystal clear and definite in its original germ, would pour a flood of new impressions that either smothered the first conception, or developed it beyond recognition. Often a short story exfoliated in this bursting way beyond his power to stop it. He began one, never knowing where it would lead him. It was ever an adventure. Like Jack the Giant Killer's beanstalk it grew secretly in the night, fed by everything he read, saw, felt, or heard. Jones was too impressionable; he received too many impressions, and too easily.

For this reason, when working at a definite, short idea, he preferred an empty room, without pictures, furniture, books, or anything suggestive, and with a skylight that shut out scenery—just ink, blank paper, and the clear picture in his mind. His own interior, unstimulated by the geysers of external life, he made some pretence of regulating; though even under these favourable conditions the matter was not too easy, so prolifically does a sensitive mind engender.

His experience in the empty room of the carpenter's house was a curious case in point—in the little Jura village where his cousin lived to educate his children. "We're all in a pension above the Post Office here," the cousin wrote, "but just now the house is full, and besides is rather noisy. I've taken an attic room for you at the carpenter's near the forest. Some things of mine have been stored there all the winter, but I moved the cases out this morning. There's a bed, writing-table, wash-handstand, sofa, and a skylight window—otherwise empty, as I know you prefer it. You can have your meals with us," etc. And this just suited Jones, who had six weeks' work on hand for which he needed empty solitude. His "idea" was slight and very tender; accretions would easily smother clear presentment; its treatment must be delicate, simple, unconfused.

The room really was an attic, but large, wide, high. He heard the wind rush past the skylight when he went to bed. When the cupboard was open he heard the wind there too, washing the outer walls and tiles. From his pillow he saw a patch of stars peep down upon him. Jones knew the mountains and the woods were close, but he could not see them. Better still, he could not smell them. And he went to bed dead tired, full of his theme for work next morning. He saw it to the end. He could almost have promised five thousand words. With the dawn he would be up and "at it," for he usually woke very early, his mind surcharged, as though subconsciousness had matured the material in sleep. Cold bath, a cup of tea, and then—his writing-table; and the quicker he could reach the writing-table the richer was the content of imaginative thought. What had puzzled him the night before was invariably cleared up in the morning. Only illness could interfere with the process and routine of it.

But this time it was otherwise. He woke, and instantly realised, with a shock of surprise and disappointment, that his mind was—groping. It was groping for his little lost idea. There was nothing physically wrong with him; he felt rested, fresh, clear-headed; but his brain was searching, searching, moreover, in a crowd. Trying to seize hold of the train it had relinquished several hours ago, it caught at an evasive, empty shell. The idea had utterly changed; or rather it seemed smothered by a host of new impressions that came pouring in upon it—new modes of treatment, points of view, in fact development. In the light of these extensions and novel aspects, his original idea had altered beyond recognition. The germ had marvellously exfoliated, so that a whole volume could alone express it. An army of fresh suggestions clamoured for expression. His subconsciousness had grown thick with life; it surged—active, crowded, tumultuous.

And the darkness puzzled him. He remembered the absence of accustomed windows, but it was only when the candle-light brought close the face of his watch, with two o'clock upon it, that he heard the sound of confused whispering in the corners of the room, and realised with a little twinge of fear that those who whispered had just been standing beside his very bed. The room was full.

Though the candle-light proclaimed it empty—bare walls, bare floor, five pieces of unimaginative furniture, and fifty stars peeping through the skylight—it was undeniably thronged with living people whose minds had called him out of heavy sleep. The whispers, of course, died off into the wind that swept the roof and skylight; but the Whisperers remained. They had been trying to get at him; waking suddenly, he had caught them in the very act... And all had brought new interpretations with them; his thought had fundamentally altered; the original idea was snowed under;

new images brimmed his mind, and his brain was working as it worked under the high pressure of creative moments.

Jones sat up, trembling a little, and stared about him into the empty room that yet was densely packed with these invisible Whisperers. And he realised this astonishing thing—that he was the object of their deliberate assault, and that scores of other minds, deep, powerful, very active minds, were thundering and beating upon the doors of his imagination. The onset of them was terrific and bewildering, the attack of aggressive ideas obliterating his original story beneath a flood of new suggestions. Inspiration had become suddenly torrential, yet so vast as to be unwieldy, incoherent, useless. It was like the tempest of images that fever brings. His first conception seemed no longer "delicate," but petty. It had turned unreal and tiny, compared with this enormous choice of treatment, extension, development, that now overwhelmed his throbbing brain.

Fear caught vividly at him, as he searched the empty attic-room in vain for explanation. There was absolutely nothing to produce this tempest of new impressions. People seemed talking to him all together, jumbled somewhat, but insistently. It was obsession, rather than inspiration; and so bitingly, dreadfully real.

"Who are you all?" his mind whispered to blank walls and vacant corners.

Back from the shouting floor and ceiling came the chorus of images that stormed and clamoured for expression. Jones lay still and listened; he let them come. There was nothing else to do. He lay fearful, negative, receptive. It was all too big for him to manage, set to some scale of high achievement that submerged his own small powers. It came, too, in a series of impressions, all separate, yet all somehow interwoven.

In vain he tried to sort them out and sift them. As well sort out waves upon an agitated sea. They were too self-assertive for direction or control.

Like wild animals, hungry, thirsty, ravening, they rushed from every side and fastened on his mind.

Yet he perceived them in a certain sequence.

For, first, the unfurnished attic-chamber was full of human passion, of love and hate, revenge and wicked cunning, of jealousy, courage, cowardice, of every vital human emotion ever longed for, enjoyed, or frustrated, all clamouring for—expression.

Flaming across and through these, incongruously threaded in and out, ran next a yearning softness of incredible beauty that sighed in the empty spaces of his heart, pleading for impossible fulfilment...

And, after these, carrying both one and other upon their surface, huge questions flashed and dived and thundered in a patterned, wild entanglement, calling to be unravelled and made straight. Moreover, with every set came a new suggested treatment of the little clear idea he had taken to bed with him five hours before.

Jones adopted each in turn. Imagination writhed and twisted beneath the stress of all these potential modes of expression he must choose between. His small idea exfoliated into many volumes, work enough to fill a dozen lives. It was most gorgeously exhilarating, though so hopelessly unmanageable. He felt like many minds in one...

Then came another chain of impressions, violent, yet steady owing to their depth; the voices, questions, pleadings turned to pictures; and he saw, struggling through the deeps of him, enormous quantities of people, passing along like rivers, massed, herded, swayed here and there by some outstanding figure of command who directed them like flowing water. They shrieked, and fought, and battled, then sank out of sight, huddled and destroyed in—blood...

And their places were taken instantly by white crowds with shining eyes, and yearning in their faces, who climbed precipitous heights towards some Radiance that kept ever out of sight, like sunrise behind mountains that clouds then swallow... The pelt and thunder of images was destructive in its torrent; his little, first idea was drowned and wrecked... Jones sank back exhausted, utterly dismayed. He gave up all attempt to make selection.

The driving storm swept through him, on and on, now waxing, now waning, but never growing less, and apparently endless as the sky. It rushed in circles, like the turning of a giant wheel. All the activities that human minds have ever battled with since thought began came booming, crashing, straining for expression against the imaginative stuff whereof his mind was built. The walls began to yield and settle. It was like the chaos that madness brings. He did not struggle against it; he let it come, lying open and receptive, pliant and plastic to every detail of the vast invasion. And the only time he attempted a complete obedience, reaching out for the pencil and notebook that lay beside his bed, he desisted instantly again, sinking back upon his pillows with a kind of frightened laughter. For the tempest seemed then to knock him down and bruise his very brain. Inextricable confusion caught him. He might as well have tried to make notes of the entire Alexandrian Library in half an hour...

Then, most singular of all, as he felt the sleep of exhaustion fall upon his tired nerves, he heard that deep, prodigious sound. All that had preceded, it gathered marvellously in, mothering it with a sweetness that seemed to his imagination like some harmonious, geometrical skein including all the activities men's minds have ever known. Faintly he realised it only, discerned from infinitely far away. Into the streams of apparent contradiction that warred so strenuously about him, it seemed to bring some hint of unifying, harmonious explanation... And, here and there, as sleep buried him, he imagined that chords lay threaded along strings of cadences, breaking sometimes even into melody—music that rose everywhere from life and wove Thought into a homogeneous Whole...

"Sleep well?" his cousin inquired, when he appeared very late next day for *déjeuner*. "Think you'll be able to work in that room all right?"

"I slept, yes, thanks," said Jones. "No doubt I shall work there right enough—when I'm rested. By the bye," he asked presently, "what has the attic been used for lately? What's been in it, I mean?"

"Books, only books," was the reply. "I've stored my 'library' there for months, without a chance of using it. I move about so much, you see. Five hundred books were taken out just before you came. I often think," he added lightly, "that when books are unopened like that for long, the minds that wrote them must get restless and—"

"What sort of books were they?" Jones interrupted.

"Fiction, poetry, philosophy, history, religion, music. I've got two hundred books on music alone."

THE MAN WHO PLAYED UPON THE LEAF

Blackwood produced many stories inspired by his years in Switzerland and one of the earliest was the following, published in Country Life *in October 1909. Its setting is precise—Blackwood provides almost but not quite enough clues to work out the location of the Holy of Holies in this story, though you can get close with the railway line that runs through Chambrelien. Not only are the locations real but so are the people. Jean Grospierre was the local pastor at Bôle whilst Louis Favre was a naturalist and archaeologist. He had been a professor at the University of Neuchâtel and had conducted experiments into the human life force. This story probably grew out of a discussion between Blackwood and Favre about a man who used to travel through the villages playing his clarinet. It did not take much for Blackwood's imagination to switch that to a human representation of Pan, not playing his pipes, but upon a leaf.*

W HERE the Jura pine-woods push the fringe of their purple cloak down the slopes till the vineyards stop them lest they should troop into the lake of Neuchâtel, you may find the village where lived the Man Who Played upon the Leaf.

My first sight of him was genuinely prophetic—that spring evening in the garden *café* of the little mountain auberge. But before I saw him I heard him, and ever afterwards the sound and the sight have remained inseparable in my mind.

Jean Grospierre and Louis Favre were giving me confused instructions—the *vin rouge* of Neuchâtel is heady, you know—as to the best route up the Tête-de-Rang, when a thin, wailing music, that at first I took to be rising wind, made itself heard suddenly among the apple trees at the end of the garden, and riveted my attention with a thrill of I know not what.

Favre's description of the bridle path over Mont Racine died away; then Grospierre's eyes wandered as he, too, stopped to listen; and at the same moment a mongrel dog of indescribably forlorn appearance came whining about our table under the walnut tree.

"It's Perret 'Comment-va,' the man who plays on the leaf," said Favre.

"And his cursed dog," added Grospierre, with a shrug of disgust. And, after a pause, they fell again to quarrelling about my complicated path up the Tête-de-Rang.

I turned from them in the direction of the sound.

The dusk was falling. Through the trees I saw the vineyards sloping down a mile or two to the dark blue lake with its distant-shadowed shore and the white line of misty Alps in the sky beyond. Behind us the forests rose in folded purple ridges to the heights of Boudry and La Tourne, soft and thick like carpets of cloud. There was no one about in the cabaret. I heard a horse's hoofs in the village street, a rattle of pans from the kitchen, and the soft roar of a train climbing the mountain railway through gathering darkness towards France—and, singing through it all, like a thread of silver through a dream, this sweet and windy music.

But at first there was nothing to be seen. The Man Who Played on the Leaf was not visible, though I stared hard at the place whence the sound apparently proceeded. The effect, for a moment, was almost ghostly.

Then, down there among the shadows of fruit trees and small pines, something moved, and I became aware with a start that the little *sapin* I had been looking at all the time was really not a tree, but a man—hatless, with dark face, loose hair, and wearing a *pélerine* over his shoulders. How he had produced this singularly vivid impression and taken upon himself the outline and image of a tree is utterly beyond me to describe. It was, doubtless, some swift suggestion in my own imagination that deceived me… Yet he was thin, small, straight, and his flying hair and spreading *pélerine* somehow pictured themselves in the network of dusk and background into the semblance, I suppose, of branches.

I merely record my impression with the truest available words—also my instant persuasion that this first view of the man was, after all, significant and prophetic: his dominant characteristics presented themselves to me symbolically. I saw the man first as a tree; I heard his music first as wind.

Then, as he came slowly towards us, it was clear that he produced the sound by blowing upon a leaf held to his lips between tightly closed hands. And at his heel followed the mongrel dog.

"The inseparables!" sneered Grospierre, who did not appreciate the interruption. He glanced contemptuously at the man and the dog, his face and manner, it seemed to me, conveying a merest trace, however, of superstitious fear. "The tune your father taught you, *hein?*" he added, with a cruel allusion I did not at the moment understand.

"Hush!" Favre said; "he plays thunderingly well all the same!" His glass had not been emptied quite so often, and in his eyes as he listened there was a touch of something that was between respect and wonder.

"The music of the devil," Grospierre muttered as he turned with the gesture of surly impatience to the wine and the rye bread. "It makes me dream at night. Ooua!"

The man, paying no attention to the gibes, came closer, continuing his leaf-music, and as I watched and listened the thrill that had first stirred in me grew curiously. To look at, he was perhaps forty, perhaps fifty; worn, thin, broken; and something seizingly pathetic in his appearance told its little wordless story into the air. The stamp of the outcast was mercilessly upon him. But the eyes were dark and fine. They proclaimed the posses-sion of something that was neither worn nor broken, something that was proud to be outcast, and welcomed it.

"He's cracky, you know," explained Favre, "and half blind. He lives in that hut on the edge of the forest"—pointing with his thumb toward Côtendard—"and plays on the leaf for what he can earn."

We listened for five minutes perhaps while this singular being stood there in the dusk and piped his weird tunes; and if imagination had influenced my first sight of him it certainly had nothing to do with what I now heard. For it was unmistakable; the man played, not mere tunes and melodies, but the clean, strong, elemental sounds of Nature—especially the crying voices of wind. It was the raw material, if you like, of what the masters have used here and there—Wagner, and so forth—but by him heard closely and wonderfully, and produced with marvellous accuracy. It was now the notes of birds or the tinkle and rustle of sounds heard in groves and copses, and now the murmur of those airs that lose their way on summer noons among the tree tops; and then, quite incredibly, just as the man came closer and the volume increased, it grew to the crying of bigger winds and the whispering rush of rain among tossed branches…

How he produced it passed my comprehension, but I think he somehow mingled his own voice with the actual notes of the vibrating edge of the leaf; perhaps, too, that the strange passion shaking behind it all in the depths of the bewildered spirit poured out and reached my mind by ways unknown and incalculable.

I must have momentarily lost myself in the soft magic of it, for I remember coming back with a start to notice that the man had stopped, and that his melancholy face was turned to me with a smile of comprehension and sympathy that passed again almost before I had time to recognise it, and certainly before I had time to reply. And this time I am ready to admit that it was my own imagination, singularly stirred, that translated his smile into the words that no one else heard—

"I was playing for you—because you understand."

Favre was standing up and I saw him give the man the half loaf of coarse bread that was on the table, offering also his own partly-emptied wine-glass. "I haven't the sou today," he was saying, "but if you're hungry, mon brave—" And the man, refusing the wine, took the bread with an air of dignity that precluded all suggestion of patronage or favour, and ought to have made Favre feel proud that he had offered it.

"And that for his son!" laughed the stupid Grospierre, tossing a cheese-rind to the dog, "or for his forest god!"

The music was about me like a net that still held my words and thoughts in a delicate bondage—which is my only explanation for not silencing the coarse guide in the way he deserved; but a few minutes later, when the men had gone into the inn, I crossed to the end of the garden, and there, where the perfumes of orchard and forest deliciously mingled, I came upon the man sitting on the grass beneath an apple-tree. The dog, wagging its tail, was at his feet, as he fed it with the best and largest portions of the bread. For himself, it seemed, he kept nothing but the crust, and—what I could hardly believe, had I not actually witnessed it—the cur, though clearly hungry, had to be coaxed with smiles and kind words to eat what it realised in some dear dog-fashion was needed even more by its master. A pair of outcasts they looked indeed, sharing dry bread in the back garden of the village inn; but in the soft, discerning eyes of that mangy creature there was an expression that raised it, for me at least, far beyond the ranks of common curdom; and in the eyes of the man, half-witted and pariah as he undoubtedly was, a look that set him somewhere in a lonely place where he heard the still, small voices of the world and moved with the elemental tides of life that are never outcast and that include the farthest suns.

He took the franc I offered; and, closer, I perceived that his eyes, for all their moments of fugitive brilliance, were indeed half sightless, and that perhaps he saw only well enough to know men as trees walking. In the village some said he saw better than most, that he saw in the dark, possibly even into the peopled regions beyond this world, and there were reasons—uncanny reasons—to explain the belief. I only know, at any rate, that from this first moment of our meeting he never failed to recognise me at a considerable distance, and to be aware of my whereabouts even in the woods at night; and the best explanation I ever heard, though of course unscientific, was Louis Favre's whispered communication that "he sees with the whole surface of his skin!"

He took the franc with the same air of grandeur that he took the bread, as though he conferred a favour, yet was grateful. The beauty of that gesture has often come back to me since with a sense of wonder for the sweet nobility that I afterwards understood inspired it. At the time, however, he merely looked up at me with the remark, "C'est pour le Dieu—merci!"

He did not say "le bon Dieu," as every one else did.

And though I had meant to get into conversation with him, I found no words quickly enough, for he at once stood up and began to play again on his leaf; and while he played his thanks and gratitude, or the thanks and gratitude of his God, that shaggy mongrel dog stopped eating and sat up beside him to listen. Both fixed their eyes upon me as the sounds of wind and birds and forest poured softly and wonderfully about my ears… so that, when it was over and I went down the quiet street to my *pension*, I was aware that some tiny sense of bewilderment had crept into the profounder regions of my consciousness and faintly disturbed my normal conviction that I belonged to the common world of men as of old. Some aspect of the village, especially of the human occupants in it, had secretly changed for me.

Those pearly spaces of sky, where the bats flew over the red roofs, seemed more alive, more exquisite than before; the smells of the open stables where the cows stood munching, more fragrant than usual of sweet animal life that included myself delightfully, keenly; the last chatterings of the sparrows under the eaves of my own *pension* more intimate and personal…

Almost as if those strands of elemental music the man played on his leaf had for the moment made me free of the life of the earth, as distinct from the life of men…

I can only suggest this, and leave the rest to the care of the imaginative reader; for it is impossible to say along what inner byways of fancy I reached the conclusion that when the man spoke of "the God," and not "the *good* God," he intended to convey his sense of some great woodland personality—some Spirit of the Forests whom he knew and loved and worshipped, and whom, he was intuitively aware, I also knew and loved and worshipped.

During the next few weeks I came to learn more about this poor, half-witted man. In the village he was known as Perret "Comment-va," the

Man Who Plays on the Leaf; but when the people wished to be more explicit they described him as the man "without parents and without God." The origin of "Comment-va" I never discovered, but the other titles were easily explained—he was illegitimate and outcast. The mother had been a wandering Italian girl and the father a loose-living *bûcheron*, who was, it seems, a standing disgrace to the community. I think the villagers were not conscious of their severity; the older generation of farmers and *vignerons* had pity, but the younger ones and those of his own age were certainly guilty, if not of deliberate cruelty, at least of a harsh neglect and the utter withholding of sympathy. It was like the thoughtless cruelty of children, due to small unwisdom, and to that absence of charity which is based on ignorance. They could not in the least understand this crazy, picturesque being who wandered day and night in the forests and spoke openly, though never quite intelligibly, of worshipping another God than their own anthropomorphic deity. People looked askance at him because he was queer; a few feared him; one or two I found later—all women—felt vaguely that there was something in him rather wonderful, they hardly knew what, that lifted him beyond the reach of village taunts and sneers. But from all he was remote, alien, solitary—an outcast and a pariah.

It so happened that I was very busy at the time, seeking the seclusion of the place for my work, and rarely going out until the day was failing; and so it was, I suppose, that my sight of the man was always associated with a gentle dusk, long shadows and slanting rays of sunlight. Every time I saw that thin, straight, yet broken figure, every time the music of the leaf reached me, there came too, the inexplicable thrill of secret wonder and delight that had first accompanied his presence, and with it the subtle suggestion of a haunted woodland life, beautiful with new values. To this day I see that sad, dark face moving about the street, touched with melancholy, yet with the singular light of an inner glory that sometimes lit flames in the poor eyes. Perhaps—the fancy entered my thoughts sometimes when

I passed him—those who are half out of their minds, as the saying goes, are at the same time half in another region whose penetrating loveliness has so bewildered and amazed them that they no longer can play their dull part in our commonplace world; and certainly for me this man's presence never failed to convey an awareness of some hidden and secret beauty that he knew apart from the ordinary haunts and pursuits of men.

Often I followed him up into the woods—in spite of the menacing growls of the dog, who invariably showed his teeth lest I should approach too close—with a great longing to know what he did there and how he spent his time wandering in the great forests, sometimes, I was assured, staying out entire nights or remaining away for days together. For in these Jura forests that cover the mountains from Neuchâtel to Yverdon, and stretch thickly up to the very frontiers of France, you may walk for days without finding a farm or meeting more than an occasional *bûcheron*. And at length, after weeks of failure, and by some process of sympathy he apparently communicated in turn to the dog, it came about that I was— *accepted*. I was allowed to follow at a distance, to listen and, if I could, to watch.

I make use of the conditional, because once in the forest this man had the power of concealing himself in the same way that certain animals and insects conceal themselves by choosing places instinctively where the colour of their surroundings merge into their outlines and obliterate them. So long as he moved all was well; but the moment he stopped and a chance dell or cluster of trees intervened I lost sight of him, and more than once passed within a foot of his presence without knowing it, though the dog was plainly there at his feet. And the instant I turned at the sound of the leaf, there he was, leaning against some dark tree-stem, part of a shadow perhaps, growing like a forest-thing out of the thick moss that hid his feet, or merging with extraordinary intimacy into the fronds of some drooping pine bough! Moreover, this concealment was never intentional, it seems,

but instinctive. The life to which he belonged took him close to its heart, draping about the starved and wasted shoulders the cloak of kindly sympathy which the world of men denied him.

And, while I took my place some little way off upon a fallen stem, and the dog sat looking up into his face with its eyes of yearning and affection, Perret "Comment-va" would take a leaf from the nearest ivy, raise it between tightly pressed palms to his lips and begin that magic sound that seemed to rise out of the forest-voices themselves rather than to be a thing apart.

It was a late evening towards the end of May when I first secured this privilege at close quarters, and the memory of it lives in me still with the fragrance and wonder of some incredible dream. The forest just there was scented with wild lilies of the valley which carpeted the more open spaces with their white bells and big, green leaves; patches of violets and pale anemone twinkled down the mossy stairways of every glade; and through slim openings among the pine-stems I saw the shadowed blues of the lake beyond and the far line of the high Alps, soft and cloud-like in the sky. Already the woods were drawing the dusk out of the earth to cloak themselves for sleep, and in the east a rising moon stared close over the ground between the big trees, dropping trails of faint and yellowish silver along the moss. Distant cow-bells, and an occasional murmur of village voices, reached the ear. But a deep hush lay over all that mighty slope of mountain forest, and even the footsteps of ourselves and the dog had come to rest.

Then, as sounds heard in a dream, a breeze stirred the topmost branches of the pines, filtering down to us as from the wings of birds. It brought new odours of sky and sun-kissed branches with it. A moment later it lost itself in the darkening aisles of forest beyond; and out of the stillness that followed, I heard the strange music of the leaf rising about us with its extraordinary power of suggestion.

And, turning to see the face of the player more closely, I saw that it had marvellously changed, had become young, unlined, soft with joy. The spirit of the immense woods possessed him, and he was at peace...

While he played, too, he swayed a little to and fro, just as a slender *sapin* sways in wind, and a revelation came to me of that strange beauty of combined sound and movement—trees bending while they sing, branches trembling and a-whisper, children that laugh while they dance. And, oh, the crying, plaintive notes of that leaf, and the profound sense of elemental primitive sound that they woke in the penetralia of the imagination, subtly linking simplicity to grandeur! Terribly yet sweetly penetrating, how they searched the heart through, and troubled the very sources of life! Often and often since have I wondered what it was in that singular music that made me *know* the distant Alps listened in their sky-spaces, and that the purple slopes of Boudry and Mont Racine bore it along the spires of their woods as though giant harp-strings stretched to the far summits of Chasseral and the arid wastes of Tête-de-Rang.

In the music this outcast played upon the leaf there was something of a wild, mad beauty that plunged like a knife to the home of tears, and at the same time sang out beyond them—something coldly elemental, close to the naked heart of life. The truth, doubtless, was that his strains, making articulate the sounds of Nature, touched deep, primitive yearnings that for many are buried beyond recall. And between the airs, even between the bars, there fell deep weeping silences when the sounds merged themselves into the sigh of wind or the murmur of falling water, just as the strange player merged his body into the form and colour of the trees about him.

And when at last he ceased, I went close to him, hardly knowing what it was I wanted so much to ask or say. He straightened up at my approach. The melancholy dropped its veil upon his face instantly.

"But that was beautiful—unearthly!" I faltered. "You never have played like that in the village—"

And for a second his eyes lit up as he pointed to the dark spaces of forest behind us:

"In there," he said softly, "there is light!"

"You hear true music in these woods," I ventured, hoping to draw him out; "this music you play—this exquisite singing of winds and trees—?"

He looked at me with a puzzled expression and I knew, of course, that I had blundered with my banal words. Then, before I could explain or alter, there floated to us through the trees a sound of church bells from villages far away; and instantly, as he heard, his face grew dark, as though he understood in some vague fashion that it was a symbol of the faith of those parents who had wronged him, and of the people who continually made him suffer. Something of this, I feel sure, passed through his tortured mind, for he looked menacingly about him, and the dog, who caught the shadow of all his moods, began to growl angrily.

"My music," he said, with a sudden abruptness that was almost fierce, "is for my God."

"Your God of the Forests?" I said, with a real sympathy that I believe reached him.

"*Pour sûr! Pour sûr!* I play it all over the world"—he looked about him down the slopes of villages and vineyards—"and for those who understand—those who belong—to come."

He was, I felt sure, going to say more, perhaps to unbosom himself to me a little; and I might have learned something of the ritual this self-appointed priest of Pan followed in his forest temples—when, the sound of the bells swelled suddenly on the wind, and he turned with an angry gesture and made to go. Their insolence, penetrating even to the privacy of his secret woods, was too much for him.

"And you find many?" I asked.

Perret "Comment-va" shrugged his shoulders and smiled pityingly.

"Moi. Puis le chien—puis maintenant—*vous!*"

He was gone the same minute, as if the branches stretched out dark arms to draw him away among them… and on my way back to the village, by the growing light of the moon, I heard far away in that deep world of a million trees the echoes of a weird, sweet music, as this unwitting votary of Pan piped and fluted to his mighty God upon an ivy leaf.

And the last thing I actually saw was the mongrel cur turning back from the edge of the forest to look at me for a moment of hesitation. He thought it was time now that I should join the little band of worshippers and follow them to the haunted spots of worship.

"Moi—puis le chien—puis maintenant—*vous*!"

From that moment of speech a kind of unexpressed intimacy between us came into being, and whenever we passed one another in the street he would give me a swift, happy look, and jerk his head significantly towards the forests. The feeling that, perhaps, in his curious lonely existence I counted for something important made me very careful with him. From time to time I gave him a few francs, and regularly twice a week when I knew he was away, I used to steal unobserved to his hut on the edge of the forest and put parcels of food inside the door—*salcimé*, cheese, bread; and on one or two occasions when I had been extravagant with my own tea, pieces of plum-cake—what the Colombier baker called *plume-cak'*!

He never acknowledged these little gifts, and I sometimes wondered to what use he put them, for though the dog remained well favoured, so far as any cur can be so, he himself seemed to waste away more rapidly than ever. I found, too, that he did receive help from the village—official help—but that after the night when he was caught on the church steps with an oil can, kindling-wood and a box of matches, this help was reduced by half, and the threat made to discontinue it altogether. Yet I feel sure there was no inherent maliciousness in the Man who Played upon the Leaf, and that his hatred of an "alien" faith was akin to the mistaken zeal that in other days could send poor sinners to the stake for the ultimate safety of their souls.

Two things, moreover, helped to foster the tender belief I had in his innate goodness: first, that all the children of the village loved him and were unafraid, to the point of playing with him and pulling him about as though he were a big dog; and, secondly, that his devotion for the mongrel hound, his equal and fellow-worshipper, went to the length of genuine self-sacrifice. I could never forget how he fed it with the best of the bread, when his own face was pinched and drawn with hunger; and on other occasions I saw many similar proofs of his unselfish affection. His love for that mongrel, never uttered, in my presence at least, perhaps unrecognised as love even by himself, must surely have risen in some form of music or incense to sweeten the very halls of heaven.

In the woods I came across him anywhere and everywhere, sometimes so unexpectedly that it occurred to me he must have followed me stealthily for long distances. And once, in that very lonely stretch above the mountain railway, towards Montmollin, where the trees are spaced apart with an effect of cathedral aisles and Gothic arches, he caught me suddenly and did something that for a moment caused me a thrill of genuine alarm.

Wild lilies of the valley grow very thickly thereabouts, and the ground falls into a natural hollow that shuts it off from the rest of the forest with a peculiar and delightful sense of privacy; and when I came across it for the first time I stopped with a sudden feeling of quite bewildering enchantment—with a kind of childish awe that caught my breath as though I had slipped through some fairy door or blundered out of the ordinary world into a place of holy ground where solemn and beautiful things were the order of the day.

I waited a moment and looked about me. It was utterly still. The haze of the day had given place to an evening clarity of atmosphere that gave the world an appearance of having just received its finishing touches of pristine beauty. The scent of the lilies was overpoweringly sweet. But the whole first impression—before I had time to argue it away—was that I stood before some mighty chancel steps on the eve of a secret festival of importance, and that all was prepared and decorated with a view to the coming ceremony. The hush was the most delicate and profound imaginable—almost forbidding. I was a rude disturber.

Then, without any sound of approaching footsteps, my hat was lifted from my head, and when I turned with a sudden start of alarm, there before me stood Perret "Comment-va," the Man Who Played upon the Leaf.

An extraordinary air of dignity hung about him. His face was stern, yet rapt; something in his eyes genuinely impressive; and his whole appearance produced the instant impression—it touched me with a fleeting sense of awe—that here I had come upon him in the very act—had surprised this poor, broken being in some dramatic moment when his soul sought to find its own peculiar region, and to transform itself into loveliness through some process of outward worship.

He handed the hat back to me without a word, and I understood that I had unwittingly blundered into the secret place of his strange cult, some shrine, as it were, haunted doubly by his faith and imagination, perhaps even into his very Holy of Holies. His own head, as usual, was bared. I could no more have covered myself again than I could have put my hat on in Communion service of my own church.

"But—this wonderful place—this peace, this silence!" I murmured, with the best manner of apology for the intrusion I could muster on the instant. "May I stay a little with you, perhaps—and see?"

And his face passed almost immediately, when he realised that I understood, into that soft and happy expression the woods invariably drew out upon it—the look of the soul, complete and healed.

"Hush!" he whispered, his face solemn with the mystery of the listening trees; "*Vous êtes un peu en retard—mais pourtant…*"

And lifting the leaf to his lips he played a soft and whirring music that had for its undercurrent the sounds of running water and singing wind mingled exquisitely together. It was half chant, half song, solemn enough for the dead, yet with a strain of soaring joy in it that made me think of children and a perfect faith. The music *blessed* me, and the leagues of forest, listening, poured about us all their healing forces.

I swear it would not have greatly surprised me to see the shaggy flanks of Pan himself disappearing behind the moss-grown boulders that lay about the hollows, or to have caught the flutter of white limbs as the nymphs stepped to the measure of his tune through the mosaic of slanting sunshine and shadow beyond.

Instead, I saw only that picturesque madman playing upon his ivy leaf, and at his feet the faithful dog staring up without blinking into his face, from time to time turning to make sure that I listened and understood.

But the desolate places drew him most, and no distance seemed too great either for himself or his dog.

In this part of the Jura there is scenery of a sombre and impressive grandeur that, in its way, is quite as majestic as the revelation of far bigger mountains. The general appearance of soft blue pine woods is deceptive. The Boudry cliffs, slashed here and there with inaccessible couloirs, are undeniably grand, and in the sweep of the Creux du Van precipices there is a splendid terror quite as solemn as that of the Matterhorn itself. The shadows of its smooth, circular walls deny the sun all day, and the winds, caught within the 700ft. sides of its huge amphitheatre, as in the hollow of some awful cup, boom and roar with the crying of lost thunders.

I often met him in these lonely fastnesses, wearing that half-bewildered, half-happy look of the wandering child; and one day in particular, when I risked my neck scrambling up the most easterly of the Boudry couloirs, I learned afterwards that he had spent the whole time—four hours and more—on the little Champ de Trémont at the bottom, watching me with his dog till I arrived in safety at the top. His fellow-worshippers were few, he explained, and worth keeping; though it was ever inexplicable to me how his poor damaged eyes performed the marvels of sight they did.

And another time, at night, when, I admit, no sane man should have been abroad, and I had lost my way coming home from a climb along the torn and precipitous ledges of La Tourne, I heard his leaf thinly piercing the storm, always in front of me yet never overtaken, a sure though invisible guide. The cliffs on that descent are sudden and treacherous. The torrent of the Areuse, swollen with the melting snows, thundered ominously far below; and the forests swung their vast wet cloaks about them with torrents of blinding rain and clouds of darkness—yet all fragrant with warm wind as a virgin world answering to its first spring tempest. There he was, the outcast with his leaf, playing to his God amid all these crashings and bellowings...

In the night, too, when skies were quiet and stars a-gleam, or in the still watches before the dawn, I would sometimes wake with the sound of clustered branches combing faint music from the gently-rising wind, and figure to myself that strange, lost creature wandering with his dog and leaf, his *pèlerine*, his flying hair, his sweet, rapt expression of an inner glory, out there among the world of swaying trees he loved so well. And then my first soft view of the man would come back to me when I had seen him in the dusk as a tree; as though by some queer optical freak my outer and my inner vision had mingled so that I perceived both his broken body and his soul of magic.

For the mysterious singing of the leaf, heard in such moments from my window while the world slept, expressed absolutely the inmost cry of that lonely and singular spirit, damaged in the eyes of the village beyond repair, but in the sight of the wood-gods he so devoutly worshipped, made whole with their own peculiar loveliness and fashioned after the image of elemental things.

The spring wonder was melting into the peace of the long summer days when the end came. The vineyards had begun to dress themselves in green, and the forest in those soft blues when individual trees lose their outline in the general body of the mountain. The lake was indistinguishable from the sky; the Jura peaks and ridges gone a-soaring into misty distances; the white Alps withdrawn into inaccessible and remote solitudes of heaven. I was making reluctant preparations for leaving—dark London already in my thoughts—when the news came. I forget who first put it into actual words. It had been about the village all the morning, and something of it was in every face as I went down the street. But the moment I came out and saw the dog on my doorstep, looking up at me with puzzled and beseeching eyes, I knew that something untoward had happened; and when he bit at my boots and caught my trousers in his teeth, pulling me in the direction of the forest, a sudden sense of poignant bereavement shot through my heart that I found it hard to explain, and that must seem incredible to those who have never known how potent may be the conviction of a sudden intuition.

I followed the forlorn creature whither it led, but before a hundred yards lay behind us I had learned the facts from half-a-dozen mouths. That morning, very early, before the countryside was awake, the first mountain train, swiftly descending the steep incline below Chambrelien, had caught Perret "Comment-va" just where the Mont Racine *sentier* crosses the line on the way to his best-beloved woods, and in one swift second had swept him into eternity. The spot was in the direct line he always took to that special woodland shrine—his Holy Place.

And the manner of his death was characteristic of what I had divined in the man from the beginning; for he had given up his life to save his dog—this mongrel and faithful creature that now tugged so piteously at my trousers. Details, too, were not lacking; the engine-driver had not failed to tell the story at the next station, and the news had travelled up the mountain-side in the way that all such news travels—swiftly. Moreover, the woman who lived at the hut beside the crossing, and lowered the wooden barriers at the approach of all trains, had witnessed the whole sad scene from the beginning.

And it is soon told. Neither she nor the engine-driver knew exactly how the dog got caught in the rails, but both saw that it *was* caught, and both saw plainly how the figure of the half-witted wanderer, hatless as usual and with cape flying, moved deliberately across the line to release it. It all happened in a moment. The man could only have saved himself by leaving the dog to its fate. The shrieking whistle had as little effect upon him as the powerful breaks had upon the engine in those few available moments. Yet, in the fraction of a second before the engine caught them, the dog somehow leapt free, and the soul of the Man Who Played upon the Leaf passed into the presence of his God—singing.

As soon as it realised that I followed willingly, the beastie left me and trotted on ahead, turning every few minutes to make sure that I was coming. But I guessed our destination without difficulty. We passed the Pontarlier railway first, then climbed for half-an-hour and crossed the mountain line about a mile above the scene of the disaster, and so eventually entered the region of the forest, still quivering with innumerable flowers, where in the shaded heart of trees we approached the spot of lilies that I knew—the place where a few weeks before the devout worshipper had lifted the hat from my head because the earth whereon I stood was holy ground. We stood in the pillared gateway of his Holy of Holies. The cool airs, perfumed beyond belief, stole out of the forest to meet us on the very threshold, for the trees here grew so thickly that only patches of the summer blaze found an entrance. And this time I did not wait on the out-skirts, but followed my four-footed guide to a group of mossy boulders that stood in the very centre of the hollow.

And there, as the dog raised its eyes to mine, soft with the pain of its great unanswerable question, I saw in a cleft of the grey rock the ashes of many hundred fires; and, placed about them in careful array, an assortment of the sacrifices he had offered, doubtless in sharp personal deprivation, to his deity:—bits of mouldy bread, half-loaves, untouched portions of cheese, *salamé* with the skin uncut—most of it exactly as I had left it in his hut; and last of all, wrapped in the original white paper, the piece of Colombier *plume-cak*, and a row of ten silver francs round the edge...

I learned afterwards, too, that among the almost unrecognisable remains on the railway, untouched by the devouring terror of the iron, they had found a hand—tightly clasping in its dead fingers a crumpled ivy leaf...

My efforts to find a home for the dog delayed my departure, I remember, several days; but in the autumn when I returned it was only to hear that the creature had refused to stay with any one, and finally had escaped into the forest and deliberately starved itself to death. They found its skeleton, Louis Favre told me, in a rocky hollow on the lower slopes of Mont Racine in the direction of Montmollin. But Louis Favre did not know, as I knew, that this hollow had received other sacrifices as well, and was consecrated ground.

And somewhere, if you search well the Jura slopes between Champ du Moulin, where Jean-Jacques Rousseau had his temporary house, and Côtendard where he visited Lord Wemyss when "Milord Maréchal Keith" was Governor of the Principality of Neuchâtel under Frederic II, King of Prussia—if you look well these haunted slopes, somewhere between the vineyards and the gleaming limestone heights, you shall find the forest glade where lie the bleached bones of the mongrel dog, and the little village cemetery that holds the remains of the Man Who Played upon the Leaf to the honour of the Great God Pan.

A MAN OF EARTH

In May 1910 Blackwood set off on his greatest adventure—to the Caucasus mountains between the Black Sea and the Caspian. He took a steamer from Marseilles which worked its way leisurely along the Mediterranean coast past Italy and Greece to Turkey. Most passengers disembarked at Constantinople (now Istanbul) but Blackwood continued along the Bosporus to Batoum (now Batumi), a rapidly growing port. It was the site of the ancient city of Colchis which had been the destination of Jason and the Argonauts in their quest for the Golden Fleece and on the journey Blackwood mused about the nature of the mythical past.

At Batoum Blackwood met a mining engineer—perhaps the same one in this story—who advised him to be cautious. Blackwood had with him an old pistol he'd acquired from his reporting days at the Tombs, but the engineer suggested that Blackwood should have a guide or two as protection. There had been several murders, kidnappings and riots in the area and it had not been long since a Georgian revolutionary called Koba had organised civil unrest. Koba had vanished but soon re-emerged under his real name—Josef Stalin.

In fact Blackwood did not encounter any problems. He found the people helpful and friendly, if a little bewildered at Blackwood wanting to walk up into the mountains, and he had a wonderful time first climbing Mount Triall and then, after a journey to Tiflis (now Tbilisi) and Vladikavkaz, venturing deep into the hills amongst the azaleas and rhododendrons. He encountered many of the local Georgians and Ossetians and, because of the coats they wore when riding, he imagined them as centaurs. It was here that he imagined a mythical Garden of Eden and the original gods and heroes of ancient Greece and in his mind a story grew which became perhaps his most remarkable novel, The Centaur.

Once back home later that autumn he was so overwhelmed by the beauty and vastness of the Caucasus that he found it difficult to write and it was a while before hearing a street musician playing a penny whistle unlocked his imagination. Before working on The Centaur *he experimented with a couple of stories such as the following which touches on the magic of that ancient land.*

J OHN Erdlieb used to tell this story—occasionally and with reluctance. It had to be dragged out of him. He seemed to feel it was telling something against himself, but that was because he didn't believe in "that kind of thing," and felt that he did himself a wrong and strained the credence of his listeners as well. Hence, probably, the strange impressiveness of the quaint recital; it had indubitably happened to him.

Though of German origin, he was English, stolid, steady, inarticulate English, and a rare good fellow, whose character emerged strongly in those difficult circumstances known as "tight places." He was a mining engineer by profession; he loved the earth and anything to do with the earth, from a garden he played with half tenderly, to a mountain he attacked half savagely for tunnelling or blasting purposes. He never left the earth if he could help it; both feet and mind were always planted firmly upon *terra firma*; figuratively or actually, he never flew. And his physical appearance expressed his wholesome, earthly type—the rumbling, subterranean bass voice, the tangled undergrowth of beard that hid his necktie, the slow, stately walk as of a small hill advancing. Moreover, you might dig in him and find pure gold—the mass of him covered the heart of a simple, tender child, honest and loving as the day. A child of earth, in the literal sense he was, if ever such existed.

"The first time," he said moving his words laboriously, as though they weighed, "was a June evening in Surrey, when I was going along a lane to catch a train to London. I was carrying a bag. It was a quarter-past ten, the train was 10.30, and I had a mile to go. I had come down in the afternoon to advise a friend about the laying of his tennis court—not professionally," he explained, with a booming laugh, "but because I knew he was going the wrong way about it—and he had persuaded me to stay to dinner. He had seen me to the gate and given me directions about short cuts. It was near the longest day, and there was light still hanging from the sky, but the lanes and paths ran along deep gullies in the sandstone, which the trees and bushes turned into tunnels of black. It was very warm and without a breath of air. Rain in the afternoon had left the atmosphere heavy, thick, and steamy. I perspired awfully, my wrist began to ache with carrying the bag, and half-way down one of the deep sandy lanes I stopped a moment to rest. I put the bag down, and struck a match to see my watch. There were seven minutes left to do a long half-mile." He paused a moment, and we concluded from that pause that he would miss his train.

"Now, I'm not the sort of man," he continued simply, "that a tramp would be likely to attack. I don't look opulent, and I'm big. Until I struck that match I hadn't passed a living soul. But my friend's wife had told me the tramps were thick about the roads this summer, and had been pretty bold as well. I'd quite forgotten all this; it wasn't in my mind. So when the glare of the match showed me a man standing close in front of me—so close I could have touched him—I got a start. He saw my watch, of course. But I saw his face. And he was looking straight into my eyes, just as though he had been staring at me in the dark before. The light, I mean, caught him in the act. There was no surprise in his face. Now I must tell you another thing as well: his face was smeared with earth." He laughed again as he said it. "The fellow looked as if he had been buried and just crawled out. It was a big bearded face, and the eyes were like an animal's—quite frank. But what struck me at the moment—I'm telling this badly, I'm afraid—was that, just as I stopped to strike that match, I noticed a strong smell of earth, of soil and mould I mean. If you've ever turned up real virgin soil you'd know exactly what it was like—same sort of smell you get when digging up a wet bit of field, only ten times stronger. A good smell; I love it.

"Well, the match went out, and the blackness after it was like a wall. I just thought I'd be getting on as quick as I could or I'd miss the train—no feeling at all that the fellow meant me any harm, you see—when I heard him say, 'I'll carry it for you. Come up this way. It's the best.' And before I could answer or object—do anything at all, in fact—the fellow had snatched my bag and made off with it. I suppose he had been waiting just at this darkest part of the lane on purpose. He went up hill, and I after him, striking angrily with my stick in the hope of tripping him up. But he had the start, and I was winded already, and uphill I'm not as quick as I used to be ten years ago. I heard his running tread along the sandy ground, light as a child; and, while I stumbled in the darkness among the loose stones and ruts, two other things flashed into my mind. I can't say what made me think of them. But it seemed to me that the fellow was very short and had been standing on tiptoe when he stared into my face; and the other thing was this: that in this sandy soil—it's mostly sand and heather and pine trees in that part—it was curious that the smell of *earth* should have been so strong. For it was rich, black earth I smelt."

John Erdlieb stopped again. He had reached a difficult place, we felt, a place where he wanted help. We gave what help we could, urging him to tell the rest, whether it seemed credible to him or not.

"He kept just ahead of me," he continued, in his growling tones that were like the deep string on a double bass, "and didn't seem a bit anxious to escape from me. He could easily—he ran so lightly—have nipped up the banks and disappeared, and I could never in this world have caught him. But he kept ten yards in front. In the patches where the trees were thinner I saw his outline plainly; he'd run a bit, then pause, then start again just when I got too close. I shouted and cursed him, but he said no word. And at length—oh, we'd been running four or five minutes, I should think—he stopped dead, and waited. It was an open space, where the banks on both sides were clear of trees or bushes, and the light from the sky, as well as the sort of radiance that sand gives out—you know—showed him distinctly, crouching in the path, the bag beside him. I came up with a rush, my stick raised to clout him on the head, when—of course, you can't believe it—he simply wasn't there. I heard his voice, but—well, I can only tell you how it seemed to me—I heard it underground. It was muffled and smothered, as though it came through earth." Erdlieb said this very low; he almost growled it; he was ashamed to tell it. "You want to know what it was he said? I'll tell you in three words: 'Now you're safe.' That was what I heard, and I heard it as distinctly as I hear my own voice now. The fellow had disappeared, as if the thing had been a dream, and I'd just wakened up." He shut his mouth with a snap, as though there was no more to tell.

A lot of questions were discharged at him, of course, but chief among them, or first, at any rate, "And did you catch your train?" He had made such a point of catching that particular train.

"Luckily," he said, "I missed it by three minutes. Yes, I did say 'luckily.' In the tunnel that begins a mile beyond the station there was a bad cave-in—it had been an exceptionally wet summer, and the first three coaches, the only first-class coaches on the train, had every occupant killed. Yes, it's a fad of mine," he answered a final question. "I always go first-class."

He gave the second incident as well. He was very shy about it; but for the dusk on the verandah, where he told it, one could have seen him blush.

"It was last year, when I was in the Caucasus—the Lesser Caucasus, some 50 miles south-east of Batoum, where there are copper mines, first worked by the Phœnicians ages ago, but covered now by a forest of rhododendrons and azaleas. The ore is visible to the eye, and they get it out with pickaxes. It's a marvellous country, wild as ever it can be, and the men wilder still, a difficult crew to manage, Georgians, Persians, Tartars, all Mohammedans, and all free with knife and pistol. We were 5,000 feet above sea-level. You could see Ararat in the distance, a pyramid of snow, and even Elbruz and Kasbek to the north, when the air was clear.

"One of my younger engineers was an American, capable as they make 'em, but with one curious drawback—he spouted Shakespeare and saw visions! A poetical sort of chap, but sober, reliable, and awfully good at his work. I think, you know, the power of the place got into him a bit—you can believe anything," he explained apologetically, "in the Caucasus—and just across the next ridge was a settlement of Ossetines. The Ossetines are said to be older than the Egyptians, and no one knows exactly where they come from; they worship the soil, pray to heaps of earth, with the idea that it expresses deity or something, offer salt and milk to open places in the ground, and all that kind of thing. They're a wild lot, too. But they didn't bother us much, although some of our workmen were afraid of them. The idea was, you see, that they resented our cutting holes in the body of their deity.

"Apart from stories, that grew big unless stopped instantly"—he said this significantly—"I had no trouble with the men at all, and the Ossetines I only saw—er—this once. My American engineer was the bother, with his imaginative talk of nature-spirits, his seeing things about the mountains, and all the rest. The Caucasus just there is not exactly the place to talk that kind of stuff. It's marvellous enough—without additions!

"Well, one afternoon this chap and I were out prospecting together— his geology was splendid, a sort of instinct in him—prospecting for new veins and outcrop and what not, and in the most gorgeously savage scenery you can possibly imagine. The mountain side was smothered with azalea bushes, all in bloom, every shade of colour, and the smell of them was almost more than I could stand. Azalea honey, you know, has a kind of intoxicating effect, like a drug, and the natives use it for that purpose, and, perhaps, the smell of these miles of blossom, taken in such enormous doses, affects the nerves a bit. I can't say about that, but anyhow, Edgar began talking his nonsense about it in his peculiar way—clear-headed enough at the same time to trace his strata with amazing accuracy and judgment—and saying that his eyes were opened, and he could see down into the ground, and talking about the Ossetines and the Powers of the Place, and all mixed up with quotations from his Shakespeare and the rest. Well, it was no business of mine to stop him. He did his work all right. I let him go on fifteen to the dozen until at last it got on my nerves, and I told him to quit it. He didn't mind a bit; just looked at me, and said, 'I've had my eyes opened by the place; I can't help it. Why, I can see your glassy essence. You're an earth-person. You ought to feel what I feel. I think you *do!*' That 'glassy essence,' you know, is in *Measure for Measure*, only I forget the whole quotation. And then he said excitedly, 'The worship of these Ossetines up here has done it. The place is all stirred up. I shouldn't be a bit surprised if we saw—'

"I interrupted him and told him to stow all that. The Ossetines, I told him—taking it that he referred to them and not to—er—other things—were over the next ridge, anyhow, five hours' climbing away—when just at that very minute he came at me like a football player on the charge. He caught my shoulders and stared at me with terror in his face. 'They're coming!' he cried out. 'Can't you hear them? They're coming!'

"And there was a curious, deep, roaring sound up in the mountains to the north, a tremendous sound. It was like thunder. Yet it was a sunny, windless day without a cloud; there was not even falling water near us. I couldn't believe my ears. And I turned and saw what at first I thought were sliding masses of earth and stones moving down towards us from the heights a mile away. There were boulders, rolling and dancing down ahead of the general mass, only they moved so slowly and with such an extraordinary kind of motion altogether that I stood and stared in complete amazement. It all bewildered me. The sound was appalling somehow. It was like an upheaval of the earth. Then Edgar shouted,

'Run, man, run for your life. They're out!' and started off downhill like a frightened deer.

"It takes a good deal to move me, however"—he smiled at us through the dusk so that his teeth were visible—"and I stood still a minute longer, watching the strangest thing I'd ever seen. For those stones and rolling boulders were not rock, but people. It was a crowd of people. Not Ossetines, though. I could see *that*. They were small and stunted. Even at that distance I could swear they were very small. They were like dwarfs. They *were* dwarfs. It took my breath away; but, I swear to you, they were just like that tramp who snatched my bag in the Surrey lane five years before, and they made the same strange impression upon me of being— er—out of the ordinary." He paused a moment, wondering most likely how much more he cared to tell. "I picked up our instruments and ran downhill after Edgar," he told us simply, "ran as hard as I could pelt. You can judge the pace when I tell you I caught him up in something under ten minutes, too." That didn't impress us much, perhaps, because we had never seen the other man, but it meant a lot to Erdlieb apparently. Edgar, of course, was a younger man. "And then we ran on together side by side, not looking back, but feeling exactly as if the mountain-side was at our heels. The roaring sound had stopped. Once within sight of the Works we stopped, too. Nothing unusual was anywhere to be seen. The heights stood out clear and sharp against the brilliant sky. Nothing moved. Not a living soul was visible in any direction upon the enormous slopes. Edgar, however, was white as a ghost, scared stiff, as he phrased it himself. He declared he had seen

'A shadow, like an angel with bright hair
Dabbled in blood.'

"I was in no mood for quotations. I could have knocked him down on the spot.

"That night, an hour after sunset, when the stars were out, and all the mountains peaceful, no wind, no noise of any kind, no hint of warning either, the landslide came. You know about it because I've already described it to you at dinner. It's why I'm in England now instead of superintending the copper mines out there in the Caucasus. The Works were smothered, the loss of life appalling. I told you how we escaped, Edgar and I, by the skin of our teeth and—er—luck. The spot among the azaleas where we first heard the noise in the afternoon—several hours before a single pound of earth had begun to shift—by eight o'clock lay under several hundred feet of fallen mountain, still slowly sliding. I doubt if the Works will ever be dug out. It would cost a fortune. I have advised against it."

A DESERT EPISODE

At some time after, or perhaps even during, his trip to the Caucasus, Blackwood met the woman who would change his life and become his literary muse. This was Maya Knoop, the second wife of Baron Johann Knoop. Knoop was extremely wealthy and ran a textile business at Narva, in Estonia. He travelled extensively. He had opened a sanatorium and health spa at Helouan in Egypt partly for the benefit of his sickly son, Ludwig, a child of his first marriage. Knoop was nearly thirty years Maya's senior. His first wife had died in 1890 and he needed someone to care for his son. He met Maya in Vienna where she performed as a violinist—she was barely twenty at that time. Knoop may have been more fascinated in the violin than Maya. He collected violins—his collection was legendary at that time. He fell under Maya's spell and they were married in 1899. Thereafter Maya's violin ended up in Knoop's collection and she was confined to being a mother to Ludwig and someone to organise Knoop's social events.

Blackwood had met the Knoops by 1910, because he uses their situation, and in particular the violin collection, in his story "An Empty Sleeve", first published in January 1911. She remembered meeting him on a Nile cruiser—owned by the Baron—but Blackwood had yet to visit Egypt, so it's more likely she met him on his trip either to, or back from the Caucasus. Either way, Blackwood was invited to visit the sanatorium at Helouan in January 1912. The effect of Egypt upon him was immeasurable. He was overcome by the sheer immensity of the desert and the scale of history. In Blackwood's imagination Egypt was immortal, preserved on a wave of eternity. He used that imagery in several stories, including the short novel "Sand". In the following story, though, we see him meld that wave of eternity alongside the immortality of love. It is easy to imagine that the couple in this story are Blackwood and Maya. He had used the name Paul Rivers in his earlier novel The Education of Uncle Paul, *and "Uncle Paul" became one of Blackwood's nicknames. He soon wrote a sequel to that novel,* A Prisoner in Fairyland, *subtitled "The Book That Uncle Paul Wrote". It is that book that gave us the image of the Starlight Express, which became the musical play adapted from the novel. But that book also describes how Maya, there called the Countess, becomes his soul-mate. Blackwood's friend, Stephen Graham, was more than aware how he had fallen under her spell. "A love affair began and lasted the rest of his life, though without physical expression," he wrote. "She was his inspiration and they were inseparable."*

Maya was a fascinating person and requires a book all of her own. The following shows just a small part of her magic.

I

"BETTER put wraps on now. The sun's getting low," a girl said.

It was the end of a day's expedition in the Arabian Desert, and they were having tea. A few yards away the donkeys munched their *barsim*; beside them in the sand the boys lay finishing bread and jam. Immense, with gliding tread, the sun's rays slid from crest to crest of the limestone ridges that broke the huge expanse towards the Red Sea. By the time the tea-things were packed the sun hovered, a giant ball of red, above the Pyramids. It stood in the western sky a moment, looking out of its majestic hood across the sand. With a movement almost visible it leaped, paused, then leaped again. It seemed to bound towards the horizon; then, suddenly, was gone.

"It *is* cold, yes," said the painter, Rivers. And all who heard looked up at him because of the way he said it. A hurried movement ran through the merry party, and the girls were on their donkeys quickly, not wishing to be left to bring up the rear. They clattered off. The boys cried; the thud of sticks was heard; hoofs shuffled through the sand and stones. In single file the picnickers headed for Helouan, some five miles distant. And the desert closed up behind them as they went, following in a shadowy wave that never broke, noiseless, foamless, unstreaked, driven by no wind, and of a volume undiscoverable. Against the orange sunset the Pyramids turned deep purple. The strip of silvery Nile among its palm trees looked like

233

rising mist. In the incredible Egyptian afterglow the enormous horizons burned a little longer, then went out. The ball of the earth—a huge round globe that bulged—curved visibly as at sea. It was no longer a flat expanse; it turned. Its splendid curves were realised.

"Better put wraps on; it's cold and the sun is low"—and then the curious hurry to get back among the houses and the haunts of men. No more was said, perhaps, than this, yet, the time and place being what they were, the mind became suddenly aware of that quality which ever brings a certain shrinking with it—vastness; and more than vastness: that which is endless because it is also beginningless—eternity. A colossal splendour stole upon the heart, and the senses, unaccustomed to the unusual stretch, reeled a little, as though the wonder was more than could be faced with comfort. Not all, doubtless, realised it, though to two, at least, it came with a staggering impact there was no withstanding. For, while the luminous greys and purples crept round them from the sandy wastes, the hearts of these two became aware of certain common things whose simple majesty is usually dulled by mere familiarity. Neither the man nor the girl knew for certain that the other felt it, as they brought up the rear together; yet the fact that each *did* feel it set them side by side in the same strange circle—and made them silent. They realised the immensity of a moment: the dizzy stretch of time that led up to the casual pinning of a veil; to the tightening of a stirrup strap; to the little speech with a companion; the roar of the vanished centuries that have ground mountains into sand and spread them over the floor of Africa; above all, to the little truth that they themselves existed amid the whirl of stupendous systems all delicately balanced as a spider's web—that they were *alive*.

For a moment this vast scale of reality revealed itself, then hid swiftly again behind the débris of the obvious. The universe, containing their two tiny yet important selves, stood still for an instant before their eyes. They looked at it—realised that they belonged to it. Everything moved and had its being, *lived*—here in this silent, empty desert even more actively than in a city of crowded houses. The quiet Nile, sighing with age, passed down towards the sea; there loomed the menacing Pyramids across the twilight; beneath them, in monstrous dignity, crouched that Shadow from whose eyes of battered stone proceeds the nameless thing that contracts the heart, then opens it again to terror; and everywhere, from towering monoliths as from secret tombs, rose that strange, long whisper which, defying time and distance, laughs at death. The spell of Egypt, which is the spell of immortality, touched their hearts.

Already, as the group of picnickers rode homewards now, the first stars twinkled overhead, and the peerless Egyptian night was on the way. There was hurry in the passing of the dusk. And the cold sensibly increased.

"So you did no painting after all," said Rivers to the girl who rode a little in front of him, "for I never saw you touch your sketch-book once."

They were some distance now behind the others; the line straggled; and when no answer came he quickened his pace, drew up alongside and saw that her eyes, in the reflection of the sunset, shone with moisture. But she turned her head a little, smiling into his face, so that the human and the non-human beauty came over him with an onset that was almost shock. Neither one nor other, he knew, were long for him, and the realisation fell upon him with a pang of actual physical pain. The acuteness, the hopelessness of the realisation, for a moment, were more than he could bear, stern of temper though he was, and he tried to pass in front of her, urging his donkey with resounding strokes. Her own animal, however, following the lead, at once came up with him.

"You felt it, perhaps, as I did," he said some moments later, his voice quite steady again. "The stupendous, everlasting thing—the—*life* behind it all." He hesitated a little in his speech, unable to find the substantive that could compass even a fragment of his thought. She paused, too, similarly inarticulate before the surge of incomprehensible feelings.

"It's—awful," she said, half laughing, yet the tone hushed and a little quaver in it somewhere. And her voice to his was like the first sound he had ever heard in the world, for the first sound a full-grown man heard in the world would be beyond all telling—magical. "I shall not try again," she continued, leaving out the laughter this time; "my sketch-book is a farce. For, to tell the truth"—and the next three words she said below her breath—"I dare not."

He turned and looked at her for a second. It seemed to him that the following wave had caught them up, and was about to break above her, too. But the big-brimmed hat and the streaming veil shrouded her features. He saw, instead, the Universe. He felt as though he and she had always, always been together, and always, always would be. Separation was inconceivable.

"It came so close," she whispered. "It—shook me!"

They were cut off from their companions, whose voices sounded far ahead. Her words might have been spoken by the darkness, or by some one who peered at them from within that following wave. Yet the fanciful phrase was better than any he could find. From the immeasurable space of time and distance men's hearts vainly seek to plumb, it drew into closer perspective a certain meaning that words may hardly compass, a formidable truth that belongs to that deep place where hope and doubt fight their incessant battle. The awe she spoke of was the awe of immortality, of belonging to something that is endless and beginningless.

And he understood that the tears and laughter were one—caused by that spell which takes a little human life and shakes it, as an animal shakes its prey that later shall feed its blood and increase its power of growth. His other thoughts—really but a single thought—he had not the right to utter. Pain this time easily routed hope as the wave came nearer. For it was the wave of death that would shortly break, he knew, over him, but not over her. Him it would sweep with its huge withdrawal into the desert whence it came: her it would leave high upon the shores of life—alone. And yet the separation would somehow not be real. They were together in eternity even now. They were endless as this desert, beginningless as this sky… immortal. The realisation overwhelmed…

The lights of Helouan seemed to come no nearer as they rode on in silence for the rest of the way. Against the dark background of the Mokattam Hills these fairy lights twinkled brightly, hanging in mid-air, but after an hour they were no closer than before. It was like riding towards the stars. It would take centuries to reach them. There were centuries in which to do so. Hurry has no place in the desert; it is born in streets. The desert stands still; to go fast in it is to go backwards. Now, in particular, its enormous, uncanny leisure was everywhere—in keeping with that mighty scale the sunset had made visible. His thoughts, like the steps of the weary animal that bore him, had no progress in them. The serpent of eternity, holding its tail in its own mouth, rose from the sand, enclosing himself, the stars—and her. Behind him, in the hollows of that shadowy wave, the procession of dynasties and conquests, the great series of gorgeous civilisations the mind calls Past, stood still, crowded with shining eyes and beckoning faces, still waiting to arrive. There is no death in Egypt. His own death stood so close that he could touch it by stretching out his hand, yet it seemed as much behind as in front of him. What man called a beginning was a trick. There was no such thing. He was with this girl—*now*, when Death waited so close for him—yet he had never really begun. Their lives ran always parallel. The hand he stretched to clasp approaching death caught instead in this girl's shadowy hair, drawing her in with him to the centre where he breathed the eternity of the desert. Yet expression of any sort was as futile as it was unnecessary. To paint, to speak, to sing, even the slightest gesture of the soul, became a crude and foolish thing. Silence was here the truth. And they rode in silence towards the fairy lights.

Then suddenly the rocky ground rose up close before them; boulders stood out vividly with black shadows and shining heads; a flat-roofed house slid by; three palm trees rattled in the evening wind; beyond, a mosque and minaret sailed upwards, like the spars and rigging of some phantom craft; and the colonnades of the great modern hotel, standing upon its dome of limestone ridge, loomed over them. Helouan was about them before they knew it. The desert lay behind with its huge, arrested billow. Slowly, owing to its prodigious volume, yet with a speed that merged it instantly with the far horizon behind the night, this wave now withdrew a little. There was no hurry. It came, for the moment, no farther. Rivers knew. For he was in it to the throat. Only his head was above the surface. He still could breathe—and speak—and see. Deepening with every hour into an incalculable splendour, it waited.

II

In the street the foremost riders drew rein, and, two and two abreast, the long line clattered past the shops and cafés, the railway station and hotels, stared at by the natives from the busy pavements. The donkeys stumbled, blinded by the electric light. Girls in white dresses flitted here and there, arabîyehs rattled past with people hurrying home to dress for dinner, and the evening train, just in from Cairo, disgorged its stream of passengers. There were dances in several of the hotels that night. Voices rose on all sides. Questions and answers, engagements and appointments were made, little plans and plots and intrigues for seizing happiness on the wing—before the wave rolled in and caught the lot. They chattered gaily:

"You *are* going, aren't you? You promised—"

"Of course I am."

"Then I'll drive you over. May I call for you?"

"All right. Come at ten."

"We shan't have finished our bridge by then. Say ten-thirty."

And eyes exchanged their meaning signals. The group dismounted and dispersed. Arabs standing under the lebbekh trees, or squatting on the pavements before their dim-lit booths, watched them with faces of gleaming bronze. Rivers gave his bridle to a donkey-boy, and moved across stiffly after the long ride to help the girl dismount. "You feel tired?" he asked gently. "It's been a long day." For her face was white as chalk, though the eyes shone brilliantly.

"Tired, perhaps," she answered, "but exhilarated too. I should like to be there now. I should like to go back this minute—if some one would take me." And, though she said it lightly, there was a meaning in her voice he apparently chose to disregard. It was as if she knew his secret. "Will you take me—some day soon?"

The direct question, spoken by those determined little lips, was impossible to ignore. He looked close into her face as he helped her from the saddle with a spring that brought her a moment half into his arms. "Some day—soon. I will," he said with emphasis, "when you are—ready." The pallor in her face, and a certain expression in it he had not known before, startled him. "I think you have been overdoing it," he added, with a tone in which authority and love were oddly mingled, neither of them disguised.

"Like yourself," she smiled, shaking, her skirts out and looking down at her dusty shoes. "I've only a few days more—before I sail. We're both in such a hurry, but you are the worst of the two."

"Because my time is even shorter," ran his horrified thought—for he said no word.

She raised her eyes suddenly to his, with an expression that for an instant almost convinced him she had guessed—and the soul in him stood rigidly at attention, urging back the rising fires. The hair had dropped loosely round the sun-burned neck. Her face was level with his shoulder. Even the glare of the street lights could not make her undesirable. But behind the gaze of the deep brown eyes another thing looked forth imperatively into his own. And he recognised it with a rush of terror, yet of singular exultation.

"It followed us all the way," she whispered. "It came after us from the desert—where it *lives*."

"At the houses," he said equally low, "it stopped." He gladly adopted her syncopated speech, for it helped him in his struggle to subdue those rising fires.

For a second she hesitated. "You mean, if we had not left so soon—when it turned cold. If we had not hurried—if we had remained a little longer—"

He caught at her hand, unable to control himself, but dropped it again the same second, while she made as though she had not noticed, forgiving him with her eyes. "Or a great deal longer," she added slowly—"for ever?"

And then he was certain that she *had* guessed—not that he loved her above all else in the world, for that was so obvious that a child might know it, but that his silence was due to his other, lesser secret; that the great Executioner stood waiting to drop the hood about his eyes. He was already pinioned. Something in her gaze and in her manner persuaded him suddenly that she understood.

His exhilaration increased extraordinarily. "I mean," he said very quietly, "that the spell weakens here among the houses and among the—so-called living." There was masterfulness, triumph, in his voice. Very wonderfully he saw her smile change; she drew slightly closer to his side, as though unable to resist. "Mingled with lesser things we should not understand completely," he added softly.

"And that might be a mistake, you mean?" she asked quickly, her face grave again.

It was his turn to hesitate a moment. The breeze stirred the hair about her neck, bringing its faint perfume—perfume of young life—to his nostrils. He drew his breath in deeply, smothering back the torrent of rising words he knew were unpermissible. "Misunderstanding," he said briefly. "If the eye be single—" He broke off, shaken by a paroxysm of coughing. "You know my meaning," he continued, as soon as the attack had passed; "you feel the difference *here*," pointing round him to the hotels, the shops, the busy stream of people; "the hurry, the excitement, the feverish, blinding child's play which pretends to be alive, but does not know it—" And again the coughing stopped him. This time she took his hand in her own, pressed it very slightly, then released it. He felt it as the touch of that desert wave upon his soul. "The reception must be in complete and utter resignation. Tainted by lesser things, the disharmony might be—" he began stammeringly.

Again there came interruption, as the rest of the party called impatiently to know if they were coming up to the hotel. He had not time to find the completing adjective. Perhaps he could not find it ever. Perhaps it does not exist in any modern language. Eternity is not realised today; men have no time to know they are alive for ever; they are too busy...

They all moved in a clattering, merry group towards the big hotel. Rivers and the girl were separated.

III

There was a dance that evening, but neither of these took part in it. In the great dining-room their tables were far apart. He could not even see her across the sea of intervening heads and shoulders. The long meal over, he went to his room, feeling it imperative to be alone. He did not read, he did not write; but, leaving the light unlit, he wrapped himself up and leaned out upon the broad window-sill into the great Egyptian night. His deep-sunken thoughts, like to the crowding stars, stood still, yet for ever took new shapes. He tried to see behind them, as, when a boy, he had tried to see behind the constellations—out into space—where there is nothing.

Below him the lights of Helouan twinkled like the Pleiades reflected in a pool of water; a hum of queer soft noises rose to his ears; but just beyond the houses the desert stood at attention, the vastest thing he had ever known, very stern, yet very comforting, with its peace beyond all comprehension, its delicate, wild terror, and its awful message of immortality. And the attitude of his mind, though he did not know it, was one of prayer... From time to time he went to lie on the bed with paroxysms of coughing. He had overtaxed his strength—his swiftly fading strength. The wave had risen to his lips.

Nearer forty than thirty-five, Paul Rivers had come out to Egypt, plainly understanding that with the greatest care he might last a few weeks longer than if he stayed in England. A few more times to see the sunset and the sunrise, to watch the stars, feel the soft airs of earth upon his cheeks; a few more days of intercourse with his kind, asking and answering questions, wearing the old familiar clothes he loved, reading his favourite pages, and then—out into the big spaces—where there is nothing.

Yet no one, from his stalwart, energetic figure, would have guessed—no one but the expert mind, not to be deceived, to whom in the first attack of overwhelming despair and desolation he went for final advice. He left that house, as many had left it before, knowing that soon he would need no earthly protection of roof and walls, and that his soul, if it existed, would be shelterless in the space behind all manifested life. He had looked forward to fame and position in this world; had, indeed, already achieved the first step towards this end; and now, with the vanity of all earthly aims so mercilessly clear before him, he had turned, in somewhat of a nervous, concentrated hurry, to make terms with the Infinite while still the brain was there. And had, of course, found nothing. For it takes a lifetime crowded with experiment and effort to learn even the alphabet of genuine faith; and what could come of a few weeks' wild questioning but confusion and bewilderment of mind? It was inevitable. He came out to Egypt wondering, thinking, questioning, but chiefly wondering. He had grown, that is, more childlike, abandoning the futile tool of Reason, which hitherto had seemed to him the perfect instrument. Its foolishness stood naked before him in the pitiless light of the specialist's decision. For—"Who can by searching find out God?"

To be exceedingly careful of over-exertion was the final warning he brought with him, and, within a few hours of his arrival, three weeks ago, he had met this girl and utterly disregarded it. He took it somewhat thus: "Instead of lingering I'll enjoy myself and go out—a little sooner. I'll *live*. The time is very short." His was not a nature, anyhow, that could heed a warning. He could not kneel. Upright and unflinching, he went to meet things as they came, reckless, unwise, but certainly not afraid. And this characteristic operated now. He ran to meet Death full tilt in the uncharted spaces that lay behind the stars. With love for a companion now, he raced, his speed increasing from day to day, she, as he thought, knowing merely that he sought her, but had not guessed his darker secret that was now his *lesser* secret.

And in the desert, this afternoon of the picnic, the great thing he sped to meet had shown itself with its familiar touch of appalling cold and shadow, familiar, because all minds know of and accept it; appalling because, until realised close, and with the mental power at the full, it remains but a name the heart refuses to believe in. And he had discovered that its name was—Life.

Rivers had seen the Wave that sweeps incessant, tireless, but as a rule invisible, round the great curve of the bulging earth, brushing the nations into the deeps behind. It had followed him home to the streets and houses of Helouan. He saw it *now*, as he leaned from his window, dim and immense, too huge to break. Its beauty was nameless, undecipherable. His coughing echoed back from the wall of its great sides... And the music floated up at the same time from the ball-room in the opposite wing. The two sounds mingled. Life, which is love, and Death, which is their unchanging partner, held hands beneath the stars.

He leaned out farther to drink in the cool, sweet air. Soon, on this air, his body would be dust, driven, perhaps, against her very cheek, trodden on possibly by her little foot—until, in turn, she joined him too, blown by the same wind loose about the desert. True. Yet at the same time they would always be together, always somewhere side by side, continuing in the vast universe, *alive*. This new, absolute conviction was in him now. He remembered the curious, sweet perfume in the desert, as of flowers, where yet no flowers are. It was the perfume of life. But in the desert there is no life. Living things that grow and move and utter, are but a protest against death. In the desert they are unnecessary, because death there *is* not. Its overwhelming vitality needs no insolent, visible proof, no protest, no challenge, no little signs of life. The message of the desert is immortality...

He went finally to bed, just before midnight. Hovering magnificently just outside his window, Death watched him while he slept. The wave crept to the level of his eyes. He called her name...

And downstairs, meanwhile, the girl, knowing nothing, wondered where he was, wondered unhappily and restlessly; more—though this she did not understand—wondered motheringly. Until today, on the ride home, and from their singular conversation together, she had guessed nothing of his reason for being at Helouan, where so many come in order to find life. She only knew her own. And she was but twenty-five...

Then, in the desert, when that touch of unearthly chill had stolen out of the sand towards sunset, she had realised clearly, astonished she had not seen it long ago, that this man loved her, yet that something prevented his obeying the great impulse. In the life of Paul Rivers, whose presence had profoundly stirred her heart the first time she saw him, there was some obstacle that held him back, a barrier his honour must respect. He could never tell her of his love. It could lead to nothing. Knowing that he was not married, her intuition failed her utterly at first. Then, in their silence on the homeward ride, the truth had somehow pressed up and touched her with its hand of ice. In that disjointed conversation at the end, which reads as it sounded, as though no coherent meaning lay behind the words, and as though both sought to conceal by speech what yet both burned to utter, she had divined his darker secret, and knew that it was the same as her own. She understood then it was Death that had tracked them from the desert, following with its gigantic shadow from the sandy wastes. The cold, the darkness, the silence which cannot answer, the stupendous mystery which is the spell of its inscrutable Presence, had risen about them in the dusk, and kept them company at a little distance, until the lights of Helouan had bade it halt. Life which may not, cannot end, had frightened her.

His time, perhaps, was even shorter than her own. None knew his secret, since he was alone in Egypt and was caring for himself. Similarly, since she bravely kept her terror to herself, her mother had no inkling of her own, aware merely that the disease was in her system and that her orders were to be extremely cautious. This couple, therefore, shared secretly together the two clearest glimpses of eternity life has to offer to the soul. Side by side they looked into the splendid eyes of Love and Death. Life, moreover, with its instinct for simple and terrific drama, had produced this majestic climax, breaking with pathos, at the very moment when it could not be developed—this side of the stars. They stood together upon the stage, a stage emptied of other human players; the audience had gone home and the lights were being lowered; no music sounded; the critics were a-bed. In this great game of Consequences it was known where he met her, what he said and what she answered, possibly what they did and even what the world thought. But "what the consequence was" would remain unknown, untold. That would happen in the big spaces of which the desert in its silence, its motionless serenity, its shelterless, intolerable vastness, is the perfect symbol. And the desert gives no answer. It sounds no challenge, for it is complete. Life in the desert makes no sign. It *is*.

IV

In the hotel that night there arrived by chance a famous International dancer, whose dahabîyeh lay anchored at San Giovanni, in the Nile below Helouan; and this woman, with her party, had come to dine and take part in the festivities. The news spread. After twelve the lights were lowered, and while the moonlight flooded the terraces, streaming past pillar and colonnade, she rendered in the shadowed halls the music of the Masters, interpreting with an instinctive genius messages which are eternal and divine.

Among the crowd of enthralled and delighted guests, the girl sat on the steps and watched her. The rhythmical interpretation held a power that seemed, in a sense, inspired; there lay in it a certain unconscious something that was pure, unearthly; something that the stars, wheeling in stately movements over the sea and desert know; something the great winds bring to mountains where they play together; something the forests capture and fix magically into their gathering of big and little branches. It was both passionate and spiritual, wild and tender, intensely human and seductively non-human. For it was original, taught of Nature, a revelation of naked, unhampered life. It comforted, as the desert comforts. It brought the desert awe into the stuffy corridors of the hotel, with the moonlight and the whispering of stars, yet behind it ever the silence of those grey, mysterious, interminable spaces which utter to themselves the wordless song of life. For it was the same dim thing, she felt, that had followed her from the desert several hours before, halting just outside the streets and houses as though blocked from further advance; the thing that had stopped her foolish painting, skilled though she was, because it hides behind colour and not in it; the thing that veiled the meaning in the cryptic sentences she and he had stammered out together; the thing, in a word, as near as she could approach it by any means of interior expression, that the realisation of death for the first time makes comprehensible—Immortality. It was unutterable, but it *was*. He and she were indissolubly together. Death was no separation. There was no death… It was terrible. It was—she had already used the word—awful, full of awe.

"In the desert," thought whispered, as she watched spellbound, "it is impossible even to conceive of death. The idea is meaningless. It simply is not."

The music and the movement filled the air with life which, being there, must continue always, and continuing always can have never had a beginning. Death, therefore, was the great revealer of life. Without it none could realise that they are alive. Others had discovered this before her, but she did not know it. In the desert no one can realise death: it is hope and life that are the only certainty. The entire conception of the Egyptian system was based on this—the conviction, sure and glorious, of life's endless continuation. Their tombs and temples, their pyramids and sphinxes surviving after thousands of years, defy the passage of time and laugh at death; the very bodies of their priests and kings, of their animals even, their fish, their insects, stand today as symbols of their stalwart knowledge.

And this girl, as she listened to the music and watched the inspired dancing, remembered it. The message poured into her from many sides,

THE WHISPERERS AND OTHER STORIES

though the desert brought it clearest. With death peering into her face a few short weeks ahead, she thought instead of—life. The desert, as it were, became for her a little fragment of eternity, focused into an intelligible point for her mind to rest upon with comfort and comprehension. Her steady, thoughtful nature stirred towards an objective far beyond the small enclosure of one narrow lifetime. The scale of the desert stretched her to the grandeur of its own imperial meaning, its divine repose, its unassailable and everlasting majesty. She looked beyond the wall.

Eternity! That which is endless; without pause, without beginning, without divisions or boundaries. The fluttering of her brave yet frightened spirit ceased, aware with awe of its own everlastingness. The swiftest motion produces the effect of immobility; excessive light is darkness; size, run loose into enormity, is the same as the minutely tiny. Similarly, in the desert, life, too overwhelming and terrific to know limit or confinement, lies undetailed and stupendous, still as deity, a revelation of nothingness because it is all. Turned golden beneath its spell that the music and the rhythm made even more comprehensible, the soul in her, already lying beneath the shadow of the great wave, sank into rest and peace, too certain of itself to fear. And panic fled away. "I am immortal... because I *am*. And what I love is not apart from me. It is myself. We are together endlessly because we *are*."

Yet in reality, though the big desert brought this, it was Love, which, being of similar parentage, interpreted its vast meaning to her little heart—that sudden love which, without a word of preface or explanation, had come to her a short three weeks before... She went up to her room soon after midnight, abruptly, unexpectedly stricken. Some one, it seemed, had called her name. She passed his door.

The lights had been turned up. The clamour of praise was loud round the figure of the weary dancer as she left in a carriage for her dahabîyeh on the Nile. A low wind whistled round the walls of the great hotel, blowing chill and bitter between the pillars of the colonnades. The girl heard the voices float up to her through the night, and once more, behind the confused sound of the many, she heard her own name called, but more faintly than before, and from very far away. It came through the spaces beyond her open window; it died away again; then—but for the sighing of that bitter wind—silence, the deep silence of the desert.

And these two, Paul Rivers and the girl, between them merely a floor of that stone that built the Pyramids, lay a few moments before the Wave of Sleep engulfed them. And, while they slept, two shadowy forms hovered above the roof of the quiet hotel, melting presently into one, as dreams stole down from the desert and the stars. Immortality whispered to them. On either side rose Life and Death, towering in splendour. Love, joining their spreading wings, fused the gigantic outlines into one. The figures grew smaller, comprehensible. They entered the little windows. Above the beds they paused a moment, watching, waiting, and then, like a wave that is just about to break, they stooped...

And in the brilliant Egyptian sunlight of the morning, as she went downstairs, she passed his door again. She had awakened, but he slept on. He had preceded her. It was next day she learned his room was vacant... Within the month she joined him, and within the year the cool north wind that sweetens Lower Egypt from the sea blew the dust across the desert as before. It is the dust of kings, of queens, of priests, princesses, lovers. It is the dust no earthly power can annihilate. It, too, lasts for ever. There was a little more of it... the desert's message slightly added to: Immortality.

THE WINGS OF HORUS

Blackwood was also fascinated by the power of flight and the freedom of birds. He had already reflected on the theme in an essay "On Wings" published in Country Life *in May 1911, and it would become the central theme to ushering in a New Age in his novel* The Promise of Air *in 1918. But there is this particular story that encapsulates in vivid imagery the possibility of flight.*

It is also set in Egypt and, like the previous story which refers to an "international dancer", may well have been inspired by Isadora Duncan. Blackwood claims to have seen her dance but it can't have been in Egypt for though she planned to visit the temples in 1913 that was thwarted by other commitments. Maybe he saw her in Paris or Venice or Florence during that year, but whenever or wherever it was, Blackwood was once again able to take a simple image and work it into a captivating story. In the late 1920s Blackwood worked with Kinsey Peile to convert the story into a ballet which was going to be produced by Anton Dolin, who was then still a young but mesmerising dancer and choreographer. Alas, the finances could not be raised but some of the sets had been created and gave some impression of what a magical treat it would have been.

B INOVITCH had the bird in him somewhere: in his features, certainly, with his piercing eye and hawk-like nose; in his movements, with his quick way of flitting, hopping, darting; in the way he perched on the edge of a chair; in the manner he pecked at his food; in his twittering, high-pitched voice as well; and, above all, in his mind. He skimmed all subjects and picked their heart out neatly, as a bird skims lawn or air to snatch its prey. He had the bird's-eye view of everything. He loved birds and understood them instinctively; could imitate their whistling notes with astonishing accuracy. Their one quality he had not was poise and balance. He was a nervous little man; he was neurasthenic. And he was in Egypt by doctor's orders.

Such imaginative, unnecessary ideas he had! Such uncommon beliefs!

"The old Egyptians," he said laughingly, yet with a touch of solemn conviction in his manner, "were a great people. Their consciousness was different from ours. The bird idea, for instance, conveyed a sense of deity to them—of bird deity, that is: they had sacred birds—hawks, ibis, and so forth—and worshipped them." And he put his tongue out as though to say with challenge, "Ha, ha!"

"They also worshipped cats and crocodiles and cows," grinned Palazov. Binovitch seemed to dart across the table at his adversary. His eyes flashed; his nose pecked the air. Almost one could imagine the beating of his angry wings.

"Because everything alive," he half screamed, "was a symbol of some spiritual power to them. Your mind is as literal as a dictionary and as incoherent. Pages of ink without connected meaning! Verb always in the infinitive! If you were an old Egyptian, you—you"—he flashed and sputtered, his tongue shot out again, his keen eyes blazed—"you might take all those words and spin them into a great interpretation of life, a cosmic romance, as they did. Instead, you get the bitter, dead taste of ink in your mouth, and spit it over us like that"—he made a quick movement of his whole body as a bird that shakes itself—"in empty phrases."

Khilkoff ordered another bottle of champagne, while Vera, his sister, said half nervously, "Let's go for a drive; it's moonlight." There was enthusiasm at once. Another of the party called the head waiter and told him to pack food and drink in baskets. It was only eleven o'clock. They would drive out into the desert, have a meal at two in the morning, tell stories, sing, and see the dawn.

It was in one of those cosmopolitan hotels in Egypt which attract the ordinary tourists as well as those who are doing a "cure," and all these Russians were ill with one thing or another. All were ordered out for their health, and all were the despair of their doctors. They were as unmanageable as a bazaar and as incoherent. Excess and bed were their routine. They lived, but none of them got better. Equally, none of them got angry. They talked in this strange personal way without a shred of malice or offence. The English, French, and Germans in the hotel watched them with remote amazement, referring to them as "that Russian lot." Their energy was elemental. They never stopped. They merely disappeared when the pace became too fast, then reappeared again after a day or two, and resumed their "living" as before. Binovitch, despite his neurasthenia, was the life of the party. He was also a special patient of Dr. Plitzinger, the famous psychiatrist, who took a peculiar interest in his case. It was not surprising. Binovitch was a man of unusual ability and of genuine, deep culture. But there was something more about him that stimulated curiosity. There was this striking originality. He said and did surprising things.

"I could fly if I wanted to," he said once when the airmen came to astonish the natives with their biplanes over the desert, "but without all that machinery and noise. It's only a question of believing and understanding—"

"Show us!" they cried. "Let's see you fly!"

"He's got it! He's off again! One of his impossible moments."

These occasions when Binovitch let himself go always proved wildly entertaining. He said monstrously incredible things as though he really did believe them. They loved his madness, for it gave them new sensations.

"It's only levitation, after all, this flying," he exclaimed, shooting out his tongue between the words, as his habit was when excited; "and what is levitation but a power of the air? None of you can hang an orange in space for a second, with all your scientific knowledge; but the moon is always levitated perfectly. And the stars. D'you think they swing on wires? What raised the enormous stones of ancient Egypt? D'you really believe it was heaped-up sand and ropes and clumsy leverage and all our weary and laborious mechanical contrivances? Bah! It was levitation. It was the powers of the air. Believe in those powers, and gravity becomes a mere nursery trick—true where it is, but true nowhere else. To know the fourth dimension is to step out of a locked room and appear instantly on the roof or in another country altogether. To know the powers of the air, similarly, is to annihilate what you call weight—and fly."

"Show us, show us!" they cried, roaring with delighted laughter.

"It's a question of belief," he repeated, his tongue appearing and disappearing like a pointed shadow. "It's in the heart; the power of the air gets into your whole being. Why should I show you? Why should I ask my deity to persuade your scoffing little minds by any miracle? For it *is* deity, I tell you, and nothing else. I *know* it. Follow one idea like that, as I follow my bird idea—follow it with the impetus and undeviating concentration of a projectile—and you arrive at power. You know deity—the bird idea of deity, that is. *They* knew that. The old Egyptians knew it."

"Oh, show us, show us!" they shouted impatiently, wearied of his nonsense-talk. "Get up and fly! Levitate yourself, as they did! Become a star!"

Binovitch turned suddenly very pale, and an odd light shone in his keen brown eyes. He rose slowly from the edge of the chair where he was perched. Something about him changed. There was silence instantly.

"I *will* show you," he said calmly, to their intense amazement; "not to convince your disbelief, but to prove it to myself. For the powers of the air are with me here. I believe. And Horus, great falcon-headed symbol, is my patron god."

The suppressed energy in his voice and manner was indescribable. There was a sense of lifting, upheaving power about him. He raised his arms; his face turned upward; he inflated his lungs with a deep, long breath, and his voice broke into a kind of singing cry, half prayer, half chant:

"O Horus,
Bright-eyed deity of wind,
*Feather my soul
Though earth's thick air,
To know thy awful swiftness—"

He broke off suddenly. He climbed lightly and swiftly upon the nearest table—it was in a deserted card-room, after a game in which he had lost more pounds than there are days in the year—and leaped into the air. He hovered a second, spread his arms and legs in space, appeared to float a

---

* The Russian is untranslatable. The phrase means, "Give my life wings."

moment, then buckled, rushed down and forward, and dropped in a heap upon the floor, while every one roared with laughter.

But the laughter died out quickly, for there was something in his wild performance that was peculiar and unusual. It was uncanny, not quite natural. His body had seemed, as with Mordkin and Nijinski, literally to hang upon the air a moment. For a second he gave the distressing impression of overcoming gravity. There was a touch in it of that faint horror which appals by its very vagueness. He picked himself up unhurt, and his face was as grave as a portrait in the academy, but with a new expression in it that everybody noticed with this strange, half-shocked amazement. And it was this expression that extinguished the claps of laughter as wind that takes away the sound of bells. Like many ugly men, he was an inimitable actor, and his facial repertory was endless and incredible. But this was neither acting nor clever manipulation of expressive features. There was something in his curious Russian physiognomy that made the heart beat slower. And that was why the laughter died away so suddenly.

"You ought to have flown farther," cried some one. It expressed what all had felt.

"Icarus didn't drink champagne," another replied, with a laugh; but nobody laughed with him.

"You went too near to Vera," said Palazov, "and passion melted the wax." But his face twitched oddly as he said it. There was something he did not understand, and so heartily disliked.

The strange expression on the features deepened. It was arresting in a disagreeable, almost in a horrible, way. The talk stopped dead; all stared; there was a feeling of dismay in everybody's heart, yet unexplained. Some lowered their eyes, or else looked stupidly elsewhere; but the women of the party felt a kind of fascination. Vera, in particular, could not move her sight away. The joking reference to his passionate admiration for her passed unnoticed. There was a general and individual sense of shock. And a chorus of whispers rose instantly:

"Look at Binovitch! What's happened to his face?"

"He's changed—he's changing!"

"God! Why he looks like a—bird!"

But no one laughed. Instead, they chose the names of birds—hawk, eagle, even owl. The figure of a man leaning against the edge of the door, watching them closely, they did not notice. He had been passing down the corridor, had looked in unobserved, and then had paused. He had seen the whole performance. He watched Binovitch narrowly, now with calm, discerning eyes. It was Dr. Plitzinger, the great psychiatrist.

For Binovitch had picked himself up from the floor in a way that was oddly self-possessed, and precluded the least possibility of the ludicrous. He looked neither foolish nor abashed. He looked surprised, but also he looked half angry and half frightened. As some one had said, he "ought to have flown farther." That was the incredible impression his acrobatics had produced—incredible, yet somehow actual. This uncanny idea prevailed, as at a séance where nothing genuine is expected to happen, and something genuine, after all, does happen. There was no pretence in this: Binovitch had flown.

And now he stood there, white in the face—with terror and with anger white. He looked extraordinary, this little, neurasthenic Russian, but he looked at the same time half terrific. Another thing, not commonly experienced by men, was in him, breaking out of him, affecting *directly* the minds of his companions. His mouth opened; blood and fury shone in his blazing eyes; his tongue shot out like an ant-eater's, though even in that the comic had no place. His arms were spread like flapping wings, and his voice rose dreadfully:

"He failed me, he failed me!" he tried to bellow. "Horus, my falcon-headed deity, my power of the air, deserted me! Hell take him! Hell burn his wings and blast his piercing sight! Hell scorch him into dust for his false prophecies! I curse him—I curse Horus!"

The voice that should have roared across the silent room emitted, instead, this high-pitched, bird-like scream. The added touch of sound, the reality it lent, was ghastly. Yet it was marvellously done and acted. The entire thing was a bit of instantaneous inspiration—his voice, his words, his gestures, his whole wild appearance. Only—here was the reality that caused the sense of shock—the expression on his altered features was genuine. *That* was not assumed. There was something new and alien in him, something cold and difficult to human life, something alert and swift and cruel, of another element than earth. A strange, rapacious grandeur had leaped upon the struggling features. The face looked hawk-like.

And he came forward suddenly and sharply toward Vera, whose fixed, staring eyes had never once ceased watching him with a kind of anxious and devouring pain in them. She was both drawn and beaten back. Binovitch advanced on tiptoe. No doubt he still was acting, still pretending this mad nonsense that he worshipped Horus, the falcon-headed deity of forgotten days, and that Horus had failed him in his hour of need; but somehow there was just a hint of too much reality in the way he moved and looked. The girl, a little creature, with fluffy golden hair, opened her lips; her cigarette fell to the floor; she shrank back; she looked for a moment like some smaller, coloured bird trying to escape from a great pursuing hawk; she screamed. Binovitch, his arms wide, his bird-like face thrust forward, had swooped upon her. He leaped. Almost he caught her.

No one could say exactly what happened. Play, become suddenly and unexpectedly too real, confuses the emotions. The change of key was swift. From fun to terror is a dislocating jolt upon the mind. Some one—it was Khilkoff, the brother—upset a chair; everybody spoke at once; everybody stood up. An unaccountable feeling of disaster was in the air, as with those drinkers' quarrels that blaze out from nothing, and end in a pistol-shot and death, no one able to explain clearly how it came about. It was the silent, watching figure in the doorway who saved the situation. Before any one had noticed his approach, there he was among the group, laughing, talking, applauding—between Binovitch and Vera. He was vigorously patting his patient on the back, and his voice rose easily above the general clamour. He was a strong, quiet personality; even in his laughter there was authority. And his laughter now was the only sound in the room, as though by his mere presence peace and harmony were restored. Confidence came with him. The noise subsided; Vera was in her chair again. Khilkoff poured out a glass of wine for the great man.

"The Czar!" said Plitzinger, sipping his champagne, while all stood up, delighted with his compliment and tact. "And to your opening night with the Russian ballet," he added quickly a second toast, "or to your first performance at the Moscow Théâtre des Arts!" Smiling significantly, he glanced at Binovitch; he clinked glasses with him. Their arms were already linked, but it was Palazov who noticed that the doctor's fingers seemed rather tight upon the creased black coat. All drank, looking with laughter, yet with a touch of respect, toward Binovitch, who stood there dwarfed beside the stalwart Austrian, and suddenly as meek and subdued as any mole. Apparently the abrupt change of key had taken his mind successfully off something else.

"Of course—'The Fire-Bird,'" exclaimed the little man, mentioning the famous Russian ballet. "The very thing!" he exclaimed. "For us," he added, looking with devouring eyes at Vera. He was greatly pleased. He began talking vociferously about dancing and the rationale of dancing. They told him he was an undiscovered master. He was delighted. He winked at Vera and touched her glass again with his. "We'll make our début together," he cried. "We'll begin at Covent Garden, in London. I'll design the dresses and the posters 'The Hawk and the Dove!' *Magnifique!* I in dark grey, and you in blue and gold! Ah, dancing, you know, is sacred. The little self is lost, absorbed. It is ecstasy, it is divine. And dancing in air—the passion of the birds and stars—ah! they are the movements of the gods. You know deity that way—by living it."

He went on and on. His entire being had shifted with a leap upon this new subject. The idea of realising divinity by dancing it absorbed him. The party discussed it with him as though nothing else existed in the world, all sitting now and talking eagerly together. Vera took the cigarette he offered her, lighting it from his own; their fingers touched; he was as harmless and normal as a retired diplomat in a drawing-room. But it was Plitzinger whose subtle manœuvring had accomplished the change so cleverly, and it was Plitzinger who presently suggested a game of billiards, and led him off, full now of a fresh enthusiasm for cannons, balls, and pockets, into another room. They departed arm in arm, laughing and talking together.

Their departure, it seemed, made no great difference at first. Vera's eyes watched him out of sight, then turned to listen to Baron Minski, who was describing with gusto how he caught wolves alive for coursing purposes. The speed and power of the wolf, he said, was impossible to real-ise; the force of their awful leap, the strength of their teeth, which could bite through metal stirrup-fastenings. He showed a scar on his arm and another on his lip. He was telling truth, and everybody listened with deep interest. The narrative lasted perhaps ten minutes or more, when Minski abruptly stopped. He had come to an end; he looked about him; he saw his glass, and emptied it. There was a general pause. Another subject did not at once present itself. Sighs were heard; several fidgeted; fresh cigarettes were lighted. But there was no sign of boredom, for where one or two Russians are gathered together there is always life. They produce gaiety and enthusiasm as wind produces waves. Like great children, they plunge whole-heartedly into whatever interest presents itself at the moment. There is a kind of uncouth gambolling in their way of taking life. It seems as if they are always fighting that deep, underlying, national sadness which creeps into their very blood.

"Midnight!" then exclaimed Palazov, abruptly, looking at his watch; and the others fell instantly to talking about that watch, admiring it and asking questions. For the moment that very ordinary timepiece became the centre of observation. Palazov mentioned the price. "It never stops," he said proudly, "not even under water." He looked up at everybody, challenging admiration. And he told how, at a country house, he made a bet that he would swim to a certain island in the lake, and won the bet. He and a girl were the winners, but as it was a horse they had bet, he got nothing out of it for himself, giving the horse to her. It was a genuine grievance in him. One felt he could have cried as he spoke of it. "But the watch went all the time," he said delightedly, holding the gun-metal object in his hand to show, "and I was twelve minutes in the water with my clothes on."

Yet this fragmentary talk was nothing but pretence. The sound of clicking billiard-balls was audible from the room at the end of the corridor. There was another pause. The pause, however, was intentional. It was not vacuity of mind or absence of ideas that caused it. There was another subject, an unfinished subject that each member of the group was still considering. Only no one cared to begin about it till at last, unable to resist the strain any longer, Palazov turned to Khilkoff, who was saying he would take a "whisky-soda," as the champagne was too sweet, and whispered something beneath his breath; whereupon Khilkoff, forgetting his drink, glanced at his sister, shrugged his shoulders, and made a curious grimace. "He's all right now"—his reply was just audible—"he's with Plitzinger." He cocked his head sidewise to indicate that the clicking of the billiard-balls still was going on.

The subject was out: all turned their heads; voices hummed and buzzed; questions were asked and answered or half answered; eyebrows were raised, shoulders shrugged, hands spread out expressively. There came into the atmosphere a feeling of presentiment, of mystery, of things half understood; primitive, buried instinct stirred a little, the kind of racial dread of vague emotions that might gain the upper hand if encouraged. They shrank from looking something in the face, while yet this unwelcome influence drew closer round them all. They discussed Binovitch and his astonishing performance. Pretty little Vera listened with large and troubled eyes, though saying nothing. The Arab waiter had put out the lights in the corridor, and only a solitary cluster burned now above their heads, leaving their faces in shadow. In the distance the clicking of the billiard-balls still continued.

"It was not play; it was real," exclaimed Minski vehemently. "I can catch wolves," he blurted; "but birds—ugh!—and human birds!" He was half inarticulate. He had witnessed something he could not understand, and it had touched instinctive terror in him. "It was the way he leaped that put the wolf first into my mind, only it was not a wolf at all." The others agreed and disagreed. "It was play at first, but it was reality at the end," another whispered; "and it was no animal he mimicked, but a bird, and a bird of prey at that!"

Vera thrilled. In the Russian woman hides that touch of savagery which loves to be caught, mastered, swept helplessly away, captured utterly and deliciously by the one strong enough to do it thoroughly. She left her chair and sat down beside an older woman in the party, who took her arm quietly at once. Her little face wore a perplexed expression, mournful, yet somehow wild. It was clear that Binovitch was not indifferent to her.

"It's become an *idée fixe* with him," this older woman said. "The bird idea lives in his mind. He lives it in his imagination. Ever since that time at Edfu, when he pretended to worship the great stone falcons outside the temple—the Horus figures—he's been full of it." She stopped. The way Binovitch had behaved at Edfu was better left unmentioned at the moment, perhaps. A slight shiver ran round the listening group, each one waiting for some one else to focus their emotion, and so explain it by saying the convincing thing. Only no one ventured. Then Vera abruptly gave a little jump.

"Hark!" she exclaimed, in a staccato whisper, speaking for the first time. She sat bolt upright. She was listening. "Hark!" she repeated. "There it is again, but nearer than before. It's coming closer. I hear it." She trembled. Her voice, her manner, above all her great staring eyes, startled everybody. No one spoke for several seconds; all listened. The clicking of the billiard-balls had ceased. The halls and corridors lay in darkness, and gloom was over the big hotel. Everybody was in bed.

"Hear what?" asked the older woman soothingly, yet with a perceptible quaver in her voice, too. She was aware that the girl's arm shook upon her own.

"Do you not hear it, too?" the girl whispered.

All listened without speaking. All watched her paling face. Something wonderful, yet half terrible, seemed in the air about them. There was a dull murmur, audible, faint, remote, its direction hard to tell. It had come suddenly from nowhere. They shivered. That strange racial thrill again passed into the group, unwelcome, unexplained. It was aboriginal; it belonged to the unconscious primitive mind, half childish, half terrifying.

"*What* do you hear?" her brother asked angrily—the irritable anger of nervous fear.

"When he came at me," she answered very low, "I heard it first. I hear it now again. Listen! He's coming."

And at that minute, out of the dark mouth of the corridor, emerged two human figures, Plitzinger and Binovitch. Their game was over; they were going up to bed. They passed the open door of the card-room. But Binovitch was being half dragged, half restrained, for he was apparently attempting to run down the passage with flying, dancing leaps. He bounded. It was like a huge bird trying to rise for flight, while his companion kept him down by force upon the earth. As they entered the strip of light, Plitzinger changed his own position, placing himself swiftly between his companion and the group in the dark corner of the room. He hurried Binovitch along as though he sheltered him from view. They passed into the shadows down the passage. They disappeared. And every one looked significantly, questioningly, at his neighbour, though at first saying no word. It seemed that a curious disturbance of the air had followed them audibly.

Vera was the first to open her lips. "You heard it *then*," she said breathlessly, her face whiter than the ceiling.

"Damn!" exclaimed her brother furiously. "It was wind against the outside walls—wind in the desert. The sand is driving."

Vera looked at him. She shrank closer against the side of the older woman, whose arm was tight about her.

"It was *not* wind," she whispered simply. She paused. All waited uneasily for the completion of her sentence. They stared into her face like peasants who expected a miracle.

"Wings," she whispered. "It was the sound of enormous wings."

And at four o'clock in the morning, when they all returned exhausted from their excursion into the desert, little Binovitch was sleeping soundly and peacefully in his bed. They passed his door on tiptoe. But he did not hear them. He was dreaming. His spirit was at Edfu, experiencing with that ancient deity who was master of all flying life those strange enjoyments upon which his own troubled human heart was passionately set. Safe with that mighty falcon whose powers his lips had scorned a few hours before, his soul, released in vivid dream, went sweetly flying. It was amazing, it was gorgeous. He skimmed the Nile at lightning speed. Dashing down headlong from the height of the great Pyramid, he chased with faultless accuracy a little dove that sought vainly to hide from his terrific pursuit beneath the palm trees. For what he loved must worship where he worshipped, and the majesty of those tremendous effigies had fired his imagination to the creative point where expression was imperative.

Then suddenly, at the very moment of delicious capture, the dream turned horrible, becoming awful with the nightmare touch. The sky lost all its blue and sunshine. Far, far below him the little dove enticed him into nameless depths, so that he flew faster and faster, yet never fast enough to overtake it. Behind him came a great thing down the air, black, hovering, with gigantic wings outstretched. It had terrific eyes, and the beating of its feathers stole his wind away. It followed him, crowding space. He was aware of a colossal beak, curved like a scimitar and pointed wickedly like a tooth of iron. He dropped. He faltered. He tried to scream.

Through empty space he fell, caught by the neck. The huge spectral falcon was upon him. The talons were in his heart. And in sleep he remembered then that he had cursed. He recalled his reckless language. The curse of the ignorant is meaningless; that of the worshipper is real. This attack was on his soul. He had invoked it. He realised next, with a touch of ghastly horror, that the dove he chased was, after all, the bait that had lured him purposely to destruction, and awoke with a suffocating terror upon him, and his entire body bathed in icy perspiration. Outside the open window he heard a sound of wings retreating with powerful strokes into the surrounding darkness of the sky.

The nightmare made its impression upon Binovitch's impressionable and dramatic temperament. It aggravated his tendencies. He related it next day to Mme. de Drühn, the friend of Vera, telling it with that somewhat boisterous laughter some minds use to disguise less kind emotions. But he received no encouragement. The mood of the previous night was not recoverable; it was already ancient history. Russians never make the banal mistake of repeating a sensation till it is exhausted; they hurry on to novelties. Life flashes and rushes with them, never standing still for exposure before the cameras of their minds. Mme. de Drühn, however, took the trouble to mention the matter to Plitzinger, for Plitzinger, like Freud of Vienna, held that dreams revealed subconscious tendencies which sooner or later must betray themselves in action.

"Thank you for telling me," he smiled politely, "but I have already heard it from him." He watched her eyes for a moment, really examining her soul. "Binovitch, you see," he continued, apparently satisfied with what he saw, "I regard as that rare phenomenon—a genius without an outlet. His spirit, intensely creative, finds no adequate expression. His power of production is enormous and prolific; yet he accomplishes nothing." He paused an instant. "Binovitch, therefore, is in danger of poisoning—himself." He looked steadily into her face, as a man who weighs how much he may confide. "Now," he continued, "*if* we can find an outlet for him, a field wherein his bursting imaginative genius can produce results—above all, *visible* results"—he shrugged his shoulders—"the man is saved. Otherwise"—he looked extraordinarily impressive—"there is bound to be sooner or later—"

"Madness?" she asked very quietly.

"An explosion, let us say," he replied gravely. "For instance, take this Horus obsession of his, quite wrong archæologically though it is. *Au fond* it is megalomania of a most unusual kind. His passionate interest, his love, his worship of birds, wholesome enough in itself, finds no satisfying outlet. A man who *really* loves birds neither keeps them in cages nor shoots them nor stuffs them. What, then, can he do? The commonplace bird-lover observes them through glasses, studies their habits, then writes a book about them. But a man like Binovitch, overflowing with this intense creative power of mind and imagination, is not content with that. He wants to know them from within. He wants to feel what they feel, to live their life. He wants to *become* them. You follow me? Not quite. Well, he seeks to be identified with the object of his sacred, passionate adoration. All genius seeks to know the thing itself from its own point of view. It desires union.

That tendency, unrecognised by himself, perhaps, and therefore subconscious, hides in his very soul." He paused a moment. "And the sudden sight of those majestic figures at Edfu—that crystallisation of his *idée fixe* in granite—took hold of this excess in him, so to speak—and is now focusing it toward some definite act. Binovitch sometimes—feels himself a bird! You noticed what occurred last night?"

She nodded; a slight shiver passed over her.

"A most curious performance," she murmured; "an exhibition I never want to see again."

"The most curious part," replied the doctor coolly, "was its truth."

"Its truth!" she exclaimed beneath her breath. She was frightened by something in his voice and by the uncommon gravity in his eyes. It seemed to arrest her intelligence. She felt upon the edge of things beyond her. "You mean that Binovitch did for a moment—hang—in the air?" The other verb, the right one, she could not bring herself to use.

The great man's face was enigmatical. He talked to her sympathy, perhaps, rather than to her mind.

"Real genius," he said smilingly, "is as rare as talent, even great talent, is common. It means that the personality, if only for one second, becomes everything; becomes the universe; becomes the soul of the world. It gets the flash. It is identified with the universal life. Being everything and everywhere, all is possible to it—in that second of vivid realisation. It can brood with the crystal, grow with the plant, leap with the animal, fly with the bird: genius unifies all three. That is the meaning of 'creative.' It is faith. Knowing it, you can pass through fire and not be burned, walk on water and not sink, move a mountain, fly. Because you *are* fire, water, earth, air. Genius, you see, is madness in the magnificent sense of being superhuman. Binovitch has it."

He broke off abruptly, seeing he was not understood. Some great enthusiasm in him he deliberately suppressed.

"The point is," he resumed, speaking more carefully, "that we must try to lead this passionate constructive genius of the man into some human channel that will absorb it, and therefore render it harmless."

"He loves Vera," the woman said, bewildered, yet seizing this point correctly.

"But would he marry her?" asked Plitzinger at once.

"He is already married."

The doctor looked steadily at her a moment, hesitating whether he should utter all his thought.

"In that case," he said slowly after a pause, "it is better he or she should leave."

His tone and manner were exceedingly impressive.

"You mean there's danger?" she asked.

"I mean, rather," he replied earnestly, "that this great creative flood in him, so curiously focused now upon his Horus-falcon-bird idea, may result in some act of violence—"

"Which would be madness," she said, looking hard at him.

"Which would be disastrous," he corrected her. And then he added slowly: "Because in the mental moment of immense creation he might overlook material laws."

The costume ball two nights later was a great success. Palazov was a Bedouin, and Khilkoff an Apache; Mme. de Drühn wore a national head-dress; Minski looked almost natural as Don Quixote; and the entire Russian "set" was cleverly, if somewhat extravagantly, dressed. But Binovitch and Vera were the most successful of all the two hundred dancers who took part. Another figure, a big man dressed as a Pierrot, also claimed exceptional attention, for though the costume was commonplace enough, there was something of dignity in his appearance that drew the eyes of all upon him. But he wore a mask, and his identity was not discoverable.

It was Binovitch and Vera, however, who must have won the prize, if prize there had been, for they not only looked their parts, but acted them as well. The former in his dark grey feather tunic, and his falcon mask, complete even to the brown hooked beak and tufted talons, looked fierce and splendid. The disguise was so admirable, yet so entirely natural, that it was uncommonly seductive. Vera, in blue and gold, a charming head-dress of a dove upon her loosened hair, and a pair of little dove-pale wings fluttering from her shoulders, her tiny twinkling feet and slender ankles well visible, too, was equally successful and admired. Her large and timid eyes, her flitting movements, her light and dainty way of dancing—all added touches that made the picture perfect.

How Binovitch contrived his dress remained a mystery, for the layers of wings upon his back were real; the large black kites that haunt the Nile, soaring in their hundreds over Cairo and the bleak Mokattam Hills, had furnished them. He had procured them none knew how. They measured four feet across from tip to tip; they swished and rustled as he swept along; they were, true falcons' wings. He danced with Nautch-girls and Egyptian princesses and Rumanian Gipsies; he danced well, with beauty, grace, and lightness. But with Vera he did not dance at all; with her he simply flew. A kind of passionate abandon was in him as he skimmed the floor with her in a way that made everybody turn to watch them. They seemed to leave the ground together. It was delightful, an amazing sight; but it was peculiar. The strangeness of it was on many lips. Somehow its queer extravagance communicated itself to the entire ball-room. They became the centre of observation. There were whispers.

"There's that extraordinary bird-man! Look! He goes by like a hawk. And he's always after that dove-girl. How marvellously he does it! It's rather awful. Who is he? I don't envy *her*."

People stood aside when he rushed past. They got out of his way. He seemed forever pursuing Vera, even when dancing with another partner.

Word passed from mouth to mouth. A kind of telepathic interest was established everywhere. It was a shade too real sometimes, something unduly earnest in the chasing wildness, something unpleasant. There was even alarm.

"It's rowdy; I'd rather not see it; it's quite disgraceful," was heard. "I think it's horrible; you can see she's terrified."

And once there was a little scene, trivial enough, yet betraying this reality that many noticed and disliked. Binovitch came up to claim a dance, programme clutched in his great tufted claws, and at the same moment the big Pierrot appeared abruptly round the corner with a similar claim. Those who saw it assert he had been waiting, and came on purpose, and that there was something protective and authoritative in his bearing. The misunderstanding was ordinary enough—both men had written her name against the dance—but "No. 13, Tango" also included the supper interval, and neither Hawk nor Pierrot would give way. They were very obstinate. Both men wanted her. It was awkward.

"The Dove shall decide between us," smiled the Hawk politely, yet his taloned fingers working nervously. Pierrot, however, more experienced in the ways of dealing with women, or more bold, said suavely:

"I am ready to abide by her decision"—his voice poorly cloaked this aggravating authority, as though he had the right to her—"only I engaged this dance before his Majesty Horus appeared upon the scene at all, and therefore it is clear that Pierrot has the right of way."

At once, with a masterful air, he took her off. There was no withstanding him. He meant to have her and he got her. She yielded meekly. They vanished among the maze of coloured dancers, leaving the Hawk, disconsolate and vanquished, amid the titters of the onlookers. His swiftness, as against this steady power, was of no avail.

It was then that the singular phenomenon was witnessed first. Those who saw it affirm that he changed absolutely into the part he played. It was dreadful; it was wicked. A frightened whisper ran about the rooms and corridors:

"An extraordinary thing is in the air!"

Some shrank away, while others flocked to see. There were those who swore that a curious, rushing sound was audible, the atmosphere visibly disturbed and shaken; that a shadow fell upon the spot the couple had vacated; that a cry was heard, a high, wild, searching cry: "Horus! bright deity of wind," it began, then died away. One man was positive that the windows had been opened and that something had flown in. It was the obvious explanation. The thing spread horribly. As in a fire-panic, there was consternation and excitement. Confusion caught the feet of all the dancers. The music fumbled and lost time. The leading pair of tango dancers halted and looked round. It seemed that everybody pressed back, hiding, shuffling, eager to see, yet more eager not to be seen, as though something dangerous, hostile, terrible, had broken loose. In rows against the wall they stood. For a great space had made itself in the middle of the ball-room, and into this empty space appeared suddenly the Pierrot and the Dove.

It was like a challenge. A sound of applause, half voices, half clapping of gloved hands, was heard. The couple danced exquisitely into the arena. All stared. There was an impression that a set piece had been prepared, and that this was its beginning. The music again took heart. Pierrot was strong and dignified, no whit nonplussed by this abrupt publicity. The Dove, though faltering, was deliciously obedient. They danced together like a single outline. She was captured utterly. And to the man who needed her the sight was naturally agonising—the protective way the Pierrot held her, the right and strength of it, the mastery, the complete possession.

"He's got her!" some one breathed too loud, uttering the thought of all. "Good thing it's not the Hawk!"

And, to the absolute amazement of the throng, this sight was then apparent. A figure dropped through space. That high, shrill cry again was heard:

"Feather my soul... to know thy awful swiftness!"

Its singing loveliness touched the heart, its appealing, passionate sweetness was marvellous, as from the gallery this figure of a man, dressed as
a strong, dark bird, shot down with splendid grace and ease. The feathers
swept; the wings spread out as sails that take the wind. Like a hawk that
darts with unerring power and aim upon its prey, this thing of mighty
wings rushed down into the empty space where the two danced. Observed
by all, he entered, swooping beautifully, stretching his wings like any eagle.
He dropped. He fixed his point of landing with consummate skill close
beside the astonished dancers. He landed.

It happened with such swiftness it brought the dazzle and blindness as
when lightning strikes. People in different parts of the room saw different
details; a few saw nothing at all after the first startling shock, closing
their eyes, or holding their arms before their faces as in self-protection.
The touch of panic fear caught the entire room. The nameless thing
that all the evening had been vaguely felt was come. It had suddenly
materialised.

For this incredible thing occurred in the full blaze of light upon the
open floor. Binovitch, grown in some sense formidable, opened his dark,
big wings about the girl. The long grey feathers moved, causing powerful
draughts of wind that made a rushing sound. An aspect of the terrible
was about him, like an emanation. The great beaked head was poised
to strike, the tufted claws were raised like fingers that shut and opened,
and the whole presentment of his amazing figure focused in an attitude
of attack that was magnificent and terrible. No one who saw it doubted.
Yet there were those who swore that it was not Binovitch at all, but that
another outline, monstrous and shadowy, towered above him, draping his
lesser proportions with two colossal wings of darkness. That some touch
of strange divinity lay in it may be claimed, however confused the wild
descriptions afterward. For many lowered their heads and bowed their

shoulders. There was terror. There was also awe. The onlookers swayed as though some power passed over them through the air.

A sound of wings was certainly in the room.

Then some one screamed; a shriek broke high and clear; and emotion, ordinary human emotion, unaccustomed to terrific things, swept loose. The Hawk and Vera flew. Beaten back against the wall as by a stroke of whirlwind, the Pierrot staggered. He watched them go. Out of the lighted room they flew, out of the crowded human atmosphere, out of the heat and artificial light, the walled-in, airless halls that were a cage. All this they left behind. They seemed things of wind and air, made free happily of another element. Earth held them not. Toward the open night they raced with this extraordinary lightness as of birds, down the long corridor and on to the southern terrace, where great coloured curtains were hung suspended from the columns. A moment they were visible. Then the fringe of one huge curtain, lifted by the wind, showed their dark outline for a second against the starry sky. There was a cry, a leap. The curtain flapped again and closed. They vanished. And into the ball-room swept the cold draught of night air from the desert.

But three figures instantly were close upon their heels. The throng of half-dazed, half-stupefied onlookers, it seemed, projected them as though by some explosive force. The general mass held back, but, like projectiles, these three flung themselves after the fugitives down the corridor at high speed—the Apache, Don Quixote, and, last of them, the Pierrot. For Khilkoff, the brother, and Baron Minski, the man who caught wolves alive, had been for some time keenly on the watch, while Dr. Plitzinger, reading the symptoms clearly, never far away, had been faithfully observant of every movement. His mask tossed aside, the great psychiatrist was now recognised by all. They reached the parapet just as the curtain flapped back heavily into place; the next second all three were out of sight behind it. Khilkoff was first, however, urged forward at frantic speed by the warning words the doctor had whispered as they ran. Some thirty yards beyond the terrace was the brink of the crumbling cliff on which the great hotel was built, and there was a drop of sixty feet to the desert floor below. Only a low stone wall marked the edge.

Accounts varied. Khilkoff, it seems, arrived in time—in the nick of time—to seize his sister, virtually hovering on the brink. He heard the loose stones strike the sand below. There was no struggle, though it appears she did not thank him for his interference at first. In a sense she was beside—outside—herself. And he did a characteristic thing: he not only brought her back into the ball-room, but he *danced* her back. It was admirable. Nothing could have calmed the general excitement better. The pair of them danced in together as though nothing was amiss. Accustomed to the strenuous practice of his Cossack regiment, this young cavalry officer's muscles were equal to the semi-dead weight in his arms. At most the onlookers thought her tired, perhaps. Confidence was restored—such is the psychology of a crowd—and in the middle of a thrilling Viennese waltz he easily smuggled her out of the room, administered brandy, and got her up to bed. The absence of the Hawk, meanwhile, was hardly noticed; comments were made and then forgotten; it was Vera in whom the strange, anxious sympathy had centred. And, with her obvious safety, the moment of primitive, childish panic passed away. Don Quixote, too, was presently seen dancing gaily as though nothing untoward had happened; supper intervened; the incident was over; it had melted into the general wildness of the evening's irresponsibility. The fact that Pierrot did not appear again was noticed by no single person.

But Dr. Plitzinger was otherwise engaged, his heart and mind and soul all deeply exercised. A death-certificate is not always made out quite so simply as the public thinks. That Binovitch had died of suffocation in his swift descent through merely sixty feet of air was not conceivable; yet that his body lay so neatly placed upon the desert after such a fall was stranger still. It was not crumpled, it was not torn; no single bone was broken, no muscle wrenched; there was no bruise. There was no indenture in the sand. The figure lay sidewise as though in sleep, no sign of violence visible anywhere, the dark wings folded as a great bird folds them when it creeps away to die in loneliness. Beneath the Horus mask the face was smiling. It seemed he had floated into death upon the element he loved. And only Vera had seen the enormous wings that, hovering invitingly above the dark abyss, bore him so softly into another world. Plitzinger, that is, saw them, too, but he said firmly that they belonged to the big black falcons that haunt the Mokattam Hills and roost upon these ridges, close beside the hotel, at night. Both he and Vera, however, agreed on one thing: the high, sharp cry in the air above them, wild and plaintive, was certainly the black kite's cry—the note of the falcon that passionately seeks its mate. It was the pause of a second, when she stood to listen, that made her rescue possible. A moment later and she, too, would have flown to death with Binovitch.

ONANONANON

When the First World War broke out in July 1914 Blackwood offered his services as an interpreter, since he was fluent in both French and German. Needless to say the authorities dithered and Blackwood heard nothing. He also offered his services to write propaganda and when nothing was confirmed he did it anyway, writing short pieces for various newspapers encouraging enlistment and reminding people of the beauty of the old world and what we were fighting for.

Whilst he waited to be summoned Blackwood continued to write, completing his children's book The Extra Day, *finishing* Julius Le Vallon *and* The Wave, *and working with Violet Pearn on the adaptation of* A Prisoner in Fairyland *for the stage as* The Starlight Express. *This ran at the Kingsway Theatre in London during the Christmas and New Year season in 1915/16 with music composed by Sir Edward Elgar. The music was a greater success than the play, and Blackwood felt it had never received due recognition. He tried for the rest of his life to get a new production, without success.*

As is so often the case, after Blackwood had waited two years to see what War work he could do, everything happened at once. He was preparing to work with the Field Ambulance Service during August 1916 when he was summoned by Military Intelligence. He met with Colonel Wallinger in London and was assigned to undertake secret service work in Switzerland. Unknown to Blackwood at the time, this operation in Switzerland had become very disorganised. The work involved rendezvousing with various agents, gathering their information, which had to be passed on to London, paying the agents and recruiting new ones. It had worked reasonably well when W. Somerset Maugham was assigned but he soon grew tired and resigned in February 1916. He fictionalised his experiences in Ashenden. *His successor was the American playwright Edward Knoblock, but he was not as fluent as Maugham in French or German and by July 1916 it was deemed that the operations should be wound down. Wallinger wanted to give it one last chance and recruited Blackwood. He was, after all, not only fluent in the languages but well known in Switzerland and had the perfect cover as a writer. Blackwood left for Switzerland in November 1916, his usual time, which would attract no suspicion. He first went to Montreux but was told his contact was dead and that the hotel was now run by a German. He retreated to Champéry where he lay low before returning to Montreux. His code name was Baker, which we encounter in the following story.*

Blackwood hated the work. He often felt he was sending the agents into danger and was overwhelmed by his usual guilt. But his instincts for under-standing individuals and their motives held him in good stead. He managed to avoid a double agent and minimised contact with another agent sent from London who acted as if the operation was a game. After six months Blackwood could cope no more and he resigned. The memories of his activities haunted him for years, with recurring nightmares, which he captured in the following story.

CERTAIN things had made a deep impression in his childhood days; among these was the incident of the barking dog.

It barked during his convalescence from something that involved scarlet and a peeling skin; his early mind associated bright colour and peeling skin with the distress of illness. The tiresome barking of a dog accompanied it. In later years this sound always brought back the childhood visualisation: across his mind would flit a streak of vivid colour, a peeling skin, a noisy dog, all set against a background of emotional discomfort and physical distress.

"It's barking at *me*!" he complained to his old nurse, whose explanation that it was "Carlo with his rheumatics in the stables" brought no relief. He spoke to his mother later: "It never, never stops. It goes on and on and on on purpose—onanonanon!"

How queer the words sounded! He had got them wrong somewhere—onanonanon. Or was it a name, the name of the barking animal—Onan Onan Onanonanon?

His mother's words were more comforting: "Carlo's barking because you're ill, darling; he wants you to get well." And she added: "Soon I'll bring him in to see you. You shall ride on his back again."

"Would he peel if I stroked him?" he enquired, a trifle frightened. "Is the skin shiny like mine?"

She shook her head and smiled. "I'll explain to him," she went on, "and then he'll understand. He won't bark any more." She brought the picture-book of natural history that included all creatures in Ark and Zoo and Jungle. He picked out the brightly-coloured tiger.

"A *tiger* doesn't bark, does it?" he asked, and her reply added slightly to his knowledge, but much to his imagination. "But does it ever *bark?*" he persisted. "That's really what I asked."

"Growls and snarls," said a deep voice from the doorway. He started; but it was only his father, who then came in and amused him by imitating the sound a tiger makes, until Carlo's naughtiness was forgotten, and the world went on turning smoothly as before.

After that the barking ceased; the rheumatic creature sniffed the air and nosed the metal biscuit tray in silence. He understood apparently. It had been rather dreadful, this noise he made. The sharp sound had broken the morning stillness for many days; no one but the boy was awake at that early hour; the boy and the dog had the dawn entirely to themselves. He used to lie in bed, counting the number of barks. They seemed endless, they jarred, they never stopped. They came singly, then in groups of three and four at a time, then in a longer series, then singly again. These single barks often had a sound of finality about them, the creature's breath was giving out, it was tired; it was the full-stop sound. But the true full-stop, the final bark, never came—and the boy had complained.

He loved old Carlo, loved riding on his burly back that wobbled from side to side, as they moved forward very slowly; in particular he loved stroking the thick curly hair; it tickled his fingers and felt nice on his palm. He was relieved to know it would not peel. Yet he wondered impatiently why the creature he loved to play with should go on making such a dreadful noise. "Doesn't he know? Can't he wait till I'm ready?" There were moments when he doubted if it really was Carlo,, when he almost hated the beast, when he asked himself, "Is this Carlo, or is it Onanonanon…?" The idea alarmed him rather. Onanonanon was not quite friendly, not quite safe.

* *

At the age of fifty he found himself serving his King during the Great War—in a neutral country whose police regarded him with disfavour, and would have instantly arrested and clapped him into gaol, had he made a slip. He did not make this slip, though incessant caution had to be his watchword. He belonged to that service which runs risks yet dare claim no credit. He passed under another name than his own, and his *alias* sometimes did things his true self would not do. This *alter ego* developed oddly. He projected temporarily, as it were, a secondary personality—which he disliked, often despised, and sometimes even feared. His sense of humour, however, made light of the split involved. When he was followed, he used to chuckle: "I wonder if the sleuths know which of the two they're tracking down—myself or my *alias*?"

It was in the melancholy season between autumn and winter, snow on the heights and fog upon the lower levels, when he was suddenly laid low by the plague that milked the world. The Spanish influenza caught him. He went to bed; he had a doctor and a nurse; no one else in the hotel came near his room; the police forgot him, and he forgot the police. His hated *alias*, Baker, also was forgotten, or perhaps merged back into the parent self... Outside his quarters on the first floor the plane-trees shed their heavy, rain-soaked leaves, letting them fall with an audible plop upon the gravel path; he heard the waves of the sullen lake in the distance; the crunching of passing feet he heard much closer. The heating was indifferent, the light too weak to read by. It was a lonely, dismal time. On the floor above two people died, three on the one below, the French officer next door was carried out. The hotel, like many others, became a hospital.

In due course, the fever passed, the intolerable aching ceased, he forgot the times when he had thought he was going to die. He lay, half convalescent, remembering the recent past, then the remoter past, and so slipped back to dim childhood scenes when the cross but faithful old nurse had tended him. He smelt the burning leaves in the kitchen-garden, and heard the blackbird whistle beyond the summer-house. The odour of moist earth in the tool-house stole back, with the fragrance of sweet apples in the forbidden loft. These earliest layers of memory fluttered their ghostly pictures like a cinema before his receptive mind. There were eyes long closed, voices long silent, the touch of hands long dead and gone. The rose-garden on a sultry August afternoon was vivid, with the smell of the rain-washed petals, as the sun blazed over them after a heavy shower. The soaked lawn emitted warm little bubbles like a soft squeezed sponge, audibly; even the gravel steamed. He remembered Carlo, with his rheumatism, his awkward gambol, his squashy dog-biscuit beside the kennel and—his bark.

In the state of semi-unconsciousness he lay, weary, weak, depressed and very lonely. The nurse, on her rare visits, afflicted him, the hotel guests did not ask after him. To the Service at home he was on the sick-list, useless. The morning newspaper and the hurried, perfunctory visits of the doctor were his only interest. It seemed a pity he had not died. The mental depression after influenza can be extremely devastating. He looked forward to nothing.

Then, suddenly, the dog began its barking.

He heard it first at six o'clock when, waking, hot and thirsty in a bed that had lost its comfort, he wondered vaguely if the day was going to be fine or wet. His window opened on to the lake. He watched the shadows melt across the dreary room. The late dawn came softly, its hint of beauty ever unfulfilled. Would it be gold or grey behind the mountains? The dog went on barking.

He dozed, counting the barks without being aware that he did so. He felt hot and uncomfortable, and turned over in bed, counting automatically as he did so: "fifteen, sixteen, seventeen"—pause—"eighteen, nineteen"—another pause, then with great rapidity, "twenty, twenty-one, twenty-two, twenty-three—". He opened his eyes wide and cursed aloud. The barking stopped.

The wind came softly off the lake, entering the room. He heard the last big leaf of the plane-trees rattle to the gravel path. As it touched the ground the barking began again, his counting—now conscious counting—began with it.

"Curse the brute!" he muttered, and turned over once more to try and sleep. The rasping, harsh, staccato sound reached his ears piercingly through sheets and blankets; not even the thick *duvet* could muffle it. Would no one stop it? Did no one care? He felt furious, but helpless, dreadfully helpless.

It barked, stopped, then barked again. There were solitary, isolated barks, followed by a rapid series, short and hurried. A shower of barks came next. Pauses were frequent, but they were worse than the actual sound. It continued, it went on, the dog barked without ceasing. It barked and barked. He had lost all count. It barked and barked and barked. It stopped.

"At last!" he groaned. "My God! Another minute, and I—!"

His whole body, as he turned over, knew an immense, deep relaxation. His jangled nerves were utterly exhausted. A great sigh of relief escaped him. The silence was delicious. It was real silence. He rested at last. Sleep, warm and intoxicating, stole gently back. He dozed. Forgetfulness swam over him. He lay in down, in cotton-wool. Police, *alias*, nurse and loneliness were all obliterated, when, suddenly, across the blissful peace, cracked out that sharp, explosive sound again—the bark.

But the dog barked differently this time; the sound was much nearer. At first this puzzled him. Then he guessed the truth; the animal had come into the hotel and up the stairs; it was outside in the passage. He opened his eyes and sat up in bed. The door, to his surprise, was being cautiously pushed ajar. He was just in time to see who pushed it with such gentle, careful pressure. Standing on the landing in the early twilight was Baker, his other self, his *alias*, the personality he disliked and sometimes dreaded. Baker put his head round the corner, glanced at him, nodded familiarly, and withdrew, closing the door instantly, making no slightest sound. But, before it closed, and before he had time even to feel astonishment, the dog had been let in. And the dog, he saw at once, was old Carlo!

Having expected a little stranger dog, this big, shaggy, familiar beast caused him to feel a sense of curious wonder and bewilderment.

"But were *you* the dog down there that barked?" he asked aloud, as the friendly creature came waddling up to the bedside. "And have you come to say you're sorry?"

It blinked its rheumy eyes and wagged its stumpy tail. He put out his hand and stroked its familiar, wobbly back. His fingers buried themselves in the stiff crinkly hair. Its dim old eyes turned affectionately up at him. It smiled its silly, happy smile. He went on rubbing. "Carlo, good old Carlo!" he mumbled; "well, I'm blessed! I'll get on your back in a minute and ride—"

He stopped rubbing. "*Why* did you come in?" he asked abruptly, and repeated the question, a touch of anxiety in his voice. "How did you manage it, really? Tell me, Carlo?"

The old beast shifted its position a little, making a sideways motion that he did not like. It seemed to move its hind legs only. Its muzzle now rested on the bed. Its eyes, seen full, looked not quite so kind and friendly. They cleared a little. But its tail still wagged. Only, now that he saw it better, the tail seemed longer than it ought to have been. There was something unpleasant about the dog—a faint inexplicable shade of difference. He stared a moment straight into its face. It no longer blinked in the silly, affectionate way as at first. The rheum was less. There was a light, a gleam, in the eyes, almost a flash.

"*Are* you—Carlo?" he asked sharply, uneasily, "or are you— Onanonanon?"

It rose abruptly on its hind legs, laying the front paws on the counterpane of faded yellow. The legs made dark streaks against this yellow.

He had begun stroking the old back again. He now stopped. He withdrew his hand. The hair was coming out. It came off beneath his fingers, and each stroke he made left a line of lighter skin behind it. This skin was yellowish, with a slight tinge, he thought, of scarlet.

The dog—he could almost swear to it—had altered; it was still altering. Before his very eyes, it grew, became curiously enlarged. It now towered over him. It was longer, thinner, leaner than before, its tail came lashing round its hollow, yellowing flanks, the eyes shone brilliantly, its tongue was a horrid red. The brute straightened its front paws. It was huge. Its open mouth grinned down at him.

He was petrified with terror. He tried to scream, but the only sound that came were little innocent words of childhood days. He almost lisped them, simpering with horror: "I'd get on your back—if I was allowed out of bed. You'd carry me. I'd ride."

It was a desperate attempt to pacify the beast, to persuade it, even in this terrible moment, to be friendly, a feeble, hopeless attempt to convince *himself* that it was—Carlo. The Monster was twelve feet from head to tail, of dull yellow striped with black. The great jaws, wide open, dripped upon his face. He saw the pointed teeth, the stiff, quivering whiskers of white wire. He felt the hot breath upon his cheeks and lips. It was fœtid. He tasted it.

He was on the point of fainting when a step sounded outside the door. Someone was coming.

"Saved!" he gasped.

The suspense and relief were almost intolerable. The touch of a hand feeling cautiously, stealthily, over the door was audible. The handle rattled faintly.

"Saved!" his heart repeated, as the great brute turned its giant head to listen.

He knew that touch. It was Baker, his hated *alias*, come in the nick of time to rescue him. Yet the door did not open. Instead, the monster lashed its tail, it stiffened horribly, it turned its head back from watching the door, and lowered itself appallingly. The key turned in the lock, a bolt was shot. He was locked in alone with a tiger. He closed his eyes.

His recurrent nightmare had ruined sleep again, and outside, in the dreary autumn dawn, a little dog was yapping fiendishly on and on and on and on.

THE LITTLE BEGGAR

As it happened Blackwood's role as a secret agent did not end there. When he returned to England he was appointed as a Searcher for the British Red Cross and served in France from February to June 1918. This affected him as much as his agent's work because of all the suffering he witnessed. When he returned home he felt he had unfinished business in Switzerland because when he had left the previous year he had made contact with an English lady who was married to a German officer and whom Blackwood believed could impart further information. It was agreed to send him back, and he dutifully returned in July 1918, remaining in Switzerland till October.

The war sucked Blackwood dry and he was never again able to write with such spiritual affinity as he had ten years before. A melancholy settled over him as he reached his fiftieth birthday. Baron Knoop had died the previous year, but Maya was not free, because the Baron's will had stipulated that the annuity he left her would cease the moment she married. Blackwood could offer her no such financial certainty. Instead she married a wealthy industrialist who was even richer than the Baron and they settled in a house in Kent that Maya promptly converted into an Italianate villa. Blackwood remained in contact but the spark between them was now extinguished.

It caused Blackwood to reflect on his life. He had always adored children and felt a closer rapport with them than with many adults. He had a six-year-old nephew, Patrick, whom he felt obliged to look after when his brother, Stevie, died in June 1917. There were also three Polish refugees whom Maya *had unofficially adopted during the War and whom he frequently played with whenever he could. He was also friends with the actor Henry Ainley and became almost a surrogate father to his children Henry, Jr. (usually called Sam) and Patsy. But with no children of his own Blackwood pondered on what might have been, out of which grew the following story.*

H E was on his way from his bachelor flat to the club, a man of middle age with a slight stoop, and an expression of face firm yet gentle, the blue eyes with light and courage in them, and a faint hint of melancholy—or was it resignation?—about the strong mouth. It was early in April, a slight drizzle of warm rain falling through the coming dusk; but spring was in the air, a bird sang rapturously on a pavement tree. And the man's heart wakened at the sound, for it was the lift of the year, and low in the western sky above the London roofs there was a band of tender colour.

His way led him past one of the great terminal stations that open the gates of London seawards; the birds, the coloured clouds, and the thought of a sunny coastline worked simultaneously in his heart. These messages of spring woke music in him. The music, however, found no expression, beyond a quiet sigh, so quiet that not even a child, had he carried one in his big arms, need have noticed it. His pace quickened, his figure straightened up, he lifted his eyes and there was a new light in them. Upon the wet pavement, where the street lamps already laid their network of faint gold, he saw, perhaps a dozen yards in front of him, the figure of a little boy.

The boy, for some reason, caught his attention and his interest vividly. He was dressed in Etons, the broad white collar badly rumpled, the pointed coat hitched grotesquely sideways, while, from beneath the rather grimy straw hat, his thick light hair escaped at various angles. This general air of effort and distress was due to the fact that the little fellow was struggling with a bag packed evidently to bursting point, too big and heavy for him to manage for more than ten yards at a time. He changed it from one hand to the other, resting it in the intervals upon the ground, each effort making it rub against his leg so that the trousers were hoisted considerably above the boot. He was a pathetic figure.

"I must help him," said the man. "He'll never get there at this rate. He'll miss his train to the sea." For his destination was obvious, since a pair of wooden spades was tied clumsily and insecurely to the straps of the bursting bag.

Occasionally, too, the lad, who seemed about ten years old, looked about him to right and left, questionably, anxiously, as though he expected someone—someone to help, or perhaps to meet him. His behaviour even gave the impression that he was not quite sure of his way. The man hurried to overtake him.

"I really must give the little beggar a hand," he repeated to himself, as he went. He smiled. The fatherly, protective side of him, naturally strong, was touched—touched a little more, perhaps, than the occasion seemed to warrant. The smile broadened into a jolly laugh, as he came up against the great stuffed bag, now resting on the pavement, its owner panting beside it, still looking to right and left alternately. At which instant, exactly, the boy, hearing his step, turned round, and for the first time looked him full in the face with a pair of big blue eyes that held unabashed and happy welcome in them.

"Oh, I say, sir, it's most awfully ripping of you," he said in a confiding voice, before the man had time to speak. "I hunted everywhere; but I never thought of looking *behind* me."

But the man, standing dumb and astonished for a few seconds beside the little fellow, missed the latter sentence altogether, for there was in the clear blue eyes an expression so trustful, so frankly affectionate almost, and in the voice music of so natural a kind, that all the tenderness in him rose like a sudden tide, and he yearned towards the boy as though he were his little son. Thought, born of some sudden revival of emotion, flashed back swiftly across a stretch of twelve blank years… and for an instant the lines of the mouth grew deeper, though in the eyes the light turned softer, brighter…

"It's too big for you, my boy," he said, recovering himself with a jolly laugh; "or, rather, you're not big enough—yet—for it—eh! Where to, now? Ah! the station, I suppose?" And he stooped to grasp the handles of the bulging bag, first poking the spades more securely in beneath the straps; but in doing so became aware that something the boy had said had given him pain. What was it? Why was it? This stray little stranger, met upon the London pavements! Yet so swift is thought that, even while he stooped and before his fingers actually touched the leather, he had found what hurt him—and smiled a little at himself. It was the mode of address the boy made use of, contradicting faintly the affectionate expression in the eyes. It was the word "sir" that made him feel like a schoolmaster or a tutor; it made him feel old. It was not the word he needed, and—yes—had longed for, somehow almost expected. And there was such strange trouble in his mind and heart that, as he grasped the bag, he did not catch the boy's rejoinder to his question. But, of course, it must be the railway station; he was going to the seaside for Easter; his people would be at the ticket-office waiting for him. Bracing himself a little for the effort, he seized the leather handles and lifted the bag from the ground.

"Oh, thanks awfully, sir!" repeated the boy. He watched him with a true schoolboy grin of gratitude, as though it were great fun, yet also with a true urchin's sense that the proper thing had happened, since such jobs, of course, were for grown-up men. And this time, though he used the objectionable word again, the voice betrayed recognition of the fact that he somehow had a right to look to this particular man for help, and that this particular man only did the right and natural thing in giving help.

But the man, swaying sideways, nearly lost his balance. He had calculated automatically the probable energy necessary to lift the weight; he had put this energy forth. He received a shock as though he had been struck, for the bag had no weight at all; it was as light as a feather. It might have been of tissue-paper, a phantom bag. And the shock was mental as well as physical. His mind swayed with his body.

"By jove!" cried the boy, strutting merrily beside him, hands in his pockets. "Thanks most awfully. This *is* jolly!"

The objectionable word was omitted, but the man scarcely heard the words at all. For a mist swam before his eyes, the street lamps grew blurred and distant, the drizzle thickened in the air. He still heard the wild, sweet song of the bird, still knew the west had gold upon its lips. It was the rest of the world about him that grew dim. Strange thoughts rose in a cloud. Reality and dream played games, the games of childhood, through his heart. Memories, robed flamingly, trooped past his inner sight, radiant, swift and as of yesterday, closing his eyelids for a moment to the outer world. Rossetti came to him, singing too sweetly a hidden pain in perfect words across those twelve blank years: "The Hour that might have been, yet might not be, which man's and woman's heart conceived and bore, yet whereof time was barren..." In a second's flash the entire sonnet, "Stillborn Love", passed on this inner screen "with eyes where burning memory lights love home..."

Mingled with these—all in an instant of time—came practical thoughts as well. This boy! The ridiculous effort he made to carry this ridiculously light bag! The poignant tenderness, the awakened yearning! Was it a girl dressed up? The happy face, the innocent, confiding smile, the music in the voice, the dear soft blue eyes, and yet, at the same time, something that was *not* there—some indescribable, incalculable element that was lacking. He felt acutely this curious lack. What was it? Who was this merry youngster? He glanced down cautiously as they moved side by side.

He felt shy, hopeful, marvellously tender. His heart yearned inexpressibly; the boy, looking elsewhere, did not notice the examination, did not notice, of course, that his companion caught his breath and walked uncertainly.

But the man was troubled. The face reminded him, as he gazed, of many children, of children he had loved and played with, both boys and girls, his Substitute Children, as he had always called them in his heart… Then, suddenly, the boy came closer and took his arm. They were close upon the station now. The sweet human perfume of a small, deeply loved, helpless and dependent little life rose past his face.

He suddenly blurted out: "But, I say, this bag of yours—it weighs simply nothing!"

The boy laughed—a ring of true careless joy was in the sound. He looked up.

"Do you know what's in it? Shall I tell you?" He added in a whisper: "I will, if you like."

But the man was suddenly afraid and dared not ask.

"Brown paper probably," he evaded laughingly; "or birds' eggs. You've been up to some wicked lark or other."

The little chap clasped both hands upon the supporting arm. He took a quick, dancing step or two, then stopped dead, and made the man stop with him. He stood on tiptoe to reach the distant ear. His face wore a lovely smile of truth and trust and delight.

"My future," he whispered. And the man turned into ice.

They entered the great station. The last of the daylight was shut out. They reached the ticket-office. The crowds of hurrying people surged about them. The man set down the bag. For a moment or two the boy looked quickly about him to right and left, searching, then turned his big blue eyes upon the other with his radiant smile:

"She's in the waiting-room as usual," he said. "I'll go and fetch her— though she *ought* to know you're here." He stood on tiptoe, his hands upon the other's shoulders, his face thrust close. "Kiss me, father. I shan't be a second."

"You little beggar!" said the man, in a voice he could not control; then, opening his big arms wide, saw only an empty space before him.

He turned and walked slowly back to his flat instead of to the club; and when he got home he read over for the thousandth time the letter—its ink a little faded during the twelve intervening years—in which she had accepted his love two short weeks before death took her.

AT A MAYFAIR LUNCHEON

After the War Blackwood's production of stories was much reduced. He completed the sequel to Julius Le Vallon, *called* The Bright Messenger *and assembled several collections of stories before turning his attention to his autobiography,* Episodes Before Thirty, *published in October 1923. He had believed that would be his last book but other opportunities arose. Working again with Violet Pearn he adapted* The Education of Uncle Paul *as a children's play,* Through the Crack, *and started to write stories for children, mostly encouraged by Patsy Ainley and her brother. They became the eponymous children in* Sambo and Snitch *(1927) and also appeared under various names in a series of stories Blackwood wrote for Basil Blackwell's* Joy Street Annuals *which were also released as little books. Titles included* Mr. Cupboard, By Underground *and* Sergeant Poppet and Policeman James—*Patsy was always Blackwood's "Best Beloved Poppet". He also wrote a novel which could be appreciated by adults as well as children about an over-philosophical parrot and a mischievous cat,* Dudley and Gilderoy.*

In addition to all these stories, Blackwood was approached by the BBC to read stories on the radio. His first story was a new one; "The Blackmailers" broadcast on 11 July 1934 and proved so popular that he became a radio regular, not only telling stories but appearing on panel shows and discussion groups, and even writing plays. It was a whole new career and it prompted him to write further stories. Many of these remained uncollected and almost forgotten, such as the following, first published in 1936 and then lost for fifty years. It shows that some of the mystique and vision had returned to Blackwood.

O N looking back, it seemed incredible to young Monson that this could have come out of such commonplace conditions. For it started while he was reading poetic stuff about the Pæstum Temples, and then about the temples of Baalbec and the worship of Jupiter Ammon, and his thoughts had run off waywardly towards Christ and Buddha, and he had been wondering vaguely—Man in the Street that he was—how such vital and terrific forms of belief and worship could ever die—when, abruptly, someone came into his study with a tiresome interruption:

"This note come by and, please, sir, and would you please answer immedshately, thank you, sir."

Monson acted immedshately and read the note:

> "*Do* forgive me, dear. I'm a man short. 1.15 for 1.30. If you *can… do.*
> FELICITY."

Now, he believed he loved Felicity. He could. He did.

"Telephone immedshately to her ladyship to say Mr. Monson will be delighted to lunch today at 1.15," he gave his answer. And in due course he went.

Further, it lies quite beyond him to explain why all the way to Curzon Street, walking leisurely this fine May morning, he was still aflame with Baalbec, the Pyramids, the Pæstum Temples, and all that sort of delicious, ancient, romantic pagan stuff. Imagination ran that way. He left it at that. Some old-world glamour caught him away into some strange, wild heaven. He found himself suddenly loathing the modern drabness, the senseless speed, the artificial mechanism, the clever, infinite invention that was smart and up-to-date, and all the rest of the rushing, uncomfortable nonsense. Machinery did everything, the individual nothing. A deep yearning possessed him for the slow, worth-while, steady liveableness of other days, when a man could believe in a mountain nymph on many-fountained Ida and worship her, by God, with a conviction of positive reaction. He heard the old, old winds among the olives and saw the spindrift blow across great Triton's horn, his sandals trod upon acanthus leaves, the wild thyme stung his nostrils…

In which ridiculous, even hysterical mood, he rang the bell in Curzon Street at 1.15 and waited upon admittance.

So ordinary was the next step, and the routine of the steps following, that he found nothing to remark upon them.

"*So* sweet of you to come and save me. Lord Falsestep had a sudden Cabinet Meeting… I think you know everybody…"

He caught instantly the usual deadly savour. The cocktails and the preliminary chatter shared this deadliness, so that he found himself harking back to Baalbec and Pæstum and his earlier foolishness, when, suddenly a late guest was announced, but in such a way that both his eye and ear were caught, held, arrested—what *is* the precise word?—startled is probably the most accurate, but, at any rate, taken with vivid painfulness.

"Painfulness?" Yes, assuredly, because it hurt. A sharp, terrible sting ran through him from head to foot. Something in him blenched, ran hot and cold, with an effect of dislocation somewhere, so that his heart seemed to stop.

Some Bright Young Thing, or its equivalent, chanced to engage him at the moment, though "engage" is wrong, because the trivial glitter held no power of any sort, and glitter is at best a surface quality. It was, at any rate, while exchanging glittering vacancies thus, that he heard the footman's voice and turned to look.

To look! Rather, to stare. Was it man or woman, this late guest? Such outlines, he knew, were easily interchangeable today. It might have been one or other. "Or both," ran like fiery lightning through him, so that he turned faint with the sweetness of some amazing apprehension.

The chatter in his ear seemed suddenly miles away, and not miles alone, but ages. Its tinkle reached him, none the less, distinctly enough: "… so you simply *must* come. It will be too adorable. Without *you* it would be just ashes. Wear anything you like, of course, and doors open till dawn…" The Bright Young Thing's invitation, yes, oozing past her violent lipstick reached him distinctly enough, though it now had a sharply hideous sound—because at the same moment he had caught the voice of the late arrival: "*Thank you for asking me,*" and the words, so softly spoken, had a quality that made them sing above the general roar.

Why, then, did a wave of life rush drenching through him as he heard them? Why did his bones seem to melt and run to gold and silver? Whence came that breath of flower-laden wind across the drowned atmosphere of smoke and female perfume? That tang as of sea and desert air that for a moment seemed too sweet, too strong, to bear?

"… you promise. I'll expect you," clanged the invitation.

"Of course, I shall be delighted," came his mechanical acceptance. "And I'll be there a little before dawn."

They turned away mutually—he, because he felt curiously shamed a trifle—she, because a young man with a lisping voice approached with a wobbling glass. Shamed perhaps, yet faint as well, faint towards the Mayfair room and atmosphere, but at the same time so alive and exhilarated towards something else that he was intoxicated. He caught at the edge of a sofa to hold him down. He had a fear that he must rise to touch a star, a nebula, an outer galaxy.

There was confusion inextricable, then somehow they were all in the ultra-luxurious dining-room, and Felicity, his friend's wife whom he believed he loved, was dropping a hurried whisper in his ear:

"You are an angel, darling, to come. A woman has failed me too—that impossible Ursula again. Do you mind terribly? No, Lovely, on your left. Just an empty chair…!"

And so it was that the space next to him was unoccupied, an empty chair, just beyond which, he realised with a lift of his whole being, sat the late arrival whose voice, with its singing beauty, had swept Today into the rubbish heap.

Now, until this moment, young Monson—young as well as simple he assuredly was—had held full command of himself, since he had eschewed strong drink and was besides frankly bored, even feeling sorry he had come at all. And boredom engenders pessimism, not optimism. At the same time, contrariwise, it awakens a sense of superiority, false of course, yet compensating, because the mind comforts itself thereby that it is superior to the cause of its boredom. And until that amazing voice had echoed across the room packed with notables and nobodies, young Monson's mood was as stated, below par—bored a little. The Bright Young Thing had exasperated with her affectations. His spirits, though for the sake of politeness to Felicity, his lovely hostess, he had forced them to spurious activity, were distinctly low. There was nothing, therefore, to account for the stupendous, gripping interest he now felt suddenly in that empty space, the breadth of an unoccupied chair, that gaped—otherwise somewhat menacingly—between him and his neighbour. The interest and stimulus lay in this: that across the narrow emptiness the stranger sat. One other thing lay equally beyond his explanation—that, instead of the sense of false superiority referred to, he was aware now of inferiority in himself that wakened a humility of heart so deep and genuine that he found no honestly descriptive words.

How calm, gentle, silent, almost meek, yet never uncomfortable nor out of place, the stranger sat there, and not in any smallest degree embarrassed. Entirely self-possessed, moreover. He might have been the host, a careless, understanding host, whose carelessness and understanding derived from the certain knowledge that all were glad to be there. Yes, it was a *he*, Monson now knew, a guest quite unimpressed by the fact that this was the luncheon of a famous social and political hostess, and that "those present" would be blazoned tomorrow with photographs in the daily press. Meek, perhaps, yet how strangely powerful, how radiant, and—the words seem childish—how beautiful, with a power and beauty beyond crumbling Baalbec and the wind-worn Pyramids. And upon some scale of mightiness that dislocated his mind perhaps a little, since a perfect blizzard of unrelated pictures suddenly swept and poured across his thoughts like an immense panorama, pictures all scaled to mightiness, so that his being seemed stretched to capacity to receive them, packed thus into a single flashing second. They roared up, passed, were gone, all simultaneously... great Stonehenge with its ache of grandeur, Pæstum with its rapture, the ghastly loneliness of the Easter Island images, the unanswerable Sphinx and Pyramids, and then, with a leap of terror, to the crystal iciness of the deserted moon, the awful depths of the nine-mile ocean bed... roared past and vanished again, as he stole a glance, wondering how for Felicity's sake, his anxious hostess whom he loved, he might approach his neighbour with a word.

On the stranger's further side, he saw, perched an empty-headed Duchess, avoiding him deliberately. He met Felicity's beseeching eye. He made a plunge across that gaping chair:

"We must bridge this empty space," he ventured smilingly, leaning over a little. "Some lady evidently has been detained. The stress of London life just now is hard upon punctuality…"

Something of the sort he said. The words rather tumbled from his mouth. There was a scent of wild thyme as he leaned over slightly.

The other smiled, lifting clear, shining eyes, so that young Monson admitted to something again akin to shock, a singular deep thrill of wonder, beauty, humility. Was it man or woman after all? shot through his mind.

"Not detained perhaps," the answer floated to him, "but unaware. Not dead, that is, but sleeping."

Oddly, there was no shock of surprise at the choice of curious words a foreigner might have found, or one unaccustomed to modern usage, and Monson felt he had merely misunderstood perhaps. The voice was soft as music, very low.

"Late, at any rate," he murmured in some confusion, his eyes upon his plate, as though in search of steadiness. "Too late," he added, his search for the commonplace still operating, "for this delicious lobster *mousse*—or whatever it may be."

That sweet, gentle smile again, that scent and purity of wild flowers, as he crumbled his bread and gazed across the narrow space towards his young neighbour, who sat unaccountably trembling before something he had never known before. Trembling, it seemed to himself, with happiness and wonder, yet with a touch of awe due to the new sense of power and splendour that rose in his heart. In his heart alone, yes, not in his mind. He established *that*, at any rate. His mind, if watchful perhaps and steady enough, seemed suddenly inoperative. What happened, what was happening, lay in the heart alone. Thus he found no explanation, as equally no doubt or question, about seeing those slender fingers radiant, the bread-crumbs shining upon the table beneath the other's touch, nor why, though raised repeatedly to his mouth, they multiplied on the cloth even while he took from them…

The eye of Felicity from the top of the long table flared at him.

Since the stranger offered nothing, Monson, making a desperate effort to get at his mind, rather than allow his heart full sway, tried again after a moment's interval. To entertain one's neighbour was the acknowledged price of admission to any feast, to sit silent, at any rate, was not permissible. Again, the words fell tumbling from his lips without reflection, or rather from his heart:

"My plans for today were otherwise," he mumbled, almost stammeringly, leaning over a little as before. "I didn't really want to come, but I'm *awfully* g-glad I did. It's so difficult to—to live one's own life and—and keep in the swim nowadays." He paused, watching a smile that opened in those glorious eyes, yet did not travel downwards to the tender lips. "I was summoned at the last moment because some Cabinet Minister and a lady failed," he fumbled on, "but I wouldn't have missed it for—for—everything in the world."

He stopped dead. The other's lips were moving. There was a light about the face and head.

"I myself was asked indirectly perhaps, but in true sincerity. And none call on me in vain."

These were the actual words, spoken so low as to be just audible, that floated across the space of the empty chair. It seemed only a glance from Felicity's eye along the table length that held young Monson to his seat.

"Poor hostesses," he thinks he heard himself murmuring, attempting a smile of charitable understanding. For at the same instant, turning abruptly, he met the other's eyes at the full. One look he saw, a look of fire and glory like dawn upon the Caucasus… and then a sense of fading, the passing away of an intolerable radiance that for a moment had forced his eyelids to drop. Yet in that fraction of a second, before they lifted again, the words came floating in a still, small voice that made them absolutely clear:

"From her heart it came. 'Oh, Christ,' she prayed, 'Do, please, come. I need you.'"

There was a stir in the room, a shuffling along the table, as Sir Thomas and Lady Ursula Smith-Ponsonby arrived with many apologies and slid gracefully into the two empty chairs on young Monson's left.

ROMAN REMAINS

The following was Blackwood's last newly published story for adults. One more for children, "Eliza Among the Chimney Sweeps", followed in 1950. "Roman Remains" was published first in the United States in the now legendary pulp magazine Weird Tales *in March 1948. Blackwood had continued to write the occasional new story, not all of which would fit into the fifteen- or twenty-minute time slot on radio, but he did little to seek publication, and his agent, A. P. Watt, seemed unaware of any new market. Ironically, Blackwood had appeared once before in* Weird Tales *with "The Magic Mirror" in 1938. It had been sold there by Watt's US counterpart and at the time Blackwood commented that it was a market worth keeping an eye on.*

It was not until November 1944, when Blackwood was contacted by the American writer August Derleth, that the US market once again came into focus. Derleth, who had been selling to Weird Tales *for almost twenty years, had started his own small publishing company Arkham House in 1939 to collect the work of H. P. Lovecraft in a more permanent hardcover edition. Derleth was expanding his stable of authors now including Clark Ashton Smith and Robert Bloch and he reached out to Blackwood to see what uncollected stories he had. Surprisingly Blackwood responded that he had only two such stories, "The Doll" and "The Trod", which Derleth published as* The Doll and One Other *in April 1946. Derleth remained in touch and when he began his small magazine,* The Arkham Sampler, *Blackwood sent him "Roman Remains", the last weird tale he completed. Derleth felt that it should have a wider readership so placed it with* Weird Tales *rather than run it himself.*

The story features a young airman on sick leave from India, which immediately suggests Blackwood's nephew, Patrick. His elder brother is called a retired surgeon, which describes Patrick's stepfather, James Eadie. Unusually it is set in Wales, which Blackwood felt was the last hiding place for Britain's old magic. His affinity with Nature remained undimmed after over sixty years.

He died on 10 December 1951, aged 82, and his ashes were scattered over the lake at Saanenmoser near Bôle.

A NTHONY Breddle, airman, home on sick leave from India, does
not feel himself called upon to give an opinion; he considers
himself a recorder only. The phrase *credo quia impossibile*, had
never come his way; neither had Blake's dictum that "everything possible
to be believed is an image of truth."

He was under thirty, intelligent enough, observant, a first-rate pilot,
but with no special gifts or knowledge. A matter of fact kind of fellow,
unequipped on the imaginative side, he was on his way to convalesce at his
step-brother's remote place in the Welsh mountains. The brother, a much
older man, was a retired surgeon, honoured for his outstanding work with
a knighthood and now absorbed in research.

The airman glanced again at the letter of invitation:

"... a lonely, desolate place, I'm afraid, with few neighbours, but good
fishing which, I know, you adore. Wild little valleys run straight up into
the mountains almost from the garden, you'll have to entertain yourself.
I've got lots of fishing rods for you. Nora Ashwell, a cousin you've never
met, a nurse, also on sick leave of sorts but shortly going back to her job,
is dying for companionship of her own age. She likes fishing too. But my
house isn't a hospital! And there's Dr. Leidenheim, who was a student with
me at Heidelberg ages ago, a delightful old friend. Had a Chair in Berlin,
but got out just in time. His field is Roman Culture—lots of remains
about here—but that's not your cup of tea, I know. Legends galore all over
the place and superstitions you could cut with a knife. Queer things said
to go on in a little glen called Goat Valley. But that's not down your street

either. Anyhow, come along and make the best of it; at least we have no bombing here…"

So Breddle knew what he was in for more or less, but was so relieved to get out of the London blitz with a chance of recovering his normal strength, that it didn't matter. Above all, he didn't want a flirtation, nor to hear about Roman remains from the Austrian refugee scholar.

It was certainly a desolate spot, but the house and grounds were delightful, and he lost no time in asking about the fishing. There was a trout stream, it seemed, and a bit of the Wye not too far away with some good salmon pools. At the moment, as rain had swollen the Wye, the trout stream was the thing to go for; and before an early bed that night he had made the acquaintance of the two others, Nora and Emil Leidenheim. He sized them up, as he called it: the latter a charming, old-fashioned man with considerable personality, cautious of speech, and no doubt very learned; but Nora, his cousin, by no means to his taste. Easy to look at certainly, with a kind of hard, wild beauty, pleasant enough too, if rather silent, yet with something about her he could not quite place beyond that it was distasteful. She struck him as unkempt, untidy, self-centred, careless as to what impression she made on her company, her mind and thoughts elsewhere all the time. She had been out walking that afternoon, yet came to their war-time supper still in shorts. A negligible matter, doubtless, though the three men had all done something by way of tidying up a bit. Her eyes and manner conveyed something he found baffling, as though she was always on the watch, listening, peering for something that was not there. Impersonal, too, as the devil. It seemed a foolish thing to say, but there was a hint in her atmosphere that made him uncomfortable, uneasy, almost gave him a touch of the creeps. The two older men, he fancied, left her rather alone.

Outwardly, at any rate, all went normally enough, and a fishing trip was arranged for the following morning.

"And I hope you'll bring back something for the table," his brother commented, when she had gone up to bed. "Nora has never yet brought back a single fish. God knows what she does with herself, but I doubt if she goes to the stream at all." At which an enigmatic expression passed across Dr. Leidenheim's face, though he did not speak.

"Where is this stream?" his brother asked. "Up that Goat Valley you said was queer, or something? And what did you mean by 'queer'?"

"Oh, no, not Goat Valley," came the answer; "and as for 'queer', I didn't mean anything particular. Just that the superstitious locals avoid it even in the daytime. There's a bit of hysteria about, you know," he added, "these war days, especially in god-forsaken places like this—"

"God-forsaken is good," Dr. Leidenheim put in quickly, giving the airman an impression somehow that he could have said more but for his host's presence, while Breddle thought he would like to tap the old fellow's mind when he got the chance.

And it was with that stressed epithet in his ears that he went up to his comfortable bedroom. But before he fell asleep another impression registered as he lay on that indeterminate frontier between sleeping and waking. He carried it into sleep with him, though no dream followed. And it was this: there was something wrong in this house, something that did not emerge at first. It was concerned with the occupants, but it was due neither to his brother, nor to the Austrian archaeologist. It was due to that strange, wild girl. Before sleep took him, he defined it to himself. Nora was under close observation the whole time by both the older men. It was chiefly, however, Dr. Leidenheim who watched her.

The following morning broke in such brilliant sunshine that fishing was out of the question; and when the airman got down to a late breakfast he was distinctly relieved to hear that Nora was already out of the house. She, too, knew that clear skies were no good for trout; she had left a verbal excuse and gone off by herself for a long walk. So Breddle announced that he would do the same. His choice was Goat Valley, he would take sandwiches and entertain himself. He got rough directions from Dr. Leidenheim, who mentioned that the ruins of an ancient temple to the old god, Silvanus, at the end of the valley might interest him. "And you'll have the place to yourself," said his brother, laughingly, before disappearing into his sanctum, "unless you run across one of the young monsters, the only living things apparently that ever go there."

"Monsters! And what may you mean by that?"

It was Dr. Leidenheim who explained the odd phrase.

"Nothing," he said, "nothing at all. Your brother's a surgeon, remember. He still uses the words of his student days. He wants to scare you."

The other, finding him for once communicative, pressed him, if with poor results.

"Merely," he said in his excellent English, "that there have been one or two unpleasant births during these war years—in my language, *Missgeburt* we call them. Due to the collective hysteria of these strange natives probably." He added under his breath, as if to himself, something about *Urmenschen* and *unheimlich*, though Breddle didn't know the words.

"Oh," he exclaimed, catching his meaning, "that sort of thing, eh? I thought they were always put out of the way at birth or kept in glass bottles—"

"In my country, that is so, yes. They do not live."

The airman laughed. "It would take more than a *Missgeburt* to scare me," he said, and dropped the unsavoury subject before the old archaeologist got into his stride about the temple to Silvanus and Roman remains in general. Later he regretted he had not asked a few other questions.

Now, Anthony Breddle must be known as what is called a brave man; he had the brand of courage that goes with total absence of imagination. His was a simple mind of the primitive order. Pictures passed through it which he grouped and regrouped, he drew inferences from them, but it is doubtful if he had ever really thought. As he entered the little valley, his mind worked as usual, automatically. Pictures of his brother and the Austrian flitted across it, both old men, idling through the evening of their day after reasonable success, the latter with a painful background of bitter sufferings under the Nazis. The chat about collective hysteria and the rest did not hold his interest. And Nora flitted through after them, a nurse maybe, but an odd fish assuredly, not his cup of tea in any case. Bit of a wild cat, he suspected, for all her quiet exterior in the house. If she lingered in his mind more vividly than the other two it was because of that notion of the night before—that she was under observation. She was, obviously, up to something: never bringing in a fish, for instance, that strange look in her eyes, the decided feeling of repulsion she stirred in him. Then her picture faded too. His emotions at the moment were of enjoyment and carefree happiness. The bright sunny morning, the birds singing, the tiny stream pretending it was a noisy torrent, the fact that "Operations" lay behind him and weeks of freedom lay ahead... which reminded him that he was, after all, convalescing from recent fevers, and that he was walking a bit too fast for his strength.

He dawdled more slowly up the little glen as the mountain-ash trees and silver birch thickened and the steep sides of the valley narrowed, passed the tumbled stones of the Silvanus temple without a glance of interest, and went on whistling happily to himself—then suddenly wondered how an echo of his whistling could reach him through the dense undergrowth. It was not an echo, he realised with a start. It was a different whistle. Someone else, not very far away, someone following him possibly, someone else, yes, was whistling. The realisation disturbed him. He wanted, above all, to be alone. But, for all that, he listened with a certain pleasure, as he lay in a patch of sunshine, ate his lunch, and smoked, for the tune, now growing fainter, had an enticing lilt, a haunting cadence, though it never once entered his mind that it was possibly a folk tune of sorts.

It died away; at any rate, he no longer heard it; he stretched out in the patch of warm sunshine, he dozed; probably, he dropped off to sleep…

Yes, he is certain he must have slept, because when he opened his eyes he felt there had been an interval. He lay now in shadow, for the sun had moved. But something else had moved too while he was asleep. There was an alteration in his immediate landscape, restricted though that landscape was. The absurd notion then intruded that someone had been near him while he slept, watching him. It puzzled him; an uneasy emotion disturbed him.

He sat up with a start and looked about him. No wind stirred, not a leaf moved; nor was there any sound but the prattle of the little stream some distance away. A vague disquiet deepened in him. Then he cupped his ears to listen, for at this precise moment the whistling became audible again with the same queer, haunting lilt in it. And he stiffened. This stiffening, at any rate he recognised; this sudden tautening of the nerves he had experienced before when flying. He knew precisely that it came as a prelude to danger: it was the automatic preparation made by body and mind to meet danger; it was—fear.

But why fear in this smiling, innocent woodland? And that no hint of explanation came, made it worse. A nameless fear could not be met and dealt with; it could bring in its wake a worse thing—terror. But an unreasoning terror is an awful thing, and well he knew this. He caught a shiver running over him; and instinctively then he thought he would "whistle to keep his courage up," only to find that he could not manage it. He was unable to control his lips. No sound issued, his lips trembled, the flow of breath blocked. A kind of wheeze, however, did emerge, a faint pretence of whistling, and he realised to his horror that the other whistler answered it. Terror then swept in; and, trying feebly again, he managed a reply. Whereupon that other whistling piper moved closer in, and the distance between them was reduced. Yet, oh, what a ravishing and lovely lilt it was! Beyond all words he felt rapt and caught away. His heart, incredibly, seemed mastered. An unbelievable storm of energy swept through him.

He was brave, this young airman, as already mentioned, for he had faced death many times, but this amazing combination of terror and energy was something new. The sense of panic lay outside all previous experience. Genuine panic terror is a rare thing; its assault now came on him like a tornado. It seemed he must lose his head and run amok. And the whistler, the strange piper, came nearer, the distance between them again reduced. Energy and terror flooding his being simultaneously, he found relief in movement. He plunged recklessly through the dense undergrowth in the direction of the sound, conscious only of one overmastering impulse—that he *must* meet this piper face to face, while yet half unconsciously aware that at the same time he was also taking every precaution to move noiselessly, softly, quietly, so as not to be heard. This strange contradiction came back to memory long afterwards, hinting possibly at some remnant of resisting power that saved him from an unutterable disaster.

His reward was the last thing in the world he anticipated.

That he was in an abnormal condition utterly beyond his comprehension there can be no doubt; but that what he now witnessed registered with complete and positive clarity lay beyond all question. A figure caught his eye through the screen of leaves, a moving—more—a dancing figure, as he stood stock still and stared at—Nora Ashwell. She was perhaps a dozen yards away, obviously unaware of his presence, her clothes in such disorder that she seemed half naked, hatless, with flowers in her loosened hair, her face radiant, arms and legs gesticulating in a wild dance, her body flung from side to side, but gracefully, a pipe of sorts in one hand that at moments went to her lips to blow the now familiar air. She was moving in the direction away from where he stood concealed, but he saw enough to realise that he was watching a young girl in what is known as ecstasy, an ecstasy of love.

He stood motionless, staring at the amazing spectacle: a girl beside herself with love; love, yes, assuredly, but not the kind his life had so far known about; a lover certainly—the banal explanation of her conduct flashed through his bewilderment—but not a lover of ordinary sort. And, as he stared, afraid to move a step, he was aware that this flood of energy, this lust for intense living that drove her, was at work in him too. The frontiers of his normal self, his ordinary world, were trembling; any moment there might come collapse and he, too, would run amok with panic joy and terror. He watched as the figure disappeared behind denser foliage, faded, then was gone, and he stood there alone dominated suddenly by one overmastering purpose—that he must escape from this awful, yet enticing valley, before it was too late.

How he contrived it he hardly remembers; it was in literal panic that he raced and stumbled along, driven by a sense of terror wholly new to all his experience. There was no feeling of being followed, nor of any definite threat of a personal kind; he was conscious more of some power, as of the animal kingdom, primitive, powerful, menacing, that assaulted his status as a human being... a panic, indeed, of pagan origin.

He reached the house towards sunset. There was an interval of struggle to return to his normal self, during which, he thanked heaven, he met no member of the household. At supper, indeed, things seemed as usual... he asked and answered questions about his expedition without hesitation, if aware all the time, perhaps, that Dr. Leidenheim observed him somewhat closely, as he observed Nora too. For Nora, equally, seemed her usual, silent self, beyond that her eyes, shining like stars, somehow lent a touch of radiance to her being.

She spoke little; she never betrayed herself. And it was only when, later, Breddle found himself alone with Dr. Leidenheim for a moment before bedtime, that the urgent feeling that he *must* tell someone about his experiences persuaded him to give a stammering account. He could not talk to his brother, but to a stranger it was just possible. And it brought a measure of relief, though Leidenheim was laconic and even mysterious in his comments.

"Ah, yes... yes... interesting, of course, and—er—most unusual. The combination of that irresistible lust for life, yes, and—and the unreasoning terror. It was always considered extremely powerful and—equally dangerous, of course. Your present condition—convalescing, I mean—made you specially accessible, no doubt..."

But the airman could not follow this kind of talk; after listening for a bit, he made to go up to bed, too exhausted to think about it.

It was about three o'clock in the morning when things began to happen and the first air raid of the war came to the hitherto immune neighbourhood. It was the night the Germans attacked Liverpool. A pilot, scared possibly by the barrage, or chased by a Spitfire and anxious to get rid of his bombs, dropped them before returning home, some of them evidently in the direction of Goat Valley. The three men, gathered in the hall, counted the bursts and estimated a stick had fallen up that way somewhere; and it was while discussing this, that the absence of Nora Ashwell was first noticed. It was Dr. Leidenheim, after a whispered exchange with his host, who went quickly up to her bedroom, and getting no answer to their summons, burst open the locked door to find the room empty. The bed had not been slept in; a sofa had been dragged to the open window where a rope of knotted sheets hung down to the lawn below. The two brothers hurried out of the house at once, joined after a slight delay by Dr. Leidenheim who had brought a couple of spades with him but made no comment by way of explaining why he did so. He handed one to the airman without a word. Under the breaking dawn of another brilliant day, the three men followed the line of craters made by the stick of bombs towards Goat Valley, as they had surmised. Dr. Leidenheim led them by the shortest way, having so often visited the Silvanus temple ruins; and some hundred yards further on the grey morning light soon showed them what was left of Nora Ashwell, blasted almost beyond recognition. They found something else as well, dead but hardly at all injured.

"It should—it must be buried," whispered Dr. Leidenheim, and started to dig a hole, signing to the airman to help him with the second spade.

"Burnt first, I think," said the surgeon.

And they all agreed. The airman, as he collected wood and helped dig the hole, felt slightly sick. The sun was up when they reached the house, invaded the still deserted kitchen, and made coffee. There were duties to be attended to presently, but there was little talk, and the surgeon soon retired to his study sofa for a nap.

"Come to my room a moment, if you will," Dr. Leidenheim proposed to the young airman. "There's something I'd like to read to you; it would perhaps interest you."

Up in the room he took a book from his shelves. "The travels and observations of an old Greek," he explained, "notes of things he witnessed in his wanderings. Pausanias, you know. I'll translate an incident he mentions."

"'It is said that one of these beings was brought to Sylla as that General returned from Thessaly. The monster had been surprised asleep in a cave. But his voice was inarticulate. When brought into the presence of Sylla, the Roman General, he was so disgusted that he ordered it to be instantly removed. The monster answered in every degree to the description which poets and painters have given of it.'"

"Oh, yes," said the airman. "And—er—what was it supposed to be, this monster?"

"A Satyr, of course," replied Dr. Leidenheim, as he replaced the volume without further comment except the muttered words, "One of the retinue of Pan."

STORY SOURCES

The following gives the original publication details for each story together with the relevant Blackwood volume in which it was first collected.

"The Empty House" and "Smith: An Episode in a Lodging House" first published in *The Empty House* (London: Eveleigh Nash, 1906).

"A Haunted Island" first published in *Pall Mall Magazine*, April 1899 and collected in *The Empty House* (London: Eveleigh Nash, 1906).

"Max Hensig", "The Old Man of Visions" and "The Listener" first published in *The Listener* (London: Eveleigh Nash, 1907).

"Entrance and Exit" first published in *The Westminster Gazette*, 13 February 1909 and collected in *Ten Minute Stories* (London: John Murray, 1914).

"The Man Who Played Upon the Leaf" first published in *Country Life*, 30 October 1909 and collected in *The Lost Valley* (London: Eveleigh Nash, 1910).

"The Whisperers" first published in *The Eye Witness*, 23 May 1912 and collected in *Ten Minute Stories* (London: John Murray, 1914).

"A Desert Episode" first published in *Country Life*, 10 January 1914 and collected in *Day and Night Stories* (London: Cassell, 1917).

"A Man of Earth" first published in *The New Weekly*, 27 June 1914 and collected in *Tongues of Fire* (London: Herbert Jenkins, 1924).

"The Wings of Horus" first published in *Century Magazine*, November 1914 and collected in *Day and Night Stories* (London: Cassell, 1917).

"The Little Beggar" first published in *Saturday Westminster Gazette*, 10 May 1919 and collected in *Tongues of Fire* (London: Herbert Jenkins, 1924).

"Onanonanon" first published in *The English Review*, March 1921 and collected in *The Magic Mirror* (Wellingborough: Thorson's, 1989).

"At a Mayfair Luncheon" first published in *The Windsor Magazine*, March 1936 and collected in *The Magic Mirror* (Wellingborough: Thorson's, 1989).

"Roman Remains" first published in *Weird Tales*, March 1948 and collected in *The Magic Mirror* (Wellingborough: Thorson's, 1989).